A NEW AGE OF MAN

A REALMS NOVEL
BOOK 1

D.A. PUTMAN

For Anderson

CONTENTS

PROLOGUE–A NEW BEGINNING

YEAR 1704 (AGE ENDING)

Valen staggered as the world around him lurched. Hands outstretched, he fell against the wall, catching himself as the vertigo threatened to overwhelm him. He wheezed, haggard breaths catching in his throat, initiating another round of violent coughs. Blood and mucous sprayed the wall.

Gods, it hurts...

He looked up through blurry eyes of pain.

The street was littered with the dead and dying. All manner of refuse from the surrounding buildings lay strewn about. Broken glass lay everywhere. Doors, either wholly busted or left half hanging, exposed the shops or homes that they had once protected. Eager fingers of fire pulsated out these new openings in its relentless search. Valen blinked furiously to clear his stinging eyes, but the smoke was everywhere, wafting down the streets in lazy plumes. He looked up. The sky was hazy and thick with ash, the sun a meager grey dot behind it all.

The pillaging had begun...was it yesterday? The day before?

Valen could not remember. His mind was as hazy as the sky. He could only remember the inn. He had to get to the inn. There was a healer.

What was the inn's name? The Crag? The Fiddle of something?

He shook his head vigorously in a vain attempt to clear his mind.

No matter. It was off the central square, and surely someone was there to help.

He pushed himself off the wall and began stumbling down the street, winding his way around the dead and debris. Great wracking waves of coughs created a slow and arduous pace. Each bout bringing up more and more blood.

How much blood can a person lose before passing out?

He let the thought go as he finally entered the central square, eyes still burning from the smoke. He blinked until his vision cleared. When he opened them, his gaze was met with only more of the same. Hands on his knees, he surveyed the square. It was a landscape of utter chaos. Carts, wagons, and their contents were everywhere. Nothing was left unscathed. Save the faint crackling of nearby fires and the distant collapsing of buildings succumbing to their fate, the courtyard was eerily quiet. Nothing stirred amongst the mass of bodies and debris.

Which inn...?

He rose, choosing the largest of the inns. He could not make out the name, but he would start there.

As he was rounding the large central fountain, a hand reached out and brushed his leg. He looked down. It was a young girl; her face a grotesque mask of pain, blood seeping from her eyes and ears. She held a small bag in her other hand, a light yellow dress spilling out, now covered with grime and blood.

"Hep...maay..." The words came out cluttered and malformed, twisting around a tongue that was too swollen, and protruding from a mouth it no longer fit. It was speckled with black, unnatural blotches, and a gurgle of blood and spittle escaped its way around the misshapen mass and down her cheek. Before Valen could respond or even pull his leg aside, the hand fell limply to the ground, the light of life slowly disappearing from her eyes.

Valen stared in morbid fascination. Her dead eyes staring back with her last desperate pleas echoing up at him. He felt...nothing.

Another wave of coughs bent him over in pain, sprinkling the young girl's face with tiny droplets of blood.

Must get to the inn...

Valen entered the inn and did not find the respite he so desired. What he saw bent him over in pain once more, only this time to vomit. His torso heaved and lurched, but he had nothing more to give, and the bitter taste of bile filled his mouth. He spat.

More than the disease had ravaged these people. A final, desperate fight for survival that would rival the bloodiest of battlefields spread out before him. Bodies, whole and stumped, lay sprawled across the entirety of the floor. Where the disease had not taken them, the fighting did. Great gashes in torsos lay open, spilling their contents. Crushed skulls had been reduced to nothing more than mounds of pulp. Arms, legs, and a few lifeless heads, eyes staring blankly at nothing, lay scattered throughout. The stench was horrific, and he struggled to hold back another agonizing retch of revulsion.

Near the back of the room, there was a makeshift barrier. Nothing more than a few of the inn's tables turned on their side. Several figures lay draped across the barrier as if in some final tragic act in a play. The slow drip, drip, drip of blood and other bodily fluids was the only sound in the room as the puddles beneath them grew, already congealing at the edges.

Valen strained and listened intently for any signs of life over the drip, drip, drip of the dead.

"Scritch...scritch..."

Valen's head jerked up, listening intently.

"Scritch..."

There!

Faint scraps across the floor coming from up above. His heart surged with hope and with a burst of energy he did not know he still had, he stumbled his way up the stairs and down the hall towards the noise.

The last door lay open and he stopped to brace himself in the doorway, wheezing from the exertion. Half a dozen ravens squawked and jumped away. They stared up at him, their solid black eyes uncaring and indifferent as they studied him, before shuffling forward and resuming their feast. Valen stumbled forward and waved his hands, managing only a pitiful yelp from his cough-ragged throat as he fell to his knees. The ravens lurched into flight and flew out the broken window.

Valen leaned forward, placing his hands on the floor in exhaustion next to the dead and partially eaten corpse, staring unfeelingly at what lay before him.

Maybe in another inn...I'll just rest here for...

Valen slowly fell to his side. He stared out the window as the darkness began to envelop him. His eyes took in the smoke hazed sky as the blackness closed in around him.

It's kind of pretty...

A raven flew in and perched on the window.

"Squawwwk!"

Spirit leisurely strolled through the field, letting her hands hover just above the tall feathery tops of the grasses. The morning was still mild, the sun just beginning to gather its intensity to burn off the morning dew. A soft breeze billowed her shift and the gentle waves of the grasses tickled her palms.

As one of the immortal Patrons of this world, she wondered why her brothers and sisters did not take more time to appreciate the simple beauty in the worlds they created. An exquisitely timed moment such as this should be savored and appreciated. She chided herself.

I must find time to do this more frequently.

Spirit lifted her head high, and slowly took in a long, purposeful breath. She did not need to breathe, but allowed herself the pleasure of the motley collection of smells from the fields and nearby forest. It was invigorating.

Standing motionless, she enjoyed the tranquility of the moment and the warmth of the light on her face. She slowly raised her arms wide, bringing her hands together at the apex, inhaling deeply through the movement. She paused for the briefest of moments, a single breath, before reversing the pose, and lowering her arms as she exhaled. As she concluded the meditative flow, her hands came together in front of her chest, fingers intertwined. She bowed her head and closed her eyes. She held the reverent pose for a few moments, and then sighed. With unenthusiastic finality, she let the short meditative moment dissolve.

As much as she would like to stay, the indulgence would have to wait for another time. Today was the day she and her brother had to inspect the last vestiges of what had been humankind's last remaining soul of this age. It was an unfortunate ending to one of the finer ages of man. The society had been progressing admirably. It was well-balanced, had no major conflicts, and a renaissance of innovation and invention had been on the threshold of emerging.

Spirit took one last look around her, regarding the beauty of the landscape. She would need to make sure she complimented Breanna. This really was a beautiful setting and should be replicated in the new age. She straightened and with a small flick of her wrist, a breath of air began to lift her. As she rose above the fields and the forest beyond, she saw her destination off in the distance. The smoldering remains of what had once been a thriving community. It was time to find her brother and complete their final obligations.

Steadily, inexorably, the sound of buzzing filled the air as she entered the city.

"Flies. Ugh, I hate flies," she muttered to herself.

So annoying.

Her brother and his fascination with death had been the culprit for these little annoying creatures. He thought they brought "balance."

They brought annoyance for sure, but balance? Not so much.

She heard him call for her just ahead.

"Spirit! Spirit, where are you?"

"On my way, brother," Spirit replied with a tinge of annoyance.

Patience had never been one of Tovin's strong suits.

She made her way over a smoldering building, locating Tovin at an inn just off the central plaza. While the rest of the continent struggled to contain the disease, this small, out-of-the-way port town had somehow been sheltered from it. The containment efforts, it turned out, had been all too inadequate and far too late. In the end, even isolated Monsk had fallen. It was here that the last soul of this age, desperate and alone, had sought refuge at one of the inns.

Spirit lowered herself down to the inn's front steps and made her way in through the main doors. The stench of rotting flesh was horrific, the blow flies buzzed everywhere. She quickly disengaged her sense of smell, wrinkling her nose in disgust. Bloated, broken, and decaying corpses were strewn everywhere in the room. Littered amongst the bodies and across the floor were all the trappings of a once bustling inn: cups, plates, chairs, tables, and barrels. Nothing was left unmolested. All lay about in various stages of brokenness.

Never to be used again.

Spirit's soul ached at the thought of all the needless deaths and the ending of another age. The scene was eerily quiet, her mood more solemn than usual at the grim task before her. She raised herself slightly above the floor to avoid the mass of bodies and debris. Swiftly, she traversed the main hall to the stairs, gliding her way up to the landing, settling softly back onto the floor. The hallway was blessedly clear, save for some broken vases and a few tables, and she made her way down the main corridor until she found Tovin in the last room on the left.

Tovin was leaning over a gaunt man of middle years, his eyes wide in fascination as he inspected the body. The blow flies were just beginning to find their new quarry as he absent-mindedly waved them away.

Spirit remained in the doorway, surveying the macabre scene. She had always found it curious the way Tovin fixated on human death. As a knight of the council, he had seen and even dealt with death on the battlefield countless times over the millennia. Yet, he was forever curious how the mortal races, in all their frailty, died of ailments so small as this. Spirit sighed heavily, growing weary of all the death that surrounded her.

"Well?" she asked.

"Fascinating."

"What is so fascinating?" She was not in the mood for her brothers 'fascinations'. Today had upset her. Angered her even. Lost in the moment, she boiled over. "He died of a disease, they all did!"

Tovin looked up at his sister, surprised at the outburst. It was not like his sister to show her anger so outwardly.

"I only...all I was going to say was that this disease was particularly virulent, so...all-consuming. The way the disease attacked the organs and shut them down. It was very systematic as it spread. It was no wonder it killed so swiftly."

"If you say so, brother. Is this truly the final human to pass?" She was growing more impatient by the second, jaws clenching tightly. She was eager to complete this grisly task. "If so, we must report back and relay our findings."

Tovin continued his morbid examination for a few more moments, then rose, reading his sister's impatience.

"Yes. He was the last. Poor soul. We must return and give our final account."

Spirit sat at her reading table, blankly staring at the mass of notes piled around her. She had lost her temper with her brother and for that, she would need to apologize. She was angry, for losing her temper, and at the scene she had just witnessed. A wave of emotions rolled over her. Anger bubbled at the top and then there was anxiety, fear, and nervousness...but she was also resolute. She calmly placed her hands on the table and closed her eyes, letting the tension ebb away until a sense of calm confidence replaced the rest.

The halls of Corpellia, the capital city of the Tal'Kier Patrons, was bustling with activity. Spirit hardly noticed as the various attendants moved to the side and bowed as she made her way, already lost in thought with the conversations and inevitable debates that were to come.

The passing of one age and the beginning of another was a time-tested process. The council would discuss the previous age; the good, the bad, and everything in between. Any subtle changes to the creation of the new age would be presented and debated until all the parameters were agreed upon. It was here that Spirit was going to draw her line and make her argument. Nothing of note, let alone extraordinary, was ever presented. Sure, there were the handful of successes. Several other ages were well into their 22nd century, achieving admirable technological success. But many, far too many... her thoughts trailed off. The universe was neither malevolent nor cruel, but it was harsh, and if there was a flaw, it would reach out with its uncaring hand and the age would end.

Spirit shuddered, remembering the scene on Galleant. All the devastation. All the untapped potential. Gone.

We can no longer keep the status quo.

Spirit pursed her lips, partly in frustration, but also determination. She was ready. Change...a step forward that would brandish hope, and for once, actually be meaningful.

Her proposal would be met with severe resistance, of that she was sure. Her arguments were sound, though, and if she could sway but a few...it might plant the seed she needed.

It has to!

All the surrounding realms were flourishing, and everyone knew of the whispers, the central realm was rife with them; Tal'kier was under scrutiny. No one, of course, spoke of it. It was the dark secret in the corner of a room, just out of the light, festering and breeding on itself, growing stronger. If they didn't speak of it, there was always the hope that maybe events would naturally change for the better. But, if they did speak of it...well that would mean admitting a failing in their charge. Hope was a dangerous thing. If you did nothing, in the 'hope' for change, without any actual change...well, that was, at the very least, naive, and at worst, ignorance. Better to admit the faults and plan a move forward, otherwise, the rumors would manifest and their realm would be at risk of being absorbed. Picked over and parceled out to the handful of more 'promising' ruling factions, like children picking sides at playtime. For her and the rest of the Tal'kier Patrons; their statuses and titles would be stripped bare, only to serve under new realm leadership.

I will not stand by and do nothing!

As Spirit approached the council chamber, she paused at the entryway, taking in the great hall. It was not particularly large as great halls went, but she had always felt it was grand in its own right. The room was circular, segmented by seven pillars. Seven pillars for the seven council chairs spaced evenly around the central round table. The edges of the room were somberly lit, a single sconce of light on each pillar. A dome above the central table lit the center, a perfect circular beam accentuating the table. It was elegantly simple.

Above the table floated depictions of all the planets currently under the purview of the Tal'kier council. Thirteen galaxies with a single planet for each were represented. Blue worlds were depicted as ones that were currently active and thriving in their current age. Those in yellow had some issue causing their age to be in question, or at the very least, in need of monitoring. Red denoted...Spirit shuddered. Her eyes fixed on the red globe suspended above the table. That was all that remained now. A single red orb, an unfeeling depiction of lives lost.

Red...how appropriate.

The human world of Galleant pulsed as if blaming her. She tore her gaze away from the table and entered the chamber. She was alone as she had hoped, and began to slowly pace around the room, taking in the murals. Between each pillar was a mural depicting various momentous events throughout Tal'kier's history. These murals were fairly static, but occasionally a new event aspired to take its place among the others. The old one would be moved to another area of Corpellia for viewing as the new one enjoyed its new prominence in the great hall. Spirit walked slowly and contemplatively around the room as the other council members began arriving. Finishing her circle, she paused near the entry, surveying the room in its entirety again.

There is great beauty in simplicity.

Letting the melancholy thought pass, she moved to take her appointed chair and grimaced at her brother. Tovin was leaning against the table next to Breanna and trying, with not much luck, to regale her with the details of their trip.

Perhaps if he had bothered to bathe before coming to the council. Men! Immortal and ancient, yet still so oblivious.

As she passed the pair, she slowed ever so slightly, laying a hand on Tovin's shoulder. As she did, he turned to address her, much to the relief of Breanna.

"Sister."

Spirit bent ever so slightly and gently whispered, "Perhaps you should rethink your hygiene and the fact that the unsavory details of our findings might not be the best choice of conversation with a woman, and the subsequent Patron of Bounty, brother."

Tovin turned towards Breanna, who was now trying desperately to seem otherwise occupied. "Ah, yes. Probably not."

Tovin stood up and away from the table. "Lady Breanna, my apologies for the breach in decorum. It was insensitive."

Breanna acknowledged the apology with a nod and then gave a short, but grateful, glance at Spirit. Her work here done, Spirit continued to her chair.

Talon was already present, sitting stoically and reading some missive of intelligence, no doubt planning for his next move in a scheme that would end up being overly complicated and fruitless. She knew that his den of intelligence spies was needed to keep up with the affairs in other realms, and all the political machinations of the central realm, but she found their methods distasteful.

Kemor, Mevane, and Bestia were all making their way to their seats by this time and the council meeting was set to begin.

Tovin stood and pointed to the human world of Galleant. Gesturing with his hands as the red orb slowly rose above the others and magnified. Its final statistics seemed to glare at Spirit with a final accusatory pulse.

Population–0

Population Peak–approximately 7 million

Technical Advancement–Typical achievement for an 18th century civilization

Religions–4 major religions across the regions

Conflicts–Minor and regional

The list went on to show that while this age of men had been advancing fairly normally, there were no major deviations from previous ages.

Spirit winced at the conclusion of the merciless statistics in front of her.

In essence, it was unremarkable.

Tovin continued with his final conclusions and their macabre trip to the inn. "The demise of the age was due to an extremely virulent disease. One, as far as I can tell, we've not seen before. The disease began in one of the subtropic port cities, most likely Karbanth or Sistelle, given their size, and quite frankly, sub-standard levels of hygiene and immoral practices. From there, the disease spread alarmingly quickly. First via normal human contaminations, then with the aid of two primary animal species, rats and birds. As we have seen before, the rats were effective carriers of the disease within a region, and the birds, well, they were the real culprit. Their migrations spread the disease across the entire continent. It was only a matter of time once this cascade began."

Spirit's shoulders relaxed as Tovin concluded his account, taking his seat. Thankfully, he did not feel the need to share his morbid fascination with the disease after such a somber recollection.

Seven million souls, we must do better. We must change! This senseless cycle of mediocrity and death has to end. It benefited no one.

Spirit slowly rose, taking in the grief clearly written on everyone's face. She steeled herself.

Now or never.

She clasped her hands reverently at her waist.

"Brothers and sisters of the council, what has happened here is horrific. Never have we seen such a total devastation of a world happen so quickly..." Spirit paused, lowering her head reverently as she whispered the last. "...and yet so avoidable."

There it was, the seed of a thought. Who would be first?

The council chamber fell silent. Spirit watched as they processed the implications. Kemor was the first to speak.

Fitting that the priest of healing would be the first to respond.

Spirit straightened. Resolute in her course of action.

Kemor's face bore an expression of incredulity as he began. "Surely you are not implying that we should have intervened directly?"

Spirit spoke calmly with the respect due a priest, and their oldest member. "No, Master Kemor. I would not break that which is forbidden. I am only implying... that we consider alternatives."

Kemor's eyes narrowed. "Alternatives?"

Spirit glanced around the table before clarifying, everyone eying her skeptically. "Alternatives...with regard to the creation of a new age." She continued quickly, before anyone could interrupt. She had to get this out. "It is obvious that we are failing in our charge. Civilizations collapse, whole worlds falling all too frequently into some manner of early demise. Should we not investigate other possibilities?" Spirit brought her hands down firmly on the table. "Not only for their sake, but for the stability and potential growth of our realm?" She let the implications of her last comment linger in the air. The dark secret no one wanted to acknowledge slowly rising to the surface in everyone's eyes.

No one spoke, but Spirit could almost hear their thoughts as if they were shouting. She had forced them to shed light into that dark corner of rumor.

What were they thinking?

The foundation for the creation of a new age had been set in place long ago. The template was simple. So simple, in fact, it had been repeated over and over without any notion of change or modification for countless millennia. The single intractable rule was simple:

after the creation of a new age, the Patrons were not allowed to interact in the natural maturation of a world. But, nothing specifically stated that the starting point had any such limitations...only taboos. It was here that Spirit hoped to lead them.

Kemor continued his scrutiny. "What are you suggesting? You've obviously given this some thought."

Spirit felt a small wave of relief and hope spread through her. *This is it.*

"I propose that we consider introducing the new age of man...to the Source." A cold shudder ran down her spine as she gave voice to the idea she had harbored in her own dark corner for so long.

The response was quick and vehement.

"Preposterous!" Talon rumbled, throwing his fists upon the table. His rebuttal still echoing in the chamber as he continued. "The mortal species are not capable of handling the Source. What would they do with it? How would they control it?" He shook his head. "No mortal species in all the realms has successfully been given access to the Source, it is too unpredictable." He slowly turned his head, staring hard at everyone around the table, making sure he had their full attention. "No realm has ever succeeded. Every effort has failed. Every...one."

Talon's words hung in the air, recriminative and true. She knew he was right. Giving mortals access to the Source would, at the very least, be unpredictable and, if taken to the extreme, dangerous.

Spirit returned Talon's gaze calmly. "I agree, but unpredictable is the point, is it not? If we are to endeavor to make our realm, and the mortals within our charge greater, should we not strive for that greatness? It is clear to me that our past endeavors are, at best, only partially fruitful...mediocre at best. Predictable and safe is not working." The conclusion was harsh and, in no small way, insulting. The time for civility was over, the reality was out of its dark corner, and it needed to be addressed.

Kemor, ever the moderator, smoothly brought the conversation back to more practical matters. "How is this even feasible? I foresee several issues. We cannot grant access to the Source from the inception of the age, the mortals would not know what they are experiencing, much less have the cognitive ability to control it." He paused contemplatively before continuing. "This would mean introducing Source cognition 'after' the creation of the Age, once the mortals were sufficiently mature. By definition, this means we would be breaking the Covenant of Intervention." He shook his head in resignation. "I do not see a way."

Spirit watched his expression soften and his tone became sorrowful. "I commend your forward thinking, I do. I too grieve at the loss of an age, but in this...I do not see a path forward."

Spirit watched as everyone at the table began silently agreeing with Kemor. She had foreseen this argument. She had struggled with it herself.

"Master Kemor. You are correct in your assessment. Mortals will need to have progressed and matured to a sufficient level before we could introduce them to the Source. The solution is to create the world with the Source present from the onset."

If Talon's eyes could throw his daggers, they would have pierced her straight through. "Not possible. The Source is not some seed that you plant."

Spirit replied with the confidence of all her long hours of study. "I have a few ideas."

Talon was not convinced. "Humph...a few ideas? I seriously doubt even your hubris is large enough to proclaim that."

Spirit let the insult go and continued. "With the Source already present, we can then control its access and to what degree. Not all mortals will be candidates. As we have seen in past ages, there are always individuals that set themselves apart, be it intelligence, inquisitiveness, or simply a proclivity for one of our own specialties. These individuals would be our prime candidates. In this way, we would not be breaking the covenant. We would simply be applying a new tenant, set at the creation of the age and extending it."

Kemor squinted his eyes suspiciously. "That is an extremely loose interpretation of the covenant. If it were found out..." He trailed off, shaking his head. "The scrutiny from the central realm would be very harsh. I am not sure they would be so agreeable with your assessment."

The other members gave no indication of their dissent or agreement to either argument. She needed time. Time for them to think, and with any hope, open themselves up to the possibility.

"Let us reconvene." Spirit said, breaking the awkward silence in the room. "We shall discuss final arguments on the morrow. Can we at least agree upon that?"

Everyone agreed somberly, and the meeting came to an abrupt end. No one sparing her a glance as they left. She was still standing at the table, staring at the red planet, lost in thought, when she felt a hand on her shoulder. She turned. It was Tovin.

"Sister." He hung his head low before raising his gaze to meet hers. "Why would you propose such a thing? It would open everyone up to reprisal, possible dismissal from the council, and any chance for advancement."

She turned her weary gaze back to the pulsing red orb and whispered, "Because it is needed."

There was silence between them for a long time. She could still feel him at her back and did not see him shake his head as he strode out of the chamber.

So there it was. The crux of the entire argument. Her little brother, the often clueless knight, divulging the heart of the matter so simply and succinctly. Granting small gifts of the Source was not the issue. She was not the first to think of it, Talon had eluded as much. No, it was the personal risk such an endeavor involved. That was the issue the members were feeling. Could they not see that 'not acting' was just as detrimental? They all knew their realm was faltering and already under scrutiny. All she could do now was wait. Wait to see if she knew her friends as well as she hoped, and that they would eventually come to her same conclusions.

Which of the two difficult conclusions would tip the scales?

Spirit retired to her room, flopping on the bed, mentally exhausted. So much time and effort had gone in to her plan, and now it was all down to one night. One last hope. A part of her was glad in the finality.

She closed her eyes and jerked with a start from her half sleep at a knock at the door. She climbed out of bed, straightening her skirt and hair to answer. Opening the door, she saw it was one of Breanna's attendants.

"Pardon, my lady, but I was instructed to give you this." The young girl handed Spirit a small note.

"Thank you."

The girl bowed and quickly left down the hall.

Spirit closed the door and sat down, opening the letter with trembling hands.

Dear Sister, what you propose is no small matter. To break ground and propose to plant such a seed takes no small amount of courage. I commend you.

I too feel the same hopelessness of our current traditions. They feel compassionless and outdated. Know that I will not vote against the full will of the council, but if the consensus is not whole, I will not stand against you.
- Breanna

Spirit stared at the note. So, she did know at least one of her friends as well as she thought. Not exactly a ringing endorsement, but also not against. That was at least a start.

Spirit received no more callings for the remainder of the night. She did not sleep.

Spirit left her room early the following morning. She wanted to walk and clear her head, taking a long circuitous route through Breanna's gardens. Afterwards, she eventually ended up at the council chamber, far earlier than she intended. Stopping at the entryway once again, she admired the room before entering. She entered and took her seat, sitting stoically while she waited for the others to arrive, studying the murals. She was intimate with each of the achievements depicted and wondered.

Were they really great?

Most of the murals depicted a victory in battle, one region triumphing over another. A few were technical in nature, a discovery here or there that advanced an age.

But were they great?

In the end, most of these ages had ended with the exploits and discoveries wasted, never achieving much more than their predecessors. Forever to be forgotten but for a mural on a wall here in Corpellia. She sighed.

Eventually, the other members began to trickle into the council chamber. Most giving her no more than a polite nod before sitting down, lost in their own reflection.

Once all had arrived, Spirit stood, gathering her thoughts.

"Friends, what I have proposed is no small thing," quoting from Breanna's note. "The thought of introducing the Source to the mortals is not a thought only I have experienced. Talon informed us that no other realm had 'successfully' introduced the Source to a mortal race. Not that it could not be done. The question of how is within our power to control. A difficult challenge...possibly. But one I believe we can achieve. The question is not one of execution, but of risk. Of fortitude. Do we have the fortitude to overcome the personal risk for the chance at creating something greater?"

Spirit scanned the room, looking at each member purposefully. "I do." She lowered her head and sat.

The hall was silent, almost eerily so, given the seven individuals seated around the table. Not a single fidget of movement. Spirit glanced at Tovin and then Breanna, both giving her an almost imperceptible nod of respect.

After what seemed liked an eternity, Mevane stood to address the council. His thick baritone voice reverberating in the chamber.

"I am but a humble engineer. I make things, and...well...sometimes I break things." This drew a chorus of weak chuckles from around the table. "But! I must endeavor the failures to achieve something greater. What our Lady Spirit is proposing is indeed no small thing, but I believe her heart is true. I, for one, am tired of the sameness, of the bitter failures and I say to hells with it! Let us see what we can make!"

As the echoes of Mevane's words died, Bestia slowly raised her hand and uttered but a single word, "Aye."

Tovin was next, quickly raising his hand, "Aye."

Breanna and Kemor looked at one another and followed in the affirmative.

Talon was all that remained. He looked around the council chamber, taking in each individual in turn. "If we do such a thing, we will need to keep it quiet. Keep it hidden for as long as we can until such a time we have something worthy of breaking the silence. Something beyond reproach. Are we all in agreement?"

Everyone nodded in agreement.

And so it was. A new age of man would begin, one with uncertainty, but also of hopefulness and potential. For the first time in the Tal'kier realm, a mortal race would have access to the Source.

Deep within the central realm, an old and ancient entity stirred.

CHAPTER 1
THE GIFT
YEAR 1303 / CALLIST'E / WEEK 1

Challand paused and peered into the barn. Through the dim haze, dust motes sparkled as they danced between the beams of sunlight. On the far wall, she could see a table. Resting in the middle, half-lit through the slats in the wall, was a box. She hesitated, looking around nervously.

Inside, Arran knelt quietly behind a few bales of hay, watching intently. He was flush with excitement as Challand stood outside the door.

So close!

In the past, the final execution of a scheme would have made him anxious. So many of his small traps and trip wires had gone wrong over the years, but he had left those days of childish pranks behind him. This was different. This time, he had created a mystery. A story for a prize. He had slowly guided Challand through a series of clues for over a week. The answer now lay in front of her. It had all led here. All the pieces had come together and now she only needed to finish. Would she walk away? Too suspicious? His years of pranks as a youth had made most in the town wary of his schemes, but this one was different. He could see it in her eyes. The mystery had her. The intrigue of following a week's worth of clues was too much for her to ignore.

Come on...

He felt the old anxiousness begin to build. Not for the spring of a trap, but the thrill of her completing his story. It had taken him a long time to find the right hiding spots and then write out all the proper clues. One small nugget of information that led to the next and then the next. It all had led here. He felt a prickle of sweat run down the center of his back.

Challand took a faltering step forward and hesitated, a sliver of uncertainty rushing across her face.

Arran watched from his hiding spot, nervous with anticipation. He held his breath. Challand took another small step forward. She was through the threshold of the barn now and she stopped, head swiveling left and right as she peered into the dimness of the barn. Her gaze finally coming back to rest on the small box. She stepped forward.

Resting her hands on the table, she bent closer, inspecting the small, rather ordinary looking rectangular box from every angle. She straightened and looked around the barn again with uncertainty before returning to the box. Carefully, as if expecting something to jump out at her, she opened the box. Inside was a small and delicate long-stem rose. It was yellow, her favorite color, and it was beautiful, not yet fully bloomed. She stared at it for several long moments and then peered around the room again. Turning back to the box, she took a moment and admired the rose's shape, its faint scent wafting up to her even in the dusty barn. She ran a finger delicately over the petals.

Arran could hear her sigh as she placed the lid back on the box, picked it up, and walked away.

He sat hunched behind the hay for several minutes after Challand had left.

I wonder if she knows...Surely she liked the rose, it's her favorite color.

Arran had never been comfortable around girls, well, young women now that he had turned eighteen, but still. He always felt tongue-tied and flush in their presence. Challand was arguably the prettiest and most sought-after young lady for miles around. She was a little over a year older than Arran, but he had known her his whole life. He had even played a few of those early pranks on her as young boys are ought to do. Young men from as far away as the towns of Pateen and Joskel had come to court her. But right now, today, she had a flower from an unknown admirer and that suited Arran just fine.

Arran brushed himself off and strolled through the village, no one the wiser, at least yet, of his latest caper.

I wonder if she will tell anyone...

Kine was not a large village, five hundred or so counting all the children. It was a small, quiet, out-of-the-way farming village. Arran had known no differently and on the occasions they would travel to one of the larger towns, he always felt a sense of relief when they returned. He could never quite put his finger on why, though. His mother said it was for the quiet. She loved the quiet. The peacefulness of long walks and her books.

Arran made his way to the entrance of his father's smithy and stepped inside. It was oddly quiet for midday. His father, Dale, had lived in Kine his entire life as the town's blacksmith, as had Arran's grandfather. It was a long line of blacksmiths that had run this family business, and one day it would be Arran's.

Dale came out from the back room and caught sight of him. "Arran, my boy, now what have you been up to today?"

"Um, not much," Arran replied nonchalantly, looking around the shop suspiciously.

"Good, good..." His father hesitated, eying him skeptically. "You sure?"

Arran's reputation still had quite a few chinks in it from all the pranks he had pulled over the years, and his father, while trusting, was still obviously a little wary.

"I'm suurrre..." Arran drew it out for emphasis and joined his father at the workbench, passing the large bellows that had so often been his punishment over the years. He picked up a horseshoe and turned it over in his hands. "I'm a changed man, Father."

"Hmmm," Dale murmured to himself. "You haven't been up to anything I don't know about, have you?"

Arran returned his father's gaze with a puzzled look on his face. "Not that I know of." He winked.

"Ha!" His father clapped him on the back. "Not exactly reassuring, but no news is good news on that front. You go on now. Your mother has been looking for you. She wants to figure out your 'ensemble' for your Source Day." Dale struggled to keep the smirk from spreading across his face. He knew his son was not one for any kind of finery, much preferring a normal set of britches and plain shirt, but he enjoyed the playful moment, watching his son squirm.

"Seriously, Father? No one in our family has ever been gifted on their Source Day. It's a waste of time."

"True, very true. It is tradition, though, and one never knows how the Patrons will bestow their gifts. I will not be the one to scorn that, or any ill winds that it might incur. So, go on." Dale waved his tongs towards the door to the house emphatically.

As Arran was leaving, he heard his father once more. "Oh, and Arran, I personally think you would look fetching in blue, if you were wondering. I have an old smock if you like." He grinned mischievously. "I think it would fit."

Arran huffed and went inside to find his mother. He would be stubborn, but he knew that there was no getting out of this particular tradition.

Arran found his mother dithering about the kitchen, even though it was between the lunch and dinner hours. His mother, Pai'ese, kept a very tidy kitchen and was considered quite the cook in the village. Maybe the best. She turned as Arran entered and gave him a smile.

"Ah, there you are. Your father sent you, I presume?" She pulled down the towel that was slung across her shoulder and began drying her hands. "So you know of what we need to speak?" A corner of her mouth twitched ever so slightly, just short of a smirk.

"Yes, Mother, but it's all such a waste of time. No one in our family has ever been..."

She interrupted him with a wave of her hand. "Yes, yes. We've heard it all before." She re-folded the towel and hung it across the back of a chair as she crossed the room. "Come, we will go upstairs and go through what we have then decide if we need to go visit Maila for any additional items." This time, she did not try to hide the broad grin that turned into a chuckle as she urged him forward.

"Shopping!" He tried to turn in protest, but a firm hand on his back kept him moving forward.

By Tovin's sword, I'd prefer the bellows.

Source Day: A day of celebration, feasting and wonderment. The festival fell during the mid-summer celebrations in the month of Callist'e, as the star of Callista finished its yearly path to its zenith, marking the new year. Arran had been to many Source Day events over the years, as everyone had. Every year, all children of age, eighteen as it goes, took their turn at the Patron's altar to be gifted, or not, as Arran had so stubbornly argued over the past few days. Arran had recently turned eighteen in June, the previous month, and now it was his turn.

It had been several days since the mystery box with Challand, and there had been no mention of it. For all intents and purposes, everything appeared as if it had never occurred. Life had been normal and, by all accounts, dull, leading up to Source Day.

Guess she must have kept it to herself.

Arran let himself be guided by his mother as they milled around the village green when he spotted Challand through the crowd on the opposite side of the Patron altar. She did not so much as give him a glance.

I wonder if she knows it was me?

Arran shrugged dismissively.

Slowly but surely, he watched as the entirety of Kine made their way to the village's center green. There weren't too many festivities that brought the entire village together, but Source Day was one of them.

Receiving a gift was not common in Kine. Challand had actually been the most recently gifted, and Arran couldn't actually remember another. Challand had been blessed by Breanna, the Patron of Bounty. After three terms at the School of Doctrine and a successful year one evaluation, she had been given the option to continue her schooling or be released to go back home to Kine. She had chosen to return home.

Arran had learned that being gifted by Breanna was very different from the other Patrons. Those gifted by Breanna rarely followed through with the four years of training that most disciplines required. Unless one wanted to excel in the arts of botany, alchemy, or the science of weather, it was enough for one to only train as long as it took for the instructors to approve one capable enough to control their powers. Once Challand had achieved this, she had returned.

Kine was primarily a farming community, Challand's family included, and so her gift had been seen as quite the blessing. She was not powerfully gifted, but her ability was still capable enough for her to achieve no small amount of success in Kine as well as in some of the neighboring villages. Her blessings to the land, seeds, and sometimes even weather prediction had become invaluable to the villages. The people of Kine looked upon her with reverence and were grateful for her blessings. Everyone benefited. "The Kine Way."

The crowd began to settle down as Mayor Burton made his way to the front of the sourcestone altar, raising his hands to quiet the crowd.

"Friends!" he shouted loudly to get everyone's attention. "Friends! Today, we gather to observe our young men and women begin their next journey. Not just for the possible endowment of a gift, but also to mark their step into adulthood."

Blah, blah, blah. Arran had heard it all before, but the mayor was not one to skip a chance to address the entire village.

How very dull. Just get on with it so I can get out of this ridiculous outfit.

Arran scratched at the itchy shirt his mother had picked out. It was unfortunately a light blue, much to his father's amusement. 'It brings out your eyes' his mother had said. Arran's mind wandered, and when he finally returned his attention back, the mayor was on the final stretch of his speech.

Finally!

Mayor Burton's cheeks flushed as he spoke the final words of the initiation, "It is time for the prayers to the Patrons, for gifts from the Source, as they deem fit: Spirit the Mage, Tovin the Knight, Breanna the Bountiful, Talon the Intelligent, Kemor the Priest, Mevane the Engineer, and Bestia the Hunter."

There were three of age this festival including Arran; Miranda, a quiet and unassuming girl; and Tok, a big hulking lad who was amiable enough, given his size, but had escaped Arran's pranks over the years for obvious reasons.

Miranda's parents quickly ushered her forward as the first. She shakily walked up to the front of the assembly and knelt before the altar of the Patrons. She looked positively petrified.

The mayor leaned over to encourage her. "Go on, Miranda, say your prayers," he whispered.

Miranda's voice trembled as she began to recite the prayer. "Thank you, Patrons, for the bounties you have bestowed upon us. We thank you for your grace and honor. I pray that you will strengthen and guide me for all that life has before me. Bless me now and forever."

The crowd hushed. Miranda continued kneeling, waiting, afraid to move or do anything assuming. One heart beat, two heartbeats, three, four, and then five. Nothing happened. The mayor leaned down, helped Miranda to her feet, and turned her around towards the crowd.

"Miranda has given her prayers and received her blessing into adulthood!" the mayor exclaimed. The crowd cheered. It was the polite thing to do, even if a gift had not been bestowed. Miranda demurely blushed as she stood next to the mayor, her cheeks slowly turning a bright red at all the attention. The mayor urged her forward, and she made her way back into her parents' arms. Obvious relief spreading across her face at no longer being the center of attention.

Tok was next. The big hulk of a lad strolled right up to the altar, knelt, and said his prayers. Again, one heartbeat, two, three, four, and five. No gift. Tok rose and turned to the crowd, arms raised triumphantly. Everyone cheered.

"Tok already received his gift from the Patron of Size years ago!" someone yelled and everyone burst into laughter, clapping him on the back as he returned to his parents.

All right...let's get this over.

Arran walked to the altar and gave the mayor a quick glance, who nodded. Arran knelt.

As he began his prayers, they came easily, almost automatically. He had been reciting them since he could first speak. As he finished the prayer, the faintest hint of doubt crept into his mind.

What if I were to receive a gift?

Arran waited and then let out the breath he had not known he had been holding.

I guess not.

Arran rose to turn to the crowd, but instead of cheering, there was silence.

What? Did I turn too early? Did I not wait for the requisite five heartbeats? Well, that would be embarrassing!

He turned to ask the mayor, and as he did, he noticed the altar. It was no longer the normal stone grey sourcestone he had known his whole life. It was now awash with a vibrant glow.

What the...?!

Arran looked at the mayor, who seemed as stunned as he was.

"What is the sigil?" someone yelled from the audience. "What Patron has gifted him?"

Mayor Burton stood transfixed, as if caught off guard, and seemingly as surprised as Arran. He came out of his stupor and leaned over to the front of the altar. In the middle of the plinth, shining ever so brightly, was the sigil of a book crossed with a single dagger.

The mayor cleared his throat uneasily. "Um...it appears our young Arran has been gifted from the Patron of Intelligence, Talon."

The crowd went silent and Arran stood rigid in disbelief, trying to digest what had just happened.

No one in their village had ever been gifted from 'that' Patron. It wasn't heard of! The Patron of Intelligence? Maybe the mayor had misinterpreted. Yeah, that was it.

Arran turned and looked closer at the altar and the glowing plinth. He blinked his eyes, then blinked again. Sure enough, smack in the middle of the stone plinth was the sigil of the book and dagger! It was Talon all right.

"What does it mean, Mayor?" a voice from the crowd asked. The question seemed thunderous in the silence.

Mayor Burton turned to face the crowd. He was obviously at a loss for words. This was unprecedented in their tiny little world. He took a moment to gather himself before continuing. "I will send word to his Lordship Baelonne. He will send a priest to finalize the gifting."

The crowd remained motionless, then someone began to clap, then another, and finally the entire village was cheering and congratulating Arran.

Congratulating? Is that what this was?

His whole life just changed. It felt like the Patrons had rolled the dice and he lost.

Talon? Seriously?

Everyone knew what Talon was really about. Oh, they called him the 'Patron of Intelligence', but did you happen to see the dagger across the book? Spies! Talon was the Patron of Intelligence, spies, and at the extreme, assassins! He was well and truly screwed.

The rest of the evening was a fog. People ate, drank (some too much) and made their rounds to congratulate all the candidates. No one lingered long with Arran, though.

They knew. Oh, they knew.

Arran stared at the ceiling of his room as the faint light of the morning sun began to make its way through the window. Sleep had been elusive. He could not stop thinking about the ceremony. His eyes became unfocused as he lay, staring up at the ceiling.

A gift from Talon!

It was surreal. The thought of actually receiving a gift had never been real to him. He would follow in his father's footsteps and take over the smithy. Sure as sunrise. He would start a family of his own...

Maybe Challand?

...and live his life in peace. Most likely never leaving Kine. Now this.

Arran blinked the blur from his eyes and rose groggily. It was not like he was going to get any more sleep and might as well face the day. He made his way to the kitchen, where his mother was busy with the morning meal.

"Good morning, Mother." Arran greeted her with a yawn.

Pai'ese turned to greet her son with a forlorn expression. Her boy...chosen by Talon. She could not believe it.

Talon! Of all the Patrons, why him?

"Come here, Arran." She wrapped Arran in a tight embrace that only mothers had seemed to perfect.

"It will be all right. We will figure all of this out. We will go to the mayor and straighten all of this out."

She released the embrace and held him at arm's length. "Now." She spoke with as much conviction as she could muster. "What do you want for breakfast?" She cupped his head in both her hands and gave him a gentle kiss on the forehead.

"I'm not very hungry, Mother."

"Nonsense, sit down and I will fix you something."

"Can I have a little something that I can take? I would like to go for a walk and be alone, if you don't mind."

Pai'ese's heart ached from the words. "Of course, dear. Let me put something together for you."

Arran took the bundle and left the village, making his way out into the fields. Somewhere he could be alone. Somewhere he didn't have to bear the pitying looks of the townsfolk.

He ended up at the large tree at the edge of the fields. He had played here many times when he was younger, and it was a common spot where his family would sometimes go for picnics. This would do. He sat down, took a biscuit from the bundle, and began to eat half-heartedly. He let his eyes close.

Arran awoke with a start as he began to fall away from the tree. He looked around blearily and found the half-eaten biscuit lying on the ground next to him.

He rubbed the sleep from his eyes, picked up the biscuit, and leaned his head back against the tree.

I guess the lack of sleep caught up with me.

He looked out over the field and bright sky. It was already mid-morning by the look of it.

He let his mind wander, lost in his own dour thoughts when he heard the faint rustling of...was that skirts? He peered around the tree to see Challand approaching.

He dusted the biscuit crumbs from his shirt as she approached.

Challand greeted him perfunctorily. "Arran." She was wearing a normal work skirt and shirt, but she made it look like feast day finery.

"Hey. So, how..." she cut him off with a wave of her hand.

She took a few deep breaths, folded her skirt beneath her and sat down.

She stared purposefully, not wavering a fraction from his eyes. "Listen...I know it was you." She let the statement hang, watching for any telltale sign of recognition. Arran did not meet her eyes. "I knew when I got the mysterious notes and the promise of a unique gift that you were probably behind it, but curiosity got the better of me. I was waiting and wary of the inevitable, but it never came."

Arran looked up, but did not respond.

She sighed. "How did you come by such a unique variety of rose, anyway?"

Arran could only shrug.

Challand looked out over the field and took a deep breath, her eyes coming back to rest on his. "As I admired the flower, I realized something. Of all the people in the world to give me my first flower... it was you. I almost had to laugh. I looked at it...and it became more than just a rose to me. It became precious. So, I went home, thankful that I didn't get caught in one of your more 'messy' pranks. That is the all of it. You are a sneaky little brat. There is no getting around that, but also, I wanted to thank you. In your own way, you gave me something I will cherish."

Silence fell between them. Arran was stunned.

Well, that took a turn I was not expecting!

He started to speak, but Challand hushed him again with a wave of her hand. "Don't say anything, Arran. You will only ruin the moment. Accept my thanks for the flower, and let us leave it at that, yes?"

Arran could only nod his head in agreement, dumbfounded.

After what seemed like an eternity, Arran summoned up the courage to speak, to say anything. "So, what did you do with the flower?"

Challand looked up, the sternness on her face replaced by sympathy? Forgiveness? Arran could not tell exactly.

"I took it home and showed my mother. She was so excited and questioned me non-stop on where I had gotten it." She chuckled. "I only told her it was from a boy and left it at that. She is beside herself trying to figure out who, and is going to help me press it for a keepsake." She ushered a weak smile.

Arran looked at her, confused. "Um, press the flower?"

"Yes, it is a method where you...never mind, it will help keep it for a long time."

"Huh." Arran had never heard of such a thing.

"Now, this matter with the flower is done. Is that something we can agree on? Between you and I? You and I...alone?" Challand emphasized the last sternly.

"I'm okay with that." Arran was starting to feel more than a little relieved, but still quite confused.

The wind rustled the leaves of the tree, and the grasses in the field swayed. Challand shifted up onto her knees, her gaze intense.

"I am not going to say I'm sorry for your gifting or give you empty congratulations. I am sure you've heard enough of that already." Her expression turned to one of thoughtfulness and caring. "I believe there is more to you than you let on. More than a life in the smithy... with your father. I cannot say why exactly, but on your Source Day, when the sourcestone lit up, I felt a rightness. That is the only way I can explain it."

Challand paused as if unsure how to proceed, fumbling with her skirt nervously. "What if there is something more for you than Kine? Or your father's smithy? What if...what if the Patrons actually 'do' see something more in you? I believe there is Arran. I honestly do."

Everything fell silent. Arran could no longer hear the wind or the leaves. All he could hear was the steady beat of his heart in his ears. Challand's eyes fell to her lap.

Then, without any hesitation, Challand leaned over and kissed him on the cheek. She stood, dusting off her skirt.

"Think about it."

Arran could only sit in stunned silence, brows furrowed with confusion as he watched her leave.

Did that just happen? Did I just get thanked for a flower and then kissed by the prettiest girl in the village? This has been a VERY strange week!

"There you are," his father said. "How are you feeling?"

Why was everyone asking me that? How do you think I feel?! I've been gifted by the most infamous Patron.

Arran wanted to scream in frustration and then sighed. "I'm fine, Father. I just needed some time to think alone this morning."

"Fine, fine." Arran could see his father was nervous as he absent-mindedly began rearranging the tools on his table. He faltered a bit before continuing, "We need to go see Mayor Burton. He will be wanting to go over your ceremony and the proper steps we need to take."

"I know."

"Okay, then let me wash up and we'll be off." He wiped his hands on a towel, eying his son. Without a word, he placed a hand on Arran's shoulder, squeezed, and then made his way into the house.

They left the house a short while later, heading towards the town hall to meet with the mayor; once again dealing with all the stupid stares and polite nods.

Ugh.

He was almost thankful when they arrived at the town hall and they could get on with this meeting and, more importantly, away from everyone.

The mayor was waiting for them in his office. He sat behind a small desk with papers neatly arranged in piles. He stood anxiously as they entered and greeted them, his eyes darting everywhere but never at Arran. He gestured at the chairs in front of the desk.

"Please, please have a seat." He circled his desk and sat down to face them. "I have sent a message to Saloanne. I expect the priest to arrive within the week."

"And if the priest verifies the sigil? What then, Mayor?" Pai'ese's voice was quick and stern.

The mayor hesitated as he settled into his chair, obvious unease shouting from his every move. "If the priest verifies the sigil...Arran will most likely be expected to return with him to Saloanne, and from there on to Meitellen, and the School of Doctrine. A gift from Talon is uncommon, rare even, and they will surely want to evaluate him at the school."

Arran grimaced at the mayor's reply.

So, there it is.

Pai'ese sat up straight and eyed the mayor severely. "And if he rejects the gift?"

The mayor visibly flinched at the question.

"Rejects the gift?" His face began to pale at the thought.

"Well, uh, it is true..." He spluttered through the words as he tried to formulate a proper reply. "Nothing is forced, mind you...but I must warn you. There will be considerable pressure from the Lord of Saloanne, Meitellen, and the school for a gift of this rarity. It is just not done, Pai'ese...tradition." The mayor sighed and continued, "Ultimately...it will be Arran's decision. He must be the one to decide."

Pai'ese sat back in frustration.

Dale patted her arm, resting a hand on hers.

The mayor, obviously unnerved by Pai'ese's reaction, offered her a handkerchief. She shook her head. He turned his gaze to Arran.

"Son." It was the first time Mayor Burton had looked at him since they entered. "What would be your decision if the sigil is verified?"

Arran sat in silence. The mayor's beady eyes unnerved him, and he got up, pacing about the room.

What do I do? I didn't even know I could reject a gift. Could I be that person? Someone who was blessed then rejected a gift from the Patrons? Could I live with that stigma? Could I live my entire life not ever knowing? What if Challand was right? What if the Patrons saw potential in me? Potential even I was not aware of?

Arran looked at his mother and father uneasily.

Could I leave them and go to Meitellen? Meitellen! The capital and most prestigious city in all of Galleant. Could I leave them to go and train in the School of Doctrine? Follow the Path of Intelligence?

Arran wandered around the office, mind reeling with the decision, before calmly retaking his seat. He returned the mayor's gaze with resolve.

"I will go."

Let's see what this famous school has to offer!

INTERLUDE

Spirit was in the council chambers and zoomed in on the human world of Galleant. The humans of this age were doing extraordinarily well. She was pleased to see how well the humans had adapted to the introduction of the Source. The speed at which they assimilated it into their societal structure was impressive.

By all measures, introducing the Source had so far been successful, at least in her eyes; but successful to her and successful to the council were two entirely different matters. The council's definition was defined only by the fact that nothing dire had yet to transpire... save the one event that had, in the end, been an oversight on their part, not any fault of the mortals. As such, they continued to allow her to move forward despite the fact that most were still uncomfortable with the riskiness of the endeavor.

Satisfied that the humans on this continent were progressing admirably, she spun the world towards the other continent on Galleant. The Patrons often created multiple continents on worlds, sometimes seeding them with sentients and other times leaving them to flourish with only natural wildlife and fauna. Spirit knew how Breanna especially enjoyed the continents left to mature in this manner.

Spirit focused the sphere down onto the continent, deep within the northern area of the vast landscape, and into a large forest. Nestled in the valley of a large mountain range was a small village of perhaps five or six hundred. The image was not a live view. Her and Mevane's creation only allowed for a few images per day, but what she saw still made her smile. The village was simple and serene. This particular race of mortals had a large affinity with nature and the earth. They tended to live more synergistically with their environs, in stark contrast to that of the humans. Spirit had always been fond of this mortal race. Without even being aware, they lived their lives based on one of Spirit's favorite tenets: 'There is beauty in simplicity'.

Spirit had introduced this race to Galleant shortly after the humans, as the attention of the council was turned elsewhere. The Tal'kier realm operated with two humanoid races in their realms. To Spirit's knowledge, this was the first time they had been placed together on the same world, during the same age. She had kept this village secret from the council and, as such, this race would not be gifted. They would simply live out their lives on a world imbued with the Source. They were, in essence, her control group.

The village was doing well, thriving even. They had proven extremely adept at attuning themselves to the Source. Given their natural synergy with nature, the villagers began taking notice when the Source levels on the planet began appearing in all living organisms. A faint aura had begun to take shape all around the world. This discovery had produced two major changes in the villagers as their attunement had matured over the last few centuries.

The first and most obvious change was their life span. Currently, the life span of these villagers was approximately five times the norm of their own race and six times that of the humans. The humans had benefited from their steadily increasing medical knowledge, and their healing gifts from Kemor, but nothing close to the magnitude of the villagers.

The second happened much more subtly, and had taken quite some time before Spirit was even aware of its existence, but it was the most remarkable. The villagers had begun to develop Patron specific abilities. She had needed to make several personal trips to the planet to verify her findings, but they were there. Several of the predetermined gifts allowed by the Patrons had begun to manifest. The effects of the Source had become more and more prevalent all over the planet; plants, animals, and the mortals, were all now imbued with some level of the Source. Most were at levels so minute it was inconsequential, but they were there, and somehow this race's natural sensitivity had allowed them to manifest gifts without Patron intervention.

Spirit's original hypothesis was slowly beginning to gain evidence, but it was all circumstantial. All of this evidence was extremely encouraging, and supported her initial assumptions about the nature of the Source, but she needed more time and significantly more analysis. She could see the outcomes, but she could not explain the 'how'. If she could do that, she would have the proof she needed. The 'evidence beyond reproach' that Talon had requested.

How? How is this happening?

Spirit softly cursed at her failed attempts at an answer.

"Spirit!" Tovin called, entering the council chamber.

Startled, Spirit swiped the world closed and turned.

"Spiirrrit?" He drew her name out in a long, questioning tone.

"Hmm?"

"What were you doing?"

"Just checking up on Galleant for my next update to the council. You startled me, is all."

Tovin narrowed his eyes. She was hiding something, but he let it drop.

"Come, a group of us are meeting for lunch and I promised Breanna that I would bring you."

"Delightful." Spirit smoothed out her skirts as she followed Tovin out of the chambers, her heart pounding in her chest.

In the central realm, the most ancient entity in the universe reached out and touched the mind of his most loyal and trusted official,
"Come."

CHAPTER 2
JOURNEY TO MEITELLEN
YEAR 1303/CALLIST'E/WEEK 4

It took five days for the priest from Saloanne to arrive. Five agonizing days for Arran to wrestle with his decision and endure the constant empty well wishes of the townsfolk. While the well-intentioned comments had diminished, the looks still spoke volumes.

He and his parents had eventually come to a begrudging understanding of his decision. They were resigned to his fate, knowing with heavy hearts that a portion of his decision was for them. Better for everyone if he went and failed, rather than reject the gift outright. So, at the end of the five days, he was ready to face his future.

The priest arrived just after mid-day accompanied by a small caravan, a handful of stewards, and a small retinue of guardsmen. He was not a large man, in height anyway. Arran watched as he struggled with his girth as he exited the carriage. His head was shaved, and he seemed to have a countenance that seemed...not pompous exactly, but obviously someone who was used to being important.

After listening to the welcome speech from the mayor, the priest bowed to the crowd and let himself be led towards the altar. Arran and his parents followed alongside the mayor. Without any hesitation, the priest began chanting, murmuring quietly as if to himself. Arran strained to hear, but did not recognize the language.

The priest's voice began to rise, speaking purposefully and slowly as he enunciated the long and complicated words. Gradually, the pace of his words began to escalate, and his voice rose in a crescendo. He began to move his arms and hands dramatically, adding them to the ritual as he waved them above his head. With a final flourish, he stopped, breathing heavily. He turned to address the crowd.

"The sigil is true! Talon, our Patron of Intelligence!" His voice was strong and booming. He let his hands drop to his sides, and turned to the mayor, beads of sweat rolling off his bald head. He straightened his robes.

Murmurs ran through the crowd.

Stepping away from the altar, the priest approached the mayor. "I would like to meet the boy before our departure."

"Yes, my lord, you may use my office." Mayor Burton pointed towards the town hall with a shaking hand.

"Thank you."

The priest gave Arran's parents a respectful glance, nodded, and with the haughtiness of a noble, followed the mayor's shaking hand.

Arran watched the priest suspiciously as he walked to the town hall.

That seemed a bit overly dramatic. Was this official realm business or a play? Maybe a bit of both?

When Arran arrived in the mayor's office, the priest was already there waiting for him. It was obvious from the way he sat in the mayor's chair that it was not properly made for a man of his size, again, not from height. The voluminous outfit he was wearing did little to help matters as he, quite frankly, overflowed from the chair. He now held a staff in his hand, upright, and to the side of the chair. It was ornately done with scrollwork up the entire length. A clear crystal was inset at the top, fitted perfectly within the wood.

Arran closed the door and stood just inside the room. They were alone.

The priest beckoned Arran forward. "Come. Come. Let me get the look of you."

Arran stepped forward to stand in front of the chairs facing the desk. He clasped his hands behind his back.

The priest observed him for several moments before locking eyes with Arran. The gaze was so intense, Arran was afraid to move. Time seemed to slow, and then with a blink of his eye, the moment ended and the priest's posture softened. "Have you ever had the occasion of doing anything particularly spectacular in your young life?"

"Spectacular, my lord?"

"Yes, a time you showed particular steadfastness during a trying time of the village? Anything you have done that would have had the townsfolk appreciate you?"

Arran's palms began to sweat, and he tried desperately to hold the surprise from his face.

By the Patrons! Does he know? Did he already hear about my reputation?

Arran paused as if in thought, as he tried to regain his composure.

"I'm afraid...that I have not." Arran's reply was clumsy, and he berated himself inwardly. He stammered out the honorific, almost forgetting. "My lord."

The priest looked at Arran suspiciously, noticing the change in the boy's countenance.

"Nothing at all?" the priest asked again, leaning forward, his tone flat with doubt.

"Nothing, sir."

"Hmm..." the priest murmured and settled back into the chair. It creaked loudly.

"Can you read?"

Regaining his composure, Arran replied quickly. "Yes, my lord, my mother has taught me the words."

"Good, good. One less thing to look after."

"What skills do you have? Anything that you have been taught during your youth?"

"My father is the town blacksmith, so I know my way around a smithy. I can do basic work, but if truth be told..." Arran paused. He had never mentioned this before, even to his parents. "...I do not think I have the manner for it."

The priest looked surprised, cocking an eyebrow. "A truthful and humble answer. If not the smithy, what skill do you have the manner for? What would 'you' like to do?"

Arran was taken aback at the question. He honestly did not know. He had never been asked what 'he' wanted to do before. Never giving a thought to anything except the smithy. He would follow his father. That was simply how it was to be.

What would I do, what could I do, if I had the choice?

The priest watched Arran stoically, face blank.

After several lengthy moments, Arran replied, "I do not know, my lord."

The priest did not answer. His face was impassive, his eyes never wavering from Arran's own.

Arran began to feel the heat of his measure, the room suddenly becoming uncomfortably warm. He began to fidget.

The priest's expression softened. "Tell me. What do you think of your gift from Talon and the responsibilities that it entails?"

Arran had thought about this very question often in the last five days and replied with confidence.

"At first I was scared...angry, even. I was confused. No one in my family had ever received a gift before. Why did the Patrons choose me? And why...Talon?" Arran paused, unsure if he had overstepped, questioning his new Patron. The priest did not show any sign of displeasure, so he continued. "But...as I thought, I began to consider...I started to view the gift as an opportunity. I have never been one to dream of grand adventures like some. I am...was, content for what lay ahead, here in Kine." Arran continued more quickly, the words coming out in a torrent, as he released all of his wandering thoughts and questions of the past five days. "I have a friend who posed a question to me not long after the gifting, 'What if?' she had asked. What if the Patrons knew of something in me which I had not yet seen? The more I thought about it, the more I became determined to see what this gifting had to offer; and if there was more to me than anyone, including myself, had ever imagined."

The priest's blank face turned to one of surprised admiration. "That might be the most humble and self-aware answer I have ever had to that question." The priest's expression turned to one of concern. "I pray you can keep that countenance, for it is rare indeed in the places you are yet to visit." He arose slowly, leaning on the staff for support.

"We are done here. We will spend the rest of today here in the village. Get your affairs in order. We will leave on the morrow, bright and early, for a good start to our travels."

Arran took one last look around his room and then descended the stairs with his small bag of belongings. His mother was in the kitchen preparing a small pouch of food, while his father watched stoically from the kitchen table. The time had come. They had said all their goodbyes the night before, and without a word, they headed out towards the main green.

To Arran's surprise, it appeared as if the entire village had turned out for his departure. Arran and his family slowly made their way towards the mayor and priest, who were already standing next to the carriage. As they passed through the gathered crowd, Arran could make out a few well wishes and even received a few pats of encouragement.

Arriving at the carriage, Arran turned to his parents, his chest quickly tightening.

Pai'ese saw his anxiety and grasped Arran in a tight embrace, whispering in his ear, "Be safe and be careful. I love you."

Arran nodded as he was slowly released from his mother's embrace. He turned to his father.

"Be strong, lad. Keep your wits about you, and..." He paused slightly and leaned forward to whisper. "...stay out of trouble." He winked slyly and then bore Arran close for a quick, strong hug.

Arran gave his father a wry smile, grateful for his ability to always find a way to lighten a mood. His tension eased as he slowly replaced it with resolve.

"Thank you, Father."

Arran gazed across the gathered townsfolk of Kine. He spotted Challand and her family. Catching her eye, he mouthed the words "Thank you," with a small tilt of his head. She smiled back. He did not know if she knew what he was thanking her for; how her simple words had helped him so much, but it felt right to acknowledge her before he left.

Arran turned and stepped up to the mayor.

"Be well, son. Know that the prayers of the people of Kine go with you." He held out his hand, which Arran shook.

"Are you ready?" the priest asked.

"Yes, my lord."

At that, the priest gestured for him to enter the coach as one of the stewards took his bag and disappeared behind the carriage.

The priest made a few final departing comments to the crowd, then entered the coach opposite Arran. He knocked on the coach wall behind him and the coach lurched forward as the small caravan made its way out of town.

Before they had even cleared the last building in town, the priest began removing his layers of garments. Sweat beaded on his forehead. Arran watched in fascination at the process in the close confines.

When he was done, there was a large pile of robes on the bench next to him and he let out a sigh.

"...silly tradition...so hot and cumbersome..." he muttered to himself.

Arran stifled a laugh. The priest furrowed his brow at this, but only replied with a soft huff of derision, rearranging himself on the bench.

The trip then slowly lapsed into silence for a long while. The priest busied himself with a book while Arran watched the slow passing of the countryside out the side window, or rested silently with his eyes closed. It was almost mid-day now, and they were making good time. He did not know how far they had traveled, but he guessed that they were now farther from his home than he had ever been. This part of the country was untouched and wild. No farmland or signs of civilization that he could see, save the road on which they traveled.

Arran turned to the priest, not sure if he should interrupt.

Lowering the book to his lap, the priest looked over the top of spectacles, eyebrows raised.

"You have a question?"

Arran pointed to the book. "What are you reading?"

The priest closed the book and handed it to Arran.

"It is the latest version of 'The History of Galleant'."

"Latest version?" Arran inquired, handling the book reverently. It was a thick book, bound in a fine soft leather with the title plainly scripted on the cover.

"Yes. As the knowledge of our world deepens, the book is updated. Sometimes adding new information, sometimes editing older assumptions. It is brought up to date every other year or so. This copy is the most current, published earlier this year."

"I should like to read it one day." Arran held the book out, returning it.

"I can look into obtaining you a copy once we reach Saloanne, if time permits."

Arran thanked him, and after a few more moments, his curiosity finally got the better of him.

"May I ask you a professional question?"

The priest looked up again at Arran thoughtfully, eyes narrowing. "You may."

"The verification that you performed. You spoke some words I did not understand, then made a lot of hand gestures..." Arran waved his hands above his head in demonstration. "...before rendering your conclusion. Were the hand movements for show, or necessary to the process of verification?"

"Ha!"

A sheepish grin spread across the priest's face, replacing his initial suspicion.

"Ah, the honest bluntness of youth. So you caught on to that, did you? I'll let you in on a little secret, my boy. We priests have a certain reputation to maintain. Yes, we can do many great things with our gifts, but they rarely require much flamboyance. Sometimes, during certain ceremonial occasions, we have been known to indulge in the innocent...let's call it, showmanship...to spice things up a bit."

Arran stared at the priest in astonishment, eyes going wide.

"You faked it?"

"I faked nothing!" Indignity sweeping across the priest's face in a flash. He hesitated, almost looking ashamed at the outburst. He continued with a much calmer bearing. "The verification that I performed did require certain priestly gift abilities. I simply embellished the process a bit. It is not uncommon in the courts. Individuals will use a bit of flourish when they can for show. It is of no harm, and for some, it is considered a game. An expression of themselves for an audience, whatever that may be."

Arran thought for a while.

Was it any different from him taking pleasure in his various schemes?

He was not sure. It felt wrong that a gift should be used and flaunted in such a manner. In the end, he let the matter drop.

They finished the rest of the day's journey, engaging in occasional small talk, but mostly in silence. The priest read his book while Arran admired the view of the never-before-seen countryside. Kine was located in an area of mostly flat land with small copses of trees. The terrain they were now moving through had more rolling hills with bluffs, valleys, and much larger stands of trees.

They made their stay on the first night in the town of Pateen, east of Kine. It was a much larger town than Kine, at least five times bigger, Arran reckoned. The priest had reserved rooms at the largest inn, on the top floor, of course, and they made their way there.

Once settled in, the priest turned to Arran. "You may go and have supper in the main hall if you like. You may order whatever you wish from the innkeeper. I will be dining in my room this evening."

Arran thanked him and hastily made his way downstairs. The inn was still fairly empty, and he easily found a small empty table in the corner. The day was finishing its slow fade into evening behind the hills and tall trees. Leaving only the evening's dusk filtering in through the few windows. Arran watched as candles were being lit, and a small fire was started in the hearth, which began to crackle and pop in earnest as the flames took hold.

A pleasant-looking barmaid approached, her smile engaging.

"May I get you something?"

Arran returned the smile easily. "Yes, please." He hesitated, not sure what to order.

"What do you recommend?"

"The main dish this evening is beef stew with carrots and pota-toes. It is the mistress's specialty."

"Sounds perfect!" Arran's mouth began watering and his stomach gave a satisfied rumble of anticipation.

The barmaid returned in short order with the beef stew, served in a 'bowl' of dark bread. Arran stared at the dish as she set down his mug of cider.

"It's what we call a trencher," the barmaid said, catching his ques-tioning stare at the bowl. She smiled proudly. "The mistress tried serving it that way a few years ago. Everyone loved it so much, now it's the only way we serve it."

"Interesting..." Arran thanked her. He was not about to argue with local customs, and began to eat. Before he knew it, he was done. The bowl of bread was also almost completely gone. Picking off already sopped bread while eating the stew was indeed quite tasty. He would have to tell his mother. He sat back on the bench content-edly with his mug of cider.

By now, the inn had gathered quite a few more patrons and was close to being full. As everyone got a little deeper into their drink, an air of genuine merriment permeated the room. There was one man in particular who was quite boisterous, often leading everyone in song. Arran could not help but smile and be taken in with their casual mirth.

Arran was so engrossed with the crowd he almost didn't notice the priest as he made his way down the stairs. He had changed out of what he guessed was the ceremonial outfit, and was now clad in a much simpler pant and shirt combination, a red sash of Saloanne around his waist.

The people parted as he crossed the floor, making way and giving a polite nod, quick bow, or curtsy in reverence before quickly going back to their revelry. He finished picking his way through the throng and sat down opposite Arran.

The priest ordered an ale and assumed a comfortable position. "So, what do you think?"

"Of what?"

"Of all this." He waved a hand at the crowd.

"It's quite a bit different than what I'm used to."

"Different how?"

Arran looked at the priest, who urged him to continue with a tilt of his head in the direction of the patrons.

Arran turned his attention back out to the main room and thought about the evening's events. "Bigger comes to mind first. More people. There are the locals, of course, but there are also strangers, travelers maybe, mixing with the locals, but everyone seems...happy. We don't have many travelers come through Kine." He paused for a moment before continuing. "Everyone is merry in their drink...not aggressive or hot-tempered. The man leading the group in song is someone of importance, I think. Someone they respect. The group responds joyfully to his directions." Arran turned in his seat towards the bar. "The barkeep is a pleasant man, but stern when needed. Especially with regard to the duties of the inn. There is pride there. The inn is clean; he has good food and drink; and treats his barmaids with a firm, but managing hand. It is...orderly...pleasant."

The priest raised his eyebrows in admiration.

"Very keen eye, Arran. Tell me, have you always had this ability?"

"What ability? I simply described it as you asked."

"Ha! So you did." He took a drink of his ale. "I know a good many people who would look at this room, its patrons, and not give one tenth the insight you just described to me. They see the same thing as you, but they do not 'see'. If you understand my meaning."

Arran shrugged indifferently. "I like to watch people. I always have." He did not mention that it was usually for one scheme or another. Often times he would watch a person for days, figuring out their habits and daily routines.

"I see," the priest replied suspiciously, returning to his ale with a grin.

"My lord, if I may ask. What is your name?" He wanted to get the conversation moving away from any topic that hinted at his past reputation.

The priest smiled knowingly over his cup and then finished his sip. "You may ask, and the answer is Qoman."

"Qoman...Is that with a K or a C?"

The priest chuckled. "It is with a Q. Not many people ask me of my name. If you like, you may call me such while we are in private company, I do not mind. However..." he leaned over the table conspiratorially and whispered. "I think it best if we obey the honorifics when we are with company. Eh?"

Now it was Arran's turn to laugh, and then he too whispered. "I understand. It is nice to meet you, Qoman."

"It has been a pleasure to meet you also, Arran."

***

They departed the following morning, and not long after they had left Pateen, the priest reached down and presented Arran with a book.

"I did not know if I would need this or not, but I did bring this."

Arran took the small book and turned it over. On the cover it had but one word 'Talon'.

Arran ran his fingers along the embossed title. "Thank you."

They both settled in and read their books, with Arran periodically peering out the window. The carriageway now wove its way through a massive forest. The enormous trunks and outstretched limbs reaching higher than Arran had ever seen. The effect created a canopy above the carriage, blocking out much of the day's light, and leaving them in an eerie mid-day gloom.

It did not take Arran long to finish the small book, and he turned to Qoman.

"There is not much history here pertaining to Talon. Most of the book is about how he is one of the seven Patrons, head of the Intelligence order, and then it goes on to repeat a lot of general knowledge about all of the Patrons."

Qoman watched as the disappointment spread across the young man's face.

Arran continued. "There is little of significance that explains Talon's gifts or how to use them. There are vague passages about Sight, Stealth, Observance, and Shadow, but nothing specific."

Qoman bobbed his head. "I'm afraid that your Patron is one of many secrets. The specific details of his gifts are not widely known. Unlike the other Patrons, whose gifts are more tangible and beneficial, with definitive and observant outcomes, the gifts of Talon are typically used in secret. You will not find many books on the matter. That is for you to learn at the school."

Arran sat back, dejected that the book did not have more to offer, but at least it had occupied his mind for a bit. As the day wore on, Arran noticed something for the first time in their travel: a group of armed guards. Three men on horseback, swords at their sides, and wearing what looked like hardened leather.

The priest smiled as Arran pressed closer to the window as he watched their passing.

"Saloanne patrols. The guardsmen patrol the main roads outside of Saloanne for safe passage. We will see them with more regularity now that we are closer to the city."

Arran looked back out the window in awe as the guards continued past. They looked so poised and impressive.

The caravan continued through the day and made its way to a small clearing not far off the road for the evening. Arran clambered out of the carriage and noticed that it must have been a common stopping point. There was a well-used firepit in the middle with plenty of room around the edges for the caravan wagons and tents. The stewards began their unpacking, and in short order, had two tents erected, and a fire blazing in the pit.

Qoman settled in with a book next to the carriage. An awning had been erected, and he sat a comfortable distance from the fire. He looked over at Arran, noticing the young boy's nervous energy.

Youth.

Qoman smiled amiably.

"If you wish to explore a bit in the woods, you should be safe enough. Do not venture far, though. Dinner will be ready in about an hour."

Arran rose quickly, not wasting any time accepting the offer. He headed out into the woods.

The rich, dense forest was magnificent. There were so many trees and their size was staggering. Arran wandered around absently, taking in the splendor of the forest. Finding some small trails, he began to follow them. He was not a skilled hunter, but he had been taught the basics of how to find a trail and track an animal. He picked one of the larger and easier trails to follow and set out. He slowed as the trail led between two bushes nestled up next to a large tree. Crouching down, he cautiously approached.

The trees here did not have leaves, instead they were some kind of short needle. They did not crunch like a leaf when stepped on, yet they did make a slight crack as the dry ones broke. He cursed himself at the noise, and continued more carefully, trying to find less dense patches for his steps.

As he was making his way around the tree, he stopped abruptly as a flash of heat erupted within his chest. Arran gasped as if he had been punched and struggled to catch his breath. The heat spread down his arms and legs. His face went flush as hot sweat immediately began to form on his brow. He grabbed at his chest, frozen in place, and as quickly as it had come, the feeling was gone.

Arran was shaking and breathing heavily. He peered around the tree and saw the trail continuing on. He shook his head.

"Go back to camp, idiot," he muttered to himself, still fingering his chest for any obvious sign of injury. There was nothing.

Turning around, he reluctantly headed back, desperately trying to puzzle out what had happened.

Was it something with his gift? But what? Was it an after effect from his Source Day?

Arran shook his head in frustration. He began to look for more trails to follow on his way back to occupy his mind. Finding a small trail, possibly a rabbit or raccoon, he began to track it as before. He slowed and crouched as he tried to remain silent. As he moved through the undergrowth, he congratulated himself on how much better he was performing. He could barely detect his own movement. He stopped and frowned in confusion. He took a few more steps... nothing. Not a whisper.

Ok, I'm not that good.

He continued following the trail, focusing on silence...not a single sound. Arran stood up, his mind racing.

Is this part of my gift?

Stealth had been one of the gifts mentioned in the book, but it did not describe how it was achieved, what it could do, or how to use it. He continued experimenting as he moved along the trail. If he walked normally along the trail, not focusing on being silent, everything was normal and he could easily hear his footsteps upon the trail. Once he focused on being silent though...nothing.

This is amazing!

He continued to experiment with the new talent on his way back to camp. It was not complicated in that it only required him to concentrate. As he got closer to camp, he began to wonder: *Should I tell Qoman? Was I required to tell Qoman? Or was this something that should wait until I get to school?*

He wrestled with the decision as he slowly made his way back to camp, before finally deciding to keep it to himself. At least for now.

Arran returned to camp and sat down on one of the chairs that had been placed around the firepit.

"How was your expedition?" Qoman asked nonchalantly, not looking up from his book.

"It was good. It was nice to get out and stretch my legs. The forest here is really amazing."

Qoman peered up over the top of his spectacles. "Discover anything exciting?"

"Not really. I thought I found a deer trail, but it was going in too far and I decided to turn back." Arran told the lie smoothly as he poked the fire.

"Hmm...too bad." Qoman returned to his book, smiling inwardly.

As the caravan broke camp, Qoman had remarked that if the weather held, this would be their last full day of travel. Saloanne would only be another day and a half.

Arran barely heard him as he stared out the window of the carriage, his mind still churning over the previous evening. He had hardly slept, and now he was tired, anxious, and disconcerted.

It had to be the Stealth gift. There was just no other explanation. I will discuss it with the instructors at school.

His mind made up, he let out a long breath, and listened to the passage of time; the uniform rumble of the carriage wheels, and the clip-clop of the horses' hooves as they beat out a steady pace.

"You seem a bit distracted today, solemn almost," Qoman said.

Arran started at the break in his reverie.

"Sorry?"

"You seem distracted."

"Oh...I'm just thinking about the city and what lies ahead is all."

Qoman did not reply and let what he knew was a lie pass in silence.

Qoman closed his book. "So, nothing happened in the woods, you say?"

Arran jerked, startled at the almost casual and indifferent tone of the question. The confines of the carriage suddenly became uncomfortably small.

The priest looked at him with amusement, his mouth quirked.

Arran sat up straight and shifted uneasily in his seat, desperately looking everywhere, except directly at Qoman.

Did he know?

Qoman continued calmly. "I can sometimes feel when a gift is received. If I am calm and my mind is not cluttered, I can sense when a gift is given. One of my own gifts from Kemor. I cannot see what gift is given, but that initial 'spark' we call it, I can feel that from time to time. I felt yours last night in the woods."

Arran felt humiliated, ashamed of having been caught in his lie.

Idiot!

Arran began to answer, but Qoman waved it away. "Do not worry. I understand your hesitancy. The first gift can sometimes be unsettling. The spark usually happens unexpectedly and can be a bit overwhelming. It has been almost seven days since your Source Day. That is a little early for one to receive their first gift, but not too uncommon...it varies."

Qoman hesitated before replying, letting the silence calm the young man. "Most gifts will come naturally, like the one last night, I'm guessing. You were doing something normal, yes? An activity familiar to you?"

Arran nodded.

"Ahh...that was probably when your gift manifested. Again, this is not uncommon. The gifts that center around skills you already possess are typically the first. The rest...well, those will require specific tutelage at the school. That is why you train." Qoman sat back, watching Arran intently.

Arran did not return the gaze. He stared out the window, focusing on nothing, lost in his thoughts.

I have a lot to learn.

The rest of their journey continued without incident. No new gifts were received and Qoman did not press him for any further information on his newly acquired gift. They arrived at Saloanne in the early afternoon as Qoman projected.

The city of Saloanne rose in the distance, with the main keep rising at its center above the perimeter walls. The caravan made its way up to the main gate; there were individuals on foot, and vendors with carts full of wares, all patiently waiting in line. It was a typical ensemble, according to Qoman. The daily markets were open until sunset and people would be coming and going throughout the day.

They were admitted through the gate and made their way down the main thoroughfare. It opened out into a large, circular area full of vendors. In the center stood a giant fountain depicting a knight on horseback. Vendors and their carts circled the outside perimeter of the area, with another circle of vendors inside, closer to the fountain, providing enough width for the passage of traffic. Behind the inner row of vendors was another open space, allowing people to walk, sit, or congregate around the fountain.

Arran was amazed at the number of people, hundreds, maybe even a thousand, all milling about. Vendors called out their wares, with people engaging them in purchases, or simply talking amongst themselves. Horses whinnied and moved through the crowd, hooves on the cobblestones ringing out. It all blended together in a cacophony of sound. He shook his head, eyes wide as the caravan made its way slowly around the market, and exited back onto the main thoroughfare on the opposite side.

They continued deeper into the city, the sounds of the market diminishing behind them, and the throng of people thinning out.

The main keep came into full view as the road emptied into a great open plaza. The keep loomed before them, behind its own inner wall and gate. Guards in gleaming silver armor accented with a red sash snapped to attention as the caravan approached.

As they proceeded through the inner wall gate, Qoman began to describe the inner keep. "The grounds of the main keep are two-tiered. The bottom tier is mainly for facilities like barracks, training grounds, stables, and warehouses." He pointed out each side of the carriage.

As the main coach passed through this lower tier, and proceeded up to the second, the support carts veered off and into the first tier grounds. Qoman continued. "The second tier is for the gardens, and at its center, the main keep. There are eight different gardens surrounding the main keep, each with their own theme and plant varieties from throughout the realms. It is one of the hallmarks of Saloanne."

Arran was awed by the sheer magnitude of it all. Never before had he seen such opulence and beauty. His head swiveled from one window to the next, trying to take it all in as the caravan made its way to the front of the keep.

"We have arrived," Qoman said with a flourish of his hands.

This made Arran smile and eased the tension he had not known was there. The priest smiled back amiably as the two exited the coach, making their way up to the main entrance of the keep.

As they approached the main doors, the guards once again snapped to attention as they recognized Qoman. He nodded politely as they passed. Once inside, they were immediately greeted by a tall man in a black suit and red sash that Arran could only guess was an attendant of some sort. Qoman removed his outer cloak and handed it to him.

"Mindell, my fine man. How have you been? I hope all has been well while I was away?"

"Fine, my lord. Lord Baelonne is currently in council with matters of state and will see you in his study after. You should have plenty of time to freshen from your trip, if you desire."

Mindell spoke in a flat, monotone manner. Arran found it a little unnerving.

"That will be splendid, Mindell, thank you. Please find accommodations for our guest here and get him settled in. Arran, I will find you later this afternoon. Mindell can assist you with the keep rules. Feel free to explore if you would like."

"This way, young master," Mindell said.

Qoman arrived at the lord's study and lightly knocked on the door.

"Come in. Ah, Qoman, back from the verification. How was your trip to the countryside? Refreshing, I hope, escaping all the hustle of the big city?"

"Yes, my lord, refreshing...and fruitful, I am pleased to report,"

Lord Baelonne crossed the study to the set of chairs at its center. "Do tell."

Qoman sat opposite. "The boy, Arran, was indeed gifted from the Patron of Intelligence. Quite remarkable, actually, for such an out-of-the-way village. Disciples of Talon are usually, how to put it delicately, from the higher families. Recipients who have already been honed towards that particular set of skills."

"Quite. What did you make of him?"

"The boy is quite keen, my lord. His mother taught him to read from an early age and he proved proficient." Qoman paused in thought, recalling their first night in Pateen. "He is very observant of his surroundings, with a good head for memory, and the reading of people. He accepts new information quickly, processes it, and asks pertinent, insightful questions." Qoman took a sip of his tea. "I have to say...I was impressed. He is very deliberate and thoughtful, especially for someone of his age."

The lord nodded his head in approval.

Qoman continued, "I believe he will make a fine candidate for the School of Intelligence. What he lacks in the martial skills he more than makes up for in mental capability. Which, I believe, puts him at least on par with any of the higher families' candidates."

Lord Baelonne chuckled lightly. "Very true. Teaching the mental is much more difficult than the physical, and being groomed can leave...shall we say, gaps in one's personal skills."

The two men shared rueful grins at this comment. Young nobility, low or high, were not typically known for their self-awareness.

"There is one more item of note, my lord. He obtained his first gift during our travels. He did not tell me what it was, but my guess would be one of the common gifts, either Stealth or Sight."

"Interesting." Lord Baelonne settled back in his chair, resting his cup on the arm, eying Qoman suspiciously. "So, by this glowing review, can I assume an offer of sponsorship is in order?"

"I believe so. As you can surmise, I was impressed with the young lad. He has the aptitude, but only time will tell if he has the desire to learn what the School of Intelligence has to offer. It takes a particular mind to walk the path of Talon."

The mood fell somber at the remark.

"Very true, but the thought of having someone of the Intelligence order from our realm...could prove advantageous." Baelonne took a sip of his tea in contemplation.

"Quite so."

"Good job, Qoman, my man. Draw up the papers, then. When do you expect to send him on to Meitellen?"

"We should make haste, my lord. New candidates arrive throughout the year, but I think it is best for him to begin during the start of a new term. The next is in two weeks."

"I should like to meet the lad before he departs. Tonight's dinner?"

"Yes, my lord."

"Thank you, Qoman, that will be all. I look forward to this evening." Baelonne stood. Qoman, recognizing the dismissal, rose and left the study.

Qoman went in search of Arran, eventually finding him in the main hall. He followed Arran's gaze. "What catches your eye the most?"

Arran turned to find the priest approaching him from across the far side of the hall.

"I think the windows. I like the stories they tell and the way the light seems to change the focus of the picture as the light moves."

"You caught that, did you? It is a little bit of imbued magic that does not change the art in any way, only in how it is perceived in the changing light."

The two stood there for several minutes, admiring the windows, before Qoman finally broke the silence.

"Lord Baelonne has invited us to dine with him this evening. I have given him my recommendation, and he has agreed to extend a full offer of sponsorship to you during your training."

Arran stared at Qoman, not sure how to react.

Qoman recommended me to Lord Baelonne?

He had thought for sure he would be accepted begrudgingly at best.

Arran nodded in acknowledgment. "Thank you for the recommendation." Arran hesitated, his face frowning in a mask of uncertainty.

Qoman waited patiently for the question.

"What exactly is full sponsorship? It was my understanding that the school provides everything the students need once accepted."

"They do indeed. The sponsorship provides two things for you. First, you will not need to go through the initial school acceptance process. The sponsorship letter that I will give you will relieve you of that duty. Second, you will receive a small stipend during your stay at the school. This will give you a modicum of means during your training. It can be used for, shall we say...entertainment purposes. Or, if used more judiciously, could be saved. The use is at your discretion."

Arran's eyes furrowed suspiciously. "And what do I owe for such an honor?"

Qoman looked at Arran appreciatively. The youth could indeed see straight to the heart of things.

"The repayment of this sponsorship entails that you will perform various duties for the lord once you have reached the proper level of training."

Arran thought on this for a few moments. "How is the sponsorship deemed fulfilled?"

Qoman smiled, once again impressed by Arran's insightfulness. "You need not worry. Once you begin your commissions, he and the school's masters will determine when your endeavors have deemed the sponsorship fulfilled. It is not a lifetime obligation."

Arran slowly rolled the thought of the commissions around for a while before nodding his head in approval.

"Good! We must prepare for dinner. Meet me back here in the main hall in one hour. Mindell should have found you something proper to wear by now and have it laid out for you."

Arran groaned under his breath at the thought of wearing something deemed 'proper' for the evening and sullenly left for his room.

Mindell had indeed already laid out an outfit on his bed when he returned.

Not too horrible

A white shirt, blue britches, calf-high boots, and a bright red sash. A bit colorful for his taste, but at least it was a simple outfit.

Oh well. Could be worse.

<hr>

Arran made his way to the main hall and looked around. He must have been a little early. Qoman had not yet arrived. Wandering, he eventually found himself once again admiring the windows. Now lit by dim moonlight instead of the day's sun, the windows had an even different aura about them. Subtle and more ethereal. Arran lost himself in the beauty of the art.

"Shall we?"

Arran jerked slightly, momentarily startled, and then turned.

Qoman gestured with a hand towards the back of the hall.

Sparing one last glance at the windows, Arran turned and followed.

The dining hall was not as big as Arran had imagined. The table was large, but not overly so. It could serve twelve by his count, and he surmised that this must be more of a private dining hall.

Arran was led to a seat next to the head of the table.

Well, that's not intimidating! Right next to the lord himself?

No one else was sitting, so he stood behind the chair, nervously fidgeting with the fine carvings. There were only five people in the room, and Arran did not believe any of them were Lord Baelonne.

Qoman conversed with two women who Arran guessed to be the Queen Mother and the young princess. The queen was pretty and stately. She portrayed confidence, bore from her station and an obvious self-confidence. The princess appeared to be several years younger than Arran. She, like Arran, was also fidgeting, her feet dancing a nervous shuffle like a horse ready to run, hands twirling at the bows on her dress.

Only a few years from her own Source Day, I'll bet.

There were two men, talking exuberantly, both using their hands to emphasize their comments. One was dressed in military finery.

A general or maybe a close friend?

The other was dressed in a similar outfit to Arran's, but far more luxurious and obviously tailored. It fit him perfectly. He was tall, lean, and fit-looking. Arran could not discern his stature or rank, but it was obviously something high enough to warrant a seat at the lord's private table.

For the most part, everyone ignored Arran until finally the man Arran instantly knew was Lord Baelonne entered the room. Everyone ended their conversations, and either nodded or bowed at his arrival.

Lord Baelonne waved his hand dismissively.

"Be comfortable, everyone," gesturing at the table and taking his chair.

Lord Baelonne! Who would have guessed I'd be sitting here not more than two weeks ago?

The High Lord of the Aaeu'din realm was a tall man, fit for his age of at least forty, and had a manner of congeniality about him. He sat and turned to Arran, smiling. It was a genuine smile, but Arran could not help but feel he was on a stage being appraised.

After everyone was seated, Baelonne stood and addressed the group. "Good evening, everyone. It is always good to see my closest friends and family together for a meal. We have a special guest this evening, as you may have noticed. Young Arran here is from the small village of Kine and has been gifted by our Patron of Intelligence, earning my sponsorship." Baelonne gestured for Arran to stand, and as he did, all the other guests stood and clapped, congratulating him.

Arran stood transfixed; he was not used to this much attention, but thankfully Lord Baelonne quickly sat down and everyone else followed, the clapping subsiding.

Baelonne turned to Arran. "So tell me about yourself, young man. All I know is what Qoman has relayed to me during your travels."

Arran took a moment to compose himself and nervously replied, "There is not much to tell, my Lord. As you have already mentioned, I come from a small village and we are not used to gifts of this magnitude. Everyone, including myself, was beyond surprised to find the sigil of Intelligence at my gifting. My family history has no record of ever having received a gift, and so I had no expectations on my sourcing day."

Arran cursed himself for such a simple and obvious answer.

He said he already knew as much from Qoman!

"Indeed," Baelonne replied smoothly. "By our records this is only the second gift from Talon that Aaeu'din has ever recorded. A very discriminating Patron, that Talon. You say no one in your family has ever received a gift. Interesting..." Baelonne trailed off in thought.

"If I may ask, my lord," Arran asked quickly, wincing at his own abruptness. "Who was the other?"

Baelonne turned to Qoman.

"It was actually a she," Qoman replied.

Even Baelonne was surprised at the statement. "A woman in the Intelligence order? Now that is interesting." His interest obviously piqued.

Qoman glanced at Arran, who looked sheepish after his small gaffe. "Sai'el was her name. Her gifting was during your...great-grandfather's reign, I believe. I am afraid there is not much known of her after she left Aaeu'din for Meitellin. There is little in the records. She rarely returned home and over time has disappeared from our histories."

The room went silent at the implied meaning of Qoman's last statement. Arran watched as the faces around the table all fell solemn.

Most likely killed in the course of her duties.

Lord Baelonne quickly broke the somber silence. "But here we are, and young Arran is now our second. May the Patrons bless your gift and all of your upcoming endeavors." Baelonne stood and jovially raised his glass. Everyone followed, toasting to Arran's future.

The 'meal' was actually a series of meals, or courses, as Qoman had whispered to him. Each was small and delicious, but by the end of the seventh, the last Arran hoped, he was sated and did not think he could eat another bite. Arran later learned that it was not necessary to finish each course, and in fact, some cultures found it an honor to the chef if some food was left uneaten.

Nobles and their odd customs.

The evening was filled with small talk during the various courses of meals, with everyone politely asking him questions about his village and his parents. They made what Arran thought were surely empty promises to visit one day, as it sounded like a wonderful place for a getaway.

The mother and daughter he discovered were indeed the Queen Mother, Mirann, and Princess Jainne. Mirann was gracious throughout the evening, while Jainne looked to be as ready for the evening to end as Arran. The two men who Arran could not place at the beginning of the evening were Relorre, General of Baelonne's army and Prince Kaelorre, Baelonne's younger brother. These two men did not engage with Arran much during the evening, preferring to discuss matters of battlefield strategies, swordsmanship, and training. This was fine with Arran. He knew nothing of these matters, and would have simply appeared the ignorant village boy.

The seventh course, thankfully, was indeed the last. Not long after Arran declined the post meal proffered sweets, the evening came to a blessed end. As everyone made their polite farewells, Lord Baelonne ushered Arran and Qoman off to a side alcove.

Baelonne placed a gentle hand on Arran's shoulder as he spoke. "I wish you well, Arran, and it is our realm's honor to sponsor you in your training. Know you carry the heart of Aaeu'din with you, and we hope to hear great things about you in the coming years. If it is allowed, of course." Baelonne winked and smiled deviously at his own joke. "Qoman here should have all of your proper papers readied by now, and it is my understanding that you leave on the morrow. Good luck to you, son." Baelonne extended his hand and Arran shook it graciously. Baelonne nodded, then turned to leave.

That boy has a precarious road ahead of him. Good luck, indeed!

Qoman and Arran left the dining hall, heading back in the direction of Arran's room.

"Get your things in order and be ready for an early rise in the morning. We will need to be at the docks by sunrise at the latest to catch the boat. Mindell will awake you at the proper time."

Arran nodded, and Qoman left him standing outside his room door.

Not wasting any time, are they?

He sighed.

Oh well, probably for the best.

The keep was grand and had a lot to offer, much of which he was not able to see in his short stay, but he was equally eager to reach Meitellen. He opened the door, finding himself anxious to begin.

Mindell arrived early as promised the following morning.

If you could call this morning.

It was still quite dark out, with the moon and stars still in full view through his window. Mindell ushered him to grab his belongings: the small bag containing the items he had arrived with, plus a surprise gift of the outfit he had worn the night before. Bag in hand, he followed Mindell out of the room.

They made their way to the backside of the keep, where Qoman was waiting for him beside a coach. This was a simple, modest coach, not the same decorative one as before. Once they were inside, Qoman handed Arran a small pouch. Examining it, he found it contained various fruits and nuts.

"You will be fed decently on the boat, but this is a little something for snacks along the way."

As the coach lurched into motion, Arran turned to say goodbye to Mindell, but he had already left.

That man is a ghost! Off to other morning duties, no doubt.

Arran sighed and reflected upon how everything moved so fast in the bigger cities.

After a short drive out of the city proper, they traveled a very curvaceous road down to the docks of Saloanne, and the river Seit-ellen. The morning dusk was just beginning to usher in the day, and the docks were already a hive of activity. Men were loading cargo on ships via hand carts, with larger cargo crates being hoisted high above, with ropes and pulleys to be stowed on the waiting ships. Arran was amazed at the coordination of it all.

They exited the coach and Qoman led them down the docks to one of the larger piers jutting away from the mainland. At the end of the pier was a towering ship. Arran had heard tales of the engineering feats about the Patrons of Mevane, but this was the first time he had ever seen one firsthand. It floated majestically in the water, with a single large column protruding up at its center, several layers of decks underneath. The top-most section was nothing but glass, with the entire deck surrounded by windows on all sides, and he could see men moving about inside. He did not know what it was called, but surmised that this would be where the captain would manage the vessel, able to see out in all directions. At the rear of the boat there was a large paddle wheel. He took it all in, utterly awestruck.

Qoman led him to a plank leading up to the ship, wide enough for five men to walk abreast. Men were coming and going. Carts full of goods went up and empty ones were coming down. As they approached the ship, Arran could make out a soft tune drifting on the air. He looked around for the source and finally realized it was the sailors. They were humming as they went about their duties.

Qoman stopped at a man with a clipboard, who was obviously managing the bustle of activity on the plank, checking items off as they passed.

Qoman cleared his throat. "Ahem."

The foreman looked up from his clipboard and greeted Qoman. "Hello, good priest. What can I do for ya?" The man's accent was slightly lilted and had a natural pleasant ring Arran had not heard before.

"Young Master Arran here has passage on your trip to Meitellen."

"Aye, let me check the rosters." The foreman flipped through the pages until he found what he was looking for. Stabbing his beefy finger down on the page, he looked up.

"Aye, Master Arran is listed right here. Papers?"

Qoman handed the foreman some papers, who looked them over.

"Aye, then." The foreman handed the papers back to Qoman, then turned to Arran. "Make your way up the plank and ask for steward Cid. He will be seeing to the comforts of our passengers during the voyage."

Qoman turned to Arran and handed him a small pamphlet bound with string. "This contains your boat passage, your papers for entering Meitellen on school business, and your letter of sponsorship from Lord Baelonne." Arran reached out to take the pamphlet, but Qoman held it firmly. He looked sternly at Arran. "Do not lose them."

"I won't."

Qoman nodded.

Arran turned to go up the plank and then hesitated, turning back to Qoman. "Thank you for everything..." Arran leaned in close and whispered. "Qoman."

Qoman chuckled at the young man's bravado and turn of humor.

"I will not forget the generosity shown to me by you and Lord Baelonne."

"You are welcome."

Arran turned and gazed up the plank and then back to Qoman. He smiled.

Qoman put a gentle hand on his shoulder.

"Good luck."

Arran extended his hand, not knowing if it was appropriate, but Qoman took it. "Be true to yourself, Arran. Do not forget that simple creed."

"I won't."

Arran turned and headed up the plank.

The boat, named Wayfarer, was on its way not more than an hour after Arran had come aboard. The plank had been drawn, and a low rumbling could be heard coming from the bowels of the boat as the large paddle wheel at the back slowly began to turn. Huge puffs of steam began to rise from the stack above.

Arran was standing at the rails on the left side of the boat; port, Cid had told him, and he watched as the docks and the city of Saloanne slowly drifted away from sight.

The trip to Meitellen would take about seven days, according to Cid. They would be stopping in several cities along the way to let people off, pick up new passengers, and either load or offload pertinent cargo.

Arran spent the majority of his first day wandering along the main deck, staring out over the rails at the passing countryside and the slow meandering of the river. It was majestic in its own way, almost mesmerizing. He could not tell exactly how fast they were going, but he'd guessed at least three, if not four, times the speed of a coach on land. The great steam-powered boat could travel quite quickly up the river and cover a large distance daily, especially given that they did not have to stop at night for rest.

On the second day, he found his thoughts turning towards the crew and became intrigued by their duties. Arran wandered the decks, finally coming upon Cid, busying himself with a set of chairs and tables used by some passengers for lounging.

"Good'ay, Cid," Arran said in the sailor's dialect.

Cid smiled at the use of the term. "Good'ay, young Master Arran."

"I'm curious, it seems to me that most of the crew spend their time managing the decks for the passengers more than performing any actual 'sailing' duties that I had envisioned. More stewards than sailors." Arran said it as a statement more than a question, but Cid seemed to pick up on his meaning.

"That be correct, young master. This here be a river steamship, not a high sea sailing ship. The duties are quite different. Most of the work needed for a steamship such as ours is below deck, in the engine room. I can see about arranging you a visit below if you would like."

Without even thinking, Arran stammered out, "Yes, please. That... that would be incredible."

Cid's face brightened at Arran's eagerness. Not many passengers showed any interest in the crew or the ship, and he knew the gesture would be appreciated.

"I will speak with the engineering foreman."

It was on the next day that Cid informed Arran that he would be allowed to visit in the afternoon, while the boat was predicted to be running normally and smoothly.

Later that afternoon, Cid led Arran down below the main deck and into the bowels of the steamship. As they descended, the rumbling of the boat became noticeably louder. After a maze of corridors and a few stairwells, they exited into a large area in the middle of the ship. At the center stood a large metal container with all manner of contrivances protruding out in all directions. There were pipes, gauges, and valves everywhere, with the crew dutifully monitoring it all.

As Arran and Cid stood at the railing looking over the center area, a man, sweaty from the humidity of the room, came up to greet them.

"Young Master Arran, I presume?" The foreman was a short stocky man, but carried himself with confidence.

"Yes, sir."

"I presume you be having some questions?" The foreman smiled amiably, belying his gruff exterior and sweaty appearance.

Arran did his best to reply to the jovial question. "J'st a few."

The foreman laughed and then began to lead Arran around the large walkway that encircled the room. There were several stations around the circular walkway where men were busy monitoring gauges and barking orders to the men below.

"Water is drawn in from the river through the pumping area o'er there." The foreman pointed to an area below and next to the boiler. "The water is steamed by heater gems, and the steam powers the wheel at the back o' the boat. The rest o' what you see is the proper maintenance of flow and pressures to keep the ol' girl running smoothly." The foreman finished, patting the railing affectionately.

Finishing their turn around the walkway, the foreman yelled at one of his crew and turned to Arran and Cid. "It was fine to meet you, Master Arran, but we need to prepare the boat fer docking. I'm afraid y'er tour must be ending here."

Arran thanked the foreman and took one last look around.

What a wonder.

Cid and Arran made their way back up to the main deck, and sure enough, he began to feel the rumble of the boat change as their speed decreased.

The stop was a short one in a town called Jhastier. After some quick onloading and offloading of cargo, the ship departed.

The following four days became routine for Arran. He wandered the decks, chatted with the crew and other passengers, and spent a lot of time watching the ever-changing landscape as the ship made its way up the river.

On the last morning of the trip, Arran packed his items and made his way to the uppermost passenger deck to view the approach to Meitellen.

Meitellen was the capital of Galleant. It sat on a large island, encircled by a huge natural moat, where the four rivers of Seitellen, Eaetellin, Neitellen, and Weitellen converged. There were bridges spanning high above the waters to provide entry to the city, equally placed on the four land areas between the rivers.

From the city itself to the elegant bridges, everything about the view was enormous and grand. Large cargo ships, passenger ships, fishing boats, and small skiffs all intermingled along the waterway, going about their day's activities. The Wayfarer entered the mouth of the interior waterway, making for the docks on the southeastern side of the waterway.

Arran had arrived.

CHAPTER 3
WELCOME TO SCHOOL
YEAR 1303 / JULY / WEEK 2

The Wayfarer reached the southeast port of Meitellen and docked. Arran slung his bag over his shoulder as he stood at the railing and stared out across the water at Meitellen. It was a massive city. A quick flicker of doubt crossed his thoughts, and his stomach tightened. He took a long deep breath, letting his tension ease before he turned, giving the Wayfarer one last look. It was an impressive vessel, and the trip had actually been fun. His tension continued to ebb as he remembered the lively crew and all of their conversations. With determination, he strode forward to leave.

As he reached the gangplank leading down, Cid was helping another passenger disembark. He looked up.

"Good'ay, Arran. It was a pleasure."

"Thank you, Cid. Please pass along to all the crew my appreciation for their patience with all of my questions."

"I will." Cid paused, his face furrowed as his expression turned serious. "Good luck in your endeavors..." He hesitated as if he wanted to say more and instead held out his hand. "May the Patrons bless you."

The two shook hands, and Cid gave him a quick nod before turning to assist another passenger.

Arran stepped down into a tumult of activity on the dock. He was momentarily startled at the chaotic bustle around him. There were people everywhere, and the din of noise was disorienting. Dock workers moving goods, passengers coming and going, and everyone pushing along as they made their way through the throng. He took a minute to catch his bearings, then headed off down the dock to the northeast, following Cid's directions for the bridge to Meitellen.

Arran traversed through the chaos that was the dock area into the lower section of the town, relieved to finally be away from the oppressive mass of people. The road that led to the bridge was, thankfully, easy to locate. There were all manner of wagons, carts, and people headed to and from the bridge's entrance. Arran got in line and waited his turn for passage across the bridge.

The guard looked at Arran indifferently. "Papers, please."

"Oh yes, sorry," Arran replied clumsily, fumbling in his bag for his city admittance letter, handing it over.

"Headed to the school, are you?"

Arran nodded.

"Good luck to you, lad." The guard handed Arran's papers back and waved him through.

The bridge was not overly wide, maybe a hundred paces, but was easily half a mile or more in length, spanning the inner waterway. Arran stopped midway in wonder at the magnificent view. In the distance, he could see the northeast bridge and the mouth of the Eaetellin river. He watched the vessels beneath him as they passed, admiring the complex patterns of movement that Cid had explained to him. 'It's like a dance on the water' he had said. Arran smiled to himself. With some reluctance, he finally forced himself to continue and pushed away from the railing.

Arran passed another set of guards at the end of the bridge and slowed, expecting more scrutiny, but none came. The guards did not address anyone entering the city and looked bored. Arran passed and stepped into the city.

He continued straight down the main road into the city. He

decided that he would stop at the first friendly-looking inn, get a drink, and ask for directions to the school. After strolling along for a while and contemplating his options, he chose The Singing Goose.

That sounds pleasant enough.

Arran stepped into the inn and made his way over to the bar, taking a seat.

The barkeep, a big, but not fat man, strolled up behind the bar, casually drying a mug in his hand. "Now what can I get for you, young master?"

"Some apple cider, please."

The barkeep moved off to fill his order, and Arran looked around. It was a fairly good-sized inn. It could probably hold close to a hundred people. There was a small stage set up by the fire in the corner for a bard, or maybe a couple of musicians. It was clean and tidy and not too crowded this time of day.

The barkeep returned and placed down a mug. "Here you are."

"Thank you." Arran picked up the mug. The pungent smell of cider wafted up. "Do you know how I can get to the School of Doctrine?"

"The school, you say? You be headed off for some training are you?"

Arran nodded as he took a drink.

"Well, you just stay on the main road to the center plaza and then head northwest from there. You won't miss it."

"Thanks." Arran took another drink of cider. "This is really good."

"My grandfather's recipe, been in the family a long time. Just the right amount of sweet vs. tart is the trick." The barkeep winked.

Arran took another appreciative sip. "May I ask as to the name of your inn? It is quite unique."

"Ah, well, I would like to say my grandfather had a grand tale behind the naming, but in truth, he and my grandmum just kind of liked the imagery and it stuck. Besides, their first choice, The Prancing Pony, was already taken." He said this as if it were a joke, but Arran did not get it, so he simply smiled politely.

Arran talked with the barkeep a while longer, learning that he was also the innkeeper and owner, as he finished his cider. Bidding the innkeeper farewell, he headed on his way. The innkeeper was a pleasant man and generous with his talk, probably a tool of the trade Arran had thought. By the time he left, he had a much better feel for the layout and a little bit of the city's history.

Arran made his way to the central plaza and then headed northwest as instructed. The streets crisscrossed about, but he made sure he stayed true, moving northwest as best he could. After a while, he began to think he might have missed the school, but as he turned the corner, he came to a stop. A large cathedral-like building came into view at the end of the street, which emptied into a large courtyard in front of the building. The large, imposing structure that stood before him looked more like a church than a school.

"I guess this is the building I couldn't miss," Arran muttered to himself, looking around.

He made his way across the plaza to the large wedge-shaped stairs that led to the front door of the building. The main building was at least five stories tall with a lone steepled tower that went even higher. The building sprawled out for another two blocks on either side of the main entrance. Scanning the three-story structures to either side, he could not make out any other entrances.

I guess this is it.

Steeling himself, he started up the staircase to the two massive front doors.

There were no guards.

Should I knock or just go in?

He looked around and decided on knocking, wrapping lightly on the door. No answer. He went to knock again and was interrupted.

"If you knock that lightly, no one is going to hear you."

Arran turned in surprise and saw a young woman, about his age, maybe a year his senior, standing behind him.

"Besides. You can just go on in. You'll be met upon entering." She smiled at Arran amiably, then pushed past him and opened the doors. Arran followed.

They entered into a great foyer. Two curved staircases dominated the space, leading up to a second-floor landing at the back of the room, then continuing up again on both sides. In the center, between the stairs, sat a large desk with several attendants, busying themselves behind stacks of papers, various writing utensils, and quite a few seriously large-looking stamps.

Arran, not knowing what to do, followed the young woman as she walked up to the attendant's table.

"Director Stejon. I believe we have a new student." She stepped aside, gesturing towards Arran.

"Thank you, Lady Elinda."

Elinda turned, gave Arran a pleasant smile, and left.

"Papers, please," the director asked.

Arran nervously handed the director his letter of recommendation from Lord Baelonne. The director's eyes never left Arran's as he took the letter. The director noted the realm seal, broke it, and began to read. After finishing the letter, he refolded it, and handed it back to Arran.

"Term will begin next week, and you are one of the first to arrive for your Patron. The Patron of Intelligence dormitory is through that door and at the last. There is no assigned bedding for first year's, so feel free to choose any not already marked so. Go and get settled in, and I will send someone to aid you in the familiarities of the school. That is all."

Okay, gruff school teacher, check.

Arran stepped out of line and headed off in the direction of his dormitory, one of the long side buildings he had noticed outside.

He passed by a basic sitting room with chairs, couches, a fireplace, and some bookshelves. Just beyond the sitting room were doors with the sigil for the Patron of Mevane above them. Farther down he came to another sitting room much like the first, and then more rooms with the Patron of Bestia's symbol above the doors.

It appeared that each section held the student dormitories with sitting rooms for each respective Patron. If he had to go through all seven before his Patron at the end, this was going to be a very long walk.

After passing the last of door for the rooms designated for Bestia, he was relieved to finally see the Patron of Talon above one of the doors.

Thank the gods.

Arran passed by the sitting room and stopped at the first door. Locked. He shrugged and moved on to the second door, which opened. It was a rectangular room with ten beds, five on each side, spaced evenly down on each side. It wasn't cramped, but it was unremarkable and a bit stark, even with the faint light coming in through the window on the back wall. Two of the beds had glowing assignment markers on the chests at their foot. Arran went over to them. A student's name labeled the bed and trunk as taken as the director had mentioned. Arran resisted the urge to grab the first open bed he found in this room and instead decided to check out the remaining rooms. The last three rooms were exactly like the first two, with only a handful of markers. Arran finally decided on the fourth room, the last in line, and which had no markers. He claimed the bed at the far end on the right.

He opened the curtains to the window and turned. There was the same small chest at the foot of the bed and a small side table with a candle. Arran crossed the room and sat on the bed, relieved to find it was decently comfortable, un-slinging his belongings.

He set to unpacking the bag, placing everything in the chest. He grimaced, noticing how little he actually possessed. He closed the chest, noticing that the medallion on the top center of the chest was pulsating with a slight glow. He looked at it inquiringly, then reached out and touched the medallion. It glowed brightly for a moment, stopped, and then his name appeared on the chest like the others he had seen.

That's handy!

As he was admiring the medallion, and congratulating himself on his cleverness, he heard a light knocking at the door. Arran went to open it.

"There you are." It was the same girl from earlier who helped lead him to the director's desk.

What was her name...Elindra? Elonda?

Arran opened the door fully. "Just getting settled in."

She walked over and looked at the chest. "Figured that out already, did you? My name is Elinda."

Elinda! That was it.

Arran snapped his fingers.

Elinda gave him a quizzical stare before continuing. "I'll be your guide, helping you get acquainted with the school. Arran, from the village of Kine, correct?"

"I am. Nice to meet you." He held out his hand.

Elinda looked at his hand and then gave him a polite nod. Arran immediately blushed in embarrassment.

Elinda smiled. "It's okay. When greeting someone for the first time, a nod is usually the accepted custom here. Handshaking is generally for men, but once you are acquainted, it can be fine for a lady, but..." She leaned in and whispered. "...I'll let you figure out the other various forms of greeting for the ladies on your own." She gave Arran a devious smile. "Shall we begin?"

He liked her already.

They left the room, and Elinda pointed to the last door at the end of the hall. "That is your section's washroom."

Arran looked at the door and then at Elinda nervously. "Just the one? For...you know..."

Elinda laughed. "Yes, it is used by both male and female students. Inside there is a common area with sinks, then individual rooms with a lavatory and washroom."

Arran let out a sigh, and Elinda moved on, noticing his obvious relief.

From a small village, indeed.

They continued down the hall. As they approached the last door in the Intelligence section, he asked. "Why is this first door locked?"

"That room is for third-year and above students. It has a sitting area, with private rooms on the second and third floors. Once you get one, the room will be yours for the remainder of your studies. You may even keep it after graduating for a small charge, if you like."

Arran looked at the door and shrugged his shoulders as they continued. Elinda explained the sitting rooms, which Arran had already surmised, and then they were back at the main entrance. There were several other students standing in line to get checked in. Director Stejon's gruff voice rising above chatter.

Elinda pointed out the stairs in the main foyer. "The upper floors are off limits to students without express permission." She continued to explain that these areas housed the instructors' living quarters, offices, and various meeting chambers for the school's staff and board.

The afternoon progressed with Elinda showing Arran the main dining area, which was off the left back of the main foyer and the library, which was off the right back. Behind the dining hall and library were two large gardens with high landscaped walls. There were sitting benches and statues sprinkled throughout the gardens.

The biggest, and by far the most interesting, part of the day was the main training area. It took up the vast majority of the school grounds behind the front main buildings. There was a path straight down the middle, splitting the grounds into two sides. On the right were areas with training dummies for both melee and archery practice. On the left were a few melee areas and then several walled-off areas with training targets inside. Arran's brow furrowed as he looked at the structures.

Elinda watched as his expression changed. "Those are mainly for the mages. Learning how to use a spell from the Fire, Water, Air, or Earth disciplines can take some practice. The wall is there to catch any wayward first or second-year's stray spell. There have been some...shall we say, unfortunate accidents in the past."

Arran's eyebrows rose at the thought of the damage a wayward spell could cause.

Elinda tilted her head to the right. "Come on."

She led them onto a covered walkway that extended around the entire perimeter of the training area. There were buildings of all sizes along the entirety of the path. Two, three, and four-story structures housed all manner of purposes for the school.

Elinda pointed out the smithy, quartermaster, and most importantly, the various discipline training buildings. Arran peeked into the Intelligence training building to find a single large room with various training equipment neatly hung on the walls.

They eventually stopped and sat on a set of bleachers near the center and at the back of the training yard. Small clusters of students who had stayed on between terms like Elinda practiced their disciplines. They listened to the ringing of swords, the steady thwunk of arrows, and the occasional whoosh of some magic being used behind a practice wall.

"That is pretty much the general tour of the school. Become familiar with the different Patron halls, you will have classes in quite a few of them. I hear Director Stejon is teaching history this term." She pointed to the Mage training hall.

Arran's head bobbed up and down as his gaze swept the buildings, recalling each.

Elinda rose. "Shall we go see what Milinda has cooked for us this evening?"

Arran hadn't even noticed how hungry he was until she had mentioned food. "Oh gods, yes."

After superb roast chicken with steamed vegetables and bread, Elinda excused herself for the evening. "If you have any questions or need anything, just ask for me at the front desk."

Arran thanked her, and they parted ways for the evening. Finding his way back to his room, Arran flopped down on the bed, exhausted.

I'll clean up in the morning.

The morning light seeped around the edges of the curtains, dimly lighting the room. Arran let out a pitiful groan and turned his back to the window, stubbornly refusing to leave the comfort of the bed. He closed his eyes in a vain attempt at more sleep, but he was awake now, and all the events and questions from the previous weeks surfaced like bubbles. Each one popping into a new question, concern, or worry.

Here he was in a room that was to be his home for the foreseeable future, and at the school that had been more myth than reality less than three weeks ago. He turned over and stared at the window with disdain, as if everything was its fault. He spared a glance around the spartan room and sighed. Lying here was definitely not going to get any of his questions answered. So, with far more effort than it should have been, he got up and went to the washroom, relieved to find it empty.

As he walked through the main foyer, he slowed, noticing that there were a lot more students queuing for check in today. There were two lines now, each several students deep. His stomach gave a loud grumble of protest, reminding him of his original destination, and he hurried his pace.

Arran placed the breakfast of bacon, eggs, and dark toast on the table and sat down. He sat alone at one of the many tables in the dining hall and observed all the other students as they milled around and sat together in huddles. It was apparent that many were old friends returning from break. Laughter and exuberant conversation permeated the dining hall. He ate his breakfast and pondered about the upcoming day.

He was getting a little low on personal funds as he remembered his stipend. He wasn't quite sure how that worked, though, having received no instruction from Qoman.

Maybe Elinda would know?

He put the thought aside, not wanting to bother her so quickly after her initial tour. She had spent a lot of time with him the previous day and had been gracious with all of his questions. He decided a bit of exploring would do. Check out the new neighborhood.

Arran wandered aimlessly through the streets of Meitellen. He stopped at an inn and ordered a cider with a portion of his remaining funds. It was good, but not as good as the one at the Singing Goose, and he made a mental note to go back and visit.

The morning trek was pleasant. The people were nice, amiable even, but they moved about as if chased by some invisible source. Everywhere he went, the people went about their business in a hurried, almost frantic pace. He was making his way back towards the school when he noticed a bookshop, 'Notable Tomes'. Arran slowed, peeking in through the window before finally entering. A small bell announced his entry. An elderly man, spectacles perched at the very end of his nose, looked up from behind a counter at the back of the shop.

He put down the papers he was sorting. "Good morning, young master. Is there anything I can help you find?"

Arran walked towards the desk, surveying the shop. "I honestly don't know. I was passing by and was curious to see what your shop had to offer."

The shopkeeper gave him a polite smile. "Peruse as you like. I will be here if you have any questions."

Arran thanked him and began wandering the shop, going down aisle after aisle. The shop was impressive. There was a book for everything from art, history, geography, biographies, cooking, and even fiction...including...romance? He chuckled softly at some of the titles.

Short on funds, he wasn't really in a position to buy anything. Plus, he didn't want to buy anything before he had time to discover what the school library had to offer. Arran thanked the owner for his time and headed back to the school.

As Arran was finishing his midday meal, he saw Elinda enter the hall. Their eyes met, and she made her way over to him.

"Hello, Arran. How was your first morning?"

"Pretty decent. I did a little exploring in the city."

Elinda placed her plate on the table and sat down, folding her napkin in her lap. "Find anything interesting?"

Arran glanced down at his unused napkin, picked it up, and wiped his mouth before answering. "I found a good bookstore."

Elinda's eyes perked up. "Notable Tomes?"

Arran's head tilted back in surprise. "Why yes, you've heard of it?"

"I have. My father has bought several rare books from Master Quil over the years. He is very reputable." She blew on a spoonful of hot porridge.

"Good to know. I'll have to remember that."

As Arran took a drink, he remembered his question about his stipend. "What do you know about stipends? My sponsor made mention of it, but didn't exactly explain how it worked."

Elinda placed down her spoon and reached for her cup of tea contemplatively. "Your sponsor will have probably set up an account for you at the Meitellen bank. There's a branch about four blocks from here. Identify yourself with your papers, and they should grant you access to your funds."

"Hmm...that's it? Sounds simple."

Arran pushed his empty plate to the side and sipped his drink. "Since you stayed between terms, what do you do in your spare time other than answer pesky questions from first year's?" He flashed her a mischievous smile.

She laughed. "I devote most of my time to my studies and training. This coming term will be my second, and I want to be prepared for the final evaluations in term three."

"Does everyone automatically go to evaluations after three terms?"

"Usually, but not always. Some get held back for one reason or another, but most take it after their first three terms. I'm hoping to pass on my first try."

Arran's face became creased with concern. "And if you don't pass?"

Elinda shrugged. "You try again. Only about twenty percent of students pass their first evaluation. Going for a fourth or even fifth term is not uncommon." She paused as if something had just occurred to her. "I guess there really are no limits. It's all income for the school."

Elinda could tell that her explanation did nothing to alleviate Arran's concern. "Listen, everyone who is gifted has varying degrees of access to the Source. Some have a strong gift, while others may be weaker. If the latter is true, the school will generally expose this; and yes, if you fail too many evaluations, the school council may decide to...let you go. There are a lot of factors that go into this decision. Don't worry yourself about that for now. You have a lot to learn between now and evaluations."

She was right, of course. Third term was almost a year away. He could worry about evaluations later. "So, how would you suggest I get started?"

Elinda smiled, pleased at the change in attitude, and Arran's eagerness. "That's the best question so far. Go to the library and speak to Master Bronsel. He's the head librarian. Ask for some volumes on first-year Intelligence lessons. Then go see the quartermaster, Master Kallion. His shop is off of the main courtyard I showed you yesterday. He can outfit you with your first-year gear and get you started on basic exercises."

They talked well past lunch, Elinda patiently answering Arran's questions.

Elinda reached to pick up her plate. "I hate to stop you, but I really must go."

Arran apologized profusely for monopolizing her time and felt a bit awkward as she left. She had been extremely helpful though, and now he had a path to plan out his remaining free days leading up to the start of term.

Arran entered the giant library and came to a sudden stop as the doors silently closed behind him. He stood in shocked silence. He understood what a library was, but this...this was beyond anything he had ever imagined. It was easily one of the largest rooms he had ever seen and it was filled with rows upon rows of books.

This is fantastic!

Arran took a few steps into the room, mouth still agape, as his head swiveled in a vain effort to take in the room. After a few moments, he headed to the large main desk in the center of the room. An elderly man with grey hair, spectacles, and creases across his face in what looked like a permanent scowl studied him as he approached. He was flanked by a much younger man, busy at... library work? Arran could not tell, but he was attacking the chore with extreme vigor.

Arran was hesitant under the glare of the older man. "Excuse me. I am looking for some books." Arran found himself pausing at the incredible stupidity of his comment. He quickly tried to cover it up, speaking quickly. "For first-year Path of Intelligence lessons."

The older man's scowl morphed into a half-questioning look. Arran squinted, not quite sure how he pulled it off.

"Path of Intelligence, you say? Interesting, don't get many of those in here." He stood up, scanning Arran from head to toe. "Benni, be a good lad and see if you can accommodate our young friend here. Maybe give him some light reading?"

"Yes, Master Bronsel." Benni stood up quickly and headed off into the depths of the library.

Master Bronsel went back to his work, totally ignoring Arran. Arran looked around awkwardly for a few moments before he decided he should probably go elsewhere.

I guess I'll just go over here, then.

Arran perused some of the closest shelves to the main desk, waiting for Benni's return. About fifteen minutes later, Benni returned, pushing a cart loaded with at least thirty books. Arran looked at the cart in shock.

Light reading?

Benni pushed the cart up next to the main desk. Master Bronsel stood and addressed Arran sternly. "You can read however many books you want here in the library." His expression turned very serious. The full weight of his scowl had returned. "But you may only check out two books at a time." As if the man's glare hadn't already been severe, it was definitely now as he continued. "The books may not leave school grounds." He paused for what seemed an eternity, holding Arran's eyes firmly. "Do not test me on this."

Arran shrank back, almost stumbling.

This man was serious about his books!

Then, just as quickly, as if a light had suddenly been turned on, his demeanor softened as he sat and adjusted his spectacles up his nose. "There are reading rooms around the edges of the library on each of the floors. If you would like to check out a book, bring it back here to the main desk."

Arran hesitated. Not sure if there was more to this conversation. It began to get a little awkward, and Arran uttered a quick thanks, eyeing the cart. He wheeled the collection of books off to find a reading room.

He spent the majority of the afternoon going through all the books Benni had gathered. He didn't really read any of them in depth, he simply wanted to get a feel for their content. He wanted to make a good choice for the two books he would be allowed to check out. He finally decided on a 'History of Talon' and one on the 'Gifts of Talon'. Returning to the front desk with the cart, he placed his two choices on the ledge of the front desk.

"I would like to check out these two books, please."

Master Bronsel did not look up, and Benni took the books. "Your name?"

"Arran."

Benni took out a piece of paper, wrote Arran's name on it, then pressed it on the inside cover of the book. Arran's name appeared when he removed the paper; the script glowed softly for a second then dissipated, leaving his name as if someone had written it in ink.

"The book is now registered to you. When you return the book, we will remove your name. As Master Bronsel mentioned, do not leave school grounds with the book." Benni did the same for the second book and handed them to Arran.

"Thank you." Arran quickly retreated towards the door, dispelling any idea of further conversation.

Arran put the two books in his dorm chest and headed for dinner.

He ate alone, only politely nodding or giving a small wave to several students he had already come to recognize.

That evening Arran began reading the History of Talon first. Like the pamphlet that Qoman had given him, the book had a lot of general information about Talon, and the Path of Intelligence, but in the end, not a whole lot of additional insight. Arran found himself skipping chapters that appeared to give much the same information as previous chapters, only written by different scholars over the years. He moved on to Gifts of Talon.

This book proved much more insightful. Similar to Qoman's pamphlet, the book spoke of the four main gifts of Talon: Sight, Stealth, Observance, and Shadow, but unlike the pamphlet, there was much more information on each.

Stealth, which Arran believed he had already been gifted, was considered a prime gift. Meaning it was almost always gifted. It explained a lot of what Arran had already figured out, but it also contained information on what it was not. Stealth allowed one to move quieter, but sound was perceived differently depending on the quarry. A deer, for example, was a non-sapient animal; Stealth, when used properly, could easily be used on such creatures. But sapient beings, humans for example, were much more difficult. Staying undetected by a sapient being took much more discipline.

The gift of Sight was straightforward. Being granted this gift allowed for one to not only have better eyesight for distance, but also granted better vision in darkness to varying degrees. This was a common gift, and it was reported that being granted this gift could eventually change the color of one's eyes, usually to pale silver.

Observance was a gift that enhanced one's awareness of their surroundings. It was also a common gift, but one's effectiveness in this skill largely depended on the individual. The keener of mind, the more effective the gift. Obtaining this gift would allow one to analyze rooms, objects, and people with accurate detail. It would also, to varying degrees based on the individual, allow one to recall situations with greater detail. Analyzing all of this information would allow one to summarize situations and behaviors. At more advanced levels, it could even help predict potential outcomes, especially during a duel or fighting situation.

The gift of Shadow was the most intriguing, and the least explained in the book. It was considered a rare gift, and the only detail on it was a vague description of blending into shadow. There was not much else known, or at least written, about the gift.

Arran lowered the book in contemplation before realizing he had read late into the night. Exhaustion hit him like a wave. He placed the books in his chest and blew out the candle.

***

Arran gathered the two books from his chest and set out the next morning. He felt that he had gleaned all he could out of them and would return them, but first he needed some breakfast.

Arran eagerly strolled into the library and up to the main desk. "Good morning, Master Bronsel. I will be returning these two books."

Bronsel looked up from the book he was reading and gave Arran a quizzical eye from above his spectacles. "Finished already, have you?"

"If truth be told, I didn't really read much of the history book. There doesn't seem to be much known of Talon."

Bronsel frowned. "Yes, he is the most enigmatic of the Patrons."

"Enigmatic?"

"Mysterious. The Order of Intelligence is the most secretive in their teachings and outward history."

"Ah yes, enigmatic indeed, then." Arran winked.

Bronsel's perpetual scowl softened as he looked at Arran. The hint of a wry smile appeared, catching the quip. He took the two books from Arran, retrieved the paper with Arran's name on it, and just as before but in reverse, touched the paper to the inside cover and Arran's name disappeared.

"I would like to look at some of the other books you have concerning first-year Intelligence lessons if you don't mind."

"As I am alone this morning, you will need to go retrieve them yourself. Third floor, section two. The first-year lessons will be in the fourth row of shelves and at the back."

Arran thanked the librarian and headed out into the library. After finding his way up to the third floor and the proper section, he began to look at the wide array of book titles. He saw many of the same books that he had been given the previous day and a few others that caught his eye. The Intelligence path trained mainly in small melee weapons, daggers to be specific; as opposed to swords, maces, or other large melee weapons. Arran knew next to nothing about daggers and ended up choosing a book that dealt with the basics.

Instead of going back to his room, Arran wandered about the school grounds to find a nice place to read. He found his way to the gardens and settled on a bench in one of the more secluded sections. He had not been reading very long before he was interrupted by a slight cough. Looking up, he found Elinda at the edge of the path opening.

"Care for some company?"

"Uh...yeah...I mean yes," Arran stammered out the words, unsure why he found himself suddenly tongue-tied. She was pretty for sure, but she had been his mentor these last few days. "Please, have a seat."

Elinda crossed the distance and sat on the opposite end of the bench.

"I see you have found my secret spot."

"Secret spot?"

"I come here to meditate, read, or just relax." Elinda closed her eyes and took in a long breath.

"I'm sorry." Arran immediately felt embarrassed. "I can leave if you would like."

Elinda giggled and let out her breath.

"No, you misunderstand. That was not an invitation to leave. If you do not mind sharing, I have brought a book of my own."

Arran let out a breath of relief.

"I don't mind at all, Lady Elinda." Arran stood and gave her a very deep and honorific bow.

She laughed at the ostentatious display. "Why, thank you, Master Arran. I think that will be agreeable."

They both enjoyed the quips with quiet laughs. Elinda opened her book and began to read, Arran doing the same.

Arran found himself distracted and unable to concentrate on the book at first. When Elinda was acting as his introductory guide, he had not been nervous at all, but now it felt awkward. Eventually he was able to get lost in his book and before he knew it, mid-morning was gone.

Arran put down his book and stood up, stretching. Elinda looked up and laid her own book on the bench beside her.

"Would you care for a stroll? I know some good areas."

"Sure." Arran stretched out his arms and leaned back. "That sounds good right about now."

They headed down a different path from the one they both had entered and slowly strolled through the various gardens. Elinda was excited to give him details about the various plants and flowers and either their medicinal or alchemical purpose. Arran discovered that Elinda was hoping to train in both areas of study while at the school. It was an ambitious endeavor.

Arran was intrigued to find out that Elinda was from Daijoon, the capital city of Valoor. Her father was the realm's head priest, as Qoman was for Aaeu'din. Her family heritage was rich with gifted individuals, mainly priests and mages.

They eventually found their way back to their reading spot, and Arran gasped at the sudden realization that he had left the book unattended on the bench. It was gone!

"Oh gods!" Arran rummaged behind and below the bench in fright. "Not even here three days and I've already lost a book!"

Elinda watched as Arran scurried around the bench and the surrounding area looking for the book. She finally could not help it any longer. "Arran, it's okay. The book is safe!" A smile spread across her face and she tried to stifle a laugh. "I'm sorry, it was a cruel joke for me not to say so sooner, but the book will be back at the main desk in the library by now."

"What? How? What do you mean?" The words came out in a panicked stammer.

"The book is enchanted to you. If the book's enchantment loses contact with you, and it is still within the confines of the school grounds, it will reappear back at the main desk of the library. You can go back and retrieve it, with no little scorn from Master Bronsel for sure, but no harm is done."

Arran sat down on the bench, relieved. He let out a nervous laugh.

Elinda looked at him with surprise. She thought for sure he would be at least somewhat angry with her.

"Arran?"

Arran took a moment to regain his composure. "You see, in my hometown, I was...well, I was known for certain...pranks. I was always being punished for my various schemes. It appears that I've come due." He smiled up at her. "Kind of ironic, don't you think?"

Elinda looked at him quizzically. "You are a strange one."

"Well, at least you know I can take a joke." Arran stood. "Now, I'd like to go get that book back, if you don't mind."

They headed back to the library, and sure enough, Master Bronsel met him with a scowl.

"Left the book unattended, did you?" His tone was sharp and his scowl deepened.

I could sharpen a blade with that look.

"Yes, sir. It was but for a short time...in the gardens. I was taking a break with Lady Elinda and..."

"On a stroll with a young lady and left the book you say?" Bronsel was trying desperately to maintain his gruffness, but eventually lost the battle.

"Not the worst excuse I've ever heard." Bronsel gave Elinda a wry smile.

Bronsel handed the book back to Arran. "Just you be careful not to let it happen again. Understood?"

"Yes, sir. Thank you, sir." Arran turned and made as quick an exit from the library as he could muster.

Arran did not slow until they had reached the main foyer. "Whew."

"See, not so bad."

"I guess not."

They parted ways and Arran decided to finish the morning by reading the book in the much safer confines of his room.

The first few chapters that Arran had already read were very basic. What was a dagger? Where was it useful? And more importantly, where it put you at a disadvantage. After that, the next few chapters had numerous diagrams and pictures on how to properly sheath, hold, and wield a dagger for rudimentary strikes. Arran was quickly coming to the understanding that he would need to practice...a lot. He placed the book in his chest, then went to lunch. It was time to visit the quartermaster.

Arran entered the training courtyard and could not help but watch some of the other students practicing. In a few short days, he would probably be out there practicing himself. It was surreal. He continued around the outer walkway until he found the quartermaster's shop, which appeared empty. There was a large counter at the back of the room with various weapons and armor mounted on the wall behind it. The remainder of the shop was divided into sections that appeared to cater to the various disciplines: cloth, leather, mail, and steel. Accompanying the appropriate armor type were weapons: staves, swords, maces, daggers, and some he could not recognize.

As Arran wandered the shop, he did not notice as a man entered from the back of the room.

"May I assist you?"

Arran turned to find a huge man standing behind the counter. He was easily a head taller than Arran, and even more muscled than his father, which was saying something.

"Umm...yes, sir." Arran fidgeted for just a moment, a little intimidated by the larger man. "Master Kallion?"

"Yes."

"I was instructed...advised, that you might be able to assist in equipping me with my first-year gear." Arran stammered through the words quickly, still somewhat in awe of the imposing man.

"That I may." His voice had a low deep rumble to it, as if he spoke from his chest and not his mouth. "From which Patron are you gifted?"

"Talon."

Kallion looked surprised. He eyed Arran up and down. "Talon, you say? You don't...I don't get many students of Talon."

"So I've been told," Arran muttered under his breath.

"You will be needing some light leather, some basic training daggers..." He trailed off as he stepped around the desk and made his way to the leather section of the room. He began picking up pieces of gear, inspecting them and turning to Arran as if in thought. Some he kept, while the others went back on the shelf. Finally satisfied with his selections, he went back to the counter, placing everything out in a neat row.

"Here you are." Kallion surveyed the gear one more time, pointing to each piece as if trying to make sure he did not forget anything. "This will get you started."

Arran looked at all the gear in amazement. A chest piece, leggings, gauntlets, boots, and the two wooden daggers. His amazement quickly turned to worry.

"This seems like it will cost a lot."

"Compliments of the school. This is all common low-tier gear. No enchantments, no enhancing special properties; plain leather garments, first-term wooden daggers, so you do not hurt yourself or others...at least too bad." Arran saw a sly smirk spread across the big man's face.

That can't be good.

"As you gain replacements, bring these back."

"Thank you."

Arran gathered up the items as best he could, thanked Kallion again, and headed back to his room.

He placed all the gear out on his bed. He suddenly realized that Kallion had not fitted him to make sure the gear would fit. The chest piece and boots definitely looked too big for him. He decided to try it all on anyway.

He tried the chest piece first, putting it on over his plain white shirt. Sure enough, it was too big. He began to take it off, when he felt a slight pull. The chest piece slowly began to shrink down to a perfect fit.

I thought he said just plain leather garments, no enchantments?!

He quickly moved on to the other pieces of gear. Sure enough, each piece slowly formed to a perfect fit.

He moved around, stretching and flexing in different positions. All of the gear was light, flexible, and did not impede his movement at all.

Nice!

Satisfied, Arran picked up the two wooden daggers and hefted them in his hands. They had decent weight, and while they were wooden, there was still a very sharp point with a decent edge. They were not as sharp as iron or steel, but he surmised that they could still draw blood with a good strike.

He retrieved the book from his chest and laid it out on the bed, opening it to the chapter on how to sheath and hold the daggers. The leggings had two sheaths on each side for holding the daggers. He put the wooden daggers in the sheaths and then practiced pulling them out. Slowly at first, to get a feel for the new motion, then faster and faster as he got used to the movement. As he became familiar with the drawing of the daggers, he began to add simple thrusts and slashes as shown in the book. He repeated the motions: re-sheath, draw, thrust, and slash. He did this until his arms ached from the new movements.

He was glad that no one was around to witness his practice. He must have looked ridiculously amateurish in his clumsy use of the weapons, but it was a start. Flopping down on the bed, exhausted from the effort, he steeled himself to practice more tomorrow.

Arran took a long hot bath in the morning to try and help soothe his aching arm and leg muscles. He continued his practice with all the basic movements in his room for the remainder of the morning until he felt he had a rudimentary competence of what he was doing. In the afternoon, he would go out to the training grounds and practice on one of the dummies in the yard. He needed to feel the stab and the slashes against something with resistance, instead of simple air.

Arran left his room, leaving the leggings on as they had the sheaths; and the boots because they were so much more comfortable than his old ones. He left the gauntlets and chest piece behind as he did not feel they added anything to his current practice movements.

After eating some lunch, he made his way to the training grounds. There were a few other students already practicing. One mage, two archers, and one other student using the melee dummies. He was practicing with a sword.

Arran made his way out to a dummy and took a deep breath. He began very slowly and deliberately unsheathing his daggers, making a thrust, a slash, and then re-sheathing them.

He had been going like this for a while when he noticed Master Kallion observing him and the other student practicing on the dummies. He didn't say anything. He simply watched from the edge of the yard, leaning on a pole. Arran went back to his practice.

After a short while, Kallion approached. "Lighten your grip."

Arran stopped and looked over at Kallion, panting from the exertion. Sweat dripped from his nose.

"Lighten your grip. It is too tight. You hold them like they are going to fly out of your hands. Lighten your grip when moving and only tighten it when engaging. You will find it easier to transition from one movement to another, fluid."

Arran nodded his head and continued, trying to keep his grip lighter during the movements, tightening only when he went to stab or slash the dummy. He found it far less stressful on his arms and it was much easier to transition between movements.

Arran stepped back from the dummy. "Thank you."

Kallion nodded. "You should also practice defensive postures during the engagement. Always be prepared for the parry or countermove."

"Parry?"

Kallion sighed heavily. "Yes, parry. It means to counter an attack aimed at you with your own daggers. You can swipe it aside, engage it directly, or move to avoid it. This is a dummy, but engage it as if it were a live person. Do you think a real person is just going to stand there and let you stab and slice them to bits?"

Arran thought on this. "No, I guess not."

"Good! Now practice as if it were a live opponent and be prepared for their countermove; think as they would think. Practice on quick stabs and slices from various angles with one hand, but be guarded and ready with the other. Expect a parry or be ready to move away from a counterstrike. To master daggers in close combat, you need to be quick, responsive, and most importantly, decisive."

Kallion watched impassively as Arran processed the new information.

"Also, you are predominately attacking with only your right hand. This is normal when beginning, as it is your dominant side and natural to you, but you need to practice every move with your off-hand as well. You need to be efficient with both hands to maximize your opportunities during an engagement."

Kallion gestured to the dummy for Arran to continue, then strolled away to observe the other students.

Arran really needed to read more of the book. He had not read anything pertaining to parrying, countermoves, or practicing with one's off-hand.

Arran spent the remaining days before the start of term, primarily in the courtyard, trying to put into practice what Kallion had instructed. It was hard, grueling work, especially with his off-hand. It did not come naturally to him and his strikes and moves were awkward.

He had finished reading the book on daggers, and sure enough, he eventually got to the sections on parrying, countermoves, and even a small passage regarding the need to practice with one's off-hand. Arran thought this odd and an oversight in the book, given how important it was. As he practiced more and began to think of the dummy as a live opponent, he realized that most of his attacks could easily be anticipated if he always came from one side. This he would fix.

He had returned the book on daggers back to the library on his last day and checked out a book on the history of his home realm, Aaeu'din. He ate dinner, read a while from the new book and went to bed, ready for his first day of real training.

INTERLUDE

The desk was a mass of disheveled papers, journals, and all manner of scraps with thoughts and half-written notes, many barely holding a coherent thought. Spirit put her head in her hands and rubbed her temples as she surveyed the collage in front of her. She knew she needed to organize it better. Using physical media for her work was untidy, but she preferred the tangibility, the solidness it offered over digital media.

All in all, she was pleased with the progress of the age on Galleant, but something nagged at her. Anomalies had begun to appear that she could not explain. Or at least that she could not explain unless it meant that another incident had occurred. It had been several generations since that occurrence and the council had gone to great measures to make sure that it could not happen again. There had to be another explanation.

She started at the sound of the door chime. It was not late, but it was well past the time she would usually expect visitors. She sighed.

Oh well, I could use a break.

"Breanna, what a pleasant surprise! Please come in."

Breanna entered, glancing at the desk across the room, and

frowned. Spirit, seeing her expression, took her arm to lead her into the sitting room and out of view of the study.

"Can I get you anything?"

"Tea will be fine."

"Of course. Please have a seat. I will be right back."

Spirit returned a short while later to find Breanna visibly irritated, staring at the fire. Spirit lowered the tray to the table between them and poured them each a cup of tea. Long moments passed as Breanna continued her silence. Spirit began to fidget.

"How are..." Breanna held up her hand, interrupting her. She took a sip of her tea and slowly turned to face Spirit. Her face was flush with regret.

She spoke deeply and sorrowfully. "I found them."

"I'm sorry?"

"I found them, Spirit! The village!" The outrage was sudden and came spilling out as if it had been bottled up for an eternity.

Silence fell upon the room. Spirit could not look up to meet Breanna's eyes. She knew the glare was there. She could feel the heat of her anger boring into her.

"You have nothing to say?"

"Honestly, I do not know what to say. I assumed that they would be found sooner or later, but I was hoping for more time before I disclosed it...them, to the rest of the council."

"More time?! More time?! Look at me!" Spirit raised her head and was taken aback at the full wrath of Breanna's glare. "Do you know what this means? The council agreed to this endeavor with specific conditions. Conditions 'you' swore would be upheld, and now I find this? You should have disclosed this immediately, but no, in your hubris, you have placed us all in grave peril of discovery!" Breanna seethed as she vented her frustration. She was breathing heavily, struggling to regain her composure from the uncharacteristic outburst.

Spirit cringed and shrank under the withering accusation. She had never seen Breanna so angry. They sat in silence, neither knowing how to continue. The fire crackled and spat, drawing back Breanna's gaze.

"I wanted to understand the effects of the Source on a race without our direct intervention. I thought..."

Breanna interrupted again. "You thought! No, I believe the right of it is that you didn't think!"

Spirit's own anger flared. "Let me finish!"

Breanna leered at her, but sat silently, arms crossed defiantly.

Spirit took a deep breath. "I thought...No. I suspected, really, that it would prove useful in my final analysis. The Source, Breanna...I believe it is more than we know. If I could somehow provide evidence, proof, that even the presence of the Source in a world...we could let the world progress naturally. That was my goal."

Breanna's eyes narrowed. Suspicion and incredulity replacing her anger. "To what end? What would this prove?"

"It would mean..." Spirit hesitated. She had not shared these thoughts with anyone. They were her own, had been her own for a very long time. She took a deep breath, understanding that she was putting a lot of faith in her friend if she continued. "It would mean that the Source is its own presence. That it alone could imbue mortal sentients."

Breanna's anger had diminished and her natural inclinations began to twirl in thought. "You mean to suggest that the Source is... sentient?"

"No. Not sentient. Maybe. I don't know. I don't believe sentience is the right of it, but alive, compelled in some way? Maybe? Think of it like nature itself." Spirit knew that using a nature analogy was a bit patronizing for the Patron of Bounty, but it was the best example to explain her findings. "It exists and is...driven to seek, find life, and grow of its own accord." Spirit shook her head in frustration and began pacing around the room. "The Source isn't simply some power that we wield and pretend to control, but a living presence that seeks out life. That it is possibly a living sentience itself..."

Spirit trailed off, not sure how to end the thought. She turned back to Breanna, watching for any hint of what she had just proposed.

"I have evidence."

Breanna's eyes narrowed as she contemplated on what Spirit had just revealed.

Spirit could see the frustration written on Breanna's face as she pondered the ramifications of the idea. "If the central realm found you out...don't you see that you are playing with all of our lives here? Our reputations? Ugh! The arrogance that you would do this without everyone's consent! We could be removed, our realm stripped apart in pieces, and your precious experiment destroyed."

Spirit flinched at the thought.

"Surely the High Council..."

Breanna cut her off. "Do not presume to know the convictions of the central realm!"

Spirit paced the room nervously as Breanna watched her. Neither spoke for a long time. Spirit was afraid and ashamed of Breanna's comments. If she was honest with herself, she knew she had been arrogant to go this alone.

Breanna stood and crossed the floor to stand in front of Spirit. "What have you discovered?"

"Follow me."

Spirit led her to the desk and began rummaging through her notes.

Breanna surveyed the jumble of papers with odd fascination. "Summarize, please." She had no intention of wading into the mess upon the table.

Spirit looked up at Breanna and then back to her desk. "Ahh. Yes, then. The villagers progressed normally, at least initially. After several centuries, though, I began to notice something odd. Their life spans were increasing. Not by much, but it was becoming noticeable. It is now close to five times that of the humans."

Spirit paused as she finally found the notes outlining the information. She handed it to Breanna.

"Why did you use the Elves? Why not another village of humans?"

"I don't know exactly. Variety? We've never created an age with two different sentients on the same planet and with the Source introduced...I would be able to observe the effects on both races."

Breanna sniffed. "Ever the inquisitive one," she muttered. She glanced at the paper in her hand, then gently laid it back down.

"And..." One eyebrow raising. "I assume there is more?"

Spirit turned, the elation of disclosing her discoveries vanishing. She continued nervously, a look of grim seriousness now etched across her face. "They have obtained Source abilities on their own... without Patron intervention."

The look of shock on Breanna's face was instant.

"You're sure? How? That isn't possible! We were careful...so sure..."

Spirit shrugged. "Several of the eldest in the village have become quite strong. It is rare, not all become that strong, but everyone in the village has abilities of some kind. Everyone, Breanna. Every single one. Their abilities appear to be attuned to their role in the village, not unlike how we gift the humans."

"Is this from the Source levels on the planet, or racial?"

"I do not know. Possibly a combination of both. I've been analyzing..." Spirit spread her arms wide over the desk, shaking her head. "I do not have an answer."

Breanna gazed over the vast array of notes. "This stays between us for now. We need to figure all of this out. And...we need to find a way to disclose this to the rest of the council. Soon."

Spirit nodded.

Breanna began walking to the door, then turned around. "And Spirit..." She gestured at the desk. "Get that mess of information in a more digestible format. We're not presenting that in the council chamber. Thank you for the tea."

CHAPTER 4
FIRST TERM
YEAR 1303 / AUGUST / WEEK 2

Week 3 of First Term

"Ugh!" Arran gasped, doubling over in pain from the strike to his stomach.

"Oh, quit whining, you git. I didn't hit you that hard, besides if you are going to continue to leave that opening, I'm going to use it."

Bran bent down and assisted Arran to his feet.

Arran glared up at him, half in anger and the other in guilt. "I know..." He winced as he straightened. "...but we are just practice sparring. You didn't have to strike so hard to get the point across."

Bran laughed. "How else are you supposed to learn then, eh?"

Arran returned the smile with a sardonic grin of his own.

Bran, officially Branford, was in his second term and closest to Arran in age, so they had been assigned together as sparring partners. The two had become close in their short time together and Bran had even changed his bunk assignment and moved in with Arran. He was from the capital city of Kimore, in the realm of Boreshone. Bran's father was a lower noble, a duke, but even this had afforded Bran certain luxuries from his father's titles. Not the least of which was weapons training from an early age. He was far superior to Arran. As a matter of fact, he was far superior to most. Of the twenty or so Intelligence students currently enrolled, Bran could probably beat most of them, and even hold his own with some of the third and fourth year's.

Bran had said that when he had been gifted by Talon, his family was more than a little surprised. Of the gifted in his family, most had always been from Tovin the Knight. It had been many generations since anyone had been gifted by Talon, but Arran could see why, and he believed Bran could as well. Bran was not just good, he was considered one of the top talents amongst all the classes. Arran was fortunate to have him as a sparring partner and friend.

It was the third week of the term and they had been training hard. Even though they had become close friends, Bran did not pull any punches. He was tough, but always quick to explain and educate Arran during their sparring.

Arran winced again as he sheathed his daggers. "Let's take a break and grab some water." Arran headed for the bleachers and the water barrel, albeit slowly. He sat down gingerly on the bench.

Bran sat down next to him and patted him on the shoulder. "You have made good progress, my friend. You have skill, but you need to be more aggressive and decisive when the opportunity presents. You had me open in the middle of that match, and you sliced moderately at my shoulder when you should have hit me much harder. I do not hold back in my strikes and neither should you. It does me a disservice."

Arran knew he spoke the truth. Hitting someone with all his force was foreign to him. Even after three weeks, it still felt unnatural to him. "I know." Arran looked up. "The strikes, the moves...everything is still too..." He fumbled for the right word. "...deliberate. I've got a dozen different thoughts bombarding me all at once."

"All in good time. You have only been training for three weeks. I've had years. Eventually, the moves will be natural, reflexive. 'If you must think about it, you are too slow'," he said in a deep, mocking tone. "A favorite saying from my old instructor from home. Now, you want to talk about a hard ass!"

The two had a good laugh and sat for a breather, watching the other sparring matches. Arran sipped his water, captivated as he watched the more advanced students. They danced and parried one another with a grace he wasn't sure he could achieve.

The afternoon continued with their sparring, Arran receiving instruction from Bran and receiving more hits than he gave. During the last match of the day, Arran finally managed to land one decisive strike on Bran's side, causing him to wince and step back. He stood up and smiled.

"Now, that's what I'm talking about!" The compliment coming out as a painful wheeze. "Let's go get cleaned up for supper."

The two friends chatted with vigor during dinner as they discussed the afternoon's sparring sessions, when Arran noticed Elinda walking over. He had not spoken with her since the term began.

Arran stood as she arrived and gave her a smile. "Lady Elinda, good to see you!"

"Good evening, Arran. How are things going so far in your first term?"

"Not too bad. I stay a bit bruised thanks to Bran here." Arran placed a hand on Bran's shoulder. "Bran, this is Lady Elinda, my initial guide when I first came to school."

Bran stood. "Lady Elinda. Nice to meet you." He gave a nod in greeting, and Elinda reciprocated.

Arran gestured to the seat beside him. "Would you care to join us?"

"No. Thank you, though. We have a group gathering to discuss our classes today. We are taking supper in our common room. It is good to see you, Arran. Bran. Good evening." She gave them a polite smile and headed off towards her dormitory common room.

Once she was gone, Bran nudged Arran. "Um, Arran?"

Having already resumed his meal, all he could muster around a mouthful of food was, "Yeaamm."

"Did you see that smile she gave you?"

"Huh? Oh yeah, it's a kind of joke. When I first met her, I offered my hand to her in greeting, and she had to give me a quick lesson in etiquette. So, whenever we meet now, it's kind of a joke when I get things right."

"Well, if a lady smiled at me that way, I'd be asking her out for a stroll somewhere nice, double quick."

"Oh, we did take a walk together once in the gardens before term started." Arran continued with his meal, not seeing the look of surprise spread across Bran's face.

"You what!"

Arran looked up in surprise.

Bran laughed and gave Arran a hearty slap on the back, almost making him spit out his food.

"You sly fox. Already taking the first step in courtship. Well done, my friend!"

Arran almost choked on his mouthful of food, looking at his friend in horror. "What?"

"Asking a lady for a walk in the gardens? Classic first courtship move." Bran began shaking his head, giving Arran a sly smile.

"No, no, it was nothing like that. We were...we were just reading together one afternoon, and it was a quick stroll to stretch our legs. That's all."

"Nice. Inconspicuous reading that led to a walk. That's brilliant, mind if I use that? Maybe that country naivety has some merit. I may need to take some lessons from you." Bran could see the look of anguish on his friend's face and laughed uproariously.

Arran could only stare blankly in utter panic.

Later that night, Arran lay in bed, dumbfounded. What had he done, and more importantly, what had he gotten himself into? Surely Elinda did not think he was trying to court her? She was from a noble family. He was only from Kine. No, it was just two friends having a chat, nothing more. He had almost convinced himself when sleep finally overtook him.

Year 1303/September/Week 1
Week 6 of First Term

As the sixth week of the term began, the school's schedule and curriculum had become a comfortable routine for Arran. So far, the first five weeks had primarily been centered around physical training: melee weapons, unarmed combat, obstacle courses, long distance running, and balance and flexibility. The balance and flexibility involved a practice of meditation and forms that were completely new to Arran. It seemed simple enough, but had proved to be quite strenuous.

Twice a day, they were required to attend classroom training. History, geography, botany, math, and alchemy were all on the list. Arran enjoyed the breaks from the physical training and the readings that were required for the classes. Master Bronsel had been more than pleased to find him visiting often on one subject or another, extending his learning past the normal curriculum.

But it was the physical training that took up most of his time. Most sessions could be done in pairs or in groups, but not all. Obvious classes, like melee weapon training, and unarmed combat, required a partner, and he and Bran were generally paired together for these sessions. The remainder, like the obstacle course and his balance and flexibility sessions, could be completed at one's own discretion as long as the predefined weekly quota was met. As Bran was a second-term student, he sometimes had other class requirements. Arran made use of this solo time, fulfilling and often surpassing his remaining weekly quota of hours; always under the watchful eye of an instructor or Kallion.

Today held something special, though. Instructor Shia had informed four students, including Arran, to meet her in the Intelligence training hall after their morning meal. Class was being held in a place officially called 'The Maze', located in the basement of their hall. The maze, affectionately called "The Dungeon" by the students, was as the name implied. It was a giant network of hallways, alcoves, hidden rooms, and traps meant to challenge the students in new and different ways specific to their Intelligence training. The room's dimensions, layout, and challenges were customized for each run. Rarely, if ever, was a run the same.

Kallion had told Arran that it had been created over a century before by a master mage and engineer at the school's request. They worked in secret and no one knows how they created the room. All efforts to duplicate it since had failed. The room was primarily used by the Intelligence order, but several of the other disciplines would reserve it from time to time for various specialized training of their own. Today was to be Arran's introduction.

Instructor Shia led the four students down to the basement's main room. There was a round table in the middle of the room with eight chairs. Barrels and crates were stacked against the walls and there were two doors, side by side, on the far wall. It was unremarkable, really, with a slightly musty odor. Everyone took a seat as Shia began to explain the details of the exercise.

"The goal of today's lesson is simple. Today, you will play tag just like you did when you were a child. There are only two ways to win. First, you are able to sneak up on your opponent and execute a blow without being detected; or two, you detect and successfully parry a surprise attack or otherwise avoid the blow."

Shia looked them over coolly, purposefully pausing on each student, making sure each one understood. "Any questions?"

No one replied, and she pointed at Arran and Victor. "You two. Each of you take a door." She stood and depressed a central carved stone in the wall behind her. There was a pause, then the stones in the wall began to part, exposing two small doorways. Both of the young men's eyes lit up in wonder as they approached their respective doors.

Shia's voice took on a low tone of patronization. "I would like to remind everyone that this is not hide and seek. You will actively seek and engage. There will be no hiding in an alcove waiting for your opponent to wander by. This is stealth training, not hiding training. Understood?"

"Yes, ma'am," the group replied in unison.

"Now then, you have thirty minutes. Today's maze is not large, so that should be ample time for the engagement. Go!"

Arran and Victor each stepped through their respective doors and into the maze.

As Arran stepped through, the stones silently closed behind him. There was a barely audible 'snick' as the last stone clicked in to place and darkness enveloped him. Arran crouched and immediately turned left. Victor had been to his left as they entered, but the hall was empty. Down the hall, he could see a small torch in a sconce on the wall. It did not provide much light this far away, but it was enough to create shadows from every corner and plunge several of the alcoves along that path into darkness. Arran concentrated and began slowly walking down the hallway in the direction of the sconce and its faint light. To his delight, he realized his Stealth ability was working well. He made little to no sound as he approached the torch. He stopped. There was a hallway intersecting his about ten paces further up.

He surmised that since this was to be a small maze, only one way would connect him and Victor. But which way? He continued forward and turned left. It did not take him long to figure out this way was a dead end.

So right it is, then.

He went back and took the other hallway. At the end of the hallway was a well-lighted room. It had a stone table in the middle with six chairs. Rubble was strewn around the entire room. Arran had an idea and picked up a handful of small pebbles and put them in his pocket.

There was only one other door leading out of the room and he slowly set off in that direction. He quickly came to an alcove, well-hidden in shadows, and stepped into the darkness, straining his ears for any sound. After hearing nothing, he exited the alcove and moved on. Another junction.

Right or left?

If his bearings were correct, right would lead back towards his side of the room. He chose left.

The hallway ended at an empty circular chamber with three other openings, none of which had doors. He could see down the hallway directly opposite him, with another junction at the end. He watched it intently until he was sure there was no movement. He slowly began edging himself left, keeping an eye on the opening to the right, until he could safely see down the hallway on the left.

There! What was that?

He strained his every sense, peering down the hallway for another sign. Nothing. But he was sure he saw something. The hint of a flicker, the subtle change of light against the far wall. He made his way over to the opening opposite from his entry and moved down the hall. He would go left at the junction and hopefully come up behind Victor from that direction...if it was indeed his opponent.

Arran worked his way to the junction corner and stopped, once again straining to hear anything beyond. He peered behind him to check his back, then down each hallway at the junction. Nothing. He turned left, crouching low and up against the wall to minimize his own shadow.

Just as he was taking his first few steps into the hallway, a flash of heat emanated from his chest. Arran audibly gasped, and just as before, it quickly vanished; exactly as it had happened in the forest. He stumbled and fell to his knees.

The spark! I got another gift!

Arran pushed the excitement from his mind and fought to bring his breathing back under control. He did not have time to think about it right now. He would inform the instructor after the exercise.

He took another moment to collect himself, then slowly continued his trek forward. He stopped abruptly, his attention intensely drawn to one of the bricks right beneath his foot. It wavered in his sight, not glowing, but easily differentiated from the other stones around it. It was slightly wedged up from the floor, and would have surely made a noticeable sound in the corridor or worse, tripped him. He adeptly stepped over it and continued down the hall, which ended with a right turn.

He stopped at the corner and listened. Nothing. He checked his back again, then slowly moved away from the corner and to the opposite wall to get a better vantage down the hallway.

He saw a small figure edge out of an alcove down the hallway, just past the opening that would have led back to the circular room. Victor was headed in the opposite direction and he was deathly silent.

He's good.

Now Arran had to find a spot to implement his plan. He backtracked from where he had just come and stepped into the first alcove he found. He then reached into his pocket to find the smallest pebble he had.

He lightly threw the pebble down the hallway and past the corner into the hallway Victor was in...and waited. He felt a bead of sweat roll down his temple, falling down his cheek.

It felt like an eternity before Arran saw the smallest flicker of shadow at the corner.

Now or never!

Slowly and methodically, Arran braced his legs and arms against the walls of the small alcove and crab-walked his way up until he was pressing his back against the ceiling. He would not be able to hold this position for long and willed Victor forward. His legs began to tremble and burn from the exertion. Victor slowly approached the alcove's entry. Arran watched from above as he crouched and peered in from a very low vantage. Sweat gathered and beaded on Arran's nose and he willed it not to drop.

Satisfied the alcove was empty, Victor began slowly continuing down the hall.

Bending his legs ever so slightly, Arran sprang from the alcove and struck Victor in the back with his forearm.

"Bloody damn hells!" Victor yelled and pitched forward to his knees from the force of the blow.

Arran lay beside him, gasping from exertion.

As if she had been following right behind them the entire time, Shia appeared and declared Arran the winner.

"That was quite clever, Arran." Shia turned and looked up and into the alcove. She rested her gaze back to Victor, who was now nursing the blow landed on his back right shoulder.

"Victor, do you know what you missed that allowed Arran to win?"

"No, I checked the alcove, and I was sure no one was behind me. It's like he dropped out of the ceil..." Victor cut off his own sentence. He glanced at the alcove and realized he had been crouching low and only looked forward into the alcove, not up.

"You were hiding up in the alcove?!" Victor gaped at Arran.

Arran raised his eyebrows sheepishly. "It was a calculated risk. I was hoping you did not think to look up. I would not have held out if you took much longer. My legs were screaming." Arran reached down and massaged his thighs to loosen the knots, wincing.

Victor stared at Arran in amazement and admiration. "That was brilliant. Really. It did not even occur to me to look up." The two clasped hands and helped each other to their feet.

Shia passively watched the exchange and began walking off down the hallway. "Come." She stopped when they got back to their entry point. With a wave of her hand, the wall separated, making an opening back into the original basement room where the other two students were talking at the center table.

"Instructor, I think I..."

She waved Arran to silence and replied, "We will talk on the matter later."

After the other two students finished their exercise, Shia had the group sit around the table and go over the tactics: what worked, what did not, and how to improve. Everyone agreed that Arran's tactic, while risky, was the best of the day.

Instructor Shia dismissed the other students, leaving only she and Arran sitting at the basement table.

"So, you manifested a gift today." It was a statement, not a question.

"Yes."

"What were you doing when it happened?"

Arran thought back, trying to remember the exact events leading up to the gift. "I had just moved around a corner after cautiously checking ahead. I was crouched low, focused on stealth, and straining for any additional sound or movement. I took a couple of steps and then it happened."

"I see. Did anything of note happen after?"

"I'm not sure. I was so intent on the exercise. I..."

The loose brick in the floor.

"There was a loose brick in the floor. I barely avoided it."

"Hmm...probably Observance, then. It is a common gift here in the maze. The exercise is set up to put a strain on all your senses."

"You will need to practice this skill. Unlike Stealth, which is a single-trait ability, Observance has many offerings. Detecting the loose stone was a simple version of a trap. You sensed something out of order in the surroundings and found it. Detecting more advanced traps, even disarming them, will eventually manifest. Finding hidden areas is another more advanced capability. Speak with quartermaster Kallion. He will procure you a basic lock picking set. Your new Observance ability will also allow you to pick locks more easily."

Shia pulled a journal out of her pocket and began to write. Without looking up, she continued. "I will add several hours to your weekly schedule in the maze. We will set up small runs with traps, hidden areas, and boxes to unlock so that you can practice. That will be all."

Arran left the basement, leaving the instructor as she continued to write in the journal. Arran stepped out of the building, into the glare of the late morning sun. The bright light stunned him and he had to shield his eyes after spending the better part of half a day in the gloom of the basement. Once he could see clearly, he saw Bran practicing on a dummy and went over to him.

"Hey."

Bran finished with a flurry and turned. "Arran. How was your time in the dungeon?"

Arran relayed his exercise and told him about receiving the gift of Observance.

"That is great! You are well on your way. It is uncommon to receive two gifts in your first term. Most don't get their second gift until much later."

Arran sighed. "I thought it would be a bigger deal, you know? I mean, Shia treated it casually, like ho hum, another gift. Have a nice day."

Bran shrugged his shoulders dismissively. "Meh, don't sweat it. Observance is a good gift, even if it is common. It has a lot of abilities tied to it. Very useful. I'm still uncovering pieces of it."

"Shia said the same. Still, it didn't feel as epic as I thought it would."

Bran chuckled. "Come on, let's get some sparring in before lunch. Want to go to the Goose tonight?"

Arran perked up. "Now, that is the best thing I've heard all day."

Arran and Bran joked about the day as they strode down the dormitory hallway, heading for the Singing Goose. As Arran reached to open the main door, it sprung inwards unexpectedly, causing him to stumble backwards in surprise.

"Arran! I'm so sorry, are you okay?" Elinda rushed forward to grab him as he stumbled.

He smiled up at her. "You almost got me there."

Elinda sighed with relief, taking a step back, looking both of them over. "Where are you two headed out on this fine evening?"

"Just over to the Goose. Would you like to come? It's just me and Bran."

"The 'Goose'?"

They both laughed at the quizzical look on Elinda's face. Arran was the first to recover. "It's kind of become our favorite spot."

Elinda's expression turned from one of question to intrigue. "You don't mind?"

Arran turned to Bran, who simply shrugged his shoulders.

Elinda grinned excitedly. "Okay. Let me go drop my packages off in my room and I will be right back." Elinda rushed off down the dormitory hall enthusiastically.

"Smooth." Bran gave Arran a shoulder bump.

"Stop it. She's just a friend."

"A pretty princess friend."

Arran shook his head, not replying. If he continued to protest, he knew that it would only entice Bran to more mocking.

Elinda returned a few minutes later, and the three headed into town. The two young men walked stolidly, almost stiff compared to Elinda's casual grace.

"So, the Singing Goose. I don't believe I've heard of that inn. Is it close?"

"Not really, but I found it when I first came to the city, and I have yet to find a better cider. I kind of always found myself heading back there, and now it's become a sort of tradition, I guess."

Bran chimed in with his own assessment. "It is a good inn. Good ale, not watered down, good food, and music on the weekends."

Elinda rolled up her sleeves as they walked. "Alright then, color me intrigued."

Arran pushed open the door as they arrived at the inn. It was already starting to get lively, and the group hustled over to the lone remaining booth.

Elinda looked around the common room approvingly. "Very nice. Not too big, not too small, and it might be one of the cleanest inns I've ever seen." She ran a finger along the table in appreciation.

Arran looked around, observing the inn more closely, trying to see it again with new eyes. He bobbed his head approvingly. "Tan and Mira do keep a fine inn." He had chosen well his first day in the city, either by luck or intuition, he wasn't sure.

Arran pointed to the bar. "Tan is the big man behind the counter and Mira, his wife, is probably in the back directing the cooking." Arran waved at the server. "And that's Cindi."

Elinda looked at Arran with admiration. "So you 'do' come here often. You know everyone on a first name basis."

Arran felt his cheeks begin to flush at the compliment. "Often enough. I like it here. It feels like an inn should feel...at least to me."

Bran agreed with a nod. "I've seen my fair share of inns, and this one does indeed have a rightness about it."

Elinda continued looking about the room in silent agreement and admiration.

Cindi strolled up to the table, wiping her hands on her apron. "What can I get you?"

"Hey, Cindi. I think you already know Bran, and this is another friend from school, Elinda."

"Nice to meet you, my lady." She gave Elinda a slight inclination, and Elinda did the same before returning her attention back to Arran. "Your regular, then?"

"Yes, please."

"Ale for me," Bran said.

Cindi looked at Elinda.

"I'll try some of this famous cider I've heard so much about."

Arran's stomach gave a low rumble of protest as he took in the smells emanating from the kitchen. "What does Mira have on the menu tonight?"

"Tonight we have roasted chicken with potatoes and, of course, her beef..."

Arran had his order out before Cindi could finish. "Oh, I'll take the chicken."

Both Bran and Elinda agreed.

"Chicken all around, then."

A short while later, Tan arrived with their drinks, placing them on the table.

"Good to see you again, Arran."

"Thanks, Tan. May I introduce another friend I've managed to drag to the Goose. This is Elinda."

Tan nodded in greeting. "Nice to meet you, Elinda, always glad to entertain a new patron to the Goose."

"And you also, Master Tan. You have a wonderful inn."

It was odd to see such a big man look humble, but Tan managed it as completely genuine. "Thank you. It is nice of you to say."

Arran leaned over the table towards Tan. "Hey, Tan...I've been meaning to ask you something. I've noticed that same man sitting over there in the corner on several occasions. Who is he? He seems so...solemn."

Tan followed his gaze. "Oh, that'd be Anders. He is a quiet old man, been coming here since I was but a lad." Tan put both hands on the table and bent down. "Rumor has it he is one of the non-gifted."

Arran's brows creased in confusion.

"Wouldn't that apply to most everyone?"

Tan thought for a moment, confused, then caught on. He chuckled. "Ha, it would at that. Non-gifted refers to someone that 'has' gifts, but was never 'formally' gifted. Some folk find him a bit weird and off-putting, but he never causes any trouble, and really likes Mira's stew."

"Does anyone ever talk to him?"

"Not usually. I've had some conversations with him over the years. Smart man." Tan waved at a customer who had just sat down at the bar. "Anyway, got to get back to work. Enjoy yourselves and nice to meet you, Elinda."

Arran bit his lip. "Have either of you heard of the non-gifted before?"

"Just rumors. Not something anyone takes seriously." Bran said.

Elinda peered at Anders. "Same here. Never actually met one before."

Arran decided to let the matter drop as neither of his friends seemed to give the non-gifted topic much thought, but Arran found himself casually glancing in Anders' direction. There was something about the man.

Elinda took a drink and her eyes opened wide approvingly. "This cider is really good."

Arran grinned widely. "I know, right?"

Cindi arrived a short while later, delivering their food. The three sat in silence and ate as the evening's music started up.

When Cindi came back to take their now thoroughly empty plates, she asked, "Another round?"

All three nodded in agreement, and as she was about to turn and leave, Arran put his hand on her arm.

"Cindi, I'd like to get Anders' next round, please."

"Old man Anders?" She looked over at the corner table.

Arran nodded

"Sure thing."

"Why did you do that?" Elinda asked.

"Not sure. There's something about him...plus, it's always nice to meet new and interesting people, and the way Tan tells it, he's got interesting written all over him."

Cindi returned a short while later with their drinks and then headed over to Anders' table to deliver the complementary ale from Arran. He watched as she delivered the drink and pointed at their table. Arran raised his mug in acknowledgment, Anders returned the gesture.

The three friends continued into the evening, enjoying each other's company. Chatting about their homes, growing up, and how they ended up at the school as they listened to the music. Bran and Elinda even went out for a dance.

Elinda sat down hard on the bench, her face flush from the dancing. Arran stood. "I'm going to go talk to Anders."

"You think that's wise?" Bran remarked.

"I don't know. Guess we'll find out."

Arran slowly picked his way through the crowd as he approached Anders' table. He was sitting in the partial shadow of the far corner of his booth, one leg stretched out on the bench and looking out amongst the crowd. He warily watched as Arran's intentions became clear.

Arran stopped at the edge of the table. "Good evening."

"Evening."

Arran fidgeted nervously. "May I sit down?"

Anders gestured to the opposite bench with his mug, and Arran slid down onto the bench.

"I'm Arran."

The old man eyed Arran suspiciously before answering. "Anders."

The silence began to stretch out, becoming awkward. Arran fidgeted with his mug and was unsure how to continue. Anders sat impassively, sipping his beer, and continuing his observation of the crowd as if Arran weren't even there.

Arran plunged forward in an attempt to spark some semblance of a conversation. "So, Tan says you have been coming here for a long time. You like the people here?"

Anders turned his head and looked at Arran blankly. His eyes were not cold exactly, they were just...there. An impassive stare. He blinked as he finally broke the silence. "I like Tan, Mira, and Cindi. They are good people, come from good families. The rest are a necessary...coincidence."

Arran shifted uncomfortably on the bench. "So you don't really care for people?"

"Not particularly."

Arran took a sip of his drink, awkwardly trying to figure out how to continue the conversation, and the question he really wanted to ask. The silence dragged on and Arran became increasingly uncomfortable. With a sigh, he was resigned to admit that this was indeed a bad idea and started to shift out from behind the table to leave.

Before he could fully rise, Anders spoke in a hushed tone barely audible above the din. "Ask your question."

Arran stopped. "What?"

"Ask your question, son. It is written all over your face. Ask me about my gifts. It's usually the only reason anyone ever wants to talk to me."

Arran sheepishly sat back down.

Arran paused, stunned at Anders' bluntness. "The way Tan explained it to me, you were never formally gifted by a Patron, but you still manifested gifts?"

"Yes. I have a few. Nothing spectacular, mind you, but I have a few gifts."

Anders turned in his seat, placing both arms on the table, his mug held in both hands. He peered at Arran intently for several long moments. "Talon. I'd guess two, maybe three, gifts have been manifested so far. The common ones I would presume, Stealth, Sight, or maybe Observance?"

Arran was dumbfounded, unable to hide the look of surprise on his face.

"That's...that's right. You can tell all of that just by looking at me?"

"I can tell by your aura." Anders watched as the new term bounced around in the young man's head for the first time. It wasn't an uncommon reaction. Aura reading was an extremely rare gift. Anders sighed heavily. "Everything has an aura. Some are fairly strong, like yours. Others are weak, like most of them." He gestured out across the room.

The hairs on Arran's neck and arms prickled with excitement. "That is amazing! I've never heard of that gift. Does it belong to a certain Patron?"

Anders sat back, his face turning sour. "I would prefer not letting the entire inn overhear our conversation."

Arran's face grew hot, his excitement dimming into shame.

Idiot!

Anders waited, considering whether to answer, then let out a small sigh. "No one knows if it is from a specific Patron. At least as far as anyone can tell me. I'm currently the only one. At least, that is what the scholars at the school told me. An interesting and rare gift, but of little real value. The school asks of my services every once in a while, but it's not something one could make a living off of. A curiosity at best."

Arran exercised more patience and purposefully paused before asking another question. "How long have you had it?"

Anders eyed Arran warily at the conversation extending question. "Ever since I can remember. I think I was born with it, but like any gift, the longer you use it, the more powerful it becomes. Like I said, everything has an aura: humans, animals, even insects, and plants, but those are pretty weak. I have to focus hard to see them, but they are there. Then there is Observance, like yourself, although my skill won't be near as strong as your gifted talent. I can do a bit of healing, but it is also weak. I can mend a scratch or a small bruise, but not much else."

Arran's excitement and eagerness flashed across his face, and Anders eyed him with scorn. Arran relaxed and leaned forward. "That is still amazing, considering you were never formally gifted."

Anders shrugged his shoulders as if it were nothing special. "I'm an anomaly. People tend to leave me alone and that is just fine by me." He leaned back into the corner, stretching his leg back out on the bench.

Sensing that the conversation was over, Arran rose.

"Nice to meet you, Anders. Maybe we shall share another drink sometime?"

"Maybe." Anders ignored him and was already gazing back out into the crowd.

Arran returned to his table and began retelling the conversation to his friends.

"That is pretty incredible," Elinda said. "Gifts, but not gifted."

"Agreed," Bran said. "Even the rumors don't tell of anyone with that many gifts."

The three talked excitedly through the evening, enjoying several more rounds of drink before finally heading back to the school.

Anders, sitting deep in the shadows of his booth, watched them leave.

Year 1303/October/Week 4
Term Break

Arran lie in bed, wide awake despite his intention of allowing himself some extra sleep now that break between terms had begun. His sleep had been restless, the thoughts of the past four months spinning through his head. His time at school had passed so quickly, and fall was beginning to take hold as the end of October neared.

The school's structure and routine, along with his new gifts, had changed him. He was no longer that naïve boy who stepped off the docks almost four months ago. He smiled to himself as he thought of home and how no one would have thought him capable of even half of what he had already learned. Under the tutelage of Bran and Kallion, his proficiency with daggers had increased tremendously. He was even winning a sparring match now and again.

I wonder what Mother and Father would think of that?

He grinned to himself at the thought.

His mind wandered to his parents. He missed them dearly from time to time, but the curriculum had been so intense, these periods of homesickness were fleeting.

I wonder what they are doing right now?

He could picture his father already up and preparing the forge while his mother began her morning kitchen rituals. He smiled at the memories.

His thoughts fell back to school. The camaraderie of his new friends had become...comfortable. He was more confident and sure of himself. All doubt about his decision to come to Meitellen had evaporated.

He rolled over, enjoying the warmth of the bed, his muscles twinging slightly at the effort. The daily physical routines were hard, but they were also beginning to show their effects. While he would never be as strong as Bran or Kallion, he was far sturdier and fit than he had ever been in his life. After four months, he could see and feel the benefits of his labors. The practices were no longer a chore, but a comforting daily ritual. His new life was falling into place and he found that he liked it.

His mind continued to wander aimlessly and inevitably came back to the dungeon. His most recent challenge. As promised, Instructor Shia had set up a weekly schedule for Arran to practice his skills. The dungeon had quickly become one of his favorites. He enjoyed the challenge that each exercise had to offer. The dungeon layouts, traps, and hidden areas were altered every time he entered. He had asked more about how the dungeon worked, but no one could give him a straight answer.

More of the lost magic that had produced it no doubt.

As the term progressed, he could tell that the instructor had been slowly increasing the dungeon's difficulty, but it only strengthened his resolve. His Stealth, Observance, and lock picking skills were all steadily increasing. Only his ability to find secret areas had been lacking by term's end. He could still not find them with any kind of regularity.

"It will come," Shia would say. "The art of Observance takes time to perfect, as it is not just about seeing and memorizing your surroundings. You have to understand what the skill is showing you. Understand the 'why' of what you see or feel."

Arran was not sure he fully understood what the instructor was trying to tell him, but he continued his practice, hoping he would come to understand her meaning.

Arran yawned and sat up on the side of the bed, running his hands across his face as his mind continued to recount all the recent changes to his life. He smiled broadly as he thought of Bran and Elinda. The three had become a tight group whose friendship had grown strong during the term. They would regularly meet for meals in the dining hall, where they talked and joked. Stories of their child-hood, or homeland, were always of great interest, but by far, the best times were had at the Singing Goose. It had become customary to spend at least one night, or sometimes two, of their weekends at the inn. For Arran, it felt like home: cozy, rustic, and warm. Arran had even begun trying the various ales that Bran and Tan would recom-mend. It became sort of a tradition over the weeks that when Tan suggested a new ale, Arran would also buy one for Anders, who was usually always present in his customary booth. A curt nod or shake of his head usually let Arran know what he thought of the new variety. Other than the complimentary round of ale, the group did not try to engage with Anders again. He had made it abundantly clear from Arran's first visit that privacy was his preference.

Arran stood up and headed for the baths. There was only one thing left for him to do, and he had resigned himself that he would complete it over the break. From the moment Bran had told him that he had accidentally engaged with Elinda in a courtship ritual, Arran had been terrified. It had not appeared to have affected their friendship so far, but he needed to clear this from his conscience and have it resolved.

By the Patrons, why were girls so hard?

CHAPTER 5
SECOND TERM
YEAR 1303 / NOVEMBER / WEEK 1

Term Break

The door to the rear gate of the school closed behind Arran with a click as he made his way for the northwest bridge of Meit-ellen. The chill air of fall felt good as he began his morning run. He glanced up at the sky, which was dark and heavy as if heralding an upcoming early snow of the season.

The run was a short one, but served its purpose in warming his muscles for the obstacle course. The course today had been challenging. On more than one occasion, he had almost missed a platform, and the precarious ten feet fall to the ground. The obstacle course, like the dungeon, changed daily. It had been forged by the same forgotten magic that enabled the dungeon and thus prevented anyone from memorizing a routine. He did not mind the difficulty, though. Challenge had become his new friend, and he embraced it.

The break between terms had begun, and he was determined to keep his training moving forward. He would maintain a weekly routine, albeit scaled back. It was called a break for a reason.

Arran stood on the last platform, looking back over the course, breathing heavily.

"That was a good one today," he muttered to himself, wiping the sweat from his face with his sleeve. He descended the stairs and headed back to school at a slow walk, letting himself cool down. By the time he had re-entered through the back gate, he was almost chilled from the bite of the fall air.

After a warm bath and a bit of breakfast, he headed out into the city. His first stop was the Meitellen bank branch. He had only visited the bank once since he arrived, to verify his account and withdraw what had proved to be enough for the entire term. Other than evenings at the Goose, he had no real use for money. The school provided almost everything he needed, but he wanted to find out how much the stipend had accumulated and refill his purse a bit.

He entered the bank and went up to an open teller, asking for a withdrawal. A blue orb appeared above the teller. A soft blue light swept across Arran's upper body, assumingly to identify him, and then disappeared. The teller opened the book in front of him, gave it a quick glance, then addressed him.

"How much would you like to withdraw, Master Arran?"

"Umm...how much is available?"

"Six gold, fifty silver."

Arran's mouth fell open in astonishment.

Six and a half gold!

That was more money than he had ever seen in his entire life. Probably more than Father and Mother had ever saved.

"Sir?" The teller looked at him with a tilt of his head, obviously confused.

Arran quickly regained his composure. "Oh, sorry. I'll take the fifty silver, thank you."

Transaction completed, Arran left the bank with more money in his pocket than he had ever had in his life and headed confidently for Notable Tomes.

Arran entered the bookstore as a light chime sounded near the back of the store. The bookshop owner, Quil, Elinda had told him, came out of the back room and stepped up to the counter.

"Ah, back again. Did you have anything particular in mind this time?"

Arran gave him a look of surprise. "You remember me?"

Quil smiled amiably. There was a twinkle in his eyes behind the scholarly spectacles.

"I remember faces."

Arran almost laughed out loud. "I bet you do! A handy gift in your line of work, I'm sure."

Quil inclined his head. "Indeed."

"As a matter of fact, I do have something in particular. I have read a basic history of Aaeu'din, but it was lacking in details about individuals. Before I came to Meitellen, my sponsor told me I was only the second gifted by Talon in my realm's history. I was hoping to find information on the other, a lady by the name of Sai'el."

Quil thought for a moment before removing his glasses and began absently cleaning them with a cloth. "Sai'el, hmmm. That does sound familiar. Specific historical details on individuals from the Intelligence order are extremely rare. That group leans towards, how shall we say, the more secretive side, but I believe I do have an unofficial tale that makes mention of Sai'el and her team's exploits." He paused for a few seconds. "You must remember, that while there will be sprinkles of fact in the book, the author will have taken certain... liberties, for entertainment value."

Arran thought about that for a moment. "Can I see it?" Which was quickly followed by, "And how much?"

Quil replaced his glasses. "It is an old book, making it somewhat rare, but then again, it is not in high demand. How about we say five silver?"

Arran hesitated, uneasy at the amount.

Quil gave him another warm smile. "It is a fair price, young master. I would like to believe that if I treat you fairly, you will be a repeat customer. Better for business."

Arran returned the smile with a half-hearted one of his own.

Clever.

"Thank you, Master Quil. I am sure it is a fair price. Lady Elinda recommended your store as quite reputable. I will take the book."

Quil raised an eyebrow at the use of his name. "You keep fine company, young master…"

"Arran."

Arran gave a small bow, and Quil responded with a quick and polite tilt of his chin.

Quil disappeared into the back room and returned a short while later with the book 'Tales of Intelligence'.

"Good day, Arran. Come back soon and please give Lady Elinda my good tidings and appreciation for her recommendation."

"I will. Good day, Master Quil."

Arran left the shop feeling pretty good about the day so far. He was rich, even if only by his own meager measure, and he had found a good book.

Not a bad day at all.

Arran forced himself to spread out the reading of the book despite wanting to finish it in one sitting. He managed three evenings. The book centered its focus on Sai'el, and while it did not focus much attention on her time at the school, it did note the time of her entry. Her final graduation to full commissions did not coincide with a full four years of terms. Arran wondered if this part was true or one of the author's liberties, as Quil had mentioned. The book painted her as a prodigy, the likes that had never been seen by the Intelligence order.

The remainder of the book went from one daring adventure to the next. Each adventure becoming more dangerous and heroic, with Sai'el and her companions succeeding in any commission they accepted. The book concluded with the team engaging a particularly dangerous foe. Only Sai'el survived. She was never seen or heard from again.

Arran put the book down on his chest. Fictional or not, that was a grand book. It was a good change of pace from the historical and instructional books that had been occupying most of his time. He set the book on his nightstand and blew out the candle.

It was the second week of break and dusk was hanging languidly across the rooftops of the city as Arran was returning from the Singing Goose. As he entered the plaza to the school, he noticed Elinda with another girl. They were just approaching the wide steps to the main door.

Arran quickened his pace and called out. "Elinda!"

Elinda halted and turned, recognition spreading across her face. "Arran! How goes break?"

"All good. Keeping up with the training and studying." Arran gave her a wry grin. "I seem to remember learning that from someone..." He rubbed his chin questioningly.

Elinda laughed. "At least you learned something!"

Arran's gaze fell to the other girl.

Elinda gestured apologetically. "Sorry. May I introduce Mare. She is of the order of Kemore and studying for priestesshood."

Arran nodded his head in greeting. "Nice to meet you, Mare."

Mare's eyes twinkled. "Well, aren't you just a fine specimen?" She reached out and gave Arran's arm a squeeze and purred. "Oooh."

Arran was momentarily taken aback, a look of utter confusion spreading across his face. Recovering, he was finally able to muster a faint, "Uh, thank you?"

Elinda tried hiding the grin spreading across her face with her hand. "Don't mind her. She's a bit unconventional, but harmless...for the most part." Elinda gave Mare a quick kick at the ankles.

"You flatter me, Elinda. Unconventional?" Mare sniffed and took in the confused looked on Arran's face. "I love my gifts and I am right good." She paused as a frown began to form. "But the whole religious and piety aspect of the order...Bah! 'Do not behave like that', 'Do not drink this'. Makes me want to scream in frustration."

Elinda laughed, watching Arran try to process and reconcile Mare's comments.

Mare's demeanor quickly turned back to mischievous as she

continued. "You and I should go get a drink sometime, handsome. The things I could..."

"Mare!" Elinda tried to speak sternly but was having trouble through a fit of giggles. "You have made your point."

Mare huffed, feigning resentment, never losing the twinkle in her eye as she gave Arran another sultry look.

The three entered the school, bade farewell, and Arran walked as briskly as he could, a pace just short of a run for his dormitory.

What in Talon's name just happened?

The next day at lunch, after a strenuous morning of training and a few hours of studying in the library, Elinda arrived and sat down across from him. She anxiously looked around at the mostly empty dining hall, before turning back to Arran. A sheepish, nervous expression on her face.

"I think I should probably explain our little meeting yesterday."

Arran pushed his plate to the side, but did not reply, and if he were honest, he wasn't sure if he could come up with anything on the topic.

Elinda fidgeted in her seat, as if unsure how to start. "Mare is a bit...eccentric, but is also extremely talented." She finished hurriedly and then paused, her expression turning serious. "Really talented. That talent alone was enough for her to pass her first-year evaluations." She paused again, obviously struggling with her explanation. Arran could see her hands wringing nervously in her lap. Looking around the dining hall again, she placed her clasped hands on the table. "Mare is struggling in second year. Not from talent, but from sheer stubbornness and attitude. She is smart enough to know she is brusque and that her personal interests lie, shall we say, outside the normal trainings of Kemore." Elinda's gaze intensified. Sympathy, mixed with concern, clearly etched across her face. "I am afraid for her. If she hopes to pass year two evaluations, she needs to find some sort of compromise with her instructors."

Elinda's eyes dropped to her hands and shifted uneasily before continuing eagerly.

"She is a good friend, and I have been trying to help. When you get to know her, you will find that she is not just talented, but insightful and keen. She has been a great help to me on numerous occasions." Elinda drew in a large breath as she finished, looking up hopefully for a response from Arran.

"I do not know what to say, Elinda. I admit I was...surprised by the encounter, but I hold no ill will."

Elinda's shoulders eased visibly, and she gave a sigh of relief. "Good. She needs more friends here at school, and it is my hope that maybe you can be added to that list. I think you would be good for her."

Arran eyebrows rose.

"Um...I don't think...that is to say..."

Elinda was momentarily confused, then realization dawned on her. "Oh no! Not that way! As a friend."

Arran visibly relaxed.

The two sat in silence for a while, and then it was Arran who began to shuffle uneasily on the bench.

Elinda sensed his uneasiness. "What's wrong?"

"It's...delicate...embarrassing."

Elinda smiled. "Well, take a note from Mare and just ask."

Arran continued to fidget, staring at his hands. He coughed lightly as if to clear his throat. "That day in the garden, when we were reading together and then went for a walk to, you know, just to stretch our legs a bit..."

Elinda listened as Arran struggled with the words, and then quickly interrupted.

"You want to know if I took that as a sign of courtship?"

"Yes!" The relief and exultation came out much louder than he intended and the handful of students in the hall looked over in their direction.

Arran held up his hand in apology. "Sorry."

Elinda could not help but laugh at the situation. She remembered the moment and after a full term of their friendship, without any mention, she had figured it forgotten. She leaned over to speak more privately. "Asking a young lady out for a walk, especially in the gardens, is a classic courtship ritual, but no, Arran. I took it for what it was, two friends having a pleasant stroll." She leaned back and looked off thoughtfully before returning her attention to Arran. "I have been courted, much to my dismay I might add, by several young men, but I am not interested at the moment. Oh, I am sure Mother and Father will want me to take on that responsibility in earnest once I graduate, but until then, I am fine to let it be. Besides, I value our friendship here at school too much to clutter it with all that courtship nonsense."

Arran let out another long, relieved sigh. "Oh, thank the Patrons."

Elinda huffed dramatically. "Well, you don't have to act like it was that much of a burden!"

"No! That's not what I..."

She laughed with a twinkle in her eye. "I'm just kidding. I guess a little bit of Mare has rubbed off on me. Seriously, though, you have been worrying about that all this time?"

"You have no idea."

Year 1303/December/Week 1
Week 1 of Second Term

Arran spent the remainder of the break with his regimen of training contrasted with lazy hours with Elinda and Mare. They talked and laughed about all manner of topics, usually at the Singing Goose. Elinda had been right about Mare. She was exceptionally smart with an extremely sharp wit. Once Arran was able to get through her unorthodox, gruff exterior, he found that Mare was a genuinely fascinating and engaging person.

As the break came to an end, Arran found himself tidying up his gear when the door to the dorm room opened. He turned excitedly.

"Bran! Welcome back! I was beginning to think you weren't going to make it back in time for start of term."

"My trip back got stymied with bad weather and we had to take to port for a few days until the storm blew over. I suspect we will see some of that snow soon." Bran flung his bag down and sat down heavily on his bed.

"How was the trip home? I bet everyone was excited to see you."

"Oh yeah, they ooh'ed and ahh'ed at me like I was some prize cow, but once the initial excitement wore off, it wasn't too bad. Father had me accompany him on some matters of house business and I got to go on a few hunts. Mostly, it was just nice for a change of scenery. The school can get a bit dreary. How about you? How did you manage to fill your time during break?"

"You know, maintain my training routine, read a book, actually I read it three times, and I spent some time with Elinda and..." Arran paused just slightly before quickly changing topics. "Pretty boring compared to grand meetings and hunting trips."

"Wait, you spent time with Elinda and..." Bran eyed him suspiciously as Arran turned away to busy himself aimlessly with the items on his bed.

Bran gave him a sideways glance, eyes narrowing. "Let me guess, you met another girl."

Arran did not look up. "Yes, and no. Yes, Elinda introduced me to her friend, Mare, and the three of us spent a lot of time visiting over break. And no-" Arran held up his hand emphatically. "-it is not what you are thinking. She's nice...okay, maybe nice isn't exactly accurate, but yeah, she is once you get to know her, and..." He trailed off, visibly flustered.

Bran laughed and shook his head. "For a small town bloke you do seem to attract the ladies."

"You'll see. I'll introduce you first chance we get."

"Wouldn't miss it for the world." He got up and punched Arran sharply in the shoulder.

"Ow!"

Bran grinned mischievously. "Good to see you again, brother."

———

Second term for Arran, and third for Bran and Elinda, began the next morning. He and Bran made their way to the training grounds to meet Instructor Shia. The previous term of seven students was now down to six. Shia informed them that third-year student Keon was on leave for his first commissions. This left Arran, Bran, and Stepf as the only first year's with Senshi, Styra, and Victor all in their second year.

For the most part, the routines of the first term were repeated, but the intensity and difficulty began to ramp up much more quickly as each week passed. Arran's talent with the blade was leading the way as his confidence and familiarity with the weapon grew. His studies in geography, history, and math were near the top of the class as well. Botany and alchemy were still a bit of a struggle, but thankfully, Elinda and Mare were helpful on these topics when he found himself struggling.

"Good spar," Bran said breathlessly as the two lowered their daggers. "You continue to amaze me, my friend. You have picked up in four months what took me years to accomplish. Your moves are more fluid and your reaction to my counters is lightning fast. I'm impressed."

"Thanks. I continued training over break." Arran took a moment, hands on knees as he caught his breath. "I think it helped my confidence."

Bran laughed. "It's much more than confidence. You have skill. I think it has become clear that it only needed to be honed. One more bout before lunch?"

"Sure, let's go."

The final match was a long one, each combatant attacking, feigning, and searching for the right opening. Arran was getting tired and Bran's strikes were hitting more frequently now. Arran grunted from a sharp jab to his thigh and stepped back, frustrated. His anger flared as he grimaced at the now complaining leg.

He charged.

Arran's daggers were a blur of motion. The flurry of strikes startled Bran as he struggled to defend against the sudden ferociousness of the attack, giving up ground until he was forced to the edge of the practice ring.

Bran stepped out of the circle, holding up his hands in surrender, panting heavily. He looked at Arran, who was seething with anger, and for the briefest of moments, was unsure if Arran was going to stop. Arran stepped back. His breaths were ragged, and there was a wildness still lingering in his eyes. Suddenly, he fell to his knees, completely exhausted.

Bran walked over to his friend and placed a hand on his shoulder. Arran looked up, and to his surprise, Bran began to laugh. No, not just laughed, he bellowed. Bran helped Arran up to his feet and wrapped him in a big brotherly hug, fists pounding him on the back.

"Well done, my friend! Well done!" Bran released the embrace and took a step back. "Kallion and I thought we'd never be able to get you angry enough!"

"Enough for what?" Arran said, still breathing heavily, his anger slowly ebbing.

"It is called 'The Warrior'. It's a term we use for when you anger someone to the point they fight with an unleashed rage. Kallion and I were beginning to wonder if it was possible to get it out of you. It can be a gift for some fighter classes, but anyone can achieve it, albeit for shorter durations than one who is gifted."

Arran didn't reply. He turned and went to the water barrel for a drink. Bran joined him, but did not say anything, wanting to let Arran process the flood of emotion, and let him calm down.

"Why is it so important?" Arran finally asked. "It felt undisciplined, angry, like I was just lashing out without thought."

"Exactly! You fought without thinking."

Arran looked at him, confused, sweat still dripping down his brow.

"Listen. When you are done here, at school..." Bran tilted his head out towards the training yard. "...your discipline with those daggers is going to get you through just about anything anyone can throw at you. There will be very few who can stand up to you toe to toe, but when the situation really gets tough...you need to know how to use that fury. How to trust in it and control it. Unfortunately, it is not just something you can turn off and on, like one who is gifted. For us, it has to happen naturally. But once you recognize it…you can use it. Controlling the Warrior in you can be a turning point in a fight. I have only truly been that angry a handful of times, but recognizing it and understanding what is happening will be invaluable to you."

Arran drank his water, continuing to calm down, and thought on what Bran had just told him. Anger, real anger, was foreign to him. He had never experienced anything like it. He wasn't sure he liked it and despite what Bran had said; he hoped he never felt that in himself again.

They finished the day with an obstacle course run, then went to get cleaned up for dinner. As usual, Elinda and Mare were already there, saving a spot for the two of them.

"There are my two strapping young warriors." Mare purred as she spoke.

Bran gave a quick flourish of a bow to Elinda. "My lady." Then he began to sit and said flatly, "Mare."

Mare did not take the bait, and the two grinned at one another. Bran and Mare had become quite accustomed to one another, and their brazen verbal banters were often the highlight of their times together. Arran and Elinda would simply sit back and enjoy the show, often times grading the two on their quips.

Mare held up her napkin and dabbed the corner of her mouth with mock delicateness. "You two are a bit later than usual this evening. Tough day?"

Bran smiled broadly and nudged Arran with his shoulder. "You could say that. Arran actually lost his temper today in a sparring match. It was a sight to behold."

Arran glared at Bran, not wanting to bring up the topic with the two women.

"It was nothing," Arran said.

The other three all looked at one another as Elinda gave her own mouth a delicate dab, trying to hide the smile on her face. "So Bran, who won the bet? I forget who had which term."

Bran looked at his plate of food sheepishly. "Kallion. He had second term."

"What?" Arran came halfway up out of his seat, aghast. "You bet on me?! On when I would…" He finished standing up, not sure if he was angry or just embarrassed.

Mare shushed him and waved her hands for him to sit. "Sit down! You're making a spectacle of yourself."

Arran slowly sat back down, and Mare put a gentle hand on his arm. "As you said, it was nothing."

Arran looked up at his friends. Each of them was looking back at him with…smiles? No, they were smirking at him, hardly able to hold their laughter. He felt his anger begin to flare once again, took another look at his friends, and then it quickly flipped off, like blowing out a candle.

He didn't like being the butt of a joke, but he had to admit it was kind of funny. Shrugging his shoulders, he accepted their mirth as they all had a good laugh at his expense.

The following week, Arran headed to the training grounds alone. Bran and Stepf were off to one of the satellite sites for four weeks of camping and training. Arran started the day with a slow routine of forms to warm up, and was just beginning to break into a sweat when Kallion strode up.

"Arran."

Arran finished his last flurry and turned to the quartermaster. "Yes, sir?"

"It is time for you to expand your weapon skills. You have progressed well with the daggers, but you will need to learn diversity."

"Diversity?"

Kallion drifted off in thought, eying Arran up and down, as if he were having an internal conversation, and then began to mutter to himself. "Of decent height, nimble and quick. Hmmm... The staff and sword, I think..."

Arran waited patiently while Kallion muttered to himself until finally he brought his attention back to him. "In order to defend against other weapons, you would do well to learn how to use them. Your daggers will always be your primary, but you need to at least know the basics of others. In this way, you will become familiar with their strength weaknesses. I want you to take the time you spend training weekly with daggers, and cut it in half. Use the remaining time on both the sword and the staff."

Arran nodded to the quartermaster, beginning to understand the logic in his request.

"Any questions?"

"No, sir."

"Good. Come see me after the morning sessions and I'll set you up."

"Yes, sir."

As Kallion turned to leave, Arran asked, "So, what did you win?"

"Win?"

"Your bet with Bran." Arran tried his best to look angry and hurt.

Kallion was a little taken aback. He hesitated a moment and then muttered, "First round is on Bran at our next trip into town."

Arran's fake glare began to falter until he could hold it no longer. He laughed. "You should have bet him two."

Kallion's expression eased as he smiled. "I should have at that." With a soft chuckle, he strolled off to attend to the other students on the training grounds.

***

Arran stumbled and grunted in frustration as his strike on the training dummy awkwardly fell across its shoulder. He had been splitting his weapon training time for a week now with the new weapons, and he ached all over. The sword was heavy, and he could not practice very long before tiring, but he felt that he was at least making decent progress. The staff, on the other hand, was a mystery. He could not understand why anyone would want to fight with a staff. It felt awkward and useless. You could at least slice and thrust with the sword.

Kallion observed from a distance, noticing Arran's frustration. He walked over. "How is the new weapon training going?"

Arran grimaced. "Not well."

"Hmm..." Kallion murmured, reaching out and taking the staff from Arran.

"The staff is a tricky one." Kallion took a step back and began twirling the staff in slow, deliberate arcs. As he continued, the movement became faster and faster until he was moving around as if in a choreographed dance. Kallion twirled the weapon in alternating high and low arcs, his feet always in motion beneath him. He was moving with a grace that Arran had never seen before. He hopped and moved, always the staff in motion, alternating between what looked like parrying moves and then attacks; his hands effortlessly changing grips as he executed the moves. With one final flourish, he made a powerful horizontal strike and the training dummy's head exploded! The shattered remains went flying through the air, strewn across the yard like kindling.

Arran stared in wonder at the display.

"Tricky...but useful." Kallion handed the staff back to Arran with a smile.

Kallion stayed on for a while longer, showing Arran four basic techniques for his practice.

"Remember, with a staff you want to avoid blocking the weapon directly; block the body part that is holding the weapon. Once you believe you have these basics to your satisfaction, come to me, and I will show you more."

Arran took the staff and nodded.

Ok, so maybe not as useless as I thought.

Later that evening, while lying in bed, Arran thought about Kallion's lessons. He began to see the usefulness and power that a staff could bring to a fight. The reach of the staff in a multi-person duel would be far more effective than his daggers, or even a sword. Plus, he loved the elegance of the staff and the precise skill that Kallion had displayed. He had looked so graceful in his demonstration. Arran decided then and there that he would strive to master the staff. He grabbed his latest book recommendation from Benni and read until he fell asleep.

It was a few days later, while Arran was taking a break from his staff training, that he spotted Mare walking towards the gardens. She looked upset, like she had been crying. Arran immediately got up to follow, then stopped.

Maybe she wants to be alone?

He watched her enter the gardens and disappear around the first corner. He sighed, cursing under his breath, and headed in after her.

Ironically, he found her sitting on the same bench that he and Elinda had shared all those months before. Her gaze was downcast and lost in thought, and she didn't even notice him until he made a polite cough.

"Ahem."

She sat up abruptly, obviously startled. "Oh!" She began wiping her cheeks with the sleeves of her robe.

"Hey." Arran gave her a moment, allowing her to collect herself. "Mind if I sit?"

Mare hesitated a moment then gestured to the bench and Arran sat down.

Arran let the silence lengthen, unsure of what to say or even how to start, but he let the time pass, giving Mare all the time she needed. Finally, he decided the best tact was to be straightforward. As Mare would have been.

"So...um...what's going on?" His voice cracking a bit as he awkwardly asked the question.

Smooth. Idiot!

Mare shrugged her shoulders. "Oh, just another spat with my

instructors." Her demeanor began to change as her voice trembled with anger. "They are so...conservative in their teachings. So obstinate. Why can't they see? Why can't...Ahh!" She spat the last words vehemently, slamming her fists on her legs.

More silence. Mare was breathing hard from the outburst. Arran waited for a few moments before continuing.

"Can I ask you a question?"

She looked at him with a sideways glance before giving a slight nod.

"Why do you argue with the instructors so much?"

"Because they are tedious and old and controlling and..." She stood up and threw her hands in the air, angrily pacing back and forth.

Arran watched as the pacing subsided and she began to regain some composure. She sat down with an audible thump on the bench. Arran gave her a few more moments until he could see her breathing calm.

"So your fight isn't against the doctrine, only their methods?"

She thought on this for a moment. "Partly...I guess. I do believe in the underlying doctrine, obviously, otherwise I would not be as gifted from Kemore as I am. I...I..." She trailed off, unable to finish the thought.

Arran thought for a second, remembering a familiar lesson from his mother. "Okay, let me put it this way. Take a step back and look at yourself through their eyes. You rebel against them and what do they see? What do they think of your belief in the doctrine? You can quote it to them forwards and backwards, but what do you think they see?"

Mare was frustrated, her anxiety clearly showing. "I don't know!"

Arran's reply was patient and calm, just like his mother. "Think."

She didn't answer.

"I think..." Arran kept his tone calm and deliberate. "...they see a student who knows the doctrine and is obviously gifted and intelligent...but at the same time, they see a student who doesn't truly believe." Arran paused. Not sure if he should continue. It was a harsh accusation, but Mare was his friend and she deserved no less. "I think they see your rebellion as not just against them, but against Kemore."

Mare turned abruptly to face him, angry conviction in her eyes. "But that is wrong! I do believe! I feel the power in the gifts Kemore has granted me. I know it!" Her shoulders sagged as she finished.

"I believe you. I really do, but I also know you." He turned, looking sharply at her. "I 'know' you." He pointed directly at Mare's chest for emphasis. "I know who you really are and can see past the rebellious nature to the person beneath. Can you say the same for your instructors? If I were them, how could I see your rebellion as anything other than a failing in your belief? In the end...how are they to 'believe' in your belief?"

They sat in silence for several long minutes. Mare's face contorted in confusion as she wrestled with Arran's statement. "So, I need to find a way to let them know that I not only know the doctrine, but how much I believe in it?"

Arran tilted his questioningly. "I don't know. Maybe? Right now, neither side has common ground. Give them one to stand on. Then go from there."

"Hmmpphh."

Mare looked at Arran out of the corner of her eye and then nudged him with her shoulder.

"That is pretty good for a country boy."

Arran laughed. "Well, thank my mother. She always taught me to try and see through another person's eyes. How do they perceive my actions? Believe me, I wasn't always the best student." Arran smiled as he thought back on all his town pranks. "But I do believe it helps me to be more open to other people."

"Smart lady."

They sat in each other's silence for a while longer before Mare got up and declared it was time to eat.

"All this serious talk has made me hungry. Shall we?" She held out her arm.

Arran stood up with a mock bow. "I think we shall, my lady."

Arran rose and took her arm.

"Ugh!" she exclaimed, pushing away from his arm. "You are all sweaty. How about you walk over there and then take a bath before we eat?"

Arran laughed. "Yeah, you're probably right."

Town of Freeholt/Realm of Valoor
Year 1304/January/Week 2

The rain had been a constant and unrelenting companion for the entire journey. By the time he reached the outskirts of town, not a single stitch was left untouched by the cold, stinging downpours, despite his gear's enchantments.

Klintoc reigned in as he crested a hill and the town of Freeholt spread out before him. Razer willingly complied with a soft whinny and a shake of her head.

Freeholt was a pleasant enough place. He had stayed here a few times in his travels through northeast Valoor. It was everything most men coveted: pleasant, peaceful, and most of all, safe. Klintoc grimaced at the lie, the illusion he knew to be false. A trick of the mind that men tell themselves so they could sleep fit at night...or at least they used to.

The people of Freeholt now understood the delicate balance between the lie and the truth. He knew the truth would not last. They would grieve, even be frightened for a while, but in the end, the lie would begin to creep back in and slowly become believable again, but that would take a while. Until then, they understood. In one evening of terror, their illusion shattered. The calm now a vacant memory and they called out...and it was he they called. So, he was sent.

"Easy, girl. Almost there." Klintoc spoke softly and patted the great mare as he spoke. He had ridden her fast and hard these past few days, harder than he probably should have, but they had arrived. Razer whinnied again at the attention, front hooves stamping out wet thuds in the rain-soaked earth. He lightly pressed his heels, and she slowly began the final stretch into town.

Klintoc entered the inn and was shocked at what he saw. The inn was completely empty save for three men at the bar. This used to be a bustling place. The handful of men all turned in unison at the entry of the newcomer.

Illusions shattered, indeed.

Klintoc shrugged out of his cloak, walked over to the fireplace, and hung it on one of the mantel pegs. As he took a seat at the bar, a mug of ale was in front of him before he fully turned around. He downed it and raised for another.

The innkeeper waved him to be patient. "Y'er supposed to drink it, savor it. Not pour it straight down ye open gul'let." He placed a fresh mug on the bar in front of Klintoc, but did not slide it over. "What word do you bring? You scholarly types fig'er out the monstrosity that killed ol' man Nielson and his boy?" Klintoc watched the other men at the bar. They grumbled and swore in agreement, not even trying to hide their dissatisfaction. They probably didn't even know what they were angry about, but he was here, he was available. They were angry, scared, and outraged. All normal emotions, but Klintoc knew he could not let this get out of control. Anger and fright, if let run to the irrational, became dangerous.

Klintoc shook his head slowly. "We do not. It is why I was sent." He kept his voice flat and even, not rising to the innkeeper's heated words. "We need more information. Has there been any more news? Any more sightings?" Klintoc was not hopeful, but he had to ask. The villagers had eventually been able to kill the beast, but not before it had killed two of their own and injured several others. They had burned the beast before its body had turned cold. It had not been a good decision...such were the choices spurned by anger and fear. Now, all they had were eyewitness accounts, and while they were consistent, they didn't make sense. The beast they described...well, it didn't exist. It was something a child would describe to his mother after having a nightmare. Klintoc needed more information, a hint of any kind, so he could act, do something, anything.

The innkeeper shook his head. "No one has gone far from the city proper. Too afraid. You here to fix that?" The innkeeper's tone had begun soft, almost frightened, but by the time he finished there was anger in his words once again. That is how quickly it can all turn.

Klintoc maintained his gaze firmly on the innkeeper, his demeanor calm. He did not waver under the big innkeeper's focused, angry eyes. The man was a boiling teapot, ready to burst. Klintoc observed the man's arm begin to tremble, his grasp on the mug of ale a vice.

Klintoc reached out and placed both hands flat on the bar and spoke softly and deliberately. "If I can, I will, but I need information, details of the attack. Which direction did the beast come from? How big was it? Anything you can remember could be helpful."

The innkeeper sighed and finally pushed the mug of ale forward.

He did not get any new or useful information, but he was not expecting any. The men needed to talk. The more they spoke, the more hopeful they became, the more useful they felt. It removed the likelihood of him having to deal with irrational stupidity.

Not generally caring what others thought of him, Klintoc knew these things mattered when he was on an official commission. In this case, he was representing the School of Doctrine, which brought... rules. So, he would put on his 'calm and play nice' with the locals. He didn't mind, not really. He put up a hard front, but a person, even a few persons like now, was usually fine and pleasant enough company. People, on the other hand...

The hard rain had relinquished overnight, and by the time he left the inn to begin scouting, it had diminished to a drizzle. After scouting in a few widening circles around the town and finding nothing, he took a break, settling down by a fallen tree, half in, half out of a small stream. The sun was finally managing to beat back some of the morning's damp fog and he relished its warmth.

Klintoc sat thoughtfully, chewing slowly on some dried beef, and letting his eyes wander around the surrounding area.

Where did you come from, my little deformed bastard? And where did your buddy go? West, I think. Or maybe north from there? Plenty of forest and hills...

Klintoc rose and began re-tightening the straps on Razer's saddles. "What do you think?" Razer raised her head and sniffed the air. He rubbed her muzzle and looked northwest.

"Going to be cold, girl."

They rode the rest of the day, moving steadily west from Freeholt towards Lake Bravin. It was a fairly isolated and unremarkable lake, as lakes went, but it was still a major water and food source for the region. He had had several fishing trips to this lake in the past. The trout and bass were fantastic. He made a note to come back when time permitted, then frowned at the empty promise. If his intuition was correct...something was about to break, something that would probably preclude any downtime in the near future.

Klintoc made camp on the northeast bank of the lake as the evening's dusk gave way to night. A small fire was meekly providing just enough warmth to stave off the chill, no more.

He sat and pondered his next move as the moon slowly rose above the trees, casting its soft glow on the still lake.

Northeast, I think. Up the river.

There were two rivers that fed Lake Bravin. One coming in from the northwest and another from the northeast. He would scout up the northeast river first.

What was its name?

He could not remember. "Shit," he muttered.

The northeast side kept him closer to Freeholt, and if the accounts of a second beast, or whatever it was, were true, maybe it didn't roam too far or cross the river.

The small fire slowly died to embers as he rolled up for the night.

They rode a few miles upriver before Klintoc found a nice patch of grass amongst the trees.

"You stay here, girl."

He removed the saddle and bags and placed them on a fallen log nearby.

"You enjoy the rest." He stroked the horse in thought for a few minutes before heading off to continue following the river on foot.

Klintoc moved silently through the forest. His Stealth skill was probably as high as anyone in all the realms, maybe even surpassing Shia in her prime.

The day was cloudless, but still had the bite of cold from the previous night as he moved from shadow to shadow. He had crossed several trails so far, but nothing out of the ordinary. Stopping, he took a drink from his flask, emptying it. He continued on through the trees, slowly making his way back towards the river to check for any other trails there, and refill his waterskin.

He noticed several of the trails he had found in the woods did indeed empty out to the water's edge. Kneeling down behind a lee of a boulder where the water was clearer from the rushing river, he filled his waterskin.

There was a soft snort and grunt from behind him, followed by movement. He froze. His body going tense and alert.

The edge of the forest was only about twenty paces behind him, but he could hear an animal rustling, rutting around in the foliage. He gently set the waterskin at his feet and with the slow practiced move of an assassin, he slid his left hand across his body and to the dagger on his right hip; out of view of whatever was behind him. He drew it out and held it firmly in front of him.

The rustling had stopped. The gurgle of the river was the only sound. Several long moments passed before he slowly began to turn his head, shifting his weight for the proper angle.

As his peripheral vision scanned across the shoreline and into the trees, something, standing just inside the treeline, came into view. He stopped his movement. It was still partially hidden in the dense under foliage, but it was there. It was sniffing the air, its great snout raised high. Tusks at least six inches long protruding from both jaws.

Klintoc calmly turned his head a few fractions of an inch further until he was able to see the beast clearly out of the side of his cowl. It had the look of a wild boar, but bigger, much bigger. Its front shoulders probably coming to Klintoc's waist or possibly even his chest. It did not have the fur or hide of any animal he had ever seen. Coarse, thick bristles covered the beast, some three or four inches long in places.

Even taking all of this into account, he noticed two distinguishing features that made this...thing even more unnatural. Starting as small protuberances on its skull, then running back along its spine, were what looked like boney spikes. They crested in the middle of its back, six inches tall.

The beast grunted and lowered its head.

Klintoc did not move as he took in the second most disturbing feature of the beast. Its eyes. They were a bright yellow and solid, no pupil, and they were now solely fixed on him. They were a malevolent yellow, chaotic and wild, and they glowed as if lit from behind.

Then chaos.

The beast simultaneously roared and launched itself out of the underbrush towards Klintoc.

Damn! That thing is fast.

He was on his feet in an instant, bracing himself, and throwing his cloak aside.

The beast was coming in low, surely in a move to skewer him with its tusks. At the last moment, he pivoted, and jumped into a flying sideways cartwheel, narrowly avoiding the strike as the tusks flew by his swinging legs.

The beast crashed into the river, howling in frustration. It turned and began sloshing through the water back to shore.

Now on firmer ground, Klintoc drew his second dagger, crouched, and readied himself for the upcoming attack. This time, the beast did not have the advantage of building up any speed, and he easily danced to the side of its clumsy attack, slashing at the beast from shoulder to flank. He pivoted to face the beast and observe his handiwork. He was not pleased. The thick bristles had protected it from the slice of the blade. Only the sharp tip of the blade had made any damage. His only reward was a long thin cut down the side of the beast. Its dark blood trickled slowly, as irrelevant as a bad paper cut.

Klintoc cursed in annoyance.

Well, shit!

The beast had scrambled to a stop and turned. Head flailing back and forth, thick gobs of spittle flying. It came again.

This time Klintoc rolled back and to the side at an angle from the attack, landing on the balls of his feet. He was instantly up and running directly towards the beast as it was struggling to bring its massive bulk to a stop and turn. Klintoc drove both daggers straight in, foregoing any slicing motion. He caught the beast as it was turning and was rewarded with two solid strikes, one into its right shoulder and the other sliding halfway up to the hilt in its neck. The beast jerked and bucked at the wound.

As Klintoc tried to disengage for a retreat, the violent thrashing of the beast's head hit his retreating left arm. The tusk piercing through his gauntlet, finding flesh. He screamed in agony as his hand reflexively loosened, his dagger falling to the ground. He grunted in pain as he quickly backed away, blood dripping down his forearm and off his fingers.

The two bloodied combatants halted, each breathing heavily. The beast stumbled as it tried to right itself, the front leg now almost rendered useless. It grunted in agony.

Klintoc stared at the wound he had inflicted on the beast's neck. Blood so dark as to almost be black, gushed from the wound. He looked at his remaining dagger. The same black, oily substance that was the beast's blood covered it.

What the...?

He flicked his blade to rid it of the substance before it could slime the hilt. As he did, he was quickly brought back into the moment as the beast raised its head to roar again, only now all it could manage was a muffled gurgle of black, frothy blood.

Hobbled and bleeding profusely from the neck wound, Klintoc knew it was done. He watched as the beast tried to manage another charge, falling forward from the injured leg. It tried to rise, only managing to thrash about and hasten its blood loss for the effort. The great beast finally lay on its side and went still, its side heaving up and down from the exertion. Gradually, the breathing began to slow and Klintoc watched as the rise and fall of breath dissipated.

Klintoc stared at the monstrous beast, still unable to process what lay before him.

He retrieved his cloak and the small medical kit. He would eventually need stitches, but that could wait until later. He needed to get Razer and the rest of his supplies. He would take as many samples as he could back to the school for analysis. Then...he chuckled at the irony. He would burn the remainder of the beast just as the villagers of Freeholt had done.

School of Doctrine/Meitellen
Year 1304/January/Week 3
Week 7 of Second Term

The days and weeks settled into a habitual routine as the days grew colder. Arran pushed himself with his staff and sword training, mainly in the confines of the training hall due to the weather. Kallion had begun slowly introducing him to more and more advanced techniques, and while he was not going to be an expert anytime soon, he was at least making progress.

Additionally, Instructor Shia continued to increase the difficulty of his dungeon runs. All of his skills were making noticeable advancements, save one. His lack of progress in finding hidden areas was becoming increasingly frustrating. It was sorely lagging behind.

Arran was settling into another reading of the tales of Sai'el when the door opened and Bran entered, looking haggard. Dark circles plainly evident beneath his eyes. He dropped his bag and fell onto his bed with a long sigh and a loud thump.

Arran sat up. "That tough, eh?"

"You have no idea."

Silence hung in the air, and Bran could feel Arran still looking at him.

Without looking up to meet Arran's gaze, "I cannot tell you anything. We were told not to speak of the training, especially to the earlier term students."

"I figured as much. I wasn't going to ask."

After a while, Bran got up to bathe, then returned and quickly fell asleep. Arran looked at his friend and became lost in his thoughts of what the training would be like when it was his turn.

With Bran back, the following weeks fell back into their normal routine of training, and Arran was happy to finally have someone to spar against with his staff. Bran was, of course, more skilled, but the gap was not great. Arran had learned from Kallion quickly and was able to hold his own almost from the beginning of their sparring practices.

It was the end of the week, with Bran and Elinda's first-year evaluations set to begin the following week. The group had decided to go out together and have dinner and drinks at the Singing Goose. They met outside the front entrance to the school, joking with each other as they made their way to the inn. Everyone was glad to have a nice distraction before their evaluations.

"What can I get ya?" Cindi asked.

Elinda smiled up at the friendly server. "Hey Cindi. Cider for myself."

Arran pointed to Mare, who ordered an ale, as did Bran.

"Does Tan have any seasonal brews available?" Arran asked.

"Not yet. He is still working on a winter ale recipe."

"Hmm...too bad. I'll have the regular bitter, and..."

Cindi interrupted with a smile. "I'll send one to Anders."

A short while later, Cindi returned with their drinks and the group settled in for the evening, Arran raising a mug as Anders received his.

Arran took a drink and decided to address the most pressing topic straight on. "So, how are you two doing with evaluations coming next week? Ready to wow the instructors with your skills and knowledge?" He tried his best to stay upbeat on the topic, knowing his friends' anxieties.

Elinda replied with a surprisingly calm air of confidence. "I'm as ready as I can be...I think. Honestly, I just want it to be over with at this point."

Everyone looked at Bran. He did not share the same confidence. "I think I'm on the edge if truth be told. Still lacking in a few skills, but mainly because I have not received the proper gift for those skills to advance properly. I'm not sure how much they will hold that against me for advancing."

Arran was quick to reply in an effort of assurance. "But you excel at all the others. You'll be fine."

Bran held up his ale in a salute of thanks as they all drank.

The inn filled up, and the evening's entertainment began. A small group playing jaunty tunes filled the air as several tables were pushed away in the center of the room, where some patrons had begun to dance.

"Would you care for a dance, my lady?" Bran stood and bowed before Mare.

"My words! Do you mean little ol' me?" she replied with feigned naivety. Then smiled wickedly. "Let's go, soldier boy." The two headed off to the dance floor arm in arm.

Elinda watched as the two disappeared into the throng of dancers. "No."

Arran turned to look at her. "No, what?"

"I'm not dancing."

"Ah. They don't teach barroom dancing in the courts?" She had danced before on several occasions at the Goose, but it was still a good poke of fun.

Elinda punched him in the arm, Arran feigning in pain. "Ow!" He smiled.

Arran took the last swig from his mug and then waved at Tan behind the bar as he acknowledged another round for the table.

Elinda leaned over. "Thank you for helping Mare."

"Helping Mare? I'm pretty sure Mare doesn't need my help. Matter of fact, she'd probably scold me for trying."

Elinda looked at him disapprovingly. "She told me about your conversation in the gardens. It really helped her. She was so focused on her own frustrations, she had never stopped to think of it from the instructors' point of view. You may have just cracked the riddle that is Mare and, in doing so, made a devilishly intelligent person...wise."

Arran laughed.

"As I told Mare, thank my mother, it is her philosophy, not mine. I just passed it along. I'm glad if it helped, though."

"Play the humble card if you want, but she is doing much better with her instructors. Discussions that before only lead to arguments, now lead to insightful debates on doctrine. She is even starting to impress a few of the instructors with her insight. I believe she is on a path that will give her a very good chance of passing her year two evaluations now. That is no small thing, Arran. So again, thank you for being a good friend to her."

Arran decided it best to take the compliment graciously and feigned a seated bow. "You and Mare are welcome."

Elinda sipped at her drink. "You are quite the puzzle, oh country boy from Kine." She gave him a smirk, and it was his turn to give her a playful punch in the arm.

Cindi returned to the table with a fresh round of drinks, and Arran and Elinda sat in silence, smiling at the patrons, and especially their two friends dancing the night away.

Back at school, Bran and Arran waved goodnight to the girls and started towards their own rooms. As soon as they turned to go down their long hallway, Arran noticed a tall figure about twenty paces ahead of them. He was clad in dark leathers and a cloak, with the cowl hanging down his back. His long hair was pulled back in a ponytail. He walked past the other common rooms and went for the first door in the Intelligence section. He turned and gave them a quick glance before entering.

Arran stared in wonder. "Who was that?"

"That would be Klintoc. He is the last person you want to meet in a dark alley. He is widely considered one of, if not the best, Intelligence agents in the realms. Receives many of the top commissions."

"I could not make out his features very well. It was like there was a fog. All his edges were blurry."

"That would be the gift of Shadow, one of the rarest gifts of Talon. Funny he would use it at school, though. I think he still maintains a room here. I've seen him a few times before."

The two continued to their rooms with Arran giving the first door a long stare as they went by.

Arran was finishing up his last bit of staff training for the week when a group of instructors entered the courtyard, followed by Bran and Stepf. They both appeared haggard and worn out. Their gear stained with mud and grime, and they looked like they hadn't slept for days.

The instructors peeled away and entered the Intelligence training hall, and Arran jogged over to greet the two fellow students as they sat down on the bleachers.

"That bad?"

Neither lifted their heads, only grunting in acknowledgment.

Arran went to the water barrel, grabbing several large ladles. The water was chilled, but not overly so. The cold of winter had been taking a break for a few days. He brought the water back to them and they both drank deeply. He went to get them some more.

After they had both drank their fill, Bran leaned back and stretched out his legs and arched his back.

"So, how do you both feel you did? Think you passed?" Arran asked.

Bran stretched his arms above his head. "Honestly. I don't know.

The instructors said they would let us know later today or tomorrow morning, but I think I did okay. No horrible fails, at least I don't think so."

Stepf nodded. "It was grueling, but I agree with Bran. I think we held our own for the most part. Unfortunately, our standards and the instructors' are not the same."

Bran and Stepf left for the dorms to clean up before heading to the dining hall for dinner. Arran agreed to meet them and was gathering up his gear to follow when he saw Elinda exit the Mage hall. She was walking around the circular path towards the dorms. He quickly finished gathering his gear and jogged over to her.

"Hey. So how did it go? Bran and Stepf looked like hell, but they think they did okay."

Elinda sighed. "I don't know. The evaluations were hard and every time I thought I was garnering some success, I was deluged with trials that made me feel like a failure all over again." She looked up forlornly. "I hope it was enough."

Mare came around the corner and saw them. She came over quickly, grabbing Elinda in a hug. Arran could just make out a faint glimmer of something as they embraced. Elinda immediately seemed calmer, more relaxed, with a measure of her weariness gone.

"Thank you, Mare."

Mare gave her a solemn smile as the two broke their embrace.

"I think I need to rest." Arran and Mare watched as she left them heading towards the dorms.

"So this is what I have to look forward to next term, then?"

"Yep. They do not make it easy to advance. Every trial is different, the instructors tailoring the trials for each student. Never the same, but just as difficult, nonetheless." Mare's gaze became distant, lost in thought.

The mood was solemn as they all gathered for dinner that evening; there was little conversation and their normal, good-humored atmosphere was absent. Bran and Elinda had both been appraised that they had passed their evaluations, but even this good news did not seem to cheer them up. No matter the congratulations or cheer that Mare and Arran tried to insert into the conversation, it did nothing to alleviate the solemness of their comrades.

Eventually Arran and Mare ceased their efforts and let the conversation fade, leaving everyone to their own thoughts. Arran observed his friends with sympathy.

What in the realms could have shaken them both so much during the evaluations?

CHAPTER 6
EVALUATIONS
YEAR 1304/FEBRUARY/WEEK 1

Term Break

Arran lay in the darkness, the room beginning to take on some of the night's chill. The term had ended the week after the main festivities of the Winter Solstice. There had been a big party in the training courtyard and was a welcome break from the normal routines of school. Even most of the instructors had taken part in some of the activities. Kallion pelting Instructor Shia with a snowball to the side of the head was the evening's highlight. But, in the end, almost everyone still wanted to go home and partake in some of the midwinter activities of their homes, including his close group of friends.

So Arran was alone. Well, not actually alone. Not at this place. There were always some students around and, of course, the staff, but the school had somehow become cold and somber without the tumult of a full term. He closed his eyes and listened intently at... nothing. Every once in a while he could make out the snow-muffled passing of a carriage outside, but mostly it was silence.

Arran did not mind the upcoming time alone. While he enjoyed the company of his friends, he was also very comfortable in his solitude. He had always been this way growing up. He had thought long and hard about spending some of his stipend to make the trip back home for break, but decided against it. He was torn between wanting to save as much as he could, and missing his parents, his friends, and the simpleness of Kine.

Home.

His mind wandered to his parents. What would they be doing right now during the holiday? His mother would have decorated the house; his father complaining all the while, stating the same argument every year, 'Why do we bother with all the work for decorations when we're just going to take them down in a month?'. Arran chuckled. He could hear his father's grumpy voice as if he were there.

I wonder what they would think if they saw me now?

He had come into his own here at school. Gone were the young boy and his pranks. In its place was a different person now. He had changed much in the last eight months since leaving Kine. Physically, he was lean and fit, the softness of his youth gone. In its place were not just the physical changes, but the self discipline and fortitude of an Intelligence student.

I've come a long way.

It was mid-way through break and Arran was practicing in the training hall. He had taken to using the meditative agility poses and forms as a warm-up for the rest of his training exercises. In the beginning, he had not given this form of training much credence, only putting in the hours which were required. As second-term training became more intense though, he began to see its value. It was calming and meditative and if he were honest with himself, helpful with his other skills, especially the flexibility. He was more balanced and grounded, more fluid with his other techniques.

He had just finished his routines and was sitting cross-legged in the center of the mat, when Klintoc and instructors Shia and Bale entered the hall. Arran opened his eyes as the group gave him a cursory glance before hastily descending the stairs to the basement. As they fell out of view Arran could just make out a few harsh whispers, 'Freeholt'...'beast'...'unknown'.

Daijoon/Capitol of the Valoor Realm
Year 1304/February/Week 2

Elinda entered the house from the back veranda, stomping off the snow from her boots and rubbing her hands together.

"Good morning, ma'am."

Elinda looked over through the open door to her left towards the main kitchen. She smiled. Estella's mere presence could light up any room.

Elinda shrugged off her coat and hung it up before making her way into the kitchen. The warmth of the room was like stepping into a sauna compared to her wintry morning ride with Spirit. Her body soaked in the warmth as she returned Estella's smile.

"What are these?" Elinda made for the table in the center of the kitchen where a variety of cookies still lay cooling on their racks.

"Don't you..." Estella turned, but Elinda had already grabbed a warm cookie and was heading out a side door and into the main house.

"Mmmph...sooo good," Elinda said through a mouthful of cookie. She waved her hand and the half-eaten cookie over her shoulder as she left. She could just make out the faint grumble of 'Incorrigible' as she turned the corner.

Elinda finished her cookie as she walked down the main hallway of the east wing, heading for her father's library. The faint sounds of a heated conversation emanated from one of the side rooms ahead of her. She slowed her pace as she walked by.

Inside, she saw her father and several other local noblemen from the court of Valoor. She could tell from the expressions and demeanor that they were not having a pleasant social chat. Her father caught her eye. He politely dismissed himself from the group and calmly walked over to the door, giving her a smile. "Realm business," he whispered, and then shut the door.

Elinda frowned at the dismissal before continuing on her way to the library.

Elinda picked out several alchemical books and settled down next to the fire in a reading chair. Several books laid out on the table in front of her, some open to a specific section while others sat stacked haphazardly. "The Flora and Fauna of Galleant" lay open in her lap as she wiggled her stockinged toes next to the fire. Her boots were drying on the hearth.

She knew that extending her studies to take on Alchemy during second term would be difficult, but she had always had a fascination with the subject. Even as a small girl, she remembered gathering all manner of plants and flowers to bring home so that her father could look up their names and uses. Right here in this very room. She stared at the fire and rolled her neck around in a stretch.

She was just about to dive back into the book when she heard the door open. Her father came in, a look of concern on his face. He closed the door and was halfway across the room towards his desk before he noticed Elinda. He immediately put on a smile that Elinda could tell was forced. She smiled wanly back.

"Good morning, dear. I didn't see you there. Did you have a good ride?"

"I did. I think Spirit enjoys the cold."

Her father nodded. "She has always been a feisty one."

Elinda closed the book, a finger holding her place. "What was your meeting about? Someone misplace their taxes again?" Elinda gave him a crooked smile, knowing the petty politics were not her father's favorite aspect of his position.

He came over and sat down in the chair opposite. "No, no. Nothing so mundane, just a bit of an issue in one of the smaller towns up north. It is being looked into and should not be anything of concern." He waved his hand dismissively, as if to emphasize its unimportance. "Now let's get you warmed up so you can change out of those riding clothes for lunch with your mother."

Her father may not have liked the politics, but he was an expert politician. Especially at changing the subject, but she did not miss the lingering concern in his eyes.

Elinda knew better than to push him on a topic that required a closed door conversation, and let the matter drop. She replaced her finger with a bookmark and stood, grabbing her now mostly dry boots. As she passed her father, she leaned over and kissed him lightly on the forehead before leaving.

Elinda entered her room and Elsie was already present, several clean outfits laid out on the bed for her to choose from.

"Hey'a Elsie."

Elsie had been Elinda's handmaiden for as long as she could remember. Elsie was six years older than Elinda. Her mother had wanted someone closer to her own age growing up, and in this she had been correct. The two had become close friends over the years and, on occasions like this, when they were in private, they treated each other more as sisters than anything else. Elinda strode across the room, already shedding her riding clothes as Elsie looked up.

"Good morning, Elinda."

Elinda gave her a lopsided smile as she headed towards the waiting bath, small wisps of steam rising pleasantly. The bathroom was muggy, with the faint hint of lilacs. Her favorite. She sank down slowly into the luxuriously warm water with a sigh. "What do you make of Father's meetings of late with the other noblemen? They seemed quite distressed about something when I saw them earlier."

Elsie was folding her discarded riding clothes and spoke as she worked. "There have been a lot of meetings of late. Even before you arrived back from school, for several weeks now. There were even several private meetings with Lord Neesan. Everyone is quite 'hush hush' on the matter."

Elinda knew that this was not the whole of it. The secrets of any keep's meetings were hard to maintain from the staff, and the rumors would be running wild by now.

Elinda let her head slip beneath the water and then leaned back, letting herself go limp in the bath's warmth. "So nothing, then?"

Elsie grinned as she finished putting away the morning's clothes and then sat down on a small stool next to the tub. "Well..." She grinned mischievously, knowing full well what Elinda wanted to hear. "They say there has been an outbreak of some kind amongst the animals north of Freeholt." Elinda opened her eyes at this. "There have even been reports of some of the animals going wild and attacking townsfolk. Perhaps even a few deaths."

Elinda sat up straight as Elsie leaned in conspiratorially. "But that isn't even the weirdest part. The beasty that was killed was said to be odd, disfigured even."

Elinda knew of Freeholt. She had been there quite a few times growing up. It wasn't a big town and was known for their fine pelts and maple syrup from the large forests in the region.

"An outbreak?" Elinda pondered on the idea. "There have been outbreaks before. Cases of rabies or the like. The stress I witnessed in the nobles' conversations earlier hardly warranted a reaction such as this. Disfigured though..."

"That's what they say."

"Hmm...strange."

School of Doctrine/Meitellen
Year 1304/March/Week I

Smooth right sweep, step back to a defensive stand, lunge, then sweep again and stand at attention.

Arran held the staff erect in front of him, one hand above the other. He stood solidly, focusing on his breath. His chest was heaving from the exertion as he concentrated on long, slow, purposeful breaths. At Kallion's recommendation, he had begun to incorporate his staff with his flexibility forms and postures. He found the combination worked well, intensifying the exercise.

Once his breathing became slow and rhythmic, he broke the stance and concluded the session in the traditional cross-legged sitting position to finish his cool down. He grabbed his gear, heading out for a drink. The slight chill of the air hit him with a refreshing wave as he exited the training hall. The last vestiges of winter were still hanging on, but spring was closing in. Arran's favorite season.

Arran had just pulled his first ladle of water from the barrel when he saw Bran enter the yard. He rushed over enthusiastically, and with just a hint of sarcasm, greeted his friend. "Welcome back, Mr. Year Two!"

"Quit it, or you'll make me blush." The two clasped hands and hugged each other with several pounds of fists on each other's backs.

Arran stepped back and gave him a crooked smile. "So, how was your break? Meet any girls at the solstice parties?" Arran held up a hand, stopping himself more than Bran's answer. "Let me get cleaned up and you can fill me in over lunch."

A short while later, the two were deep into the explanations of their breaks as they finished their meals.

Arran grinned maniacally. "So, you never answered my question. Did you meet any girls? Surely you met someone that touched your fancy at all of those parties?"

Bran returned the grin, almost sheepishly then with his normal vigor. "Maybe...just a few." He held out his hand and looked up as if in thought as he began lifting his fingers, one, two, three, four...

Arran punched him in the shoulder. "All right, all right. Do tell. Come on now, details. I want details."

"Nothing to tell, my friend. You know I have a no courting rule until after year two. It's driving my mother mad."

"I see, so...no one caught your eye, then?"

A wry grin spread across Bran's face. "I didn't say that! Your turn. Tell me, how many courtships did you manage to have, or at least stumble into over break?"

Arran had to laugh at the joke. "Not a one...that I'm aware of, anyway." The two were still laughing as Elinda and Mare walked up. As they approached, Elinda leaned over to Mare. "I wonder, what could have these two so worked up?" She began rubbing her chin questioningly.

"Their lack of girlfriends, maybe?" Both boys' laughter came to a sudden halt.

"Now that is just hurtful," Arran replied.

"Hurtful...but scarily on the mark," Bran said admittedly.

Elinda and Mare sat down as the round of subdued chortles quieted down. "So, how was everyone's break?" Elinda asked.

"That's actually what we were talking about," Arran replied. "I did what I always do and Bran met a lot of girls he had no interest in." Arran nudged Bran playfully. "How about you, Mare?"

Mare shrugged her shoulders. "Same ol', same ol' for me."

There was a lapse in the conversation as everyone waited to see if Mare would continue. She did not. Arran had noticed that with all of her forwardness in just about every other topic of conversation, her home life was never a subject she cared to talk about.

Elinda broke the silence. "Arran? How many courtships did you engage in over break?" The joke had become a common point of jest, and he endured the laughs at his expense once more.

"Nothing on that front, I'm afraid. It was pretty much the same for me. I didn't do anything of note beyond training and some light reading." Arran got more than a few raised eyebrows at the 'light reading' comment. Everyone knew of his voracious appetite for books. He paused, suddenly remembering the day in the training hall. "The instructors seemed awfully busy about something though, come to think of it. There were a lot of meetings upstairs. Oh, and one day I saw Klintoc and instructors Shia and Bale go down into the dungeon while I was working out. They barely noticed me as they headed down, talking all quiet. I overheard something about Freeholt, a beast and...something else. I can't remember."

Elinda's eyes went wide as Arran finished. "Wow, that is eerily similar to a story I heard. My father, several other nobles and even Lord Neesan, seemed very worked up about a rumor of an outbreak in Freeholt. Something about animals gone wild. Everyone is saying it's a rabies outbreak, but I'm not buying it. I could tell my father was concerned." Elinda's face turned somber. "There were rumors of a couple of deaths."

The conversation fell at the mention of the two deaths. Bran shifted in his seat, brows furrowed. "It sure sounds like the two are related, given they both mention Freeholt, but...why would the school instructors and Klintoc care about a rabies-like outbreak amongst some wildlife in northern Valoor? Could the deaths be from something else?"

"I don't know," Elinda remarked. "But something has them concerned."

<hr />

Week one of Arran's third term was just a few days old when Arran and Bran were approached by Kallion on the training grounds. He was followed by another student carrying a sword. He was tall and broad and he carried the sword with a practiced confidence.

"Gentlemen, I'd like you to meet Rayneer. The three of you are going to assist one another."

Bran looked at Arran quizzically and then back to Kallion. "Assist?"

Kallion stopped in front of them as Rayneer stepped to his side. Kallion was a big man by anyone's standard and Rayneer was easily his equal. "Rayneer is a Knight of Tovin and a good swordsman." Kallion glanced at Rayneer, the barest twitch of a grin forming. "He needs practice against other weapon types, as do the both of you. I believe sparring with each other will help advance your skills. Arran and Bran, you are both good with daggers and staff. I want you to spar using both weapons against Rayneer. Rayneer, I want you to concentrate with your sword against these other weapons. Once I feel you have progressed satisfactorily, I'll move you on to another weapon. Any questions?"

All three students nodded their heads in acceptance, and Kallion strolled away to administer to other students.

Arran held out his hand. "Nice to meet you. I'm Arran."

"Likewise." Rayneer shook Arran's hand and then Bran's. "Shall we have a go?"

Bran and Arran both looked at one another. "Age before beauty?" Arran said mockingly.

Bran raised his eyebrows and then shrugged. He walked over to take his mark opposite Rayneer in the circle.

Rayneer was taller than Bran by at least five inches, standing easily over six feet tall, and had a build that would rival a heavyweight brawler. Thick was the first word that came to Arran. Rayneer held his medium training sword with ease and, Arran noted, looked very light on his feet for a young man his size. Given Rayneer's advantage in size, strength, and weapon against Bran's smaller stature and daggers, Arran was very curious to watch the match.

The match started slowly as Rayneer tested out Bran's guard with some basic swings and frontal attacks. Bran either moved to avoid the blows or attempted to brush the sword aside with his daggers in a parry. The parries proved difficult though, given Rayneer's heavier weapon and gift of Strength. As the match wore on, and Rayneer began to press with more vigor, Bran took a blow from the sword in the ribs. His parry attempt had failed with the strong of his dagger and the blow went through to his side.

"Ugh!" Bran grunted, bending over from the blow. "Okay, that one hurt."

Rayneer walked over and placed a hand on Bran's back. "The advantage is mine in weapon and strength. You are fast, though. I believe mobility is your best defense. Dodging my blows is much more advantageous than trying to parry them, and it provides an opportunity for a counter. Parrying does not. It is a much riskier move."

Bran straightened up with a small wince and a curt nod to Rayneer. "Arran, your turn."

Arran stepped into the circle and set his daggers in guard position. Rayneer started the fight in much the same way he had with Bran. Heeding Rayneer's advice to Bran, Arran stuck with dodging his attacks instead of trying to parry them. As the matched progressed, he began to get a feel for the bigger man's moves, and it slowly became easier to anticipate his attacks. After a while, Rayneer seemed to become a little frustrated. Arran had yet to even try an attack of his own. The sparring session had turned into a one sided cat-and-mouse match. Arran noticed a shift in Rayneer's weight and anticipated the forward attack. He stepped to the side and then in, slicing Rayneer across the chest.

They stepped back from one another. "A good strike, my friend. You anticipated the thrust at just the right moment to attack yourself. Very impressive."

"One of my gifts," Arran said between several deep breaths. "As a fight progresses, I can begin to pick up on the shifts in your body positions. I'm still learning, but done properly, it allows me to antici-pate a move."

"A handy gift indeed." Rayneer grinned widely, giving Arran a clap on the back.

They continued sparring through the afternoon. Bran and Arran taking far more hits than they gave, but by the end of the afternoon, the training had proved useful. Everyone had learned a little more about the other's techniques.

Arran and Rayneer had just finished a lengthy spar with Rayneer clipping Arran's leg with a clever counterstrike. Arran was breathing heavily. "Let's call it a day, shall we?" The other two agreed, and they walked over to the bleachers for a rest and drink.

Bran took a large drink of water and wiped his mouth. "So, be honest, Rayneer. How easy did you take it on us today?"

Rayneer was silent for a few moments as he gave the question some thought. "Truthfully? Probably half."

Arran spit out his mouthful of water, aghast. "Half! We are going to look like we rolled down a hill of rocks with all these bruises. You look like you have barely broken a sweat."

Rayneer smiled amiably. "One of 'my' gifts, Resilience. I can fight an abnormally long time with minimal tiring. Coupled with my gift of Strength, it proves a useful combination. Both are primary common gifts of Tovin."

"Great," Bran said. "This is going to be a long and painful term."

Rayneer chuckled. "Do not worry, Bran. I can see the potential in your daggers. Coupled with your other skills, it will not be long before you are testing me proper. I think that is what Kallion is trying to achieve, more well-rounded individuals."

"I don't know about well-rounded, lumpy and bruised, maybe." Bran grimaced as he gingerly felt at his ribs. Rayneer laughed so loud several of the other students stopped to stare at them. Arran noticed Kallion smiling from across the yard.

The three parted ways for the day. Arran and Bran slowly made their way to clean up, with what ended up for each being a long, soaking hot bath.

That evening in the dining hall, Arran noticed Rayneer enter with what he guessed were a few of his fellow students of Tovin. He caught Rayneer's eye and motioned him over.

Elinda noticed Mare's eyes bulge as Rayneer approached the table. He absolutely towered over them.

"Maarre," Elinda said, elongating her name accusingly.

Mare looked back at Elinda, feigning complete innocence. "What? I was just going to ask Mr. Tall and Handsome here if he was the culprit who pummeled our two friends." She motioned across the table at Bran and Arran.

Rayneer gave a polite nod at the two young women, introducing himself. "Rayneer. A pleasure to meet you, and yes, I am said culprit." Then, much to everyone's surprise, he gave Mare a wink.

Arran's eyebrows rose sharply as he looked up at Rayneer and then to Mare. It was not often that someone could unnerve Mare, but that wink had done the trick. Arran believed it was the first time he had ever seen her actually dumbfounded and at a loss for words.

Elinda, either missing the exchange or simply ignoring it, picked up in the greeting. "A pleasure. I am Elinda, and this is Mare." Elinda nudged Mare and then leaned over and whispered.

"Close your mouth, dear. You don't want to drool all over your nice dress."

Mare clamped her mouth shut and huffed.

Elinda continued smoothly. "You must excuse our friend. She sometimes has issues keeping her thoughts on her internal voice…if you know what I mean."

Rayneer chuckled at this, even his light chuckle feeling like it would shake the rafters. "I have a sister who…how shall I say, suffers from the same."

This got a chorus of laughs from the group and another exasperated huff from Mare.

"Would you care to dine with us?" Arran asked.

"Perhaps another evening." He motioned to his friends' table, who all were watching the exchange. "It was a pleasure meeting you all." He bowed and went to join his friends.

Elinda watched him leave, moving lithely through the crowd to his table. "He was much more amiable than his size would predict. How did you meet him?"

"Kallion felt we needed to spar with him for extra training. Worst idea ever." Bran tenderly probing the bruises on his ribs.

Elinda and Arran both laughed, Arran grimacing from the outburst as he too gingerly put a hand to his own ribs.

They all finished dinner with Mare uncharacteristically quiet for the remainder of the meal.

Year 1304/March/Week 4
Week 4 of Third Term

Arran arose quietly and dressed, not wanting to disturb Bran. It didn't work.

Bran rolled over sleepily. "Where you headed so early?"

"Got an early dungeon run with Shia. I'll catch up with you later."

Bran grunted something unintelligible and was already back asleep before Arran had closed the door.

Arran entered the Intelligence training hall following Instructor Shia down the back steps and into the maze. The instructor had prepared this morning's dungeon specifically for Arran and would be observing him to judge his progress.

Shia stood before the door and turned to Arran.

"Pickpocket four guards, unlock six chests, disarm twelve traps, and find six hidden areas."

Arran groaned at the objectives for this morning's exercise. His best tally for hidden areas in any exercise thus far had been two. He knew that she was placing the total at six to challenge him. He needed to improve. He knew it, and she knew it.

"Yes, ma'am."

Arran entered the maze and immediately scurried down a hallway to find the first shadowy alcove from which to begin. The instructor had not mentioned how large today's maze was, or how many guards would be patrolling. He would need to be wary until he could scout the area out.

Arran made his way from alcove to alcove and down hallways. As he finally finished scouting the layout to his satisfaction, he paused on what he was calling the south end, hidden well back in an alcove. He had two successful pickpockets, disarmed four traps, and found one chest, which he successfully opened. The maze seemed to be of medium size, probably two hundred and fifty paces by one hundred. He would start on this end and methodically work his way to the northern end.

He had made his way to the far right and was just about to exit one alcove for another when he heard a guard coming from around the corner. He slid back into the shadows of the alcove and listened. Sure enough, the guard was heading his way.

The alcove was too shallow for him to remain hidden. If the guard was to look in, he would be easily seen. Using one of his previous tricks, he crab-walked up the alcove and suspended himself at the top. His back against the ceiling of the alcove, muscles straining.

The guard walked by, slowing to inspect the alcove, and then continued down the hall. Arran silently came down and crept up behind the guard, successfully pick-pocketing another. Arran grinned.

That was three.

He slipped into the nearest alcove behind the guard and waited until he turned and continued on. He was in the perimeter hallway on the south side. In each direction, he could see the other two perimeter hallways heading north. The one the guard had just gone down and the one in which he had just left. There were two other entries, or exits, he thought, equally spaced, heading inwards to the interior space of the maze. Other than the two smaller alcoves which Arran had already explored, there was only one other alcove. It was perfectly placed in the middle of the hallway on the perimeter wall and contained a statue depicting some sort of bird.

Looks like the perfect place for a hidden area.

Arran made his way to the statue and fell in behind it. He stopped and listened for any other movement. Satisfied that he was alone in the hallway, he began inspecting the statue. It was not very large, maybe three feet tall, sitting on a small cubicle pedestal. Arran started inspecting the pedestal, finding nothing special. He strained, concentrating all his will as he continued examining the bird. He was just about to give up when he noticed a slight glimmer out of the corner of his vision. His eyes darted towards the tiny glint, focusing. Climbing slowly up onto the pedestal, he focused all his attention on the head of the bird. He was sure that the glint had come from there. He inspected it intently.

There!

He saw the faintest of glimmers in the right eye of the statue.

"Ah!" Arran gasped and his hand went to his chest. The sudden shift of his weight nearly causing him to lose his balance and fall from his perch. A flash of heat spread through his chest, and then it was gone.

Another gift!

He was breathing hard. In his excitement, he almost didn't hear a guard making the turn into his hallway from one of the interior hall-ways. Arran scrambled down behind the statue as quietly as possible, hoping he had not given himself away in his excitement. The guard had evidently not detected Arran and walked past the statue, giving it only a cursory glance. Arran took the opportunity to grab another pickpocket before returning behind the statue, waiting for the guard to move on. The guard made his turn at the other interior hallway and Arran let out a long breath.

Another gift had been granted, but there was no time to think about that now. He would discuss it with the instructor after the exercise.

Making his way back up onto the pedestal, he began inspecting the bird's head again. This time, and with much less effort, Arran was able to detect the glimmer in the eye of the bird. He reached out and touched the eye, probing around it. Nothing. He tried again, this time pushing directly into the eye itself. He heard a faint snick in the wall behind the statue. He slid down the statue and started inspecting the wall; sure enough, a middle stone now had a faint glimmer, pulsating silently.

He pushed on it, hoping it did not make too much noise. As he pushed on the glimmering stone, it and three others slowly slid back into the wall, thankfully making little sound. When the stones were done moving, they revealed a small crawlway into another room. Arran dropped to his belly and crawled into the room.

Arran stood and took a few moments to inspect the room. It was small and rectangular, perhaps six paces wide and ten paces long. The room was lit by two torch sconces, equally spaced in the middle of each side wall. There were loose stones on the floor that had apparently fallen from the ceiling, and broken earthenware lay strewn about the entire room.

Near the far end of the room, a few paces from the back wall, there was a small pedestal with a chest on top. There were no other visible exits.

He concentrated and began looking for traps. To his surprise, the room's floor and walls were covered in various stun and alarm traps.

Arran readied himself and began meticulously disarming the traps on the floor, slowly making a path to the pedestal. His trap total had climbed to eight by the time he had finished.

He stood in front of the pedestal, inspecting it for any additional hidden traps. Finding none, he set to unlocking the chest. It took quite a bit longer than normal, but eventually he heard the satisfying snick of the lock. Arran slowly opened the chest, and to his surprise, found a pair of gauntlets resting inside.

"What?"

All of the chests he'd opened during his previous training exercises were empty, just for training, or so he had thought. Should he take the gauntlets? He couldn't carry them, they would just get in his way. Put them on? He shook his head. No, while the gauntlets looked to be of finer quality than his school issue, it could be another test. Much to his dismay, he opted to leave the gauntlets behind. He would ask about them later.

Arran heard a faint noise behind him and turned. The stones that led back into the maze began slowly returning to their original positions in the wall, essentially closing the crawlway. He had a momentary sense of panic believing he was trapped, but as soon as the stones completed their path, he could see the glimmer on the center stone as it finished moving into place. He breathed a sigh of relief, assuming it was there to reopen the crawlspace.

Probably for the better.

Despite the claustrophobic feeling now permeating the room, a passing guard could have seen the opening's light on the other side.

Arran turned and inspected the room again, intently focusing on all of its surfaces. Against one of the side walls, there seemed to be a mass of traps near the floor. He made his way over and inspected the area. The traps started about waist high and spread downwards in a semicircle to the base of the wall. There were faint scrape marks on the floor at the base of the wall beneath the cluster of traps. Working slowly and deliberately, Arran disarmed all the traps clustered in the area.

There!

After disarming the last trap, a glimmer appeared on one of the stones.

Those sneaky devils put a hidden area inside another!

He took a moment, admiring the cleverness of the room. He turned his attention to the traps he had just disarmed. Was it a path to another hidden area? But what to make of the marks on the floor? He followed the marks into the room from the wall, disarming a few more traps along the way until they ended, almost dead center of the room. He was now well past his needed trap total.

He grinned as a satisfying thought came to him. Going back to the wall, he pressed the stone bearing the glimmer. He had to step aside as two stones moved out from the wall, and as the first set of stones fully entered the room, the next two in the wall began to come out, creating a stone staircase. When finished, the stairs were over halfway up the wall, with the first stones ending exactly at the end of the markings in the center of the floor. Arran grinned.

Ok, so now I have some stairs. Is there another hidden area at the top of the wall? Into another chamber?

Arran looked up and, as if on cue, he saw another glimmer in the ceiling of the chamber above the top of the stairs. He ascended the stairs and inspected the sections in the immediate area around the new glimmer in the ceiling. Once satisfied that there were no traps, he took a deep breath and pushed on the glimmering stone in the ceiling. The stones ascended upwards and moved to the side, revealing an opening in the ceiling. Unlike the chamber he was in, it had no light. It was pitch black inside.

Kneeling down, he was able to grab the torch from the side wall sconce and hold it up into the hole. He stood up on his toes as best he could, torch held high. From his vantage point, he could only make out the ceiling and the top portion of the walls. The space seemed extremely small.

Nothing to do now but go on up.

He reached up and gave the torch a light toss. It landed just inside the lip of the opening. Crouching, he jumped up and got a good handhold on the edge of the opening. He hauled himself up and into the room. Thankfully, there were no traps at the edge of the opening. He grabbed the torch and held it aloft. The room was indeed extremely small, only a few paces square, and the ceiling was so low he had to crouch down to move about. In the middle of the room, there was another chest. He diligently inspected the floors and walls. Finding nothing, he moved over to the chest and began picking the lock.

As before, the lock was more complex than normal, but after careful maneuvering, he finally heard a faint snick. He wiped the sweat from his brow and slowly opened the chest. To his surprise, there was another piece of gear inside. This time, it was a pair of leather boots. Like the gauntlets, the boots looked to be of much finer quality than his current school issue.

In the name of the Patrons!

Arran became frustrated with his indecision. Was he just to leave new gear in boxes or take them? He bent down and pulled the boots out of the chest, admiring them when he heard a noise from the room below.

"Arran!" Instructor Shia called. "Come down and bring the contents of the box, please."

Was the exercise over?

He had not finished with his objective counts. Maybe he was found out by a guard having stupidly left the initial crawlspace open. Sighing, he dejectedly descended the stairs with the boots, offering them to her.

The inspector took the boots and turned them over in her hand. "Well done. Very few students find the double hidden glimmers, much less solve the trap, and locate the hidden stairs to the room above." She handed the boots back.

"But...but I did not finish the objectives."

Shia eyed him curiously. "You have proven more than proficient at accomplishing today's objectives."

Arran could only nod in relief.

Arran retrieved the gauntlets from the first chest and followed the instructor as they exited the maze. As the walls closed behind them,

Arran turned. "Ma'am, I received another gift today. I believe it might be the gift of Sight."

"Hmmm...very fortuitous, wouldn't you say?" She turned and gave Arran a smile. Shia actually gave him a slight smile.

Arran blinked in surprise.

Shia smiled!

Arran had never seen so much as a slight grin from her before.

"Yes, ma'am. I don't know if I would have been able to find both rooms without it."

"Take both pieces of gear and report to the quartermaster for inspection. He will be able to give you more information." Smile now gone, she turned to leave.

Arran exited the Intelligence hall to find that it was already mid-afternoon. He had started the exercise so early. Had he been in there all day? He suddenly felt extremely exhausted as he made the realization. The constant stress of the exercise washed over him like a wave.

He entered the quartermaster hall and walked over to the counter. Kallion was nowhere to be seen, so he placed the boots and gauntlets on the counter and waited, relieved to find a chair.

"Taking a quick nap, are we?"

Arran's eyes snapped open as Kallion strolled into the room.

"Sorry, Master Kallion. Just really tired from today's exercise." Arran tried to wipe the grogginess from his eyes.

"So I hear. Found the ceiling chamber, very impressive."

"I discovered these two items in a couple of chests I unlocked." Arran gestured at the two items on the counter.

Kallion walked over and picked up the gauntlets first. "Let's take a look, shall we? Gauntlets, fine hardened leather, very nice." He handed them to Arran. He picked up the boots and inspected them for a moment, and grinned excitedly. "Now these are the find of the term. Leather boots with an enchantment!"

"Enchantment?"

"Yes, a very nice find for a first year. Looks to be a common stealth enchantment."

"What exactly does it do?"

Kallion continued inspecting the boots closely. "It enhances your Stealth ability. When you are actively using Stealth, it will now be enhanced for even quieter movement. Not a bad enchantment for an Intelligence student to find, eh?" His grin broadened as he handed the boots to Arran.

"Both pieces of gear are nice upgrades for you. After you clean up those filthy pieces you have on, remember to bring them back. These other two are yours to keep."

"Thank you." Arran looked at both of the items, knowing that he should probably be more excited about the new gear, but he was just too tired. He needed a nice hot bath, food, and some sleep.

That evening at dinner, the others were excited to hear of Arran's new acquisitions and his accomplishment in the maze.

Rayneer came over when seeing the group's excitement, congratulating Arran. "An enchanted gear find in your first year! That is quite the accomplishment. I only have one piece myself and it was purchased for me by my father."

"Same here," Elinda remarked. "Enchanted gear of any quality is expensive and to find it during a maze run, very impressive. Those hidden rooms must have been an extremely hard accomplishment."

Arran's face grew hot at the attention. "Receiving the gift of Sight during the exercise didn't hurt. I honestly don't know if I would have caught all the signs without it."

"Whatever the reason, well done, my friend," Bran said, giving him a clap on the back.

Mare shook her head, half in admiration and half in amazement. "Damn, Arran, you receive a gift; you find enchanted gear; and accomplish a feat in the maze only a handful of Intelligence students have ever achieved. That is one hell of a day!"

Elinda laughed. "As elegant as ever, Mare, but accurate. One hell of a day, Arran." She raised her cup in salute, the others following.

***

Year 1304/April/Week 2

Week 6 of Third Term

Arran put a final few items in the small bag he was being permitted to carry with him on this training exercise. He was going on the same four-week exercise that Bran and Stepf went on in their third term. He was not looking forward to it, remembering how the two had looked when they returned.

Bran watched Arran from across the room. "You'll be fine."

"Mmmhmm."

"Really, I mean it. You are ready, probably more so than I was."

Arran did not respond. He knew his friend was just trying to be helpful, but he found little consolation in the words. Satisfied with his packing, he turned to leave. "Let's go eat, eh? I need to get my mind off leaving tomorrow."

"Sure, let's go." Bran sighed, grateful to do something to break the strain he knew Arran was feeling.

The dining hall was fairly empty as the two grabbed some breakfast. They ate in silence until Rayneer sat down to join them.

"Morning, fellas." Rayneer greeted them cheerfully.

Bran stared up at him. "Tell me, are you always so cheerful in the morning?"

Rayneer laughed and noticed Arran's sullen mood.

"Mmmm, so the four-week exercise got you anxious? Don't worry, my friend, I've seen your skill. You will be fine." He gave Arran such a hard clap upon his back it almost made him choke up his food.

Rayneer instantly looked apologetic. "Uhh, sorry about that."

Arran looked at Rayneer and, try as he might, he could not be angry with his big friend. He smiled weakly. "Guys, I appreciate the encouragement. Really. But let's not talk about it, okay?"

Both friends nodded their heads as Elinda and Mare joined them at the table.

"Four weeks without 'Country'. Ahhhhh." Mare sighed mockingly. "Elinda, can I request that Arran have this training every term?"

Bran and Rayneer looked at each other alarmingly and then at Mare.

"What?"

Bran motioned with his eyes at Arran, then back to Mare. "Um, we just agreed that we weren't going to talk about it."

"Not at all?" She pouted.

"No."

"Fine, fine, the topic is out of bounds. How about this, then?" She leaned over the table as she spoke softly. "I saw a stream of instructors headed up to the second floor again this morning. Think they are still meeting on that secret outbreak or whatever?"

"Maybe," Elinda said. "I haven't heard anything more from home."

Rayneer looked at them all questioningly. "Meetings?"

"Oh, sorry Ray," Elinda said and then gave him a quick rundown of Arran's and her stories during the term break.

After Elinda finished, Rayneer sat back in his chair, his eyes going distant in thought, then his expression turned concerned.

Elinda looked at him, brows furrowed. "Rayneer? What is it?"

Rayneer took a moment before he replied. "When I was home during break, I too heard of an outbreak amongst some wild animals. I didn't think anything about it at the time, but now hearing this..." he trailed off.

The group sat in silence, digesting the new information.

Mare leaned into the table again. "Two incidents, possibly not even related, are one thing, a coincidence. But three?"

The group finished their breakfast in silence, each lost in their own thoughts. Whatever was going on was starting to point towards something related across two realms now, and who knew how many more?

Arran was nervously sitting on the bleachers in the training courtyard, one leg bouncing up and down unconsciously as dawn broke the following morning. He watched indifferently as the sky lit up with all the myriad hues and colors of the sunrise. It was a beautiful scene, but it did little to assuage his mood. His night had been fitful, with his dreams waking him frequently. Various disconnected visions of failure and pain. He eventually decided to get up and prepare for the day, eventually ending up in the courtyard, brooding over the upcoming exercise.

It was like this that Instructor Shia found him a short while later, accompanied by a female student he recognized, but could not remember her name. He turned his attention to the pair as they approached. Shia was not wearing her typical instructor's robes and instead had chosen a simple outfit of black riding pants and boots with a white shirt and pale blue tunic. The student accompanying her was shorter than Arran and small, almost petite, but lithe. She walked with a sure grace and confidence, carrying only a small bag, a bow and quiver slung across her back, and a knife sheathed at her side. She wore simple brown leathers, each piece a slightly different shade than another. Her cloak was a mottled patchwork of dark greens, browns, and blacks. Everything fit her perfectly. He wondered how many were enchanted.

"Good morning, Arran." Arran turned to the instructor and stood. "This is Cassandra. She is a third-year student from our Patron Bestia and will be joining us."

Arran nodded in greeting. "Cassandra."

Cassandra spoke with a voice that belied her stature. It was firm and slightly huskier than Arran would have imagined. "Cass, if you don't mind."

"Very well," Shia said as she turned and led them to the stables.

After Shia procured their horses for the trip, she led the group over the northwest bridge out of Meitellen. It was a full day's ride to the base camp they would be using during the training exercise. Arran was familiar enough with riding a horse, but it had been a while since he had ridden. By the end of the day, his entire backside was complaining for the effort. He was relieved when they finally reached the camp.

The camp was in a small clearing, just inside the beginning of what Arran believed was the Blackwood forest, if he was correctly recalling his geography. In front of the cabin was a circular clearing with a stone-lined firepit surrounded by three logs laid out in a triangle. There was a small shed to the side of the cabin, a horse pen, and a privy set off a short distance away. Arran could faintly hear the sounds of a small stream somewhere east of the campsite.

"Put your bags in the cabin, then water, and pen the horses," Shia instructed.

The two students grabbed their gear and entered the cabin. The cabin was a one room affair and spartan. There were four beds, two to a side, with a table placed in the middle, just in front of the fireplace.

Returning outside, Arran was relieved to find that the chores provided a much needed reprieve for his sore backside from the day's ride.

He and Cass had just finished and were stretched out, leaning on the logs around the firepit when the instructor exited the cabin and joined them.

"Cassandra, I believe there is still enough light in the day for you to procure us some dinner. Would you be so kind? Take Arran along so that he may observe."

"Yes, ma'am." Cass went inside the cabin, retrieved her bow and arrows and headed out straight north of camp. She did not look back and Arran scrambled along behind her as they delved into the woods.

They walked purposefully for about a quarter of a mile before Cassandra began to slow. She crouched, motioning Arran to do the same. She quietly pulled an arrow from her quiver and nocked it with practiced ease.

That was smooth.

They remained silent and motionless for several long moments. Then, with slow precision, Cass pulled her bow up for a shot. She held the bow in front of her, undrawn as she surveyed the area. Then, with the bare minimum of movement, she drew, and the arrow leapt from the bow with barely a whisper.

She rose and went to retrieve her prey. "That's one." It was a rabbit, and she handed it to Arran. "One more should do us."

Cassandra quickly found another trail and a second rabbit. She turned and began leading them back to camp. Along the way, Cass started pointing out various nuts, berries, tubers, and herbs that were useful. They picked a few as they walked. More importantly, though, she pointed out a variety of berry that they did not want.

"It's not poisonous, but you will almost wish it was after spending the better part of a day in the privy." She gave Arran a sideways glance and a crooked grin.

Arran chuckled, glad to find that she at least had a sense of humor.

When they returned to camp, Shia was inside the cabin, a pot already simmering near the fire. Cassandra prepped the rabbits, while Arran was instructed to chop the tubers and some of the herbs. Everything went into the pot for a stew.

As they ate, Shia explained the curriculum for the first three weeks of the exercise. "The first week is all about tracking. Cassandra will teach you how to track, how to read the markings of what you are tracking, and most importantly, provide us with our meals. We will only eat what we provide."

Arran had some knowledge of tracking growing up, but knew from just the one short excursion with Cass that he was far below her skill. He could definitely learn a few things from her and looked forward to the exercise.

Shia continued. "The second week will consist of trapping and basic survival skills. The third week, you will put the lessons from the first two weeks into practice. You will leave camp and survive on your own for three days and nights, then return to camp. Cassandra will answer questions and instruct you on any issues you may have had. You will then go back out for three more days and nights."

Shia did not continue, and Arran frowned in confusion. "What about week four?"

She looked at Arran gravely, clearly exasperated by the question.

"Worry more about your first three weeks. You will be well served in week four by doing so."

Ok, that didn't sound ominous at all.

He took the small admonishment in silence, determined he would learn as much as he could from Cass in his allotted three weeks.

Breakfast consisted of what remained of the stew from the previous night. Arran exited the cabin to find Cass sitting by the firepit. She waved him over, holding out a bow.

"It's been in the shed for too long and needs some tending. I'll show you."

She began guiding Arran through an inspection and preparation of the bow. He had performed all of these routines growing up, but what Cass showed him made Arran understand just how little he knew about archery. They spent the better part of an hour going over the bow before she deemed the bow hunt worthy. Refurbished bow in hand, they set out.

The first week was nothing short of amazing. Cass was an endless fountain of information. She knew more about tracking game and identifying trails than anyone Arran had ever known. She showed him how to identify all the telltale signs of an animal's passing and the particular habits of each, so that one knew where to look. Rabbits, squirrels, boars, deer; he could now distinguish between them all.

Mid-way through the week, they had stopped for a brief break. Cass had her back to a tree and was prying off a piece of dried meat absently. "You have learned well. I'm impressed."

Arran had a pretty good idea that his gifts of Observance and Sight played a large role in how quickly he could learn what Cass was teaching him. Even so, his insatiable eagerness to learn directly from a skilled individual such as Cass fueled his enthusiasm.

Cass looked around, frowning as she lifted her nose to the air, tossing a small piece of meat in her mouth. "Hmm...one thing we haven't covered yet. Predators. I'm surprised we haven't found a fresh trail yet." She pursed her lips and scrunched her face up in concentration. "Wolves usually hunt in packs, so if you see one, there are probably a handful you haven't seen close by. Give them space. Same for bears and cats. They are more solitary, but just as dangerous. Lastly, there are wolverines." She let out a loud breath before continuing. "I hate wolverines. They are nasty little sons of bitches. We are a fair distance from the mountains where they are typically found, but it would not be too unheard of for them to range this far south." Cass shook her head and looked at Arran intently. "Don't be fooled by their size. They are vicious."

Arran nodded his head in understanding.

They finished the week having found plenty of prey animals for Arran to practice his new skills on and had even finally found several sets of wolf tracks. There had only been one set of old bear tracks, no cats, or the hated wolverines. Arran soaked it all in.

Week two had Arran taking what he had learned from the previous week and added traps, snares, and basic survival. Cass instructed him on how to devise everything he would need from the various resources in the forest. She showed him where to place the traps and snares for particular prey; make a fire from the resources in the forest; pick a suitable camp site; and build a lean-to if needed.

"Most importantly, know where your closest fresh water source is. You can go without food for a bit; or live on roots, berries, and nuts for days; but if you don't have water, you will dehydrate and slowly become useless."

By week's end, despite Arran's enthusiasm for the tasks, it quickly became obvious that making traps and snares was a skill that took more than a week to properly learn. Tying the knots needed from the forest materials for most of the traps and snares was tricky. Most of his attempts either failed or were shoddy examples of the craft. At the end of the week, even after constant coaching from Cass, his skill was rudimentary at best.

At the start of the third week, the group was relaxing next to the firepit, enjoying some hot tea that Shia had brought with her. "Do you remember the parameters of this week's exercise?"

Arran nodded his head, but his eyes were unconvincing.

Shia repeated the instructions. "Go out for three days and nights, return, and give us a detailed report. You will then repeat it once more."

Arran nodded with much more confidence. "Understood, ma'am."

Arran finished his meal and left camp with nothing but his bow, a quiver of twelve arrows, and a hunting knife. As he made his way deeper into the forest, he ventured northeast. He and Cassandra had trained little in that direction and had decided that exploring a bit during these three days of freedom would be a welcome side benefit.

The week passed quickly and with surprising ease. Cass had been an excellent teacher, and he put her training to good use. He enjoyed the solitude and quiet of the forest, using his down time to practice his forms and meditation.

Upon returning to camp after the second excursion, Arran thought he had done well, despite Shia's disappointment in his ability to effectively build and use traps.

The next morning, Arran saw Cassandra packing her bag.

He playfully asked, "Leaving so soon?"

Cassandra looked up and gave Arran a small smile.

"My task here is done. You did well." She threw her bag over her shoulder and left the cabin.

Shia was waiting outside, holding Cass' horse, prepped and ready for her journey back to Meitellen.

Cassandra stopped a few strides from her horse and turned to Arran. She whispered solemnly as she placed a hand on Arran's shoulder. "Good luck next week." Arran watched her leave as he remembered the state that Bran and Stepf had returned in after this exercise.

Later that afternoon, and much to Arran's surprise, Victor and Stepf arrived at the camp.

Arran ran over to greet them, grabbing the horse's reins as they slowed. "Hey guys." They only nodded curtly and remained silent.

As if on cue, the instructor exited the cabin. "Gentlemen. Please stow your bags in the cabin, and give Arran and I moment, if you please."

The two students complied, and instructor Shia motioned for Arran to join her by the firepit.

Her face grew dour, and her words were hard and serious. "For the next six days, those two are not fellow students. In fact, for the purposes of this exercise, they are your enemies. They will hunt you with the intention of either incapacitating you or successfully demonstrating a killing blow." She paused, her stare managing to pierce him as sure as any dagger. "By any means necessary." She let the statement hang for a moment before continuing. "The exercise is broken down into sessions. A session ends when either you eliminate both or they eliminate you. At that point, Victor and Stepf will return to camp, and you will have two hours until they begin hunting again."

Arran thought for a moment, then questioned, "What if I am able to evade them for the duration of the exercise?"

"It has been done before, but it is highly unlikely and not the intention of the exercise. You would do well to actively engage them as they will you."

It slowly began to dawn on him the difficulty of this final week. Up until now, it had been fun. He had trained and learned new skills, but now...now he had to use that knowledge not just for survival, but to hunt his fellow students. It was going to be a long, long week.

With quiet unease, he asked, "How do I pass?"

"There is no pass or fail for this exercise. I will be keeping track of everyone's progress and all the captures. This is only for purposes of gauging your current skill level. Your upcoming evaluations are pass/fail; this week is more of a measuring stick, if you will."

Arran thought for a few moments and then replied, "So, when do we start?"

Shia gave him a quizzical gaze, raising her eyebrows with a lopsided smile. "If that is all, we shall begin immediately. You may take your bow, arrows, hunting knife, and one waterskin." She then reached down into the bag at her feet and pulled out one of the wooden training daggers. "Do not attack with the bow or knife. You may only strike with this." She handed Arran the familiar wooden dagger.

"The training area is a semicircle, approximately two miles east, west, and north of this camp. Try to stay within those parameters. If you venture too far, there is a small enchantment that will alert you. You will feel a slight tingling in your legs."

Arran rose and left to gather the rest of his gear before rejoining the instructor.

"You have this evening to prepare. Victor and Stepf will leave in the morning to begin the session." She watched as Arran secured his bow. "My only advice is this: forget school sparring rules, forget gentlemanly conduct, use whatever means necessary to survive. Now go."

Arran did not acknowledge her. He turned and headed straight north out of camp, steeling himself with every step. He walked at a brisk pace for about twenty minutes, what he estimated to be just over a mile. Turning, he then headed northeast for ten minutes, then southeast for another fifteen minutes. He stopped to catch his bearings and then made straight south, making small efforts to mask his trail, but not fully. He also took the time to set a few false trails, knowing that a skilled tracker would figure it all out eventually, but he didn't care. He wanted to be followed. He began making his way back to the original campsite.

Night had fallen, and Arran watched the camp, well hidden within the forest. He could make out all three individuals around the camp's firepit. He was too far away to hear any conversation, but that was okay. Come morning, he would be ready and in place to turn the hunter into the prey.

Arran was awake and studying the camp well before sunrise the next morning. He had hardly slept the night before. He knew eventually he would need to remedy this, but for now, he was alert and running on adrenaline, ready to execute his first plan.

Victor and Stepf exited the cabin, surely having slept far better than himself, and quickly spoke to Shia before leaving the camp. Stepf headed northwest and Victor headed straight north.

Arran cursed under his breath.

He had hoped that they would leave together so he could keep track of them both, but that was now out. He opted to follow Victor, as he was heading towards Arran's original path and would soon find his trail.

Arran followed Victor for several hours as he tracked Arran's trail from the previous evening. Secure that Victor would follow the trail to its conclusion, Arran broke off and headed towards a section he knew had a few trees he could climb.

Arran found a location that suited his needs and then walked around the big tree to the opposite side, obscuring his trail as he went. Satisfied, he turned and began climbing. He found a suitable branch that wasn't too high and offered good concealment. He waited.

An hour had passed, and he was beginning to become anxious.

Did he lose my trail?

He had been in the tree long enough now that he had to constantly shift his weight to keep from becoming too stiff. Finally, he saw the barest shift of a shadow from up the trail. Arran tensed as he watched, barely breathing. Sure enough, he saw Victor moving slowly and cautiously towards the tree.

Arran maneuvered ever so slightly to make sure he was behind cover in the tree. He lost his angle to view Victor from a distance, but now had a clear view beneath him. He drew his dagger, focusing intently for silence. His breathing slowed.

A few moments later, Arran regained sight of Victor. He was kneeling down, inspecting Arran's tracks. Victor followed the tracks with his eyes, his brows furrowing as he saw the trail disappear as it led towards the tree. He stepped to the side and away from the tree, giving himself space to make a wide circle. He held his dagger at the ready in front of him as he crept. Satisfied that Arran wasn't lying in wait, he approached and knelt down at the spot the trail ended. Victor inspected the ground for several long moments, trying to pick up the trail. He then continued moving around the tree, gazing intently at the ground and his surroundings.

Just as Victor had moved into a position for Arran to strike, Victor must have either deduced what was happening, or he heard Arran as he shifted, but either way, he barely had time to raise his arms as Arran fell from the tree.

Victor yelled in surprise as Arran fell on top of him.

"Argh!" The combined screams of both melding together in a cacophony of surprise and anguish as they fell to the ground.

Arran had hoped to get a clean killing strike from the surprise attack, but Victor had been able to slap the strike aside at the last possible moment. Arran's dagger falling to the ground.

They landed in a heap of tangled limbs as they hit the ground. Victor was first to react and maneuvered to climb on top of Arran as the two rolled. Victor was a little taller than Arran and, more importantly, heavier, and he was able to bring that weight to bear as they rolled, securing the dominant position. His hands quickly went to Arran's throat.

Arran gasped for breath as Victor bore down. Desperately, Arran released one of his hands, feeling around for his dropped dagger. Victor smiled as his hands continued to tighten around Arran's throat. Arran did not have much time left. His vision began to blur at the edges.

Then, as quickly as it started, everything stopped. Victor's smile quickly vanished as he felt the point of the dagger at his throat.

Reluctantly, Victor released his grasp on Arran's throat. "Conceded." He stood up dejectedly and backed up with hands on knees, panting heavily.

Arran took a few moments to catch his breath and let his vision return to normal. He rose to his knees, still breathing heavily. "What gave me away?"

Victor looked up and eyed him warily. "I was trying to figure out the meaning of the path around the tree when I remembered the dungeon exercise. It was just in time to see you falling on me from the branch above."

Without another word, Victor collected his fallen gear and departed.

Arran stayed for a while longer, taking a few gulps of water and eating a few of the nuts and berries he had collected. Then he headed straight west, hoping to pick up Stepf's trail before sundown.

Dark had fallen, and Arran had been unsuccessful in finding Stepf's trail. He decided to bed down for the remainder of the night. A fallen log across a small gully proved perfect. It offered good protection from one side and a clear line of sight out of the other. He ate the raw roots, berries, and nuts he had collected during the day and finished what was left of his water. He was exhausted from the day's events and the lack of sleep from the previous evening had caught up to him. He quickly fell asleep.

Arran awoke with a sudden shock. "Shriek!...Shriek!" He scrambled for his knife.

Wh...what...the hell was that?

Deep sleep still had his mind muddled. He finally found the knife where it had fallen to his side and got to his knees, knife held out in front of him. All of his senses were shakily coming to full alert as the fog of sleep broke under the onslaught of his adrenaline.

He listened intently, and then he heard it again.

"Shriek!"

He sighed and lowered his knife with a curse of frustration and fatigue.

It was a bird he concluded, probably an owl. His heart was pounding in his chest. He slowly crawled out of his hiding place to investigate. How long had he slept? He looked up at the sky and could just make out the faint glow of the moon through the canopy, still high in the sky.

Probably only two or three hours. *Well, crap.*

The rest of the night brought very little sleep, every small sound shocking him awake, and then the adrenaline forbidding his attempts at any further rest. Dawn was breaking when he finally decided he would get no more sleep and went to find the stream to refill his waterskin.

He breakfasted on nuts and berries again during his cautious trek to the stream. This stream was the only source of fresh water in the training area and would be a likely place to be discovered. Once he arrived at the stream, he studied the area carefully before venturing down to refill his waterskin and then quickly fell back into the safety and cover of the woods. He drank his fill, then refilled it once more before heading out to try and pick up Stepf's trail.

He found what he thought was Stepf's trail around mid-morning and followed it. A few hours later, he was confident he was on the right trail, discovering where Stepf had bedded the night before. It was also in a gully with cover on one side and a single point of entry. Arran grinned.

He continued tracking and was rewarded a short time later, finally catching sight of Stepf ahead of him. He was tracking parallel to the stream. Arran had been lucky that Stepf had already passed by his eventual point of entry earlier that morning. Now knowing where Stepf was, he put his plan in motion.

Arran spent the remainder of the afternoon keeping a watchful eye on Stepf, and set to gathering trap materials and, most importantly, a rabbit for dinner.

Arran set up his camp about a half mile southeast of where Stepf was preparing his own camp for the evening. He made a handful of crude traps, knowing that Stepf would most likely detect them, even at night, but that was not the point. They were bait number one.

As dusk was ending and the darkness of full night descended upon the forest, Arran started a small fire and cooked his dinner. The fire was only lit for about fifteen or twenty minutes, but that should be more than enough time for Stepf to pick up the smell of smoke and head his way. Arran ate his dinner, grateful for the respite from nuts and berries. Now he waited.

He set up his vigilance on the southeast side of his makeshift camp, kneeling behind a tree with thick shrubs on one side. He did not have to wait long.

"Ugh!" came a small muffled cry from the northwest side of the camp.

Arran grinned maniacally.

Gotcha!

He hadn't thought that Stepf would trigger a trap, so that turned out to be a bonus. Arran was now focusing all his attention towards the sound and that area of the camp. Silence. Nothing.

Was Stepf's Stealth ability so advanced that he couldn't detect him? If so, this might have been the dumbest idea ever. He had essentially invited him in.

The minutes crept by...Five? Ten? Then Arran saw it rather than heard it, a faint movement of shadow to the northeast and away from the initial area of disturbance.

Smart.

Arran could no longer make out any movement, but kept his eyes trained towards the eastern side of the camp. Sure enough, he finally saw movement. Stepf had circled the entire camp, essentially approaching from the opposite direction from the initial disturbance. Arran had put no traps on that side of the camp, but Stepf was wary and approached carefully. Arran watched as he surveyed the camp and any possible hiding places amongst the surrounding shrubbery. Arran never heard a sound.

He is good.

Stepf slowly and methodically worked his way around the camp looking for any trace of Arran. Arran had not moved a muscle, afraid that it might give away his position. He focused all his attention to his right and, hopefully, Stepf's approach. Stepf was extremely talented and Arran almost didn't catch the barest hint of movement, only ten paces away.

Arran forced himself to loosen his grip on his dagger. Sweat was forming in his palms.

Stepf moved back and away from the camp and began to circle away. Then he began to move back in, straight towards Arran's position.

Arran cursed inwardly, more at himself for this fool plan, than at Stepf.

Stepf was in a perfect trajectory towards Arran. He would need to move or risk being exposed.

Stepf stopped, now only a handful of paces away, but unable to see Arran in his hiding place and the sheer darkness of the night. Arran willed himself silent. Stepf spent several long agonizing minutes surveying the area in all directions. Seemingly satisfied, he headed towards the camp and the tree closest to Arran. Arran watched as Stepf sat crouched behind his own cover. Arran slowly raised his arm, dagger ready for the throw.

Stepf slowly rose and began coming around the foliage, heading towards Arran.

As soon as Stepf was clear, Arran let the dagger fly. With a loud crack, the hilt of the wooden dagger struck Stepf in the forehead, staggering him.

"Argh!" Stepf cried out, both hands reaching instinctively to his head.

Not wasting any time, Arran stepped forward, bending low and swung out his leg, sweeping Stepf's legs out from under him. Arran leapt on his chest, grabbing the fallen dagger, and holding it to Stepf's throat.

Stepf's eyes were watering from the hit on the head. He blinked a few times to clear the blur as the slow realization came into focus. "Conceded."

Arran relaxed and rolled off to the side, breathing heavily.

Arran awoke groggily, shivering from the cold dampness of the night. He was sleep-deprived, hungry, battered, and bruised from the week's brutal regime. His clothes were torn and covered in dirt and grime. As was he.

Was this the last day?

He had lost count of the days and was finding it hard to focus. He took a long drink from his waterskin and then struggled to his feet. He stared blankly at the now empty container, realizing he would need to replenish it soon. He sighed. That should probably be his first task of the day before he once again began the arduous task of tracking his foes.

With another long and heavy sigh, he cleared his bedding spot as best he could and headed off towards the stream. It should only be a half-hour walk from his current position.

He had not traveled far when a shout sent all his senses on high alert. He stopped and crouched reflexively, staring intently in the direction of the sound.

"Arran!" came the shout again. "Arran!"

Was that Instructor Shia?

Arran scrambled for cover.

"Arran!" The shout came again, this time much closer.

"The exercise is over. Time to return to camp."

Arran saw Instructor Shia coming through the trees.

Slowly and cautiously, Arran rose from his hiding spot and warily eyed the instructor.

"There you are. Come, the exercise is over."

Arran let out a long sigh of relief and shambled towards the instructor, following her back to the main camp.

They arrived at camp and he took in the site that had been his home for the last four, well, three weeks. The horses were packed, and the camp had been broken down. He was given the last remnants of the morning stew before the group headed back to Meitellen.

They arrived at the school stables, and Arran struggled to dismount and gather his things.

Shia watched him intently, a pang of pity for the young boy tinged her voice. "Take tomorrow off to recuperate." She placed a reassuring hand on his shoulder before turning away.

Arran stood stoically, almost unable to stand on his own two feet as he watched her leave. Victor and Stepf each came up to him, giving him a reassuring pat on the back, saying nothing. Arran barely managed a weak nod to the two as they also departed.

Arran made his way back to his room, garnering more than a few stares along the way. He disrobed and forced himself to take a bath. Upon returning to his room, Bran was there, waiting for him.

"I heard that you had returned. How did it go?"

Arran grunted as he fell onto his bed. "I honestly don't know." His voice came out in a hoarse croak. He barely recognized it as his own. Before Bran could ask anything else, Arran fell asleep.

He awoke the next day to find that he had slept until almost noon. He grimaced as he rose. His body ached from head to toe, and he was instantly aware that he was ravenous. He bathed again for good measure, dressed, and headed off to the dining hall.

He went through the line, grabbing an obnoxious plateful of food and went to sit down. As he was finishing off the huge meal, he noticed Mare headed in his direction.

"Damn, Country, you look horrible." She sat down next to him, looking him over with what Arran thought was genuine concern.

"Thanks for noticing. I feel just as bad. You should have seen me yester..." He stopped and looked up at her questioningly. "Um, Country?"

"It just came to me. Fitting I think." She waved a hand dismissively. "Hmmmm..." Mare muttered quietly to herself. "Do you mind? She opened her hand, palm out towards Arran."

Arran looked at her skeptically, but nodded in approval.

Mare looked around to make sure no one was paying attention as a small glow began forming in her hand. She placed her hand gently on Arran's chest and the soft glow quickly spread out, permeating his entire body. It was over in a matter of seconds.

Mare looked around to make sure no one was paying attention. "We're not supposed to practice healing outside the infirmary. Rules and all that." She smiled maniacally.

Arran shrugged his shoulders and moved his head from side to side. The majority of his aches were gone, and he felt...decently refreshed. He stared, openmouthed, at Mare.

"Just a little refresh spell to help with the small aches and pains. I didn't heal you completely. Your bruises and cuts will still heal naturally. I didn't want it to be too obvious, just in case." She winked.

Arran stood, stretching out his entire body and flexing. He could indeed still feel his bruises and see all the small cuts about his arms, but overall he felt much better.

"Thanks, Mare. This is amazing."

"You are welcome. It's kind of my thing. Besides, I don't want to have to listen to you moan on about it for days." She gave him one of her patented crooked smiles.

Arran smiled back and headed off for another plate of food.

Year 1304/May/Week 2
Week 10 of Third Term

Instructor Shia stood looking out her office window contemplatively. It had only been a few days since their return, but the boy had shown admirable resilience. She suspected the young priestess friend of his had something to do with it, but still...it had been an impressive outing. Her eyes fell to a sparring session, watching intently as the sounds of the practice weapons echoed in the courtyard. She took a sip of the still too hot tea and let her eyes wander, eventually finding Kallion, ever present and watchful, as he made his rounds.

A knock came at her door.

"Enter."

Klintoc sauntered into the instructor's office calmly, closing the door and coming to rest in front of her desk.

"Please, sit. Can I get you anything?"

He sat down and waved a hand. "I'm fine, Instructor."

There was a pause as Shia took a sip of her own tea. "What do you know of first-year student Arran?"

Klintoc's expression was one of confusion as he tried to recall the name. "Not much. I haven't even spoken to the lad. I've only seen him in passing. A friend of Bran's, I think."

"I see." Shia blew on her tea before taking another sip. She watched as Klintoc's mood shifted to annoyance.

"What is this about?"

She looked at him calmly, yet spoke with authority. "I want you to participate in the boy's evaluations next week."

"Instructor, I do not have the time..."

Shia cut him off. She knew he had little patience for school training. He had repeatedly refused all offers to become an instructor himself since graduating, but in this, she would hold fast.

"You still have investigations and inquiries here in Meitellen before you need to head back out into the field. A day, maybe two, is all I ask."

Klintoc eyed the instructor suspiciously. "Why?"

"There is something about this boy. He's proving an exceptional first-year student, maybe even better than you in first-year terms." This brought a grunt of derision from Klintoc, but she continued. "We recently returned from his four-week survival exercise and he scored six kills to only three against."

She thought she saw his eyes widened just a fraction at this news. It had been an impressive showing.

"His foes were both several terms ahead of him and he bested them. Would you like to know how he began the exercise? He spent the entire first day trekking through the forest, laying false trails, and circled back to the camp. He watched the next morning as Victor and Stepf left and then tracked Victor into a trap of his own making. Instead of hiding, he immediately took the tact of hunting them."

Klintoc nodded his head approvingly. "Still, is this worth my time with everything else that is going on?"

Shia's own temper flared for just a brief instant at his obstinance, but let it go before answering. "I believe so. I want your assessment of him, and..." She hesitated ever so briefly. "...I want a second opinion of what I have seen thus far before...before I move forward."

"Move forward?" Klintoc's brow furrowed, eying the instructor suspiciously for several long moments. "You mean to advance him."

It was not a question, and Shia did not answer.

"You think he is that talented?"

"I do."

Klintoc's brow furrowed in frustration, then abated. "Fine. I will participate."

Now it was Shia's turn to be surprised. Her eyes widened.

"What? If you feel this strongly about the lad, I'll give you my assessment."

"Thank you." A small measure of her tension eased at his acceptance.

Shia rose from behind her desk and walked around as the two strode towards the door. "I honestly thought this conversation was going to take much longer."

"Hmmph."

As Klintoc reached for the door, she put a gentle hand on his arm. "Keep this between us for now."

Klintoc made no reply as he left the room.

"What can I get you tonight?" Cindi asked, approaching the table.

Arran smiled. "What does Tan have on tap?"

"Bitter and wheat tonight."

"Nice, I'll have a wheat and send one to ol' Anders also, please."

"Can do." Cindi finished taking orders for the rest of the group and headed for the bar.

When she returned with their drinks, Arran waited for her to deliver Anders'. He raised his mug and Anders reciprocated the gesture. Anders took a long draft of the beer and then nodded his head in approval. Tan's unfiltered wheat was a favorite they both shared and was just coming into season.

As Arran returned his attention to his friends, he found them all staring at him. He let out a long, exasperated sighed.

"Okay, everyone, get it out." He knew his friends meant well, but he had never been one who liked being the focus of conversation.

Elinda mocked taking a drink. Speaking over the top of her cup to hide her face. "Soooo...evaluations." The cup did little to hide the smile spreading across her face.

"First-year eval's. It's kind of a big deal." Rayneer remarked. "I was a nervous wreck my first evaluations."

Mare looked at Rayneer speculatively. "I find that hard to believe."

She waved her hands up and down Rayneer's body. "I mean, just look at you!"

Rayneer chuckled at Mare's obvious baiting, but did not take it. "I was confident in my physical abilities, yes, but mentally I was a mess. There was, is, a lot of pressure on me...from my family." Rayneer looked away and down at his mug. "Especially my father." He hesitated before looking back up at the group. "My entire life has been filled with constant reminders of how my grandfather rose to prominence as one of the finest knights in the realms." Rayneer waved his hands high above his head grandiosely and with no small amount of sarcasm.

The group fell silent at the personal revelation from their friend and the implications.

"So, your father was not gifted then?" Arran asked.

Rayneer looked up sullenly. "No. It has bothered him his entire life. I think that is why he has put so much pressure on me to succeed. I sometimes wonder if things are worse because of it."

The mood turned somber as everyone sipped at their drinks.

"Well, I think Country will do just fine," Mare said assuredly, trying to lighten the mood.

Arran accepted Mare's lead to steer the conversation away from Rayneer. "Thank you, Mare. Can we change the subject? Have we heard any more news about the goings on in Valoor?"

This got everyone's attention.

"Not much," Elinda replied. "I have not heard of any other incidents as serious as the one in Freeholt. There have been several scouting parties sent out. If they have found anything, they are keeping it very quiet."

"I was wondering..." Arran began nervously and looked over at Anders. He leaned over the table and spoke quietly. "The outbreaks have been mainly focused on animals, from what we have heard. I remember Anders saying that everything has an aura, even animals. That means they have a connection to the Source, just like us. What if the animals' connection has become corrupted somehow, or it is manifesting differently, causing them to behave erratically?"

"Interesting theory," Mare replied. "That is a big if...but it would account for the heightened reaction Elinda saw at court and the response at the school. If the Source is involved, there would definitely be larger ramifications at play."

"I don't know," Elinda said, shaking her head. "It is interesting, but do we know enough about the Source to really come to that conclusion?"

Arran looked out over the inn, finding Anders again, sitting in his corner. He got up from the table.

"Where are you going?" Elinda asked.

"I'm going to go talk to Anders. If he can see auras, maybe he's seen something that could shed some light on something like this. I don't know. Call it a hunch."

He rapped the table with his knuckles, looked at his friends, and steeled himself for the upcoming conversation.

Anders did not acknowledge Arran's approach, never taking his eyes off whatever he was looking at out across the room. "I was wondering if you would come back."

"May I sit?"

Anders gestured his consent with a hand and Arran slid down onto the bench opposite.

Anders turned and leaned out over the table, both arms forward, clasping his mug and staring at Arran intently.

Arran was a little unnerved at the intense response and fidgeted in his seat before cocking his head to the side in question.

"What?"

Anders just stared at him. It was unnerving. He wasn't looking at Arran, not in his eyes like conversational, but up, down, and around his body.

Finally, he broke the intense stare and leaned back, looking down at the table. "My mug is empty."

"Huh? Oh! Your mug. Right." He held up his hand to get Cindi's attention, then two fingers.

Now Anders' focus was squarely back at Arran's eyes and his big eyebrows came together.

"What are you kids up to over there, whispering so intently with one another?"

Arran began fidgeting again, then forced himself to stop. "Funny you should ask. Well, that is kind of why I wanted to talk to you."

Anders did not answer, so Arran continued.

"Auras. I have a question about auras."

"And here I thought you came all this way for my charming personality."

Anders sat back in the booth, crossing his arms over his chest.

Cindi arrived, and Anders thanked her. He then took a long pull from his mug.

"Go on."

"Have you heard about the disturbances in northern Valoor?"

"I have. Vague reports of erratic behavior in animals. An attack where a few people died."

All of Arran's tentativeness evaporated as he dropped eagerly into the retelling of their information. "Right. Well, ever since the first report, the school officials and several of the top tier graduates have been meeting very secretively. If it were simply some wild animals, why all the fuss?"

"So you and your friends..." Anders nodded over in their direction. "...believe there is some conspiracy going on? A cover up?"

Arran shook his head. "We don't know. Maybe not a full on conspiracy, but something is strange about it, no?"

"Maybe."

"So, my question is, have you ever seen an aura that was, I don't know exactly how to put it. Wrong? Off? I don't know, different somehow?"

Anders looked at Arran with dead pan eyes for several long moments. He leaned back over the table, his voice turning hoarse and gravelly, just above a whisper.

"You want to know if the Source is involved?"

Arran nodded uneasily. Once again, Anders' intense glare unnerving him, his black eyes deep and penetrating. A cold shiver prickled the back of his neck and then it was gone.

Anders leaned back. "That is quite the intuitive leap."

Arran did not respond and busied himself with his beer, letting the strange moment pass.

Anders let out a long sigh and looked out across the inn for a long time before answering.

"I've had my suspicions...But!" He pointed his bony finger emphatically. "Do not take that as confirmation. All I have are observations and guesses."

Arran nodded in assent, sensing the gravity of what he was about to hear.

"At first I didn't give the differences in auras much thought. It happened only with an animal here or there, so I dismissed it. An animal's mind and their nature are different, so it made sense that their auras would also be different."

Arran leaned forward in anticipation.

"When I was younger and out fishing, I heard a rustle along the opposite shore. A wild boar came rushing out of the woods, tossing its head about, snorting and running erratically in different directions, seemingly heedless of its surroundings. The aura coming off the boar was...how did you put it? ...off. Usually, an aura is stable and soft. A faint glow, for lack of a better term. The boar's aura was inconsistent, pulsing wildly. I watched in fascination. It thrashed about on the shore and in the water for several minutes. Then, like it had discovered some purpose, began running down the shoreline at full speed. Without breaking stride or even aware of what it was doing, the boar ran head first, straight into a large boulder. I heard the crack of its neck. I sat stunned, not understanding what I had just witnessed. As the body sank to the ground and lay still, I watched as its aura slowly disappeared to nothing. I had never seen an aura like that before, nor have I since."

The two sat in silence for a long time, Anders' eyes unfocused and staring at nothing.

Anders returned from wherever he had gone in his thoughts and looked hard at Arran.

"I have thought about that incident many times over the years and yes, I have wondered if the Source could have somehow been connected. Still, it would be hasty to draw such a conclusion. We simply do not know enough about the Source, its makeup, its reason for being, or the machinations of the Patrons. There are too many unknowns."

"Have you ever spoken of this to any of the scholars at the school?"

"No." His reply was quick and flat. "I've never spoken of it to anyone save you just now."

Arran bobbed his head in thought. "You have to admit. The stories coming from northern Valoor and yours are eerily similar."

"Possibly. Or it is a coincidence and the issues in Valoor have a completely different cause?" He shook his head. "Too many unknowns."

Arran sat back, frustrated. He knew that Anders was right. They didn't have any solid evidence to link the two events and point to the Source as the link.

Arran took a deep breath. "I should be going."

"I trust that you will keep this private, no? I do not want to be dragged into whatever is going on. Do you hear me?"

"I promise."

Arran rose and pointed to Anders' half-empty mug. "Enjoy the wheat while you can."

Arran returned to his table and sat down. His friends all looking at him anxiously, taking in his grave look.

"So?" Mare finally asked.

Arran looked up at his friends. "Let's go back to school first."

Everyone nodded in assent as they finished their drinks.

Back in the Intelligence common room, Elinda busied herself making tea, while the rest of the group settled in, waiting for Arran to begin. When he finally retold Anders' story, no one spoke. A story about the Source such as this was unprecedented. Unheard of. The implications...far reaching.

"That's pretty horrific," Rayneer finally said. "I mean to watch an animal do that to itself and have the ability to see its aura. I mean..." He trailed off, not finishing the thought.

"He said he never saw that kind of aura again, right?" Elinda asked.

Arran nodded.

The group dropped back into silence for a long while, everyone lost in their thoughts until Bran stood up.

"Okay, we've had enough brooding for one night. To successful evaluations." He raised his cup.

The group rose in unison, welcome for the release of tension, and clinked their cups to Arran's future success.

Year 1304/May/Week 4
Week 12 of Third Term - Evaluations

After a hearty breakfast, Arran made for the training hall to begin the day. The nervous energy he had needed an outlet. As he was finishing the last of his movements, he saw Shia through the open door. He gathered his things, wiped his brow, and headed out to face the first day of his evaluations.

Day one was entirely physical in nature. The morning began with a ten-mile run. It was longer than he usually ran, but Rayneer had pushed them often enough that it wasn't too bad. It felt like a decent time, or at least 'he' thought so.

Four obstacle course runs followed, a different course each time, and twice as long as their normal runs. Noon was approaching, and he was allowed thirty minutes for a lunch break. The afternoon consisted solely of the obstacle course. There were four more runs, each one increasing in difficulty with the fourth being held after sunset. He had never run the course after nightfall, and it was by far the most challenging. The course was the longest of the day and he had incurred several penalties. Each one forcing him to retreat back to a predetermined starting position based on his progress.

The day had been an obvious test of his physical endurance and agility, and Arran had to admit, even with all of his training, he had been pushed to his limits. Only after returning from the four weeks at camp had he ever felt so fatigued. After a quick bath and a late meal by himself, he fell into bed.

Arran was shaken awake for what felt like only minutes later. He did not know what time it was and was told to dress and gather his gear before he was led out of the room.

Bran opened his eyes and quietly murmured, "Good luck." Arran did not hear the faint whisper of encouragement as the door quietly closed behind him.

As Arran was led through the training courtyard, he looked up at the night sky. The moon was only halfway through its nightly arc.

What time was it? Two? Maybe three?

They crossed the courtyard and Arran was led down into the maze and given instructions very similar to his previous exercises. Avoid detection, and achieve a requisite number of pickpockets, disarmed traps, chests, and hidden areas.

The maze was huge, by far the largest that he had encountered. The exercise was painstakingly slow, given the vast area and increased number of guards. Once his last hidden area had been found and the chest opened, Instructor Shia ended the exercise and led him out. He squinted at the bright light of the noonday sun.

After a quick meal, they immediately began the afternoon trials, which consisted of sparring matches. The matches varied his opponent, his weapon and his opponent's weapon, going through all the various iterations one could obtain between dagger, sword, and staff. It became evident in the last few matches that the lack of sleep and his fatigue were wearing him down. His form became sloppy, and he was bested numerous times. Dusk was falling when they finally finished and Instructor Shia approached him.

"That is all for today. Eat, rest, and meet me at the stables tomorrow morning at dawn."

Arran went to bed early, forgoing his friends' urging to relax with them in the common room. He was too tired. Additionally, if the upcoming trial was anything like his previous visit to the camp, he wanted to get as much rest now while he still could.

Arran arrived at the stables, as instructed. Shia was already there waiting for him, horses saddled and ready to go.

The trip to the camp was uneventful and boring. Shia did not engage him in any conversation and the few times Arran tried, her replies were terse and short. He gave up, and they finished the trip in silence.

They arrived at the camp and, other than a few mundane instructions, the instructor was eerily silent, seemingly lost in her own thoughts.

The next morning, Arran was instructed to gather only his daggers and staff. They departed, heading straight north. After about an hour, they began to turn towards the northeast. They were well past the designated area of his previous exercise.

About midday they came upon an old, abandoned fort. It sat nestled in what probably used to be a large clearing, but was now overgrown as the surrounding forest had slowly reached out to reclaim it. Arran was mesmerized by the slow decay of destruction that lay before him. The outer stone walls of the fort were mostly broken. Large heaps of stone lie around the clearing with only a few stubborn walls left standing with any resemblance of their former glory. Inside the outer walls were the remains of a handful of other structures, all in a similar dilapidated state. Not a single roof remained. In the few walls that remained, windows were nothing more than gaping holes, serving only as footholds for the creeping vines.

They made camp inside the walls in a small area that had been cleared of debris. It had obviously been used before. A small, well-used firepit sat in the middle.

They unpacked in silence. Arran sat opposite Shia as the fire's light flickered off the fort's crumbled remains, creating a myriad of dancing shadows within the confines of the ruins.

Shia studied Arran as he surveyed the ruins.

"Fort Samil."

Arran brought his attention back to the instructor as she continued.

Shia looked around the interior of the structure before continuing. "Samil was a knight of legend many generations past, four or five hundred years ago, if memory serves. When he retired, this land was granted to him and he constructed this fort. Isolated with only his thoughts and memories of a long career, Samil became increasingly paranoid. He began to build vast tunnels underneath the fort. Twists and turns, dead ends with traps, and exits scattered all around this area. Some as far as a mile away." She gazed off into the distance. "Once Samil passed away, he had no family to inherit the fort, and it was left abandoned. The school petitioned it for rights and we have used it for training ever since. A good majority of the tunnels have collapsed over time, but it still serves us well. It is a more natural environment that we cannot always duplicate in the dungeon scenarios."

Arran listened intently, engrossed with the instructor's story. It was the most she had said to him since they left Meitellen.

Shia picked up a short stick and poked at the fire, sending embers afloat as the flames regained some of their former strength. "Tomorrow's exercise is simple: traverse the tunnels, find the hidden chest, and return its contents back to me. The chest will be guarded by one other individual. You are not to engage the individual, the goal is for you to stay undetected as much as possible. If you are detected and dealt a killing blow or concede, hold position for five minutes, then continue. Questions?"

Arran shook his head. This exercise's objectives seemed far simpler than many he had already completed in the maze. He was missing something. There had to be a catch.

Arran spent the rest of the afternoon exploring the fort and meditating, trying to figure out the hidden difficulty of the exercise. Finally conceding that he would not come up with an answer, he retired early. The last thing he saw as he closed his eyes was the instructor. She sat impassively by the fire, eyes closed.

At first full light the next day and with a good morning meal, the instructor led Arran to the largest of the interior buildings. Inside, and at the back of the broken down structure, was a stairway.

"Any last questions?"

Arran shook his head, and the instructor motioned for Arran to enter the tunnels.

Arran paused as he entered the stairwell, letting his eyes adjust to the dim light of a single sconce at a landing, maybe twenty steps down. There was another set of stairs leading off to the left. He descended cautiously, scanning for traps. He traversed four sets of stairs, each turning left, until he finally exited into a room roughly twenty feet square. A single sconce on the right wall eerily lit the room. The other three sconces were broken, two lay on the floor, and one still hanging stubbornly awkward on the wall. There were two exits apart from the one he just entered. One against the far wall, door hanging ajar, and one to his left with no door at all.

He began by surveying the room, slowly walking around while looking for traps or anything else of interest. Two simple detection traps were located in front of each the doors. He disarmed them both. He mentally flipped a coin and chose the entry to his left.

The hallway past the entry appeared to go straight for some distance, but he could not be sure. The light from the main room barely illuminated the initial room, much less the hallway. His increased dark vision assisted him, but as he made his way down the hall, it began to curve, eliminating any assistance from the dim light of the room. Darkness enveloped him less than two dozen paces in.

He crept down the hallway warily, right hand outstretched as he felt his way down the right wall. The darkness was as pervasive as any he had ever encountered and it unnerved him.

Getting discovered this close to the beginning of the trial would be stupid.

He stretched out with all of his senses as he progressed and then stopped. There was something on the opposite wall ahead of him. Was it a glimmer? His Sight ability was good, but in the pitch black he was hard-pressed to make it out. He approached the source slowly and found that it was a moss or lichen of some kind, giving off a faint glow. It wasn't much, but it offered some respite from the total blackness of before.

He continued past the dim light and back into darkness, right hand still out against the wall. Suddenly, his hand fell away into an opening. He froze, looking in the direction of the open space beside him. Several small patches of the moss glowed along the new juncture as it curved to the right. A faint light painted the left wall as the hall curved right out of sight. The hallway he was in continued forward, but he made up his mind quickly. He went right.

The passage was not horribly long and as he made the turn of the curving tunnel, he was greeted with the source of the faint light. Ahead of him was a small room. The door was hanging by a single hinge as the faint light spilled out around its frame. Arran approached the entrance, inspecting the door for traps and surveying the inside of the room. The sconce providing the light was hanging loosely at an angle on the same wall as the door. In the middle of the room was a stone...table? No, it was more like an altar, solid and tapering up from the base. There was one additional exit on the opposite side of the room. The door was closed. Satisfied there weren't any detectable traps, Arran slowly approached the altar, circling it, and inspecting for traps.

Arran's head was violently pulled back as someone grasped him by his hair! The cold steel of a blade came to rest on his neck. He froze. The blade pressed hard into his neck, on the verge of drawing blood.

Arran's shoulders slumped. "Concede."

Nothing happened. The blade did not retreat and the grip on his head tightened. Then he was shoved violently into the altar, his chest hitting the edge with a sting of pain. He gasped for air as his lungs emptied. By the time he righted himself and looked back, his assailant was gone. The door that had been closed was now open.

But which way did he go? I didn't hear a single footfall!

He leaned against the altar, replaying the scenario in his mind. There had not been the barest hint of sound. He had made an assumption about the closed door and the protection it provided him. He would not make that mistake again.

After five minutes, Arran continued through the now open door behind the altar. He closed the door behind him, shutting off the light of the room. He didn't move, letting his eyes adjust back to the darkness of the tunnels. Unlike the maze, he was unable to figure out the configuration of these passages. The maze was always square or rectangular, but here the passages seemed to curve and turn back in too many directions to get a feel for where he was at or where he had come from. He guessed that was what Shia had meant about a more natural environment that the maze could not replicate.

Time lost all meaning as he progressed through the passages. Four times he found himself back in the main entry room, never finding any hidden areas or the chest. The only consolations were that he had not been detected again since the first mistake in the altar room and the pervasive moss that helped stave off the worst of the darkness. Despite this, his nerves were fraying. The need for constant vigilance and the darkness were beginning to take its toll.

Arran cursed at himself in a whisper after reaching the main entry hall once again. He should have had the foresight to use something to mark his way, a mark on a wall, or maybe place stones in recognizable patterns. He had been down here for hours and he could still start using the markers, but he had lost a lot of valuable time not thinking of the idea from the beginning.

He decided to try the left tunnel once more. He came to the first junction and glared down the passage that led to the room of his earlier mistake. He had not followed this passage straight, though. Had he? He knelt and placed three stones side by side on the right wall of the passage he had gone before and then continued straight.

Arran stopped when he thought he caught the faintest shadow of movement forward and to his left. Was there an alcove there? Another hallway? He crept his way in that direction and it was indeed another passage to the left, and it was long. The faint glow of the moss speckled the walls and disappeared into the distance. It was the longest straight passage he had yet to come across. He placed his three stones at the base of the right wall and moved down the passage.

As he moved down the hall, he could see a faint glow. As it became more prominent, he saw that a sliver of light was coming from the base of a door. He looked around in the feeble light and noticed that the hallway had gotten larger. The ceiling was much higher, at least twice his height now, and it had widened out by several paces. Near the top of walls, right before reaching the ceiling, there were several alcoves running parallel to the floor, just long enough for a man to lay down in.

He shuddered at the implications.

He could not see any way to climb up to investigate the alcoves, nor was it possible to see if they contained anything, or, more importantly, anyone. He would need to keep a watchful eye on his back.

He eased his way to the door, inspecting it for traps. Satisfied, he slowly opened it halfway and peered into the room. It was surprisingly well lit and appeared to have been a study. It was a good-sized room with numerous shelves and a large desk near the back wall. A broken chair lay behind. There were no other visible exits from his vantage. He entered the room, sliding against the wall just inside the door and then turning back to survey the passage behind him. He shut the door. He looked down and found some debris and spread it around near the base of the door.

Not going to get me that way again.

He spent a considerable amount of time investigating the room, believing it was a good spot for something hidden, but in the end, he found nothing.

He leaned against the desk with a heavy sigh. He begrudgingly decided he had spent enough time in this room, but could not shake the notion that there was something here he missed. It seemed too perfect. He took one last look around and headed for the door.

Very deliberately, he removed the rubble he had placed at the base of the door, opened it just enough to peek out, and then slid back into the hallway, shutting the door behind him. He took a moment to let his eyes adjust, wishing he could have found a way to get to the small alcoves near the ceiling. The chair in the room had been broken, and the desk was far too large to move, and would have made too much noise. He resigned himself to come back if he could find something to boost him up.

Arran cautiously made his way back down the hallway. He stopped. He strained all his senses, something...he dove forward into a roll and came up on his knees, facing back the way he came. There was nothing. Just the faint light emanating from the door. His heart was pounding, ringing in his ears despite the silence of the dungeon. As he knelt, body tense, he began to feel foolish for his skittishness. He rose, took a few calming breaths, and turned to continue back to the main hallway.

As he returned to the junction with the main hallway, he knelt and found the three stones he had placed earlier and then continued left. After a few dead-end hallways that had been blocked by cave-ins and a handful of traps, which he disarmed, he stopped. He had been following this hallway for a long time now with nothing to show for it. He was just about to turn around when he heard a faint noise in the dark ahead. Arran knelt and pressed himself close to the wall, listening. He listened for what seemed like forever, but he did not hear the sound again.

Grimacing at the obvious bait, he followed in the direction of the sound. After all this time, he couldn't turn around at the first encounter of anything halfway worthwhile in this mess of hallways.

He didn't know how long he had been going, but a sense of hopelessness began to edge back into the corners of his mind. Had he imagined the noise? The hallway had become nothing more than a bare, rough tunnel, obviously not maintained, or as cared for as the previous passageways. It was noticeably cooler and light was scarce. The moss had become much more intermittent, and he was forced to feel his way along in some sections. As he began to give in to the thought of turning around, the tunnel ahead took a sharp turn to the right. His stubbornness was finally rewarded. The tunnel's sides flared out several paces on both sides and the ceiling rose as before. At its end was a massive set of double doors. Faint light was seeping out from the crack in between. The doors were tall, stretching from floor to ceiling, and each was easily five feet wide.

Arran examined the newly enlarged tunnel, no alcoves, no other exits, just the rough hewn rock and earth of a tunnel. Arran approached the doors. There was no discernible lock that he could find, simply two large vertical iron handles, each adorned with a lion's head at the top. Finding no traps on this side of the door, he grabbed the handle of the left door and slowly pushed it inwards. Wary of traps, he cautiously entered the room, pressing his back against the opposite door as he closed it.

The room appeared to be another study or...

Library.

There were rows upon rows of shelves with rotting books and scrolls in various stages of decay. Even in the faint light and his obscured view, he could feel the vastness of the room. It was the largest single area he had come across so far. In front of him was a path to the center of the room between the shelves of books. At the center was a round table, two chairs, and a single candle burning in the middle. He cautiously made his way to the center and towards the table. His heart was pounding in his ears as he nervously checked every corner and every aisle of shelves as he crept forward.

The table had a few stacks of books and various papers scattered about. A few of the books lie open, covered in dust, as if someone left them there, bookmarked for a further read, never to return. He walked around the table, surveying the room. The room was circular, with the rows of shelves spiraling outwards from the center table. Some areas seemed orderly, the shelves lining up with precision, while in other sections the shelves were facing at odd angles, some even tilted over and resting upon one another.

This room is going to take forever to investigate.

Resigned that he could not pass up such a find, he collected a stack of blank papers from the table and rolled several pieces together tightly lengthwise for a makeshift light source. It wasn't ideal, but it would do.

He went back to the entry doors, remembering his earlier

mistake, and spread out some debris at the base of the doors. He decided to survey the perimeter of the room first. Turning left from his entry, he began examining the perimeter. There were alcoves with small statues about every ten paces, mostly of animals in various vicious poses. Most were in some state of disrepair with missing heads, arms or legs half broken, and the like. The room was easily several hundred feet across. He had almost finished the perimeter and made his way back to the entry doors when he felt the sharp sting of a dagger at his side. As he tried to turn and face his assailant, another cold blade followed quickly at his throat. This time drawing a trickle of blood.

Arran gasped in surprise and pain as he whispered the dreaded words.

"Concede."

The dagger stayed pressed sharply against his side for a few moments longer; the tip pressing past his armor with a prick of pain, and then it was gone.

In a voice as cold and hard as Arran had ever heard, his assailant spoke. "Come. The exercise is over." In a flurry of dark robes, the assailant swept past Arran and threw back the cowl covering his head, and pulled down the mask that had covered the bottom half of his face. As he approached the doors, he turned to face Arran.

"Why the left door?"

Arran started at the question and the first real sounds he had heard in hours. He looked up from the small wound in his side that was already staining his shirt red.

Klintoc!

He stood there dumbfounded, in shock, surprise and, if he was honest, a little bit of infatuation with the direct question from the man.

Klintoc sighed with exasperation.

"It's not a hard question."

"Uh, sorry, it's just that. I mean, you're..."

"Yes, yes. Why the left door?"

Arran took a deep breath and centered himself. "Most people are right-handed, and I thought that if a trap was set, it would most likely be behind that door, assuming they didn't just trap both. It was pointless. I didn't find anything."

Klintoc looked at him curiously.

"Hmmm..."

Klintoc closed his eyes and, with one quick motion, opened the right door as a bright flash went off, blinding Arran and incapacitating him for a few moments.

"You made a sound decision, then followed it up with bad tradecraft, and an even poorer assumption."

Klintoc eyed Arran piercingly, and he shrunk beneath the glare.

"Where did you search for traps?"

Arran pointed to the floor and the space between the doors where they met.

Klintoc pointed to the top hinge of the door.

Arran groaned. He had not thought to check that high.

"One more thing before we leave this room: How was I able to obtain your concession?"

"Because you are better than me." Arran's reply was quick and matter-of-fact.

Klintoc rolled his eyes. "Try again. I've been tracking you all day, and this is only the second concession I obtained. Why?"

Arran hesitated, giving more thought before answering. He finally gave up and shrugged his shoulders.

"I don't know."

Klintoc let out a long sigh and muttered, "What the hell are they teaching you then?"

Klintoc's voice took on a slow, soft cadence as if he were talking to a child. "What were you doing when I caught you?"

"Searching the perimeter of the room."

"If you suspected someone might be in the room, what do you think they might be doing?"

"Probably observing me."

"Correct. So, as you 'methoodicalllly'..." Klintoc drew out the last word dramatically, "...searched the perimeter, you made yourself..."

He trailed off, looking to Arran expectantly for the completion of his thought.

"Predictable."

Arran finished the statement dejectedly, sagging in upon himself as he answered.

Klintoc stood up straight. "Exactly. Never be predictable." He turned and led Arran out of the dungeon.

———

Instructor Shia sat at her desk, staring at the mountain of reports strewn in front of her.

So much information and yet so little.

A knock came at her door.

"Come in," she said more brusquely than she had intended.

Klintoc entered and moved across the room in his typical lithe manner to stand in front of the desk.

The instructor looked up without saying a word as the two exchanged glances that conveyed far more than words. After a few moments, Klintoc simply nodded.

"So, you have confirmed my suspicions, then?"

"Yes." The reply was short and curt.

The instructor shifted through the papers on her desk, found the one she was looking for, and held it out for Klintoc.

"That is a historical list of students who have been evaluated ahead of schedule."

Klintoc took the list and studied it. The list contained only six names, with the majority from early in the school's history. The Intelligence order was younger then, and the leadership had been eager to get their agents into the field. It did not go well. After a few early and unfortunate deaths, the school tightened their qualifications, realizing that there was no substitute for proper training. So much so that the last such advancement had been over a hundred years ago.

"This is a very short list."

"So, you see my dilemma. If I choose to submit his advancement, it will not be without serious scrutiny."

Klintoc sat down and placed the list back on the desk. They sat in solemn contemplation for several minutes before Klintoc broke the silence.

"Would you like me to personally present my findings to the board?"

Shia looked up in surprise. "That would...be appreciated. Reading your findings is one thing, but having it presented to them in person would be far more persuasive."

"Mmmhmm."

"Have you finished your report then?"

"I have not. It will be done by the end of the day and delivered to you."

"And..." Shia's eyebrows rose expectantly, pausing for him to continue, obviously not wanting to wait for the written report.

Klintoc smiled at his old instructor. "Patience never was your strong suit, was it, Instructor?"

Shia could only manage a forced smile at her former pupil.

"Given that he is a first-term student, his skills are extremely advanced. Even students with formal training prior to attending the school are not near his level. He was what? A blacksmith's son? Either his skills were intrinsic, and the training brought them out, or he has an abnormally strong gift from the Patrons. Or both. If you were to ask me without any prior knowledge of the lad, I would probably place him firmly in third year."

Klintoc saw a gleam in Shia's eyes. She was obviously pleased that her assumptions were proved correct.

"As for the evaluation exercise, I subdued him twice. I probably could have gotten a few more, but he was extremely wary after the first concession. I have not participated in many evaluations, but the simple fact that I had to work for the concessions I did get speaks volumes. Additionally, he came very close to detecting me on one occasion, even while I was using Shadow. I would venture that no other student in the entire school could have done that."

Shia's eyes widened at the last. "Good. Can you present this to the board with the same conviction?"

Klintoc chuckled. "I've never been one to mince words. I think I can manage. Will there be anything else?"

"No. I trust I still have your discretion for now?"

Klintoc gave her an evil grin as he rose. "As always, Instructor."

Shia watched as her former pupil, and if she were honest with herself, friend, leave. She turned in her chair and stared out the window, wondering how all of these events seemed to be converging.

Coincidence?

She shook her head unconvincingly. There was only one problem with that conclusion. Shia did not believe in coincidence.

"Congratulations!" the group cheered as Arran entered the common room. Arran made a grand flourish of a bow to his friends and then began clapping his hands high in thanks. They cheered even louder at his gesture.

Arran walked over and fell into a chair as Rayneer handed him a cup of cider, which he took and quickly half-drained, settling back lazily into the chair.

First year was complete!

He could finally relax for a bit and simply enjoy the company of his friends. He looked around at the group that had come to be his new...family. Arran had never really thought of it that way before, but they had become much more than just friends or fellow students. He had relied on them for support and they on him. It felt good. It felt right. Arran drained his mug as Mare finished a raunchy joke that made Rayneer's ears turn red. Everyone laughed. It felt good to laugh. They never seemed to have enough time to just enjoy a simple thing as laughter as of late.

No, no somberness tonight. Tonight would be fun.

Rayneer refilled his cup.

Arran stretched out, resting his crossed feet on the table. "So what are everyone's plans for break?"

Bran answered first. "I have to go back home. Father wants me to attend some gatherings. I think he is beginning his push for me to court someone with a bit more vigor." He grimaced. "Of his choosing, of course. It will be tiresome."

Several of the group nodded in agreement.

"I will be heading home, also," Elinda replied. She looked down and away from everyone as she said it, like she had something more to say. Everyone turned to her expectantly.

Hesitantly, she raised her head. "I wanted to ask everyone if they would be up for visiting Valoor with me during next break? I was going to ask father if he would sponsor the trip while I was back."

Mare beamed with excitement. "Why so cheeky? That would be fantastic! A free trip to Valoor and a chance to check out the princess' home grounds? Done!"

"I believe my father would agree, if for no other reason than to forge ties with another house," Bran replied.

"I'd also need to ask my father, but I don't believe he would object," said Rayneer. "Politically speaking, he would probably jump at the chance, same as Bran's."

Arran just shrugged his shoulders. "I don't typically have anything else going on during breaks. I'm in. Sounds like fun."

Elinda let out a sigh of relief. "Good. I'll ask father and see if he will approve."

Mare looked at Elinda suspiciously. "Why are you so nervous?"

Elinda looked up sheepishly at Mare.

"Elllindaaa."

Elinda stared at her hands, which were nervously curling in and out on her lap. "Okay, I might have another reason for asking all of you to come." She looked up at Mare. "I want to go and visit the town where the outbreak occurred." She looked down again, feeling everyone's eyes on her. "I thought it would seem less suspicious with everyone going."

"So you want to mess around in realm affairs?" Mare said indignantly.

"Not mess around so much as...take a little trip up to Freeholt, sample some of the local fare. Their maple syrup is to die for, by the way, and you know, maybe partake in a little of the town gossip."

"Syrup and gossip?" Mare said, cocking her head to the side mockingly. "For an innocent-looking mage princess, you sure have a devious side."

"Why, Mare!" Elinda said, feigning shock and putting a hand to her chest. "That might be the nicest thing you have ever said to me!"

Elinda scanned the room expectantly. "So it's settled then?"

Everyone agreed, and Elinda relaxed back in her chair, looking quite pleased with herself.

INTERLUDE

Spirit stood at her desk, anxiously surveying the mountain of compiled notes. She was dreading this moment, but knew it was necessary. Her study of the anomalies was at a standstill and she needed help.

A light knock came at the door. She turned and looked at the door with reluctance. With a heavy sigh, she went to answer it.

"Morning, Breanna."

Breanna entered the room without replying, striding stiffly to the couch.

"Tea?"

"No." Breanna's tone was terse and curt as she sat. Then she stared at the floor in front of her and her shoulders sagged. Her demeanor slowly relaxed. "I'm sorry, sister. This escapade of yours has me on edge." Breanna looked up sullenly. "When you called… well, I immediately feared the worst."

Spirit did not meet her eyes.

She doesn't know how right she might be.

Breanna tilted her head, her curiosity and suspicion suddenly aroused. "So, I was right, then? Something is wrong?"

Spirit sat down across from her and lifted her eyes.

"Yes...and no? More...odd. I cannot figure it out, and I was hoping that you could help."

Breanna shook her head sadly. "Oh, Spirit, what have you gotten us all into?"

Breanna straightened herself, assuming her usual confident countenance. "Tell me."

Spirit took a deep breath and began.

"Do you recall the incident with the adventuring team and the cave where we had initially placed the sourcestone?"

"Yes, the team followed a group of unruly bears into the cavern of the sourcestone. They were on a commission to subdue the animals. They were successful, but at great cost. Only one survived. We later discovered that the animals had been adversely, affected...changed... by prolonged and direct proximity to the sourcestone. It is why we moved it farther into the mountain and closed it off."

Breanna looked up at Spirit in distress. "Has it been discovered?"

"No, no, I have checked. The sourcestone is undisturbed and undiscovered. It is not the issue, at least I don't think so, not directly. But the behavioral and physical changes that we observed in the bears...it is happening again. On a much smaller scale, but the evidence is there."

Breanna took a few moments as she thought.

"So erratic behavior in some animals, but no such evidence in the humans?"

"Correct. The first incident was in northern Valoor, near the mountains containing the sourcestone. A beast, the remnants of what used to be a boar, entered a village in a frenzy, attacking anything that got in its way. The villagers were able to put it down, but...there were a few deaths." Spirit paused.

"Are you sure you wouldn't like some tea?"

The sudden look of annoyance from Breanna was enough of an answer.

"Right, then. My first inclination was, of course, the sourcestone. Maybe its power was beginning to seep out, affecting the general area due to its proximity. We've observed how much stronger it has become. But...that didn't seem to fit the more I began to investigate." Spirit rose and began pacing around the room as she continued. "I started to notice similar anomalies across the continent. The distances became too great and so I have been forced to dismiss the sourcestone itself, at least for now. More and more incidents began to appear. Once I knew what to look for, it was easier to track them down, but there does not seem to be any discernible pattern. Additionally, once I find an incident, whatever anomaly caused the issue had already occurred. I cannot pinpoint a source." Spirit stopped her pacing and turned back to Breanna.

"If you would like, I can show you on the map."

"Maybe later." Breanna was already deep in thought with the information from Spirit. "How about the other continent? Have you discovered anything there?"

"I have not, but until we have a reasonable explanation, I have not ruled out the possibility."

Breanna leaned back deep into the couch, arms crossed, while one hand twirled with a strand of her hair.

"I think I will take you up on that tea, if you don't mind."

"Of course."

Spirit returned a short while later, placing the serving tray on the table, steam silently rising between them.

Breanna leaned in to pick up the cup, blew across its surface, then took a sip.

"Have any seafaring animals been affected?"

"No, not that I have found so far, but I have to admit, I have only given the oceans a cursory pass."

"What manner of animal tends to be affected from your analysis?"

"Small to midsize. The boar in northern Valoor is the largest I have seen so far." Spirit's brow furrowed, wondering where she was going with this line of thought. "What are you getting at, Breanna? Do you think type and or size of animal makes them susceptible?"

"I don't know." She took another sip of tea contemplatively. "We are missing something."

The two sat in silence for a long while, sipping their tea, before Breanna finally sat forward and rubbed her eyes.

"I need to rest. I will do some analysis of my own and we can speak later to compare our notes."

"Of course."

They rose together, and Spirit gave Breanna a hesitant smile.

"What?" Breanna said incredulously.

"There might be one other small consideration."

Breanna sighed. "What now?"

"One of the villagers has been exploring and, if their progress continues, I believe they may discover the other continent."

"Hmm...this was always a possibility. Bah, there isn't much we can do about it now, we'll have to wait and see." Breanna's face became furrowed in question. "Do they already have the means to make such a trip between continents?"

"Possibly. The villagers have extended their reach across a vast majority of the continent, primarily via the rivers, and have become avid mariners. Making the leap to sea travel is a big jump, but they are a resilient and cunning people, even without their Source abilities."

"Interesting. Is there anything else?" Breanna said derisively.

"No. That is the whole of it."

As they made their way to the door, Spirit rested her hand on Breanna's arm.

"Thank you."

Breanna nodded wearily and departed.

CHAPTER 7
SECOND YEAR
YEAR 1304 / JUNE / WEEK 2

Week 2 of Term Break

"Hey." Rayneer tilted his head up in greeting as he sat down across from Arran, attacking his breakfast with vigor. "What's going on today?"

It was the second week of break, and the two friends had spent the majority of their time together. Primarily, this meant training and Rayneer's insufferable penchant for long distance runs. This was offset by Arran insisting that they also continue their classroom studies, which meant books.

"I thought we could train a bit this morning, then head into town and visit the bookstore." Arran acted very nonchalant as he spoke, suggesting the trip through a mouthful of eggs.

Rayneer eyed him warily. "Bookstore?"

Arran set down his fork and continued enthusiastically. "Yeah, it's called Notable Tomes, and Quil, the owner, is quite knowledgeable. I've never come away disappointed."

Arran had become a regular customer of the bookstore, just as

Quil had anticipated from the first time he had visited. He was always on the lookout for any new finds from Quil on Sai'el and, much to his surprise, any other old and obscure history Quil recommended. History had become a growing interest for Arran, and he now had a small collection of books growing in his dorm chest.

Rayneer sneered at the suggestion. "I think I'd rather run extra laps than go to a bookstore."

"Come on. Expand your horizons a bit. I'll bet you first round at the Goose that you find something interesting."

"A cup of ale against my disdain for reading? You are on, my friend."

"So, did I just hear a bet?" Mare plopped down beside Arran, snagging a piece of bacon off his plate.

"Yes, you did. Rayneer is going to take the dangerous quest to the bookstore today," Arran said in a mockingly scary tone.

Rayneer glared, while Mare grinned mischievously.

"Mind if I come along? I think I would like to see this."

"Sure," Arran replied. "We're going to get a run in and maybe some sparring after breakfast, then we will meet out front after?"

"Sounds good." Mare grabbed a piece of toast and dodged Arran's half-hearted slap of her hand as she rose. "See you then."

Arran was sitting on the front steps of the school, watching the townsfolk go about their everyday activities while he waited for his friends to arrive. He enjoyed watching people, wondering what they were thinking, what task they were on, and observing their interactions with one another. His Observance skill working overtime as he took it all in.

Arran suddenly felt a nudge in his back, turning to see Mare with Rayneer right behind her.

"Let's go, book geek," Mare said with a wink.

The familiar tinkle of a bell announced their entry to Notable Tomes as the trio entered the bookstore. Quil was at the counter near the back of the store unpacking an arrival of new books. He looked up at the sound of the bell, a smile breaking out on his face as he recognized Arran.

"Welcome back, young Master Arran." His smile was genuine and stretched out across his face.

"Thank you, old Master Quil." The affable greeting was now a ritual every time Arran came to the store.

Mare quickly peeled off and began combing through the bookshelves for something of interest, as Arran and Rayneer approached the counter.

"Quil, I would like to introduce a fellow student and friend, Rayneer."

"Welcome. It is an honor, young sir." Arran grinned at the greeting.

Ever the politician and salesmen.

"And to you, Master Quil," said Rayneer, returning the gesture.

Arran eyed the new arrival of books with eagerness. "So, I see you've received some new books. Anything I'd be interested in?"

"I'm afraid not. These are more instructional and hobby in nature, rather than historical."

Arran's enthusiasm deflated. "Oh well, we'll just look around then and leave you to your unpacking." Arran headed off towards the history section. Rayneer followed along, obviously unsure of himself.

As Arran reached the familiar section, he turned and noticed Rayneer standing stoically a few feet away, not actually looking at anything.

"You can at least try to look at the books, you know?"

He shrugged his shoulders. "What for? I told you, books are not my thing."

Arran thought for a few seconds and then strode past Rayneer, heading back to the front desk. "Follow me."

Arran returned to the counter where Quil was finishing up his work.

"Quil, my friend here is finding it difficult to enjoy the art of perusing. Maybe you would like to help?" Arran gave him a small wink.

"I see. It can be a bit overwhelming at first if you do not know where to start. Tell me, what interests you? Did you have a hobby as a youth, or maybe an activity that you enjoyed?"

Rayneer looked at Arran suspiciously, then turned back to Quil.

"My training is, of course, my focus, and the instructors are more than capable in that regard."

Rayneer grinned at Arran, proud that he had avoided whatever it was Arran was playing at.

Quil continued unperturbed at the young man's casual dismissal. "True...very true. They are quite knowledgeable." Quil rubbed his chin thoughtfully. "How about your youth? Was there anything you enjoyed doing or something that piqued your interest?"

Rayneer turned to Arran, then back to Quil as he thought for a few moments.

"Maps."

"Hmmm...maps. Anything in particular about maps?"

"I liked studying the detail of the terrain and how my father would play out a battle, trying to figure out the tactics before they occurred."

"So, maps and battle tactics..." Quil trailed off in thought before stepping out from behind the counter.

"Come this way." Quil headed off into the shelves, stopping near the history section where they had previously begun their journey. He extended a long and delicate finger across the books with reverence.

"Here we are." Quil pulled out a massive leather bound volume, handing it over to Rayneer with both hands.

Rayneer took the book and looked at the cover, reading aloud. "A Treatise on Geography and Battle."

"Yes, I believe the author spent several years on that one, interviewing many notable generals and copying various maps used during their campaigns."

"Hmm..." Rayneer muttered, opening the book.

Quil gestured to a reading table at the end of the row. "Might I suggest the use of one of the reading tables? It is a big book and you'll find that many of the maps need to be unfolded."

Rayneer quietly headed off to the table, book in hand, head down as he went.

Arran leaned over and whispered. "That was expertly done, if I do say so myself."

"I've been at this a while." Quil grinned and headed back to the front counter.

Arran still had not found anything fruitful and was back at the counter talking to Quil when Mare arrived, setting a book down in front of Quil.

"I'll take this one."

"Very good. Ahh, very popular that one. A good choice, if I may say."

Arran bent over to look at the book, "Adventures from Afar: A Romance Novel." Arran could not help the grin spreading across his face.

Mare turned on him abruptly. "What!"

"Nothing. Nothing at all." Arran raised his hands in defense. "I just...well, never would have guessed you for...umm..."

"For what, Arran!" Mare interrupted, hands on hips defiantly. Her face furrowing.

"For...uh, an avid reader of adventures," he stammered.

Mare glared. "Hmmph. One word my country friend, layers. Everyone must have layers, my dear Arran." She quickly retrieved her book, turned and tucked it in her satchel.

"Lay..." Arran was about to reply when Quil rested his hand on Arran's arm.

"Probably best to leave that be, son," he whispered.

Arran looked at Quil dumbfounded, but took the advice, never finishing the comment.

Mare turned back, looking around. "Where is Rayneer?"

Arran gestured over his shoulder with his thumb, pointing at the reading table where they had left him.

Mare's eyes widened as they approached. Rayneer looked completely out of place. His huge frame bent over and totally engrossed, like a small child trapped in a man's body. He crouched over the book. A massive map unfolded. The map was easily three times the width of the book, almost taking up the entire length of the table. Rayneer was gently running his finger across the map in thought, flipped back a few pages to read some text and then returned to the map.

Arran and Mare stood in utter amazement for a few moments until it was obvious Rayneer was not going to acknowledge them.

"You know, this isn't a library, Rayneer. If you like the book, you should buy it." Mare said.

Rayneer looked up at the two of them and relaxed back with a sigh. He began quietly folding the map back into the book and closed it.

Rising from the chair, he muttered angrily. "Ugh! Now I have to buy the book and first round at the Goose." Shaking his head, he made his way back to the front counter.

The trio of friends made their way to the Singing Goose for lunch and, as promised, Rayneer bought the first round.

"I'm going to beat you!" Rayneer yelled over his shoulder. "Better hustle up, little man."

Arran was lagging behind, as usual, on the long run Rayneer had set out for them this morning. He was good for shorter distances and sprints, but in these long runs, Rayneer was far superior, his Resilience an unfair advantage. Arran struggled to find a last bit of energy for the final push, but could not overtake the larger man.

"By the Patrons," Arran panted, leaning over and taking long breaths in an effort to try and overcome the nausea he felt rising in his throat.

Rayneer smiled down at him, clapping him on the back.

"You are getting better, my friend. I almost had to try this time."

"I...hate...you," Arran managed between breaths.

Rayneer laughed.

"Come on, let's grab some water." Rayneer helped Arran upright as they made their way back across the bridge to school.

The two sat in silence for a while as they enjoyed the cold water and rest after the long run.

Having recovered a bit, Arran asked. "How long was that run?"

"That was about twelve miles today."

Arran nodded. "Let's not do that again."

Rayneer laughed. "It's good for you. Builds character and stamina."

Arran sat up, glaring at his large friend.

"I think I will go practice some meditation and poses in the hall. Catch up with you for lunch?"

"Sure." Rayneer headed off towards the sparring dummies.

Arran took a few more blessedly cool drinks of water, then made his way over to the Intelligence hall, which was empty given the term break. He grabbed a mat from the wall and sat down, crossed his legs and concentrated on his breathing until his rhythm was even.

"I hear you let Rayneer talk you into one of his distance runs."

Arran opened his eyes and saw Kallion standing in the doorway.

"Yeah, remind me not to do that again...ever." Arran grimaced from the stiffness in his legs as he rose.

Kallion smiled as he crossed the room.

"You should stop by and see me before term starts. Second year will have you graduating to steel daggers. Bring in your old wooden and iron ones from first term and we'll get you outfitted."

Arran had figured at some point the use of the wooden and dulled iron blades would eventually conclude. He nodded up at the quartermaster.

"Keep practicing your poses and sparring with the new blades over break to get a feel for them and their sharpness. You will need to learn how to execute your moves, and discern the difference between a strike that is a simple knick, versus one that will be a solid cut. That level of skill with the blade will be one of your evaluation items."

Kallion gave Arran a clap on the shoulder. "You will do just fine. Continue to practice like you did in first year."

"I will."

Arran left the quartermaster, deciding it was time to clean up and then get some lunch.

"So how was that manly run this morning?" Mare was quick not to let any opportunity to goad Arran pass by as she nibbled at her bread.

Picking up right where Mare left off in the torment of their friend, Rayneer replied. "Oh, it was okay for a mid-distance run. I think I broke a sweat there towards the end."

Arran glared at both of them. "Well, next time Mare can join and we'll see how well she does."

She feigned shock; her face becoming the picture of innocence. "And get my new skirts all dirty?"

"Humph...you are a bad influence on him. You know that, right?"

"I prefer to think that I simply facilitated the release of Ray's inherent sarcastic nature. Like a gift from the Patrons, only from me." She smiled triumphantly at the analogy.

"So, what's up for the rest of the day?" Rayneer asked.

"I'm headed over to the library after lunch, then Kallion's, to swap out the old blades for new ones required for second year," Arran said.

"No," Rayneer replied curtly.

"No, what?" It was Arran's turn to feign innocence.

Rayneer tilted his head and frowned. "The library?"

Mare and Arran looked at one another and could barely keep from laughing.

"I was not planning on inviting you," Arran replied with a chuckle. "I'm doing some research, is all. I would not have expected you to enjoy this trip. Buuut..." Arran said, trailing off.

"Just stop it. I'll catch up with you later, after you've seen Kallion. You are going to want to practice with your poses and the dummies before sparring. Those steel bladed weapons are wicked sharp."

"Well, if you boys are going to just prattle on about blades and such, I think I will go and make do with some of my own training. Maybe goad an instructor into another debate." Her eyes twinkled.

Rayneer shrugged. "I have some errands in the city. I guess I'll get those done while the two of you are busy."

Mare and Arran shared a glance. "Just some errands around town that might take you, say, to a certain bookstore?" Mare said mockingly.

"Oh, by the Patrons, you two just don't give up, do you? Just errands."

Arran gave his friend a clap on the back as he got up. "Tell Quil I said hello." He made for the exit before Rayneer could usher a retort.

Arran entered the dusky ambiance of the school library, enjoying the now comfort and familiarness of the place as he made his way over to the front desk.

"Good afternoon, Master Bronsel."

"Arran." The librarian looked up over his spectacles with a small smile. "What can I do for you today?"

"Quil made a suggestion to me and thought you might be able to help."

"Oh he did, did he?" Bronsel said, amused. "What could an old librarian offer that the great Quil could not? Please enlighten me."

Arran smiled at the comment. Arran had learned that Quil and Bronsel were old friends and often called upon one another for advice or just an evening of wine and discussion about rare or interesting books. It seemed like a fitting friendship, given what Arran knew of the two lovers of books.

"It's about Sai'el."

"Ah, yes. As I have mentioned, Benni and I have looked, and we cannot find any books pertaining to her exploits, commissions, or other activities."

"I remember, but what about class information, school roles, or anything of that nature?"

Bronsel put his hand to his chin in thought.

"We do keep records of that sort, but they are not part of the main library. Those records are kept in the sub-basement area, and we do not keep account of them like the books in the main area. They are also notoriously incomplete and unorganized."

"Would you mind if I took a look around?"

"You may. I'll have Benni show you the way."

A short while later, Benni and Arran were headed down a flight of stairs located at the rear of the library.

"So why does this Sai'el hold such fascination to you?" Benni asked.

"I don't know. Curiosity? There is something about how she was considered a prodigy in the Intelligence community and all of her exploits. Then poof, she mysteriously disappears after the death of her group. The mystery won't let go of me."

Benni did not reply as he continued leading them down.

They emerged into a large room, the only light that of Benni's orb lantern. He turned. "What time frame are we looking at?"

"It would have been about one hundred or so years ago."

Benni led them down one row of shelves, then another, searching for a section of records dating back to that approximate time frame. He finally stopped near a stack and hooked the lantern on a peg on the shelf.

"This section seems promising. Let's start here." Benni touched the base of the lantern and it brightened.

The two began combing through the books, one after another, looking through class scrolls until Benni finally found something and gasped.

"I think I have something! Here in the notes of this class, it makes mention of Sai'el testing ahead of schedule in term one of her second year." Benni continued reading from the page. "Impressive..."

Arran leaned over. "Let me see the year on that book. Yeah, that fits. Now we can narrow down our search. Look for any books in the following years."

The two set forth with new vigor after the discovery, and Arran found another entry stating her advancement again to year four.

Benni was reading through their findings and whistled in admiration. "She evaluated out through third year in less time than it takes most people to advance in two."

"Yeah, prodigy indeed."

They continued searching for another hour, coming up with nothing additional for their efforts. Arran sat down on the floor, exhausted and frustrated. The information that they had found only confirmed Sai'el's prodigy status, which he already knew.

Benni stood and stretched. "It is getting late in the afternoon. Master Bronsel is probably wondering if we got lost. We should probably head back."

Arran sighed dejectedly. "You are probably right. I don't think we are going to find anything else. These records are too jumbled and incomplete." Arran rose slowly from having sat for so long and the stiffness from his long run earlier in the morning. He grabbed the lantern, holding it up as Benni replaced the book he had been studying back on the shelf.

Arran's eyes wandered to the shelf opposite of the one they had been scouring and stopped. He held the lantern closer and read the date on one of the books. It was another in the right time frame, but in the wrong section.

"Wait a minute." Arran handed the lantern back to Benni. "I found a misplaced one."

Benni took the lantern from Arran, holding it up for him to see. Arran began scrolling through the pages and stopped. On the page in front of him was a drawn picture of a graduating class. It was an exquisite illustration, extremely detailed. He admired the picture for a few moments, then began to read the names of the individuals listed below the picture. There, in the center of the list, standing out like a beacon, was Sai'el. He glanced up at the picture to find the corresponding person in the picture from the list. Arran froze.

"Give me some more light!" He turned and Benni held the light lower.

The girl was about his age, slender, with long blonde hair, and she was smiling for the portrait. But that is not what made Arran catch his breath. He focused in on her face and features. Sai'el looked stunningly like Arran's mother! The resemblance was uncanny.

Arran's heart began to race, his thoughts a jumble.

"Can we take this?" His voice quivering in an urgent plea.

"We can take it back to the front desk and ask Master Bronsel." Benni looked at Arran hesitantly, not understanding what had made him become so frantic.

"Let's go." Arran bolted for the stairs, book firmly in his grasp.

They made their way back to the front desk and Arran put the book down in front of Bronsel. He opened to the picture he had found.

"Can I get a copy of this picture?"

Bronsel looked at the picture, studying it.

"Someone skilled in the art of drawing could probably make a facsimile of the picture. A magical one could also be purchased, but they can be tricky and costly. A drawn copy would probably be best."

Benni leaned over and examined the picture. "I can do it."

The two turned and stared at the young man.

Benni looked up, surprised at their reaction. "What? In addition to being a scribe here in the library, I hobby at art and drawing. I could make a good copy, even enlarge it if you would like."

"That would be amazing, Benni!" Arran enthusiastically clapping him on the shoulder. "How much for your efforts?"

"Meh, don't worry, it will be good practice for me and the enlargement would be a nice challenge. Besides, I'd be helping a friend." Then he smiled sheepishly. "I wouldn't turn down a nice dinner, though."

Arran grinned broadly. "Done! One dinner and as much ale as you want. I have just the place. How long do you think it will take?"

"A few weeks if Master Bronsel doesn't mind me working in my free time here at the library." Benni looked over hopefully at the librarian.

"Fine, fine. But only in your spare time." The hint of a small smile forming at the edge of his mouth.

Arran thanked the two and headed out of the library, his mind racing at the potential possibilities, and all the questions that simple picture had evoked. Was Sai'el related to his mother? Could his family line indeed have source lineage? Did his mother even know about Sai'el and if she did, could she shed some light on her mystery?

As he exited the library, he was surprised to find that he had spent the better part of the afternoon there, and the sun was near setting. Kallion would need to wait until tomorrow, and he hoped Rayneer had not been waiting on him all afternoon.

Year 1304/June/Week 4
End of Term Break

As Arran, Rayneer, and Bran entered the common room, they found Elinda and Mare already sitting on the couch, enjoying a cup of tea. Arran poured himself a cup and sat down with a plop.

Taking a sip of his tea, he noticed everyone looking at him.

"What? Do I have something on my face or something?" He wiped his mouth and chin.

"Happy Birthday, Arran!" Elinda shouted.

Arran looked around at his friends, stunned.

"How did you even know?" He was properly surprised.

Elinda smiled maniacally. "I 'may' have glanced at your entry papers. It didn't say the exact day, but I knew your birthday was sometime in June sooo, here we are...Happy Birthday, Arran."

Elinda raised her cup in salute, and everyone drank.

"So what does that make you, old man?" Bran quipped.

"Ha, just old enough to whip you."

"Good one. In your dreams."

"I actually prefer an older man." Mare sipped at her tea nonchalantly.

The three young men stopped their laughter so suddenly you could have heard a pin drop. They all turned and looked at Mare, mouths agape.

"I don't think that is what she meant," Elinda said hurriedly. She turned to her friend. "Did you Mare?"

She shrugged. "A girl has her secrets."

Desperate to change the topic, Arran turned to Elinda.

"So, Elinda…how was your break home?" Arran asked the question awkwardly, everyone knowing what he was really asking about.

"You can just ask plainly. My break was fine, other than my parents trying to get me to accept suitors again. But I think what you mean is, did he approve our group's visit next term break? I am pleased to say that he did. He was excited to have visitors from so many different realms and actually thought it was a great idea."

"Nice!" Rayneer said. "I have never been that far east. Would we have time to go to the shore in addition to our, uh hmm, other endeavors?"

Elinda smiled at Rayneer's awkwardness. "Yes, I believe we could fit in a trip to the shore."

"Yes!" The exuberance of the big man got a round of chuckles from everyone.

"So, is everyone able to come?"

Elinda watched as everyone nodded their heads. All that was, except for Bran.

"Bran?"

"I'm afraid I cannot." He hung his head sullenly. "Father already has plans for me next break. He is arranging several events of which I am to attend. He was very adamant that I be present and attend to the duties of the house."

Elinda's face soured. "I'm sorry, Bran. I was really hoping everyone could come."

"Maybe next time." Bran replied, obviously dejected.

Arran leaned over and put his hand on Bran's shoulders. "Sorry, buddy, it won't be the same without you."

"Yeah," Rayneer said in agreement.

"So, what troubles did the three of you manage to get into during break?" Elinda asked, trying to lighten the mood.

Mare instantly perked up. "Rayneer found books!"

Rayneer raised a hand, one finger held aloft. "Book. I found 'a' book."

"Oh, I can't wait to hear this. Out with it, then. What book could entice the mighty Rayneer, hater of all things bound?"

Rayneer sighed. "Master Quil had a book on the geography of battles and I...found it interesting. Happy?"

Everyone laughed.

Arran hid his mouth behind his mug. "Mare even found a book to her liking."

She turned to him with a withering glare.

"Oh?" Elinda turned. "Do tell."

"It was just an adventure novel. Sometimes I like a good adventure tale, that's all." She continued to stare at Arran, daring him to continue.

Elinda's eyebrows rose, and she followed her gaze back to Arran.

He cupped a hand to his mouth and in a conspiratorial whisper said, "Romantic adventures."

"Romance, you say?" Elinda slapped her legs with her palms in delight.

Mare glared at Arran. "Leave it, Elinda."

"Sure, sure. Older men, romantic adventures, and to think I thought I knew you." Elinda leaned in close and whispered, "Just make sure if you find any 'good' parts, you let me know, okay? I might want to borrow it." She nudged Mare with her shoulder.

Mare sank into the couch, sipping her tea, and did not reply.

Arran smiled at his friend and inwardly thought of his own discovery. He would keep that one to himself. At least until he had time to think it through and eventually speak with his mother.

Year 1304/Callist'e/Week 2
Week 2 of First Term

Arran was sitting on his bunk, a single candle burning at his bedside. Bran was already asleep across the room. He was having trouble sleeping, and his mind was still racing with all the possibilities and questions since he had found the picture of Sai'el. So many questions he desperately wanted answers to. Benni had outdone himself and actually completed two copies for him. One was an enlarged image of Sai'el, as he had promised, and then another of the full team, also slightly enlarged. Arran stared at the enlarged image of Sai'el. The likeness to his mother was now even more remarkable. Constant thoughts of his mother being related to Sai'el seemed impossible, yet it was hard to put aside the evidence he now held.

He carefully folded the parchments and put them in the protective leather pouch he had procured for them. He blew out the candle and hoped that sleep would come easier this night. He needed to put aside this distraction. His training was beginning to suffer because of it and the lack of sleep did not help. He knew it and he could tell that the instructors knew it. He needed to finish his year two evaluations and hopefully be cleared for his first commissions with Lord Baelonne. Maybe, just maybe, he could find time to visit Kine while back in Aaeu'din and speak with his mother about the photo and finally get some answers.

He closed his eyes and tried to put the photo and all thoughts of Sai'el out of his mind. If he did not pass evaluations, all of his plans would be for not. With this thought, he resolved to redouble his focus on his training and upcoming evaluations.

The next day, Arran, Bran, and Rayneer rested at the water barrel, each breathing heavily and enjoying the cool water.

"You seem to have come with more vigor today," Bran said.

Rayneer stretched out his leg on the bench. "About time."

Arran looked up at his two friends, not replying. They knew something was bothering him, and yet he had kept his discovery from them. He felt bad not sharing it with his friends, but not yet, maybe when he found the right time, but not yet.

Kallion approached. "How are the new blades working out, Arran? I haven't heard of any major incidents, so can I assume you are adjusting?"

"Yes, sir. I am still working on control and accuracy, but I think I am getting the hang of them."

"Good, good. Show me."

Kallion looked out over the training courtyard. "Victor!" He waved his hand. "Over here."

Victor jogged over to the group.

"You and Arran, sparring circle. First blood or uncontested disabling blow."

"Yes, sir." They both replied in unison and headed for the sparring circle.

Victor was two terms ahead of Arran, a year older, and the experience with blades to match that difference. Much like Bran, he had been training before he even reached the school, but as the match progressed, Arran was holding his own and the matchup proved fairly balanced. Victor had the experience advantage, but Arran was quicker, and his Observance skill had been progressing steadily, allowing him to anticipate Victor's moves.

The match was approaching five minutes when Victor scored a blow on Arran's forearm, drawing blood with a deft flick of his wrist during a countermove by Arran.

Kallion stepped into the circle. "Not bad. That was well fought by the both of you. Thank you, Victor, that will be all."

Victor gave a small bow, which Arran reciprocated, and then left.

Kallion turned to Arran. "Well fought. Keep at it. Some of your moves still look clumsy with the new blades. Your shifts are not as smooth as they should be."

Arran thanked the instructor and made his way back towards Bran and Rayneer.

As Kallion watched Arran leave, Instructor Shia approached him in the sparring circle.

"How is he doing?"

"I was beginning to wonder if we had overestimated the boy's talents, or overworked him. His effort has lagged of late. He has been going through the motions, but not with the same intensity or advancement of first year. That was a good match, though. Victor is one of the best second year's we have with the blade, and he held his own for a good while. If he can resume his rate of advancement from first year, he might be ready from a martial skill perspective. We shall see."

Shia turned her gaze and watched the group. "Those three have formed quite the bond."

"Yes, they have, along with the two young ladies. We could have the makings of a fine team, if family and politics don't get in the way."

Shia shook her head angrily. "Nobles and their politics. How much talent has been wasted over the years to those posturing fools?"

"Too much," Kallion agreed. "Any word from the north?"

Shia stared out across the yard and replied calmly, not bothering to look at Kallion while she spoke.

"We have had a new discovery. Klintoc was able to track and kill another one of the beasts. It was even more malformed, mutated somehow. Its behavior even more erratic and hostile. It could mean nothing...or it could mean everything. We need more information. We need to figure out the how and the why of this. It is beginning to scare some people. Even some of those 'fools' with no small amount of power."

Shia turned and looked at Kallion gravely. "And scared people do stupid things."

The two stood in silence for several long moments, lost in their thoughts.

"I'll leave you to it, then. Good day, Kallion."

Mare could already taste the upcoming evening meal as the group made their way to the Goose. "I am so looking forward to Tan's ale, Mira's cooking, and some music."

"Agreed," Arran replied. "With New Year's celebrations going on, I'm hoping that he has some new brews."

"I was thinking..." Elinda said, trailing off.

Rayneer gave a quick glance at Arran. "Never a good sign."

"You!" Elinda pointed a finger at Rayneer ominously. "Shut it."

"As I was saying, I was thinking...what if we asked Anders to accompany us during break?"

Arran laughed. "You mean ask Anders if he would come along and use his Aura reading to muddle about in realm business?"

Elinda huffed. "Well, I wouldn't put it quite that way, but yeah. You have to admit, his skill is uniquely qualified for what we are planning on doing."

Arran shook his head. "He'd never come. He said to keep it quiet and was very clear that he did not want to get dragged into anything political. I don't think making a trip to Valoor is going to be high on his list of things to do."

"Can we at least try? Maybe he would have a change of heart after thinking about it for a while."

"Maybe, but I doubt it."

The group settled in to their favorite table, with Cindi catching sight of them and turning in their direction.

"Anything special on tap yet, Cindi?" Arran asked.

"We have our regular wheat, standard bitter, and a very strange fruit beer that people are saying isn't bad. It is a wheat beer with a hint of watermelon."

"Interesting, fruit in my beer. I'll take one and send my customary round to Anders of the same." He turned to Mare. "A copper says he hates it."

Cindi lowered her head. "Sorry, Arran, Anders isn't in this evening. As a matter of fact, I haven't seen him all week."

Elinda appeared stricken at the news. "Is he all right? He isn't sick or anything, is he?"

"I don't know. All I know is he hasn't been around lately," Cindi shrugged and finished taking everyone's orders.

Arran looked over at Anders' customary table. "I hope the old guy is all right. Let me go ask Tan. Maybe he knows something."

Arran found a seat at the bar and patiently waited for Tan to finish serving another customer.

"What can I get ya for, Arran?"

"Oh, nothing. Cindi took our order. I was just wondering about

Anders? Cindi mentioned he hasn't been around much lately. Is he okay?"

Tan tilted his head as he dried off a glass. "As far as I know. Rumor has it he has left town. Packed up and headed south. I only heard about it the other day, but I think he's been gone a few days."

Arran took the news harder than he thought he would. The old man had become a tradition at the Goose. It wouldn't be the same without him.

"Thanks, Tan." He went to leave, then turned back around. "What do you think of this watermelon ale?"

Tan wrinkled his nose. "That one isn't for me. I don't need sweet or fruity in my beer. I'll stick to standard bitter, thank you very much, but it's selling alright. Let me know what you think, eh?"

"Sure thing, Tan, thanks."

Arran returned to their table and relayed Tan's information to the group.

"So we bother the old guy. He tells us an obviously important and tragic story from his youth, and ask him outright if he thinks it's related to current events, and then he takes off in the opposite direction? Did I pretty much get that right?" Mare swept her gaze across the group sarcastically.

No one bothered to answer her.

CHAPTER 8

VALOOR

YEAR 1304 / AUGUST / WEEK 4

First term of second year passed by in a blur. Arran threw himself into his studies and training in an all out effort to push the mystery of Sai'el out of his mind. He had done well. Kallion was impressed with his eventual adaptation to the heavier steel blades and Arran was holding his own against students well ahead of him in experience and age. He had gained no new gifts, but the ones he had were all advancing far faster than even the instructors' expectations. All in all, he was proud of the gains he had made. Now it was time for a much needed break and vacation to Valoor.

The mood in the common room was lively as everyone, save Bran, who had already left for home, was anxious on the night before they were to leave.

"Everyone should pack a few cold weather garments," Elinda said to the group. "It will probably still be warm in the capital and at the shore, but when we go up north to Freeholt, it's possible they could get an early fall spell and it could be a bit colder."

"Sounds good. We're still on for a trip to the shore, right?" Rayneer tried to act nonchalant, but no one missed the eagerness in his voice.

Mare laughed. "I can't wait to see our menfolk frolicking in the surf." There was just the hint of a mischievous twinkle in her eye. She winked at Elinda.

Rayneer brushed aside the obvious comment meant to embarrass him and Arran. "Have you seen the ocean before, Mare?"

"Only to the southeast, closer to my home. We traveled a few times when I was younger. It has been a while."

"Well, hopefully the weather will be kind and we'll have a nice day or two to enjoy the views from the beach house." Elinda knew the others did not have the means that she enjoyed from her family's wealth. She typically went out of her way to downplay her family's wealth while at school, but she had to admit she was looking forward to sharing some of the comforts with her friends.

Arran was first to arrive the following morning, and sat ready and waiting on the front steps of the school. He had already withdrawn a few gold from his account for the trip, just in case. Even with the withdrawal, he was amazed to find he still had almost ten gold left. His expenses at school were low, with only an occasional book bought from Quil, and their trips to the Goose. All in all, he was pleased with his savings, but knew that he would need every bit of it if he wanted to upgrade his gear once he started commissions.

Rayneer was next to arrive, clapping Arran on the back in greeting.

"Hey'a. Ready for the journey?"

"I am. It's the first time I've left town, save for the time to the training grounds, which I don't think counts as a proper trip."

"You're right. That does not count," Rayneer replied ruefully.

Both of the girls arrived soon after, each carrying two bags to the boys' one.

Arran and Rayneer looked at one another, then Rayneer punched Arran sharply in the shoulder.

"Told you!"

Arran winced at the larger boy's punch, as both girls looked at them in confusion.

Rayneer turned and noticed their confused looks. "I bet him that each of you would have two bags or more for the trip."

Elinda huffed. "Men."

Despite their joke, each boy offered to carry one of each of the girls' bags as they headed off east towards the docks.

The group passed over the easternmost bridge in Meitellen and towards the closest docks that would serve the ships headed east on the Eeitellen river.

The docks were the customary bustle of activity that Arran remembered from his own trip. As the group passed through the throng of people, he wondered which ship they had purchased passage on, but to his surprise, they did not stop. Arran slowed down and looked over his shoulder as Elinda continued moving on towards the end of the dock. She stopped and looked back at Arran.

"Come on." She waved her hand, ushering him forward. "This way."

Arran complied and not too much further along, Elinda stopped at a gangplank to one of the most elegant and sleek looking boats he had ever seen. It was gorgeous. Polished wood in dark hues gleamed in the sun. It was as majestic a boat as Arran had ever seen.

"My cousin happened to be in the neighborhood on business and agreed to hold over and give us passage."

Rayneer looked the boat up and down in admiration. "Just happened to be in the neighborhood?"

Elinda gave an awkward smile and started up the gangplank. "Come on."

At the top, a lean, well-tanned man greeted them as they boarded. He had dark brown hair, well cut that hung to his shoulders, slightly tousled. He wore a loose red shirt with the sleeves rolled up just above his elbows, fitted brown pants, and boots. It was simple attire, but obviously well tailored.

He greeted Elinda warmly with a hug. "So good to see you again."

"Thank you, Raif. I really appreciate you holding over for us."

"Not a problem at all. So, who are my guests for this little voyage?"

Elinda stepped aside to let the others board and made introductions for everyone.

Raif greeted everyone amiably, with the courtesy and manner of a polished nobleman or, at the very least, someone with means. "A pleasure to have you all aboard. If you will follow me, I'll show you to your rooms and get you settled in."

Raif led them down a small set of stairs in the middle of the deck and into what looked like the dining area with a small kitchen on one side and a table for eight on the other. Everything gleamed like it had just been installed and polished with a silk cloth.

Following the corridor towards the back of the ship, there were three rooms, two on one side, and one on the other, with the final space reserved for the bathing room. There was another room at the end of the corridor, presumably Raif's room.

"The ladies will each have their own room and you two get to bunk together here." Raif pointed to the second door on the left, across from the bathing room. "I'll let you all get settled. We will be underway shortly. Welcome aboard, everyone."

Elinda observed her friends soaking in the obvious opulence of which they had just been introduced. "It's just a boat." Desperately trying to downplay the opulence and realizing that she had probably failed.

"My uncle's fishing boat is 'just' a boat," Rayneer replied. "This is a whole different class." Trying, but not succeeding, in keeping the grin off his face.

"You boys fight over the bunks. I'm going to go bury myself in my bed," Mare said mockingly.

Even Mare's jibe did not put a damper on the moment. Arran would have never thought he would experience such luxury. He had to admit; it was more than a little intoxicating.

The trip to Daijoon took six days, and the group enjoyed every minute. Raif was the consummate host throughout the voyage. He pointed out landmarks along the river, escorted them into town at several ports of call, and introduced them to local delicacies. He even managed to teach some basic mariner skills to Arran and Rayneer.

The girls laughed at their mistakes, and everyone enjoyed the moments.

When they arrived at the capital, Arran was almost saddened for the voyage to end. He had not felt so relaxed in a very long time. Not since before the Source Day that had changed his life. He did not regret the path his life had taken, but he also had not realized how stressful and tense the last year had been. Until now.

Raif expertly guided the boat into its berth, as gently as if it was drawn by a magnet, snicking into place as the deck hands secured it. On the dock stood a handsome couple, arm in arm. The man was tall and lean, with light brown hair. His simple pants and shirt hung impeccably. A sash of green was worn across his chest. Arran's eyes were then drawn to the woman at his side. She was breathtaking. She wore a simple, light blue dress with a gold embroidered rope at her waist, tassels hanging delicately at the ends. She had the same long, golden hair as her daughter, bundled in a weave down her back. There was no mistaking it. Elinda's parents had come to greet them on their arrival.

As soon as the gangplank was set, Elinda rushed down to the dock, wrapping her parents in an embrace.

"So good to see you, dear." Elinda's mother said, grasping her face with both hands and placing a kiss on her forehead.

"Thank you, Mother."

"Elinda," her father said. "No hug for your father?" He winked, and Elinda complied.

Releasing from his daughter's hug, he gestured behind her. "I believe introductions seem to be in order."

Elinda turned.

"Mother, Father, may I introduce my closest friends from school: Mare, Arran, and Rayneer." She pointed to each in turn.

"Everyone, my parents, Lord Colston and Lady Jolyn Frambroe."

Then, without any hesitation, Mare made a perfect curtsy. "So very nice to meet you, my lord." Then deftly angled towards Jolyn and made another. "And to you, my Lady."

Arran thought to ask what had the perfectly polite young woman in front of him done with his friend, but thought better of it as he and Rayneer both respectfully greeted Elinda's parents. Maybe he would bring that up later, he thought with a smile.

"Jesker," Lord Colston said, "Would you please make arrangements for the bags?"

"Right away, sir."

"That won't be necessary," Arran said as Jesker came for his bag. "It's just the one for me."

"It would be my pleasure, sir." It was the most polite and sincere tone Arran may have ever heard.

Now feeling a little foolish, Arran accepted the gesture and let Jesker gather his bag.

Lord Colston stepped forward and shook hands with both boys. "Now, I'm betting you are all tired after having to spend six days with Raif. He no doubt put you to work?"

"They may have learned a few knots and some basic skills, cousin," Raif replied with a smirk.

"Of course they did."

Leaning over conspiratorially to Rayneer and Arran, he whispered, "I'm not sure if he does it to get out of the work, or if he truly enjoys the teaching."

Elinda's parents, despite their obvious wealth, put off none of the airs of it and were extremely charming and welcome. He glanced at Elinda and now knew why the rich princess from Valoor was so grounded and easily likable.

The lord and lady led them down the dock with each of Elinda's parents taking turns asking each of them about themselves, where they were from, and how their schooling was progressing. They guided the conversation so calmly and effortlessly that by the time they reached the carriages, everyone was perfectly at ease.

The carriage ride led them up near the main gates of Daijoor, but they did not enter the town proper.

"Colston and I prefer the countryside. Our estate is east of the capital," Lady Jolyn explained.

"My father feels the same," Rayneer replied. "He says he gets enough of the court and nobles during the day and prefers to make a getaway at least once a day."

"As do we. You will need to tell us of your father. We hear he is a fine man."

"Thank you, my lady. I'm sure he would be pleased to hear it."

The carriage ride skirted the edge of the city and then headed east, where the landscape turned from fairly flat into rolling hills. It did not take long before the Frambroe estate came into view. It sat on a small hill, trees lining all sides but the front. A long graveled path led up to the main estate, lined with a variety of flowers and shrubs. The path ended at a large fountain that split to either side, forming a circle around the fountain. They turned right at the fountain and came to rest at the front door.

Everyone disembarked, and Jesker was there to greet them. Arran wondered how the man beat them to the estate.

He must be related to Mindell.

They stood at the entry once everyone had exited the carriages. Colston turned at the top of stairs to address them. "Dinner will not be for several more hours, and I'm sure Elinda would like to show you around. Your bags will be in your rooms, and we shall see you again at dinner. Enjoy your stay at Frambroe estate." He turned and opened the door.

The group thanked Elinda's parents profusely, and after they had left, Arran hadn't even noticed that Jesker had already managed to whisk away their bags.

Definitely related to Mindell.

Elinda let out a long breath. "So, what would you like to see first?"

Arran was looking around the grand foyer, replying absently as he stared. "So I'm just going to get this out of the way. I mean, Wow! Just wow, Elinda!"

Elinda blushed at the compliment. "Thank you. I know that my parents' wealth afforded me a lot of opportunities. I'm not naïve to that fact, but I've always tried to not let that wealth define who I am. When I was gifted, I jumped at the opportunity to go to the school for training. There I could just be Elinda. Be myself."

Mare scoffed. "But not a bad spot to come back to, eh?"

Elinda chuckled. "No, I suppose not. Come on, if no one cares, I'll show you my favorite place."

She led them through the manor and out onto a large veranda off the back of the house. After a short walk through several gardens, they came to a large building. It did not take Arran long to realize it was the stables.

Elinda led them in and directly to a stall in the middle. Inside was a beautiful white horse with just a touch of black in its mane and around its hoofs. It was gorgeous.

Elinda grabbed an apple from a nearby bin and held it up for the horse. "This is Spirit." The horse took it greedily as Elinda stroked its muzzle.

"I was hoping that we could ride out on our trip to the shore. It is an easy day and a half ride and we can camp out for the night. The stars are magnificent."

"Sounds good to me." Arran looked at the others, who all agreed.

Elinda clapped her hands. "Great!" She turned to Spirit. "I will see you tomorrow." Spirit responded by rubbing her head against Elinda's hand.

Elinda guided the group through the grounds, pointing out spots of significance, most with some childhood story attached. Through the gardens which, for a personal estate, were pretty impressive. Arran began to understand where Elinda's fascination with herbs, flowers, and the time she spent in the school's gardens came from.

They finished their tour and made their way back to the main house. Elinda guided them up the main front stairs to the second floor and to their rooms. They had to peek in and check the baggage to know exactly whose was whose.

They had just found Arran's room when Elinda turned. "Dinner should be in about thirty minutes if you would like to freshen up. It will only be us and my parents, so feel free to keep it casual." She grinned at Arran. "So there is no need to wear that one good shirt you have."

"Ha ha." Arran escaped into his room, shutting out the echoing laughter in the hall.

Dinner was indeed a casual affair, with Elinda's parents regaling her friends with one embarrassing story after another. The food and the wine were exceptional, and by the end of the evening Arran could feel the exhaustion of the day catching up with him.

"I think that is enough storytelling for one night," Colston said. He smiled at his daughter. "We have to save some stories for later." Elinda rolled her eyes at him and he laughed, standing to pull out Jolyn's chair. "I hear you will be heading out to the shore for a few days. Hopefully, the weather will hold." Jolyn took his arm. "I believe we will take our leave." They both graciously made their exit, leaving the friends with their privacy.

Rayneer watched the couple depart and stated. "You have fine parents."

"Thank you. They could have stopped a few stories ago, though."

Mare laughed with a joyful menace. "Now where is the fun in that? I have enough material here to last the rest of the year."

Elinda sighed, defeated and resigned to the fact that Mare would indeed make good on her promise.

The group made their way back to their rooms, and Arran was barely able to undress before collapsing onto the single most comfortable bed he had ever felt. He barely had time to register it all before the wine and his exhaustion carried him off to sleep.

The first thing Arran felt when he awoke the next morning was how extremely relaxed and well rested he was.

Is this all from a bed?

The room was still mostly dark, and he rolled over, putting several of the spare pillows over his head to block out the faint hint of morning light seeping in around the curtains. He closed his eyes, trying to eke out just a few more minutes of comfort and warmth.

"I need to get me one of these beds," he muttered to himself.

He had almost faded back into the embrace of sleep when a knock came at the door.

He groaned. "Yes?"

The door slowly opened halfway and Jesker peeked through. "Sir, breakfast will be served shortly on the back veranda."

"Thank you, Jesker," he muttered. His muffled reply coming from beneath the swathe of pillows.

Arran lie there for several more minutes before rising and throwing his legs over the side of the bed, giving a brief shudder at the cooler air in the room. He walked over to the window and opened the curtains. The morning dawn across the rear gardens of the house was serene.

He turned and surveyed the room at length. He had been so tired the night before, he barely had time to take it all in. The room was not overly large, but it was well appointed; sitting chairs next to the hearth and now dead fire, a sitting table for two, and a small desk against the wall. Everything perfectly placed around the bed at the center. He sighed contentedly and headed for the side bath.

As Arran made his way down to the veranda, he walked slowly as he marveled at the Frombroe house. The house and its decorations were obviously expensive, but it did not scream flamboyance. Understated, that was what he was trying to think of. Expensive, but understated, as if the rooms were saying, "I know I'm expensive, but I don't have to scream it."

Arran finally arrived out onto the veranda, noticing he was the last to show.

"Welcome back to the living," Mare said. "Too much wine?"

"Maybe a little, but I think that bed sucked me off into another world. I had a hard time waking up."

"They are extremely comfortable," Rayneer agreed around a mouthful of food.

Arran sat down and began filling his plate, suddenly hungry at the sight and smells of the meal laid out before him. "So, what is on the agenda for today?"

Elinda laid down her fork, pulling up her napkin and dabbing at the corners of her mouth. "I thought after a nice breakfast, we could have a leisurely morning to prepare for the trip to the shore. Leave around noon? It is a day and a half ride, so we should arrive by tomorrow afternoon."

Everyone agreed as they attentively went back to their breakfasts.

After breakfast, everyone retreated to pack their bags; meeting up again at the stables. Elinda introduced each of them to the horse that would be theirs for the trip. They spent some time brushing and feeding them before going out on a short exercise trot around the yard.

Arran's horse was named Storm, and he and Arran were quick to form a bond. Storm had a good temper and was lithe and strong. Arran was not an expert when it came to horses, but he knew a fine horse when he saw one. Storm was all that and more. He was sure that if he let the reins free, this horse would move like the wind. As Arran was stowing his staff to the side of Storm, Jesker entered the stable carrying a basket.

"My lady, your mother insisted on a day pack of food." He began handing everyone a small bundle contained within the basket.

"Thank you, Jesker. Tell her it is much appreciated."

Jesker gave a slight bow as he handed out the last of the bundles. "Have a safe and memorable trip, my lady." Then he turned and made his way back up to the house.

"Shall we?" Elinda said.

Arran could see her eyes begin to gleam with the anticipation of the ride.

Everyone led their horses out of the stable, mounted, and followed Elinda towards the main road, headed east and to the shore.

The afternoon was pleasant, and Elinda kept the pace smooth and even, letting her friends take in the countryside while still being able to maintain a conversation.

As dusk began to take over the horizon, she guided them to a small valley between a couple of knolls that had a lone, tall oak tree growing at the bottom. They made camp and ate from their prepared bundles of food. They talked and joked amiably, as they always did.

As the night slowly set in, the stars began to twinkle into existence, populating the sky.

"Come on," Elinda said to everyone as she rose from the fire. "Let's go enjoy the stars."

She led them up the side of one of the knolls making up their small valley and searched around until she found the right spot.

"Here we go." She sat down and motioned for everyone to spread out around her. "Leave enough room so that you can lie flat on your back."

Mare looked at her skeptically. "Just do it, Mare."

Everyone shuffled around, eventually finding a spot and lay down in the soft grass.

"Now wait for your eyes to adjust to the darkness," Elinda said.

As their eyes adjusted and the night sky grew even deeper, the heavens began to light up. The absence of light in such a remote location gave the group a whole new version and appreciation of the night sky. Arran had done this as a boy, but the soft grass and present company made the experience all the richer.

"This...it's impressive," Rayneer said over a yawn.

"I know, right?" Elinda said.

The group sat in silence admiring the view and lost in thought until Arran heard Rayneer give a quick snort.

"Looks like the big guy is ready to turn in," Arran said, kicking him in the leg.

"Huh? What?"

"Time for nighty-night," Mare said.

"Oh, sorry. I must have nodded off."

Elinda snorted a laugh and rose, leading the way back to their campsite.

The next day's ride was as pleasant as the previous afternoon. Elinda kept the pace much the same for most of the day, with a handful of gallops sprinkled in when the road was agreeable. Arran marveled at

Storm's speed and strength, enjoying the breeze across his face as the horse moved effortlessly beneath him. Stopping only once for a light lunch, they reached the shore by mid-afternoon. Elinda led them on to the sandy beach and right up to the edge of the ocean. The lapping waves breaking against the hooves of their horses.

Elinda turned Spirit to the south. "We're this way." She lead them down the beach towards a small cliff. A house was perched at the top, overlooking the ocean and the beach.

"Let me guess," Arran said, pointing to the house. "That is your family's little getaway house on the shore?"

Elinda blushed sheepishly, not replying.

"You complaining, Country?" Mare asked.

"Nope, just appreciating the location."

As they approached the cliff, Elinda led the group off the beach and on to a small trail that led up to the house. A large horse pen was set off to the side of the house and the group made their way there.

Elinda dismounted and pointed to the open-sided shed located at the back of the pen. "Why don't you men go throw some fresh hay down from the loft while we unpack and take care of the horses?"

Once the horses were properly quartered, Elinda led the group up to the house, opening the door and striding across the large living area towards the stairs. "Make yourself at home. Grab any room, save the one at the end of the hall. That would be my parents' room. If you want, we can change and take in what remains of the afternoon down on the beach." She looked at Arran, who was standing in the middle of the room, head on a swivel. She took a couple of large strides back to him and nudged him hard in the side.

"Don't. Just enjoy."

"Wha...oh. Yeah. Sorry. It's just...so..." Elinda nudged him again, even harder.

"Ow! Okay, I got it." He rubbed his ribs.

Mare shouldered past him and was first up the stairs to claim a room.

They spent the rest of the day on the beach, followed by a fireside dinner and another enjoyable evening laying in the sand, enjoying the stars, and the lapping sounds of the ocean waves.

The next morning, after a light breakfast, they were headed down to the beach for the day when Arran saw a man coming up the trail.

"One minute, go on ahead and I'll catch up," Elinda said as she hurried over to the approaching man.

As she rejoined them on the beach, Arran asked, "Who was that?"

Elinda did not meet his gaze, staring out over the ocean, eyes unfocused. "What? Oh, an old local family friend. He watches the house for the family and noticed our arrival. He was coming by to investigate, or in this case, say hello. Father helped out their family during some down years in the fishing market a long time ago. The two families have been exchanging favors ever since. Watching the house while we are away is just one of the many unspoken arrangements. I've known Michal and Elouise my entire life."

She turned and looked at Arran gravely.

"What is it?"

Her voice came out in a tremor. "Another attack."

"Here? At the shore?"

"No. A small inland village a few hours away. Michal said no one was injured, but Arran..." She paused. "Klintoc was here. He interviewed everyone. He only left a few days ago."

Arran pursed his lips, face turning dour.

They did not speak as their attention was eventually drawn to their friends running in the surf and diving through the waves. Mare was splashing Rayneer with water, mocking him the entire time.

Arran turned to Elinda. He smiled awkwardly. "You don't think... you know...Mare and Ray..."

Elinda looked at him in question, then quickly caught on to his meaning. "No!" She hesitated. "I mean, I don't think so. She's never said anything to me and anyway, how can you tell? She flirts and carries on with everyone."

Arran raised his eyebrows as he watched his two friends. "It does provide good cover for one's true feelings. 'Layers' and all that." Laughing at his own joke. "Come on, we can't dampen that mood.

We'll tell them tonight." Arran grabbed her hand and guided a reluctant Elinda down into the surf.

That night over dinner, Elinda relayed Michal's story and their last evening at the shore had turned into an unfortunate, grim affair.

<hr>

The following day, as the group headed back to the Frambroe estate, the mood was dark. Even another relaxing evening under the stars did little to assuage anyone's countenance. As they approached the stables, Jesker appeared from within, patiently waiting for them near the entry.

That guy is everywhere.

He greeted them as they approached. "Good day. I trust the trip was enjoyable." He took Spirit's reins from Elinda as she dismounted.

"It was. Thank you, Jesker." Elinda easily moving out of their sullen reverie.

They finished stabling and feeding the horses, and then made their way up to the main house. Elinda's mother was on the veranda as they approached.

"Welcome back, dear. How was the coast?"

"Quite pleasant. Just cool enough in the evenings for the fire and warm enough during the day to enjoy the water. We should go in late summer more often. It was nice."

Arran stepped up to the table beside Rayneer, grabbing a grape from a fruit bowl. "I think Rayneer had the best time. When he wasn't frolicking in the water he stood and stared at the ocean for hours." Arran quickly stepped aside from the incoming blow aimed at his shoulder.

"I did not frolic."

Jolyn covered her mouth as she attempted to stifle a laugh. "Well, I'm glad you enjoyed your trip. Go get cleaned up. Dinner will be ready shortly."

The following morning, after everyone had finished breakfast, and they were alone, Elinda casually asked, "When would you like to head up to Freeholt?"

No one answered. Everyone knew what she was really asking: when would they like to go investigate the incident?

Elinda's face darkened. "Oh, come on. It's just a little questioning. No harm ever came from that."

Arran shrugged his shoulders. He saw Elinda set her shoulders and knew there was no preventing her plans, even with the recent news. "How far is it?"

"About three days if we take our time. If I ask the drivers to hurry a bit, we could probably make it in just over two."

"I'm good whenever."

"Me too," Mare said.

Rayneer only grunted as he reached for another morning bun.

Elinda clapped her hands excitedly. "Great! We'll leave tomorrow. I'll make all the arrangements. Feel free to explore the grounds and enjoy the day." She turned to Arran with a wry smile. "Father has a wonderful library, if one was so inclined."

Rayneer groaned.

A short while later, Arran was wandering the house, deciding to take Elinda up on her offer.

As if by magic, Jesker appeared. "May I help you, sir?"

Startled, Arran turned around.

That man could teach stealth techniques at the school!

"Uh yes," Arran said, regaining his composure. "I was wondering if you could point out the lord's library."

"The library is at the end of the east wing." He pointed down the hallway leading east.

"Thank you."

Arran headed down the hallway, passing several doors, and a few open sitting chambers before coming to the end. Two massive wooden doors stood before him.

Should I knock or just go right in?

He decided to try knocking first. No answer. He knocked again.

No answer. He pushed on the right door and slowly opened it, stepping inside.

As he peered around the room, he hesitantly asked. "Hello? Anyone here?"

There was no answer.

The lord's library was larger than he thought it would be. He had thought to find more of an office space or study, but this was far from that. The room spanned the entire breadth of the house from front to back and was at least another fifty paces across. The room was open and high, spanning up the two-story height of the house. Shelves lined every available space on the walls. In the middle of the room was a circular staircase that led up to a central platform with two chairs and a table. Four walkways led off from the platform to each side of the second floor space.

"Impressive," Arran whispered to himself.

He turned left and began perusing the closest shelf, running his fingers along the spines in admiration. He continued his way around the room, past the desk that sat under the window facing out over the front yard. The back wall had a central fireplace with two sitting chairs. He ran his hand over the soft embroidered material as he passed. The final open area of the room held two couches with a center table. He admired how well the library was organized. History was by far the largest collection here on the first floor. Sections were organized by the various realms and then by year, with the earliest titles at the top. The only remaining section on the first floor appeared to contain fiction titles.

Arran smiled to himself and wondered if he would find an "adventure" novel for Mare.

He climbed the circular staircase up to the central platform and made his way around the walkways of the second floor. The second floor was more oriented to applied learning. There were books on all manner of topics: botany, cooking, horse care and breeds, landscaping, blacksmithing, and weapon making. There seemed to be at least a handful of books on all manner of topics.

Arran found a book in the weapon section on daggers and pulled it out, thumbing through the pages delicately. He made his way over to the central platform and sat down.

As he was slowly drawn into the book, he discovered an entirely new appreciation for his given weapon. He found that his daggers were of the most basic type in design and composition.

No surprise there.

He was so engrossed in the book he barely heard the door to the library open.

Lord Colston entered, looking around.

"Up here, sir," Arran said, observing a soft tone as if he were in the school library.

Colston looked up as he closed the door.

"I hope I am not intruding. Elinda mentioned your library to me..."

"Not at all," Colston interrupted with a wave of his hand. "What are books good for, if not to share and read? Find anything of interest?"

Arran looked down at the book in his lap. "Yes, sir. A book on dagger making and design."

Colston thought for a moment, then jerked slightly as it came to him. "Ah yes. That is a good one. I prefer the sword myself, but I find daggers to be quite interesting. Elegant in their simplicity."

Arran put the book on the table and went to the railing. "You have an impressive collection."

"Thank you. It does tend to grow, though. I might have to add on another room soon." He chuckled to himself. "Jolyn wouldn't let me hear the end of it if I did that."

Arran smiled along at the personal jest. "I know what you mean. I've only been collecting for a little over a year now, but if I let him, Master Quil would have me purchasing one of his personal spaces. My chest at school is starting to get a bit cramped."

"You've met Master Quil then? Fine man. He is well?"

"He is, sir."

"Good, good. Well, I simply wanted to stop by and see how you were getting along. Feel free to browse. I will leave you to it."

Arran thanked the lord as he left, overhearing him mutter.

"If we removed the fireplace and extended..." The door closed softly, cutting off the remainder of Colston's musings.

Arran spent the rest of the day in the library. He ended up reading the majority of the book on daggers, fascinated at the various designs and compositions. He discovered that the most rare and sought after material for any blade was a substance called 'star steel'.

He became so engrossed in the books that he didn't realize until midway through the afternoon that he had missed lunch. His stomach began protesting at his lack of attention.

Arran replaced all of the books reverently and made his way out to the veranda where Mare and Elinda were enjoying a tea in the shade. He joined them.

"We missed you at lunch," Elinda said.

"Yeah, I was in your father's library and lost track of time."

"You and your books," Mare said, shaking her head.

"There are worse things I could be doing with my time."

Mare huffed and let the conversation drop.

"Everything set for tomorrow?" Arran asked Elinda.

"All good."

"Nice." Arran sat back in his chair, enjoying the pleasant weather and company of his friends. "Where's Ray?"

"I think he's holed up with Father going over his collection of swords and such."

"Sounds about right."

Dinner that evening was delicious, as expected. After some time visiting, and enjoying a very nice red wine from the house cellars, everyone wearily made their way to their rooms. Elinda's excitement and exuberance for the upcoming trip finally beginning to permeate the group.

Elinda's mother saw them off the following morning. "Have a fun trip and be careful." Jolyn waved her hand goodbye as the carriage began to roll.

Poking her head out the window, Elinda shouted back her reply. "We will, Mother." She settled back in the seat next to Mare.

"Liar," Mare said. "You have no intention of playing it careful if you get your way."

"True, but Mother doesn't need to know that." She turned and gave one last wave to her mother, smiling mischievously.

Late in the morning on the third day, they arrived in Freeholt.

"Finally," Rayneer said, climbing out of the carriage and stretching his arms high. "I know we planned for the shortest time, but it would have been nice to stop a bit more frequently."

"Big baby," Mare retorted.

Rayneer shrugged and walked around to the back of the carriage to grab their bags. Arran followed.

They checked in at the local inn. The owner remembered Elinda and her family well from previous visits and welcomed them all warmly.

Rayneer threw his bag onto the bed and turned to Arran. "Hey. You want to go for a little run? I bet the girls will just want to wander the shops, and if I know Elinda, maybe sneak in a few innocent questions about the incidents. They don't need us getting in the way."

Arran glanced up sideways. "Little run?"

Rayneer held up his forefinger and thumb closely.

Arran laughed. "Actually, that actually sounds pretty good. I could use a good run. Been a bit lazy recently."

"Well, we are on vacation."

After changing, they headed downstairs, where Mare and Elinda were already chatting up the local barmaid. No doubt already on their fact-finding tour.

Arran caught Mare's eye and mouthed, "Going for a run."

She rolled her eyes and went back to the conversation with the barmaid.

Once outside, they walked north out of town, then settled into a light run to warm up. As they followed the trail, it became apparent that it was going to enter the woods. There was a well-marked trail that seemed like it had good use.

"Looks like the locals like to hike," Rayneer said between breaths. "Hopefully, we'll have some good trails to follow."

They jogged lightly for about an hour, Rayneer not creeping up the pace like he normally did, seemingly content to enjoy the coolness from the shade of the trees and the light sweat from the run.

They came to a fork and Rayneer turned right, stopping abruptly. About a hundred paces in front of them, the trail had been marked off limits, with several saw horses blocking the way.

Rayneer looked at Arran. "Want to investigate?"

Arran shrugged. "Might as well. It'll give us something to tell the girls."

They approached the makeshift barrier, seeing nothing out of the ordinary. They continued following the now off limits trail for about a quarter mile, still finding nothing to indicate a reason for the barriers.

Rayneer stopped and looked around. "You want to go on?"

"I don't think so. Let's head back."

Rayneer agreed, and they headed back the way they had come. They slowed to a walk just outside of town to cool off and greeted the villagers with a polite wave or nod as they made their way back to the inn.

The girls were nowhere to be seen, and they decided it best to go get cleaned up before dinner.

Sitting idly at the bar with a mug of the local ale, which was quite good Arran thought, they enjoyed the slow pace that was Freeholt. It was a nice town. One could hardly believe the atrocity that had besieged them just months ago. It must have been chaos.

Mare and Elinda eventually returned, heading for a booth at the back of the room. Elinda motioned for them to join.

Arran tilted his head up to acknowledge her, then held up a finger to the innkeeper behind the bar. He ordered two more ales for himself and Rayneer, then headed over to join the girls.

"So, how was the afternoon for you two? Discover any dark secrets?" Arran said in a mocking, scary tone.

Mare glowered at him, but it was Elinda who replied, "No. No, we did not. As a matter of fact, you would think that nothing had happened at all. We could not unearth even the smallest hint of a rumor." She looked positively dejected.

"We found a blocked off trail during our run," Rayneer said. "Could be something."

Elinda sighed. "Yeah, maybe we head out and take a look tomorrow."

Arran and Rayneer tried to lighten the mood and bring some levity to the conversation after the girls' demoralizing afternoon, but to no avail. Both girls picked at their dinner and retired early, leaving Arran and Rayneer at the table.

"That was depressing," Rayneer said as he finished his stew.

Arran nodded. "One more?" Rayneer smiled, and Arran ordered one more round of the local ale before retiring for the night themselves.

The following morning Elinda had regained some of her original enthusiasm as the group trekked out to the sight of the closed off trail. They all foraged around for several hours in all directions, finding nothing of major interest.

Elinda sighed as everyone gathered around at the only thing of interest they had found. "I don't see anything other than this old campsite." She kicked at the dirt around the disheveled firepit. "Let's go back to town."

At this point, it did not take much to convince the group. They had all become frustrated and bored with their search.

As they entered town, Elinda laid out her plan for the remainder of the day.

"Arran, you and Rayneer make some inquiries with the menfolk.

Blacksmith, pub talk, and the like. Mare and I will see if we can make any more headway with some of the women."

By the end of the second day, their luck proved to be even less effective than the first. It was evident that word had gotten out about the four young students asking questions about the incident, and no one was willing to talk.

They had another sullen dinner, with no one harboring any excitement about obtaining any better results the following day.

Arran was first to arrive downstairs in the morning and grabbed a booth, ordering a cup of coffee. Rayneer was next down, followed by Elinda and Mare a few minutes later.

They ordered breakfast which, for Arran, had ended up being the highlight of each day so far in Freeholt. Elinda had not been lying about the pancakes and local maple syrup of this region.

"These are sooo good," he said over a mouthful of pancakes.

Elinda muttered something he couldn't hear and picked at her food. It was going to take more than maple syrup to get her out of her sour mood. She looked up.

"I just don't understan..."

Elinda was abruptly interrupted by shouting in the common yard outside the inn.

"Monsters!" someone shouted. "They've returned!"

Arran and Rayneer both bolted upright and headed for the door. Arran grabbed his staff that was leaning against the wall.

They exited the inn just in time to see a huge "something" ram its tusks into a man, who was most likely the one shouting and trying to get away. The man crumpled to the ground, a huge gash in his lower back.

Arran looked around and saw another beast headed their way from down the street.

He tossed Rayneer his staff.

"You take that one." He pointed. "I'll see if I can grab this one's attention."

Rayneer grabbed the staff out of the air and headed up the street to engage the oncoming creature.

Arran pulled his daggers out and ran straight at the creature, who was now turning around to make another run at the villager, who now lay completely still, blood pooling beneath him. The creature turned its head, now aware of the second man running straight at it.

As Arran approached, he could make the beast out more clearly. It was about half as tall as a man at the shoulders, with sharp quills running down the length of its back. Its head was huge, with a large gaping snout and wicked looking tusks protruding out on each side. As grotesque as it looked, the most unnerving thing about the creature was its eyes. Yellow, bloodshot eyes glared at him with all the hate of a predator that had just been challenged.

The two charged one another head-on, the beast snarling and shaking its head as it ran forward. Arran gauged the distance as he ran and at the last possible moment, dove above the beast, just barely clearing the upraised head and tusks, raking his daggers down the back of the creature. The thick spines on the back of the beast deflected one of his daggers, which did little damage, but the other found soft flesh and tore a long gash down its back. It had not been a good slice, with only the tip of the dagger able to penetrate. The creature howled in equal parts pain and frustration as it was denied the satisfaction of its attack.

Arran tucked, rolled to a stop, and turned. He was down on one knee, daggers poised in front of him, one dripping with the black blood of the creature.

"That got its attention," Arran muttered, breathing heavily. Arran felt a rush of adrenaline as he felt the Warrior begin taking hold. Unlike the first time Arran had been overcome by the Warrior adrenaline, he had learned to control it, harness it, and use it to his advantage, just as Kallion and Bran had instructed him. It felt good as all of his senses sharpened into focus.

Arran looked over at Rayneer, who was deftly beating the other creature mercilessly with the staff while evading its head and the sharp tusks that tried to rip into him. He watched as Rayneer took a hard kick from the creature as he dodged behind it. Arran knew he would only be able to distract the beast with the staff. He would need help soon to put it down. Arran returned his attention back to the beast in front of him. He needed to end his fight and end it quickly.

The creature in front of him snorted loudly, shaking its head and howling, spittle flying in all directions. It charged again.

This time Arran did not run. He slowly walked forward as the creature barreled towards him.

Arran pirouetted to his right just as the creature lowered its head to ram him with its tusks, and on the reverse pivot viciously stabbed the back left flank of the beast with both daggers. Just as he had hoped, the creature lost function of the injured back leg and, with all of its forward momentum, toppled to the ground.

Arran turned and sprinted after the fallen creature. Before it could find purchase and rise, he leapt upon its back and rammed both daggers into the taught muscles of its neck. He held his daggers strongly, pinning its head down with all his strength. The beast thrashed viciously, its spines tearing into Arran's legs, but he squeezed his legs tighter, ignoring the pain. Slowly, the creature's struggles began to ebb. It twitched for a few more seconds before finally succumbing to the injury.

Arran was panting heavily from the exertion, but could hear his instructors' training kicking in. "Never rest during a fight, evaluate your surroundings, and always be looking for the next engagement." He quickly took stock of himself. The creature had managed to swipe one of his tusks across Arran's pivot leg, leaving a nasty gash across his thigh. He could feel the blood running down his leg. It was not a threatening injury, but painful as hell. He was sure it would hurt a lot more later.

No time. Have to assist Rayneer.

He dislodged his daggers and sprinted towards Rayneer when he saw a third creature making its way down the main road into town.

"Elinda!" he shouted, pointing at the third creature barreling down the road.

Elinda looked and turned gravely, stepping out fully into the yard. Without any hesitation, she began focusing her will at the beast as it ran wildly down the road. She waited until it was within striking distance and thrust her hands forward. The beast was hit with a wall of air that stopped it dead in its tracks and then launched it backwards in the opposite direction. It flew at a frightening pace, eventually hitting a nearby tree with a loud thud and an audible crack. It did not get back up.

Arran watched as Elinda fell to her knees, gasping, as he raised his eyebrows in admiration.

She just laid that thing out with one spell!

Arran made his way over to Rayneer, and the two made short work of the last beast, confusing and finally overpowering it, as Arran again sank his daggers in its throat while Rayneer had it distracted.

Arran looked around, scanning for more threats. Finding none, he limped his way over to Mare, who was kneeling on the ground next to the fallen villager.

He tore off his shirt and wadded it up, using it to apply pressure to the grievous wound in the man's back. Mare's hands glowed with an intensity he had never seen before.

"Come on, Mare," he pleaded, tears of frustration and anger streaming down his dirty face.

"I...I can't." She slumped down onto her knees. Her voice was a soft whimper, tears forming in her eyes. "His wounds are too severe. He has lost too much blood."

Arran pressed harder at the cloth. He watched as more blood than he had ever seen in his entire life flowed down and around his knees. He couldn't stop. His mind told him the man was dead, but he continued to hold the bloodied rag down with all his might. His face streaked where the tears had washed away the grit of battle.

He finally eased away, slumping to the ground as Mare rested a hand on his shoulder. He could only stare in horror at the lifeless man before him, tears flowing freely. He cried for a man he did not know, but had fought to save. He did not move. Could not move. Did not want to admit the death before him. Finally, he lowered his head and sagged into himself.

"Come on," Mare said, gently grabbing his arm. "Let the villagers take care of their own."

Arran looked up at her with bloodshot eyes, turned and embraced her.

Mare slowly stood up, placing her arm around Arran's shoulder, urging him away from the fallen man. Reluctantly, he rose, and they made their way to the steps leading into the inn before sitting down.

Mare knelt before him. "Let me see the wounds on your legs."

Arran did nothing to dissuade her and straightened his legs, staring off at nothing, eyes unfocused.

Rayneer, holding Elinda up for support, guided her over to sit down next to Arran. No one spoke a word, still reeling from the emotional aftermath of the chaotic fight. The adrenaline slowly receded as they all came to grasp the horror of what had just happened. It was no longer a guess or a story they told each other around the comfortable confines of a fire in a common room.

Arran didn't know if it had been minutes or hours when a group of the local town officials approached.

"We would like to thank you for all that you did today," one official said.

Elinda stood. "You are welcome, but it is not necessary. We are only glad we could assist." Elinda spoke with a humbleness that honored them all.

The official turned to look out over the carnage that still lay in the courtyard. "That was more than an assist, my lady. You and your friends took down three of those creatures. That is no small thing. The school will be receiving a very congratulatory letter on all of your behalves from the city of Freeholt."

Elinda did not protest and took the compliment with grace and a simple nod. Her composure slipping as she sat back down.

The rest of the day was a blur, and before he knew it, they were all sitting down for dinner. The mood was somber and the four friends, usually so exuberant, did not know how to act or what to say to one another.

The server approached the table tentatively. "Can I get you anything?"

After a few uncomfortable moments of silence, Arran asked. "I don't suppose I could get some pancakes?"

Everyone at the table looked at Arran incredulously.

He shrugged. "I'm hungry."

"If you eat any more of those, you'll be running for weeks to pull off that weight," Rayneer said, slapping his friend on the back. And that was all it took. It was as if a veil had been thrown aside. In that simple gesture, the somber mood was broken.

"Pancakes all around, if you please," Elinda said. The first glimmer of a smile forming for the first time all day.

"And mugs of that local ale for me and my friend here," Rayneer said.

"Ale and pancakes?" Mare said, wincing.

Rayneer gave Arran another slap on the back. "If you are going to have an unconventional dinner, why stop there? Eh, Arran?"

The server curtsied politely and hurried away to fulfill their order.

"Did she just curtsy at us?" Arran said.

"She did," Elinda replied. She gave a small tilt of her head towards the rest of the patrons in the inn.

Arran looked up and around, finally noticing that everyone was looking in their direction. A man at a nearby table stood slowly and raised his mug in salute. As if on cue, one patron after another joined him, and within seconds, the entire inn was raising a mug in salute to the young students.

Arran was awestruck at the generosity of the gesture and found himself blushing at the attention. He rose, taking his own mug from the waitress, saluted back and in one draw, drained his drink. The inn instantly broke out in raucous cheers, as if they too needed something to break the reverie of the horrible day.

They were about halfway through their meal, which was taking longer than normal as everyone wanted to come by and thank the group, when the door to the inn burst open. The inn went silent as everyone turned to see who had entered so abruptly.

Arran turned to look with a mouthful of pancakes and almost spit them out on the floor as he recognized the newcomer.

Klintoc furiously surveyed the room. Locating the four students, he stalked in their direction, his huge strides eating up the distance to the table.

In a hoarse, almost shouted whisper, he hissed, "What in the Patrons' names are you four doing here?" His fists were clenched and pushing hard into the table.

No one spoke. No one wanted to speak or answer the obvious angry question.

Arran swallowed his food and answered meekly. "Um, we're on vacation, sir."

This must have been the exact wrong thing to say, because Klintoc's eyes flared with renewed anger. "Vacation?" He shook his head and made eye contact with each and every one of them.

He leaned in and hoarsely whispered. "Upstairs! Now!" He paused, looking down at the table.

"Are those pancakes?"

"Yeah, they're really go..." Arran did not finish his reply under another withering glare and rose with his friends.

Gathered in Arran's and Rayneer's room, the four students stood just inside the door, shoulder to shoulder as they watched Klintoc pace back and forth.

Finally, he came to a stop, and in a very deliberate tone, asked, "Now tell me how the four of you come to be here and everything that happened. Every detail."

The four looked at one another as Mare took the lead, explaining their vacation and then the events of the day.

"I think that is all." She exhaled and looked at her companions for approval. They all nodded in agreement and stood in silence as Klintoc processed the story that he had been given.

"So I'm to believe that you just happen to be visiting in the town where the incidents first occurred...on a vacation? I know what the rumors are, and I'm sure you and the rest of the school do, too. Do not deny it."

No one spoke. Everyone looking down at their feet, not wanting to meet Klintoc's glare.

Klintoc shook his head, now seemingly more out of frustration than anger.

"You have no idea of the danger...much less the obvious meddling with supposedly secret realm affairs..." He shook his head in obvious frustration. "I want you all to go back to the Frambroe estate first thing tomorrow, and then make best speed back to school. Is that understood?"

"Yes, sir!" they all said in unison.

He gave them one last look, making sure his orders were understood, and taken as gravely as he intended. He shouldered Arran aside and left without another word.

There was an audible sigh of relief from the entire group as the door shut behind him.

"That was pleasant," Mare said mockingly.

Arran looked worriedly at the closed door. "I just hope we don't get expelled."

Elinda went to the bed and sat. "I don't think they will expel us, but we are sure to catch a lot more grief when we return to school. I'm sorry for dragging you all into this."

"We're big boys and girls," Mare replied. "We knew what we were doing, and we were just as curious as you."

Elinda sighed. "I'm tired."

Everyone agreed, but Elinda did not rise.

"Uh, that's my bed," Rayneer said sheepishly.

Elinda looked down and, without a word, rose as she and Mare left the room.

***

After everyone had packed their bags, they met in the dining hall for one last glorious breakfast. The pancakes were delicious as expected, but the mood was somber, the conversation stilted and uncomfortable. They had been caught in their lie and now would have to face the repercussions.

As they made their way outside to the carriage, they were greeted with a surprise. The vast majority of the village had gathered outside in the courtyard and around the carriage.

The town official Arran recognized from after the attack came forward and once again thanked them for their courage in defense of their town.

"It is a small thing, but we had several cases of the syrup we know you grew fond of during your stay packed for you." He motioned towards the carriage.

Arran almost laughed out loud and thanked the official, shaking his hand.

The three-day journey back to the Frambroe estate was tense and bereft of the excitement of the previous journey. Each jostle of the carriage and hoofbeat of the horses drew them one step closer to the uncomfortable confrontation with Elinda's parents and, eventually, the school officials.

Once they arrived, Elinda had the unenviable task of explaining the events to her parents. She could never pass a lie to them, and had begrudgingly admitted their original intentions for the trip to Free-holt. Her parents were not happy, to say the least, but in the end, grateful that no one was seriously injured.

Colston rose from his chair and stood before the group. His face was tightly drawn with frustration and disappointment. "I will try to find passage back to Meitellen for you tomorrow."

As he passed, Elinda reached out for his arm. "Father." Her voice was low and tremulous. "I...I only wanted to see what we could find out. I never intended for all of this to happen."

Colston sighed heavily.

"I know. When you graduate, it is possible that you may be called upon for school or realm business...eventually. Your mother and I know this, but were not prepared for news that you had been put in harm's way so soon. We should have been."

He paused as several awkward seconds ticked by. "We understand this. We may not like it, but we understand." He squared his shoulders and looked intently at his daughter. "But to lie to us. That is the worst. You lied to us and in that...I cannot abide." He turned, Elinda's arm falling away as he held out a hand to Jolyn.

The disappointment on her parents' faces tore at Elinda, and she began to tear up.

"I know, Father. Never again."

Arran, Rayneer, and Mare stood awkwardly as they witnessed the very personal exchange between Elinda and her parents. No one spoke.

Colston spoke over his shoulder as they left the room. "You and your friends get cleaned up and prepare for passage tomorrow. We shall see you at dinner."

The following morning, the group had gathered in front of the house and were ready to leave.

"Goodbye, my dear," Jolyn said. She reached out and wrapped Elinda in a tight hug before releasing her and placing a loving kiss on her cheek. "Please be careful."

"I will, Mother."

Jolyn then faced the rest of the group, her face becoming very stern. "And the rest of you...take care of my daughter...and each other."

There was a quick chorus of "Yes, ma'ams" and "We will."

Jolyn gave them each a parting hug and stepped back. "Go on now," she said, gesturing to the carriage. "Your father is waiting for you at the docks."

As the group walked down the dock to the waiting ship, Elinda saw her father talking with someone she presumed was the captain.

"Your passage is set and the captain only has two stops along the way. You should be back in Meitellen in five days." His voice was flat and terse.

Elinda could tell that he was still very cross with her and felt a pang of guilt.

"Thank you, Father."

Arran stepped forward. "Lord Colston. Thank you. I believe all of us would agree that you have been a most generous host. I hope that in better times we can visit again?" Arran let the open-ended question hang as he held out his hand.

"In better times," Colston replied, taking Arran's proffered hand in his.

Elinda gave her father a hug and then followed her friends onto the ship.

INTERLUDE

Breanna threw down the papers she had been reading in frustration. "I cannot see how these anomalies are related to the sourcestone!"

Spirit nodded wearily. "Nor can I. The patterns simply do not fit." She sat back dejectedly, twirling her hair in thought. "If not the sourcestone...then what?"

Breanna sat up and began to fidget nervously in her chair. She slowly began absentmindedly straightening the notes she had just thrown to the table and answered so softly, Spirit could barely hear her. "I believe we need to expand our possibilities."

"Expand? To what? We've covered every angle from the sourcestone."

She looked askance at Spirit. "It's not the sourcestone. I think we have established that. I'm talking about...other possible interferences or..." Breanna paused. Her gaze turned soft, almost forlorn as she continued. "...Interferers."

Spirit sat up straight, taking a moment to comprehend what her friend had just inferred.

"You think an outside source is at fault?"

"It's possible, however distasteful. We need to start looking at the humans. They have always been a rash race, eager in their inquisitiveness, almost to a fault. We've seen it before."

Spirit shook her head, not wanting to believe in this course of inquiry, but knowing as she did that Breanna was correct. If a human had found a way to twist the Source gifts to something malevolent, it would change everything. Any attempts at corruption of the source by the humans would not be tolerated. The other council members would be quick to respond, and, at the extreme, possibly bring this age to an abrupt end.

They had only one major anomaly, and it had occurred well over a century ago. It was directly attributed to the sourcestone itself and was concluded to have been deemed a Patron oversight. They had not foreseen the effects that direct contact with the stone would incur. The stone had been well hidden, but essentially unprotected. Once they had fixed this oversight, the age was allowed to continue. But this...if the humans began purposefully and maliciously affecting the Source, that would be an entirely different matter.

Spirit's face contorted in thought as she went over the scenarios in her mind. None of them were good. Finally, she resigned herself. It had to be done. "What do you propose?"

Breanna stood and walked around the table to give herself time to think. "We are going to have to start investigating deeper into the individual lives of those with the means to execute such an anomaly. Highly talented individuals that have been gifted will be our primary suspects."

The Patrons typically never bothered to investigate individuals unless it was out of pure curiosity or on the official business of identifying potential candidates for gifting. It was not part of the cycle. They could not be tempted with favoritism. An age, once begun, was meant to proceed under the auspices of free choice. Be it good or bad.

Spirit refreshed their teas and sat back down. The long moments of silence ticking away slowly. Spirit held her cup with both hands and sipped as she watched Breanna pace behind the table. Eventually, Breanna sat, joining Spirit in her tea, still deep in thought.

When Breanna finally spoke, she did not look up. "There is one more thing. It is time we let the rest of the council know about this..." Breanna turned in her chair and looked at Spirit gravely. "...about everything."

Spirit inclined her head almost imperceptibly in acknowledgement. She had known this was coming, and she had been preparing herself. She could deal with the outrage and admonishments, but the disappointment was going to sting the worst.

"At the next council gathering, then?" Spirit asked.

"I think that would be for the best. In the meantime, we continue our investigation and hopefully have more answers than questions when we disclose...all of this." She gestured widely at the scattered papers on the desk, then bowed her head and took another sip of her tea in contemplation.

CHAPTER 9

ADVANCEMENT

YEAR 1304 / SEPTEMBER / WEEK 3

Week 3 of Term Break

Instructor Shia paced across her office, silently flipping through the pages of the report as Klintoc sat silently, waiting for her to finish.

Once she concluded, she purposefully took her time as she tidied the papers and placed them in a folder neatly on the desk.

"So, in essence," she began, resuming her steady walk across the room; hands clasped behind her back as she spoke out into the room. "We had another attack on the village of Freeholt. We are no closer to finding the cause of the mutations, and on top of all that, we have four of our students fully involved and engaged in the latest incident. Does that about sum it up?"

"That about sums it up, yes. On the plus side..." He stopped abruptly, hearing her quick and most likely agitated turn. He could feel her eyes on him. "Listen, the students' actions were extremely well received. All accounts from my interviews show they did not hesitate, were well organized, and acted with the highest regard towards the village civilians. I gave them a pretty good dressing down for having poked their nose in where it didn't belong, but it is hard to argue the results."

Shia waved her hands about irritably. "Yes, yes, I read the report."

Klintoc turned in his chair to face her, irritated at the dismissal. With defiance in his voice, he continued coldly. "No! I don't think you do understand. I've seen these beasts." Klintoc's voice became a low growl. "I've fought one single handedly. The three in this most recent attack were the largest and most malformed we've seen to date. Those students took them down without hesitation and, in my opinion, with great efficiency. It was..." His voice calmed, the burst of anger gone. "...impressive." He sagged back down in the chair and spoke out across the empty desk. "Putting aside the fact that they went poking around where they shouldn't, they acted admirably. More than admirably, in my opinion."

Shia stared at Klintoc's back and she raised her eyebrows. "Praise from the mighty Klintoc? High praise, indeed."

"Do not mock me, Shia." His voice returning to a low growl. "Those four are damn near ready to graduate, and you know it. They are as good as most of the other agents we have in the field. I do not take field results such as this lightly."

"I know." Shia's shoulders sagged noticeably as she crossed the room and sat down behind her desk. "I am proud of the way they conducted themselves, despite the initial subterfuge they engaged in." She sighed heavily. "My frustration is with the incidents themselves. We are no closer to finding the cause, or the why, than we were months ago."

Klintoc did not answer, staring blankly out the window behind the instructor, knowing that he could not argue the point and disappointed in himself for not having produced any results.

Shia placed her arms on the desk and began stroking the feathers of a quill. "Well, I cannot just graduate a bunch of year two's and one year three, but with Arran's advancement to pass year two evaluations this coming term, that would just about put them all on even footing as year three's, if I'm correct. That is at least a start."

Klintoc's eye's narrowed at the comment and he waited until Shia returned his gaze before answering. "You are thinking to assign them to the same commissions during their third-year terms." It was a statement, not a question.

Shia smiled appreciatively at her old student. He had always been quick to pick out underlying patterns, the words between the words. "I do. But first, I would like to see how the boy conducts himself individually on his upcoming commissions."

"You already know my thoughts on his readiness."

"Hmmph." Shia sat back. "We shall see. It is settled, then. Now, could you please go find me some evidence on the how and why of this?" Frustration thick in her words.

"Oh, I'll hop right on that. I wasn't aware it was a priority." He uncurled himself out of the chair with a smirk and made for the door.

"Smartass," Shia muttered as he left.

***

"Why haven't we been called to the office?" Arran asked, flexing his hands in and out into fists on the arm of the chair. "Let's just get the reprimand over with already."

"Maybe they are trying to keep it quiet and betting that we'll keep our mouths shut," Mare said.

"I don't know," Arran replied, getting up from his chair as he began pacing around the common room. "I don't like it and the not knowing is driving me insane."

"Well, you pacing around and complaining about it is not going to fix anything," Elinda said. "Just calm down. We're not expelled. They would have already done that...I think. The worst that can happen now is a reprimand on how stupid we were. Don't do it again and so on."

Arran flopped back down in a chair with a loud thump and the group sat silently as the slow tick of the clock measured out the long moments.

"Ahem," came a voice from the doorway.

Everyone turned.

"Instructor!" Arran said with surprise, rising from his chair.

"No need," Shia said, waving Arran back to his seat as she continued into the room to stand before them. Her eyes became slits and her voice was flat, almost menacing. "I trust you know why I am here?"

They all nodded in affirmation.

"This is all I am going to say and I'm going to say it but once. What you did was stupid and reckless. You are not to speak of the incident with anyone, save your instructors, and only when called upon. Is that understood?"

"Yes, ma'am," they said in unison.

"Good." She swept her head across every member of the group, enforcing her statement with her gaze before leaving the room.

Once the echoes of the instructor's steps had faded down the hall, Arran looked around at everyone. "That's it?"

Mare raised her eyebrows. "Evidently so." Then her brow quickly furrowed as she thought.

"What is it?" Arran asked.

Mare did not immediately answer, her eyes unfocused as she finished her thought process. Then she smiled wickedly.

"Maarre..." Arran said suspiciously.

Mare turned to Arran. "I think they're covering their asses."

Elinda snickered at the comment, and it even got a chuckle out of Rayneer.

Arran stared at her questioningly, obviously not catching on.

Mare straightened up in her chair. "It's simple. Punishing us would undoubtedly raise more suspicion than just telling us to shut up about it. They want to keep this quiet, so what better way than to gag us instead of trying to trump up a lie of four students' punishment while on vacation break?"

Arran shook his head. "I don't know..."

Rayneer stood and placed a hand on Arran's shoulder. "It's a good theory and in the end, what does it matter? All we have to do is keep our mouths shut. Term starts in a few days and we'll get back to our routines." He rubbed his hands through his hair in frustration. "Anyway, all this worry has given me a headache." Rayneer got up and left.

Mare watched Rayneer leave, then leaned over the table towards Arran to whisper. "Way to go, Arran. You just managed to annoy the one person I didn't believe possible to annoy."

Back in his room, Arran took out the photo of Sai'el and stared at it for a long time before putting it up. He blew out the candle and lay staring into the darkness deep into the morning. His mind refusing to shut down as it raced between the events at Freeholt, the meaning of the Sai'el photo, and how everything had become so complicated.

***

Year 1304/October/Week 1
Week 1 of Second Term

The new term had started, and luckily Rayneer had been right. The routines of their training took Arran's mind off of the events over break and he was able to push them, for the most part, to the recesses of his mind.

Rising early one morning during first week, Arran headed to the training hall to work on his forms and enjoy the solitude before first class.

He was sitting meditatively, eyes closed, when he heard the soft steps on the stairs leading into the hall.

"Arran," Shia greeted, entering the hall.

"Instructor," Arran replied, starting to rise.

"No, please sit. I wanted to have a private word with you." She moved across the room, sitting down on bended knees in front of Arran.

Shia settled into the pose, closed her eyes and took several long, even breaths.

She opened her eyes. "It has been decided that you will take evaluations for year two one term early. This term."

Arran's eyes widened.

"Early, ma'am?"

"Yes. You have done well and with the evidence and results from... your vacation... we feel you are ready."

"I don't...I mean...can I do that?"

"It is not unheard of. When appropriate, we have escalated certain individuals who show the aptitude and proper growth." She kept her voice calm and even, downplaying the rarity of the advancement. "You have progressed well and we believe that you are ready."

Several long moments passed as Arran's eyes darted around the room, anywhere other than at the instructor, as he came to grips with the unexpected news.

Shia interrupted him, bringing his attention back to her. "Do you feel that you will be ready?"

"Yes, ma'am!" Arran's reply was quick with excitement.

"Good. Keep this to yourself for now. I will announce your early evaluation when the time comes."

"Of course, ma'am."

"Now, shall we continue our meditations?"

The instructor stayed for another hour, finishing the meditations, and then practicing various forms together. First with daggers, and then with the staff. Shia had never directly instructed him before, and Arran accepted the practice and her advice eagerly.

They both stood together in the center of their mats breathing heavily and then, to Arran's surprise, she bowed. "That was invigorating. Thank you for allowing me to participate on your time."

"Thank you, ma'am," Arran said, returning the customary bow.

Shia muttered under her breath. "I definitely need to practice more often." She wiped her brow with her arm as she turned to leave.

Arran watched her go, still standing stoically in the middle of the mat. If he took evaluations one term early, he could, if he got approved, set off on his first commission for Lord Baelonne. He could be back in Aaeu'din by January and with a little luck be home for Winter Solstice with his family.

Invigorated by the news, he set himself even more determinedly to his training. He 'would' pass his evaluations early.

While the personal news of his advancement was great, the highlight of the first week of term for the school was, without a doubt, the weekend's breakfast. At Arran's suggestion, everyone had agreed to donate the cases of maple syrup to the matriarch of the kitchens. She had proclaimed that the first break day of term would be a special pancake and waffle day. Students from all the disciplines filed in for the event. The dining hall was the most crowded Arran had ever seen. Additionally, and by Arran's rough count, the majority of the instructors had also attended. For one glorious morning, the four friends were the culinary heroes of the school.

Year 1304/December/Week 3
Week II of Second Term

The final week of training before evaluations had arrived, and Arran was beginning to wonder if Instructor Shia was ever going to announce his early evaluation.

Had the instructors changed their minds?

Every day that went by only heightened his anxiety, but the training regimen that he, Rayneer, and Bran had outlined for themselves helped keep it mostly at bay. They had been training relentlessly for the entirety of the term. Following Arran's lead, all three had thrown themselves into their training like never before. Arran's insistent passion spurred the three to train and push one another constantly. It was not long into the term when it became clear to anyone observing that the three were quickly adding themselves to the short list of the school's top fighters.

As their training regimen, and its obvious results, became more apparent, other students began to ask permission to participate. No one was turned away, regardless of year or Patron class, in an effort to push themselves and learn. Even students two years their senior were drawn in. What began as a trickle, with students of Tovin and Talon leading the way, soon blossomed to include participants from almost every other Patron.

Students of Spirit and Kemor even joined, Elinda and Mare included. The preferred training from these groups was usually staffs, but the unique hand to hand martial technique of Kemor's students soon began to gather favor. The style had an art to it, and Arran had found that many of the forms he used for his dagger and staff training were easily translatable.

Mare had become quite formidable with the staff as had Elinda. When not training the martial arts, Elinda held sessions on how to defend against mage casters, including how to distract an opponent or otherwise interrupt a spell casting.

As all of this slowly unfolded, Arran and Rayneer approached Cass around mid-term and asked if she would be interested in teaching a session on archery for all who wanted to attend. She had agreed and, much as Arran remembered from his first year of survival training, Cass was an excellent teacher. She was patient and thorough, but tough when needed. No one escaped her stern instructions, but she was always sure to follow with encouragement when needed.

The lines between classes blurred as the instructors, and Kallion watched in wonder and approval. Never before had they seen such cross disciplinary training between students occur, especially in their free time. The atmosphere of learning and training had become infectious.

Finally, as the end of the week approached, Instructor Shia called Stepf, Bran, and Arran together in the training hall.

She stood in the middle of the mat as the three boys approached and stood shoulder to shoulder in front of her, their hands clasped at their waist.

"Evaluations are next week, and I wanted to inform the two of you that Arran will be joining you for year two evaluations."

Bran grinned broadly, giving his friend a congratulatory slap on the back.

"Well done, Arran!"

"Yes," Stepf agreed. "Well deserved. You have proved to be an exceptional student and mentor, if I may add. I myself am grateful for the time you have given me this term."

Stepf was referring to his struggles with the staff. Arran had noticed the same mistakes he had made when Kallion handed him the unwieldy piece of wood not so long ago. Over the course of the term, he had assisted Stepf in this very training hall, passing along the knowledge that Kallion had given him, as well as his early mistakes.

Arran inclined his head in thanks.

"That is all," Shia said.

The three students bowed, turned, and left the training hall.

Shia watched them leave and heard the faint step of a boot hit the top stair behind her. She tilted her head, acknowledging the presence.

"So it is done," Klintoc said, stepping into the room.

"It is. I only hope we are not rushing him and making a mistake."

Klintoc sniffed just short of a laugh. "Are you serious? Have you been paying attention to the transformation of your school? You know you are going to have to re-examine the training regimens now, right? What those three boys have done is nothing short of miraculous. If I had not watched it myself, I wouldn't have believed it. Anyway, Bran and Arran are probably close to graduate level by my estimation." Shia turned fully and eyed Klintoc with a wary glance. He held up his hands in defense. "But I defer to your discretion. Let us see how he performs."

Shia turned back to gaze out on the courtyard and the pockets of students training together. "You will assist next week?"

"I can stay for a day or two before I need to leave for Mharfan."

"Good, I want you to push him. I want you to push him to the point he believes he has failed. Better to do it now in the controlled confines of the evaluations instead of...out there," she said, gesturing with one arm widely.

Klintoc's face became stern and his reply was curt. "Agreed."

News of Arran's evaluation advancement did not take long to

spread. That evening at dinner, many students and well-wishers stopped by to congratulate him.

"Well, would you look at that?" Mare said. "Country has become quite the celebrity."

"Very exciting, Arran," Elinda said. "This will make us all third year's next term. We can finally move into the individual section of our dorms. We get our own room!"

"It's about time," Mare said sarcastically. "I was beginning to wonder if I should still be seen running around with a bunch of second year's."

"Please, even you cannot put a damper on this news," Elinda retorted. "Second to third year is a great milestone. Graduating is probably the only major event left."

"I have to pass first," Arran said solemnly. "I hope I'm ready."

"You will be fine," Bran said. "I'm more ready now than I could have hoped for after this last term's level of training. Having had you and Rayneer as my training partners, plus all the other sessions with everyone else...we are going to be just fine."

Rayneer nodded in agreement. "He's right. I've advanced my skill and learning more in this past term than any previous two or three combined. We are ready."

Arran looked at his two friends whose eyes, posture, and tone radiated confidence. "Guys, it's not that I'm not confident...I just...I don't want to be over confident. I have a feeling we're going to be tested hard. Really hard."

Arran, Bran, and Stepf walked into the training courtyard where Instructor Shia and two other students stood talking by the sparring circle. Arran recognized them both from the previous term's training. Gal, a first-term fourth year and Shay, a second-term fourth year. Arran had only sparred with them once or twice, as they were rarely at school, off on commissions. They were both extremely talented and either would be a stiff challenge in a duel. Arran let the thought pass and disappear as they approached.

Instructor Shia turned to greet them as they neared.

"We will start the morning with physical training." She turned to Gal and Shay. "If you would be so kind to begin."

With the two older students leading the group, they set out for a six-mile run. The older students kept a brisk pace, but having trained with Rayneer, Arran and Bran had no problems keeping up. Stepf, on the other hand, began to lag a bit towards the end of the run.

After taking a small break and some water, the group went to the training hall where they went through all the various weapon forms for dagger and staff. Each trainee moved through all the long forms they had practiced so diligently. The session was slow and methodical with Shia or one of the older students occasionally interrupting with a correction or piece of advice.

The morning ended with two timed runs on the obstacle course, coupled with shorter normal runs that were also timed. They would traverse the ever-changing obstacle course, then either Gal or Shay would pace them on a two-mile run and then return to the obstacle course. Three executions of this routine were deemed a single run.

The obstacle portion of the evaluation proved the most difficult of the morning. The combination of the courses and the runs proved challenging for Arran. His legs were straining from all the exertion. Additionally, the rate at which the obstacles appeared and departed had been vastly increased, making the courses extremely difficult. One second, a platform or obstacle was there and then it was not. Arran and Stepf had each fallen twice while Bran had three.

Arran could see Instructor Shia high above in one of the observing towers, ever watchful.

It was a grueling physical examination that had all three of the students totally exhausted by the noon break. They were allowed a thirty minute break for lunch before they were directed to the sparring circle. The bleachers were near packed with other students coming to watch the evaluations. Arran let them disappear from his mind as he focused on the upcoming matches.

The two older students stood stoically outside the circle, faces impassive and grim.

Did Shia instruct them to look so dour?

It seemed unnecessary, but he shrugged it off.

"We shall start with daggers," the instructor said, motioning for Bran to take the circle.

The afternoon matches began, much as Arran had anticipated. Each of them would spar with one of the older students until a conceding blow was marked, but that was when the afternoon took a sudden twist. At the end of the one-on-one weapons rotation, the three were then instructed to spar with both older students at the same time. Arran had watched a few evaluations of his own over the previous terms and he had never seen a two-on-one scenario before. It was a grueling and painful experience for all three as they progressed through the various weapon disciplines.

Bran grimaced as he raised his cup for a drink of water. "That was more than a bit humiliating."

Arran grunted in agreement. "The two-on-one sessions. Have either of you ever seen that before?"

Bran and Stepf both shook their heads.

"I think that might be the point, though," Stepf said. "They need to throw the unexpected at us during the evaluations to gauge how we will react and perform. They know we understand the basics."

Arran reluctantly nodded in agreement. All of them had been thoroughly beaten and outclassed in the two-on-one sessions. All the confidence they had at the start of the day had now literally been beaten out of them.

That evening at dinner, Arran listened to similar humbling stories from Rayneer and Elinda. Rayneer's first day was very similar to his. A lot of physical training and weapons sparring. Elinda's, however, was very different.

"I had to perform various spells from all four disciplines three times, with each requirement increasing in intensity. All while being bombarded with distractions to break my concentration. After each session, I had to recite the origins and nature of the spell to show my understanding of its underlying essence. My brain is mush. I just want to go to bed."

Mare had offered a secreted heal, but everyone declined, not wanting to tempt being caught during evaluations.

The meal and scant conversation over, they all retired for the evening.

The following morning, the three students, still sore from the previous day's exercises, trudged to the training courtyard for day two of their evaluations. Instructor Shia sat quietly on a bench, waiting for their arrival.

As the three approached, she looked up.

"Today's exercises will be in the maze and customized individually. Stepf, you will be first, then Arran, and finally Bran. If we cannot get through all three exercises today, we will continue them tomorrow."

Shia gestured, rising, and pointing towards the training hall. "Stepf."

Stepf gave a semi-confident glance to his two friends and headed off towards the hall behind the instructor.

Bran and Arran walked over to the bleachers on the far side of the courtyard to wait.

"So what do you think they have in store for us?" Arran asked.

"Don't know. Could be anything. One thing is for sure, that dungeon has more secrets than we've even come close to seeing."

Three hours later, Stepf exited the training hall. His face was pale, hair matted to his brow with sweat. He sat down next to the water barrel and began taking huge gulps, most of it falling over his chin and down onto his chest.

Arran and Bran ran over and sat down next to him.

Stepf wiped his face. "Can't speak to you," he whispered. "Not until after everyone is through. Instructor's orders."

Arran and Bran nodded and rose, not wanting to put Stepf in a bad position sitting with them.

Instructor Shia entered the doorway of the training hall.

"We need to reset for the exercise. Return here in one hour," she said.

"Yes, ma'am."

Arran returned a little ahead of schedule and was waiting in the training hall in a meditative pose when Shia came for him.

"We are ready now."

Arran rose and followed the instructor down the stairs. The cellar of the training hall had become like an old friend to Arran over the last year and a half. He had spent countless hours in the maze honing his skills, but somehow this time he felt a great unease sweep over him as they descended.

Shia stopped at the side wall that opened into the maze. "As usual, incapacitate as many guards as you can, obtain pickpockets, find traps, and any hidden areas. Do this until you are discovered or receive a decisive blow."

Arran did not reply. The instructions were routine, and he entered without hesitation as the wall opened.

Arran crouched, looked around, and dove quickly into the first alcove he could find across the hall and to his right. He disappeared into the shadows as best he could and listened. He calmed his breathing and focused, eyes and ears coming to bear on anything that would begin to give him the lay of this iteration of the maze.

He remained hidden for at least ten minutes as guard after guard passed his alcove. Garnering a few pickpockets while he surveyed their patterns.

How many guards are down here?

When he thought he had figured out a semblance of a pattern, he edged out of the alcove, turning left and down the hall to the first junction.

Clear.

He turned left again and then into the first alcove he came to, just barely managing to slip in as a guard came around the corner at the far end of the hall.

Sweating profusely now from the dankness of the maze and his own exertion, he again waited and observed. The guard that he had barely evaded did not pass by.

Did he go down another passage? I don't remember seeing one. Did he turn around? That would be new.

Guards had always followed patrol patterns for him to discern. Arran ventured forth to scan the hall. It was clear. There were no other passages leading off of this hallway.

There was only one more alcove on the opposite side of the hallway from where he was and towards the end where the guard had entered. Arran scrambled down the hallway, barely evading a trap that was set in the center of the floor. He did not stop to disarm it, passing it by, and entering the alcove.

Sweat was now running down his face as he blended in to the back of the alcove.

With this many guards and their new behavior patterns, this could take me all day!

Coming to this realization, Arran took three long breaths and began focusing on what he had seen so far, which was not much. He had effectively come right and into the first junction after entering the maze. He entered the first hallway towards the middle and was now in an alcove close to the far hallway, which was probably the backside of the maze.

He made up his mind to continue moving right to find the end of that side of the maze. He listened for several more minutes as he saw three guards pass by in the side hallway, but none had entered his junction. Easing his way out, he took a look into the side hallway for another alcove and cover with which to observe.

Just as Arran had made a move to exit the alcove, he saw it, the smallest flicker of shadow from the direction he had previously come. He turned just in time to see the shadow form into a man.

Arran quickly brought up his blades to defend the incoming blow.

Dumbass, why didn't you already have your blades out!

The attacker had caught him off guard and he began quickly back-stepping to try and put some space between himself and his attacker. The attacker did not relent, continuing to force Arran backwards so that he had to stay on the defensive. It was all Arran could do to avoid the harrying amount of incoming blows.

Then, with a quick flick after one of Arran's parries, he took a sharp cut to his forearm, almost making him lose his grip on that hand's dagger, and in that moment he stumbled.

The attacker was on him in a flash, another slice to his other arm near the shoulder. This time, his dagger fell, as he desperately continued to fight off the incoming blows with his one remaining weapon. His attacker feigned and Arran lashed out to parry the attack as he felt his legs getting swept out from under him. He hit the ground hard, his head rocking back with a crack on the stone floor. His vision blurred as he threw his arms up to defend what he knew was the incoming blow. Stars danced across his sight as his arms were thrown aside.

The fight was over. Arran felt the cold tip of the attacker's dagger touch his throat, piercing him.

Recognizing the warm sensation of blood trickling down his neck, he gasped, "Concede."

The attacker did not take the dagger from his throat, blood now flowing down his neck and into his shirt.

Arran blinked and finally got his first real look at the attacker as he lay frozen on the ground. Clad in all black from head to toe, cowl of the cloak up and face covered in a full mask, he could only see the black-rimmed attacker's eyes. Those eyes bore into him with silent determination. The attacker tilted his head as if examining him like a piece of meat and then, as quickly as the attack had come, the dagger retreated and was deftly sheathed. The attacker turned and strode down the hallway without a word.

Two guards were quickly at his side. They hauled him up and led him out of the maze.

Shia was waiting for him as he exited. She looked Arran up and down, noticing the cuts on his arms and the blood on his neck.

"Go see to your wounds."

Arran could only silently comply and with great resignation

made his way up the stairs, realizing that he had probably just failed his evaluations.

I didn't even make it an hour!

As he exited the training hall, he made his way over to the water barrel for a drink, not saying a word to his friends. The look on his face, his wounds, and the fact that he had only been gone for about an hour was more than enough to quell any conversation.

Arran rose and made his way to the medic facilities, not even having the presence of mind to wish his friend well on his upcoming trial.

As he entered the medic facility, the first attendant took one look at him and ushered him to the first empty bed.

"Someone will be with you in just a moment," he said, hurrying away.

It wasn't long before he heard a familiar voice. "Damn, Country, what does the other guy look like?" Mare said, coming up to his side.

"Not now, Mare," Arran said more tersely than he intended.

"Hmm...not now? Sorry, not my style. Now turn so I can take a look at that arm."

Arran turned as Mare cut off the sleeve of his shirt and cleaned the cut in his upper arm, which was the worst of the injuries.

She placed a hand over the injury, and the familiar small glow began to appear. When she removed her hand, all that remained was a pink pucker of red flesh where the wound had been.

"That will be tender for a few days, so don't go getting stabbed again."

She repeated the process for his other two wounds.

When she was done, she grabbed a towel to clean her hands, then put two fingers under Arran's chin and held his head up so that he was forced to look at her.

"I've seen worse from training exercises."

Arran did not reply, his eyes looking at her, but not seeing.

"Look...at...me...Arran," Mare snapped.

He blinked at the small outburst and his eyes refocused, now staring intently into Mare's.

"Do not presume to know your fate," she said, recognizing the defeat in his eyes.

"They..." She opened her arms in a wide gesture. "...did not present you for early evaluations to set you up for a fail. They are grooming you. For their own purposes, no doubt, but they are grooming you. They are going to push and prod and pound on you to see how far they can go."

Mare let out a long sigh, looking warmly at her friend.

"Believe me, I know. More than one of my instructors would love nothing but to see me give into despair and fail, or worse yet, quit. They have been unkind and unfair in several of my trials. But I would not, will not, give them the satisfaction. Now I want you to gather yourself, and rid that pretty little head of yours of that despair. When you leave here, I want you to present yourself with the utmost dignity and as much confidence as you can muster. Do...I...make...myself... clear?"

Arran blinked and was taken aback under Mare's withering and determined glare. He shakily nodded.

She scowled. "I'm not convinced. Try again."

Arran took a deep breath and let it out slowly.

"Yes," he said more confidently. "Thank you, Mare."

She held his gaze intently for just a moment longer, and then it was gone. She stepped back and shrugged her shoulders. "Meh, I'll let you buy me an ale, though."

Arran let out a light chuckle.

"First round is on me."

"Go on. I've got more important patients to attend to." Arran saw the twinkle in her eye as she headed off down the aisle.

Arran returned to the courtyard, definitely feeling better than when he had left, but the nagging feeling of his failure had not totally abated, despite Mare's best efforts. He did appreciate his friend's words and if he were honest; they did help.

He sat down next to Stepf, who was looking far better than when he had exited the maze, and the two waited in silence for Bran to finish.

It was two more hours before Bran and Instructor Shia emerged from the training hall. Bran looked much like Stepf had earlier, and the two came over to where Arran and Stepf were seated.

"Evaluations are completed," Shia said. "We will inform you of the results tomorrow."

"Only two days, then?" Stepf replied.

The instructor turned her head to Stepf without a word. The look quickly conveying that the topic was concluded. They sat in silence as Shia left the courtyard.

Shia made her way up to her office, where she found Klintoc already present, wine in hand and sitting comfortably by the fire with his feet resting on the center table.

"Make yourself at home," she said sarcastically. "Now get your feet off my table."

Klintoc scoffed, but removed his feet from the table. "This is some really fine wine, if I may say so." He gestured to the chair opposite him where a second glass of wine was waiting on the table.

"Hmmph. So, what is your evaluation of the three?" Shia said, relaxing in the chair and holding the wine up appreciatively to her nose.

"Stepf is a very good second year. Bran is better, though. He's probably close to fourth-year talent, I'd say. I observed them both at length and put the fear in them a few times to gauge their responses. They both responded well and their tradecraft was solid. I don't see anything that should hold them back if you don't."

"And Arran?"

Klintoc sat a few moments, gathering his thoughts.

"Arran did well. I did not..." He stopped, noticing the surprise on Shia's face.

"What?"

"You dismantled him in less than an hour and he did well?"

"If you would let me finish." Klintoc widened his eyes and tilted his head as if asking for permission.

"Proceed," she said sarcastically.

"Thank you. I did not observe anything to refute our notion that he is as advanced as we believe. I could have taken the other two out in the first few minutes of the trial if I had been as aggressive with them as I was with our young Arran."

"Aggressive?" Shia remarked with disdain. "The boy came out of there with not one, but three wounds."

"They were but scratches," Klintoc retorted. "They will receive much more grievous injuries in the field and to be honest, Arran already did with that beast in Freeholt."

"I still don't like it. It is not a good look when a student comes out from a trial with that much blood."

Klintoc waved his hand dismissively. "I'll leave the politics of the school to you. Which brings me to my next observation. These three, especially Arran, should be released for their first commissions as soon as possible. They have all the skills they need for third-year level commissions, probably higher in Bran's and Arran's cases. They need the unpredictability of the real world to advance. Especially Arran. He received his first gifts quite quickly if I remember, and progress on that front has slowed. If we want them to succeed and advance, they all need to be pushed, and the controlled confines of the school's training can only do so much."

Shia reluctantly nodded in agreement.

"I concur. I will make the recommendation."

Klintoc sat back, taking another drink. "So, my work here is done, then?"

Shia did not reply.

"Good, but first I'm going to finish this wine. It really is good."

Everyone sat in sullen silence the following morning as they mostly picked at their breakfast. Everyone except Rayneer, who was already on his second plate. But while his appetite was still intact, his normal implacable facade was not. He looked haggard and worn out. Arran could not remember another time when he saw his friend so utterly drained, physically and emotionally. Arran knew that the evaluation must have been grueling to tax his Resilience to the point of this level of fatigue.

Elinda was much the same, but he knew her fatigue was more mental than physical. Nevertheless, it still wore heavily on her and was no less apparent.

Finishing their meals, the group bid each other good luck and began to depart. Bran and Arran waited a few more minutes for Stepf and the three made their way to the courtyard. Instructor Shia was at the steps of the training hall, conversing with Kallion. They slowly walked over to receive their outcomes.

"Thank you, Kallion," Instructor Shia said.

Kallion nodded as he saw the three students making their way to what he knew they felt was inevitable doom. He remembered his own walks and inwardly smiled at the memory.

Shia acknowledged the group and ushered them into the training hall. They followed as if prisoners being led to an execution.

"Have a seat," Shia said, gesturing to the mats already laid out on the floor.

The three did as asked, and Shia followed them to the floor in a cross-legged pose.

"So that I do not have to look at those forlorn faces any longer, I'll tell you all that you passed."

The obvious relief was instantly realized as all three let out a long breath, looking at one another. Smiles replacing their previous dour demeanors.

"But..." Shia said sternly. "...this is not without some observances of your shortcomings and how we are to address them."

The smiles disappeared immediately at the seriousness of Shia's last remark.

Good. They realize there is still work to be done.

"You will be released for your first commissions and, as such, third-year activities will be delayed until you return. Commissions will be selected by your lords and me, and will be geared toward your further advancement. Hopefully, it will address said short-comings. Primarily of which is your lack of real world experience."

Arran's and the instructor's eyes locked for just a fraction of a second, but the message was clear: keep the incident in Freeholt out of this conversation.

"You are to complete your commissions, observe, listen, and use your skills to the utmost best of your abilities. Use this opportunity to hone your skills, and after any engagement, be it passive or otherwise, I want you to evaluate yourself on what you felt you did well, and what you could have done better. I want full reports written and on my desk when you return."

Shia swept her eyes across each student, pausing slightly upon each to make sure they understood the gravity of her instructions.

Arran was sure that the 'otherwise' in her previous statement was meant to drive home the importance of her words.

All three students nodded.

"Take some time to rest, and I will give you the details of your commissions in the next day or two. That will be all."

The three students rose, bowed, and left the training hall in much better spirits than when they had arrived.

That evening in the common room, the mood from the morning breakfast was vastly improved. Everyone had passed their evaluations and was excited for the term to be over.

"Let's see," Mare began. "Country will, of course, be assigned to find the bandits responsible for the atrocious pig stealing cartel in Kine. Rayneer will get to join a local militia and get to swab out toilets and do all of those important marching in line drills while Elinda... hmmm..." She paused, thinking for a bit.

"Ah, yes, Elinda will be assigned to the Capitol Library to scribe those ever important botany books she loves."

Everyone had a good laugh at Mare's predictions, drinking to her cleverness.

"So, Mare," Arran said. "What did you do on your first commissions?"

"Yeah, Mare, do tell," Elinda quipped.

"My much needed skills were used to help establish a new church in one of the cities in my home realm. I got to unpack hymnals, candles, and all manner of stock for the new church. Oh, and let's not forget the most important bit, play secretary to the new head priest. He was a giant peacock, so full of himself and arrogant as hell. I'm pretty sure one of the instructors put me on that assignment, knowing full well it would annoy me. If I had to listen to one more of his condescending 'Aren't you just precious?' remarks, I was going to die."

Arran sat in silence for a while as he listened and watched his friends. He was once again reminded of how lucky he was to have come by this circle of friends. The pressure release of the evening, after the tremendous stress of the week, was exactly what they all needed.

***

Arran had slept well. The anxiety of early evaluations now gone. He was strolling across the training courtyard when a young servant boy found him and delivered a note from Instructor Shia. Arran thanked the boy and opened the letter. He was to report to Lord Baelonne as quickly as possible. He read on and it turned out that passage for the trip was to be charged to the school.

Yes! I'm going home!

He went quickly to his room and began packing his bag. He hesitated as he picked up the small pouch containing the picture of Sai'el. He took the picture out and looked at it for the thousandth time, wondering what his mother would say. Would she even know who this was? All the questions that had plagued him these last months came bubbling to the surface.

Soon enough.

He gently refolded the picture and placed the pouch in his bag.

Confident that he had packed what he needed, he left the school and headed into town. He wanted to retrieve some money for the trip and for his parents.

That evening, the friends sat at their customary table at the Singing Goose.

"So how long do you think you'll be gone?" Elinda asked.

"Not really sure," Arran replied. "I have to think at least four weeks, if not a bit more. I don't really know if it's one long commission, or several. Guess I'll find out."

"Thank the Patrons that mine was only set for the length of term break," Mare said, taking a drink of ale. "This is good. What is it again?"

"Some winter fruit berry ale," Arran replied, sticking out his tongue. "I'll stick to Tan's bitter, thank you very much."

"How about you, Rayneer? You know what you'll be doing yet?" Arran asked.

Rayneer looked down sheepishly at his beer.

"I got it right, didn't I?" Mare said with glee.

Rayneer squirmed in his seat, which, for a guy as large as Rayneer, was something comical in and of itself.

Rayneer looked up. "Unfortunately, Mare was probably not far off the mark."

"Ha!" Mare exclaimed, drawing a few stares from the other patrons.

"Elinda? How about you?" Mare asked, now eager to see if another of her predictions would prove true.

"I haven't heard anything yet," she replied haughtily. "I have only been told to report to the head mage of Daijoor for unspecified duties. I'm really hoping for something Alchemy related, given my studies."

Tan approached the table with a fresh round of drinks.

"I hear you are off on your first commissions. A round on the house to wish you the best of luck." Tan placed the drinks on the table.

"Why, thank you, Tan," Arran said. "I will spread the wonders of the Singing Goose all along the shores of the Seitellen during my voyage."

Tan laughed. "Thanks." His face turned serious as he scanned the group. "Seriously, best of luck and...be careful out there."

The group nodded and raised a fresh mug to Tan as he left.

"Good guy, that Tan," Rayneer said.

"Yep," Arran agreed, taking a long pull of bitter from his mug.

CHAPTER 10
COMMISSION
YEAR 1305/JANUARY/WEEK 1

Week 1 of Term Break

The group all met for breakfast before bidding each other farewell. Arran's thoughts turned solemn. It all felt so surreal. Had it really been a year and a half since all of this started? It didn't seem possible that he was already leaving on his first commission.

Everyone said their goodbyes and well wishes, each eager to head out on their first commissions. Arran felt a pang of mournfulness as he watched the group split up and go their own way.

We'll all be back before we know it.

He slung his pack over his shoulder, grabbed his staff, and headed for the docks.

Finishing the morning roll he grabbed on the way out of the dining hall, Arran found himself entering the bustling docks. He stopped and began scanning the area, looking for the dockmaster. He approached a burly man holding a clipboard and barking orders at anyone and everyone on the docks.

"Excuse me, sir, might you be the dockmaster?" Arran asked.

"Aye."

"Do you know if the Wayfarer is in, or if not, when she will be in?" Arran asked. He had hoped to book passage on the Wayfarer again on his passage back to Saloanne, but he would not delay his trip if it wasn't possible.

"Aye, she made dock yesterday," the dockmaster replied, pointing down the docks.

Arran thanked the dockmaster and headed off in the direction he had pointed. The voice of the dockmaster immediately returning to its previous bluster of commands behind him.

Arran walked along the docks, scanning the ships until he came upon the Wayfarer. He smiled.

"Good'ay, Cid," Arran said, remembering the lingo from his previous voyage.

Cid turned and looked at Arran, brows furrowing, then recognition spreading across his face.

"Arran!" Cid exclaimed, holding out his hand. "What brings ya 'round?"

Arran took his hand, and Cid shook it vigorously.

"Well, I appear to be in need of passage back to Saloanne and I was hoping to book the Wayfarer again. When do you depart? I'm in kind of a hurry."

Cid thought for a moment. "Well, we just arrived yesterday, and we finished unloading this morning. We should be able to finish reloading later today, or early tomorrow morning, and then we will be off. We do not have a scheduled stop in Saloanne for any goods, but if you book, I'm sure the captain would be obliged."

"So tomorrow morning then and seven days as before?" Arran asked, wanting to obey the 'as quickly as possible' aspect of his letter.

"Nay, should be more like five. We won't have any stops along the way. Saloanne would be our first port. Our goods are for delivery further south."

"Perfect," Arran replied. He had been planning on seven days, and even with the short delay, he would still be making good time.

"Book my passage," Arran said. "Oh, I was told you could charge it to the school."

"Intres'ting. Shouldn't be a problem tho'. See you in the morning, then."

"See you in the morning."

Arran spent one last evening in his dorm room. It was quiet. Everyone else had already left, and many students were going home since this was the last break before the Winter Solstice next month. He enjoyed a peaceful evening of reading in the abnormally quiet common room.

The sun was lazily making itself known as Arran made his way back to the docks the following morning. He watched as the street lighters made their rounds, snuffing out the lamps for the day. The docks were already awake with a bustle of activity.

When do these guys sleep?

"Good'ay, Cid," Arran said, approaching the gangplank to the Wayfarer.

Cid turned and smiled. "Good'ay, Arran, come aboard. We should be off shortly. All the goods are aboard and the lads are securing things for the voyage."

About an hour later, with only two other passengers coming aboard and the ship secure, the Wayfarer began slowly departing from the docks.

Arran went to a railing and enjoyed the majesty of being on the water again. Meitellen spread out across the northern horizon on the starboard side of the ship as they entered the inner circular channel towards the Seitellen. Arran leaned over the rail, taking in the morning breeze.

The five days seemed to take forever, but Arran managed to keep busy talking to the crew and, of course, Cid. On the morning of the fifth day, Arran found himself lazily gazing southward as dawn broke. In the distance, he could just make out the keep of Saloanne, high upon the hill overlooking the river.

Arran hastily made his way to the gangplank once the ship had docked. He didn't want to delay the Wayfarer.

"Thank you, Cid. It was another fine trip. With some luck, maybe I can catch you on the way back."

"Good'ay, Arran," Cid said, shaking his hand. "Best of luck to ya."

With that, Arran walked down the gangplank to the dock. Not wasting any time, the gangplank was drawn in behind him as the Wayfarer continued its voyage south.

Arran looked around until he found the familiar path that led to the keep and set out at a brisk walk.

***

Arran nervously approached the main entry to Saloanne keep, surprised at his anxiousness. He didn't know why exactly. He was, in almost every way, not the naïve boy that had left here almost two years ago. Steeling himself, he strode confidently up to the guards.

Arran handed his letter of commission to the guards, stating his business with Lord Baelonne.

"Hold here," said the guard, brandishing Arran's letter as he left to go inside.

Moments later, Mindell appeared, now holding Arran's letter.

"Master Arran, so good to have you back. Follow me, please."

Mindell led Arran inside and to a small chamber just off the foyer.

"If you will wait here. Master Qoman and Lord Baelonne will be with you shortly. May I take your items? I can put them in your room."

Arran instantly cringed at letting his bag out of his possession, thinking of the picture, but then eased.

"I think I'll just lay them here until after I speak with the lord if you don't mind. I don't know what my plans are quite yet."

"Very well." Mindell politely bowed and left, shutting the door behind him.

A few moments later, Qoman entered the room.

"Arran!" he said excitedly. "So good to see you again."

"And you also, Master Qoman."

"Well, well, it looks like school has been treating you well. You have grown into a fine-looking young man. Your parents will be proud." Qoman crossed the room, grasping Arran's shoulders, smiling broadly, as if 'he' was the proud father.

"Thank you, sir. Do you think I will have time to make a trip to Kine? I would very much like to see them."

Well, that was subtle.

Arran grimaced. He had hoped to ease his way into asking for time to visit home, and here he was blustering it out like he was that same small town boy from before.

Qoman rested a light hand on Arran's shoulder. "Let's bring it up with the lord, and we'll see what we can do. I don't think he would begrudge you some time to visit your parents."

The door opened abruptly, and Lord Baelonne entered the room, shutting the door behind him. He looked distracted and distraught.

"Welcome back, Arran."

Arran gave a slight bow. "Thank you, sir."

"I am sorry I don't have much time for pleasantries, so let's get right down to the business of your commission." Baelonne crossed the room and took a seat on the couch. Arran and Qoman followed, taking the two chairs opposite.

The lord began speaking almost immediately. His voice was quick and terse. "We have had issues with bandits along the southwest road to Morc'ier. They have been extremely clever in their attacks, leaving no trail to follow and very little to no evidence. I would like you to investigate the attacks, and if possible, track the ruffians down for capture. I cannot abide with bandits on the main road to Morc'ier. It sends a bad message to the populace that we cannot protect the realm and it damages commerce." Baelonne's lips were tight. His tone and his face both showing his disgust and anxiety from the attacks.

"Understood, sir," Arran replied. "Is there a local constable or mayor that I may contact for information?"

"There is. A good man..." Baelonne trailed off in thought, trying to recall the name, snapping his fingers.

Qoman interjected smoothly. "Cole, I believe it was, sir."

"Ah yes, Cole. He has been assisting the militia. I had Relorre send out a team of militia not long after we learned about the attacks. Go and see Relorre. He can give you the details of the militia and the route." Baelonne rose.

"I'm sorry to be off with such a curt conversation, but I have other matters to attend. Best of luck to you, and I hope you can find the little bastards."

Arran rose and bowed, a bit surprised at the venom with which Baelonne spoke.

"If I may, sir," Arran said as Baelonne was heading for the door.

Arran looked at Qoman, who gave a slight nod of his head as if to say, 'Go ahead'.

"Yes," Baelonne said, obviously eager to be moving on.

"I was wondering, if time permits, of course, if I could make a trip home to Kine to visit my parents while I'm here?"

Baelonne thought about the request for a moment, then sighed heavily. "I want you focused on these attacks. Is that understood?"

Arran nodded dejectedly.

The lord saw the disappointment in the young man's eyes and pondered the thought for a few more seconds.

"Hmm...After. Once the issue with the bandits is resolved. I want rid of these damn troublesome bandits. Am I clear?"

Arran was taken aback at Baelonne's uncharacteristic outburst, but immediately perked up and glanced at Qoman, then back at Baelonne. "Yes, sir. Thank you, sir."

"Very well." Baelonne turned and hurriedly left the room without another word.

Arran let out a long breath.

"So it looks like you have your orders, then," Qoman said. "You should be able to inquire after General Relorre in the training grounds. They should be back from their mid-morning exercises."

Arran began gathering his belongings. "Thank you, Qoman." As he reached for the door, he came up short.

"Arran." Qoman's voice was soft and filled with concern. "Be careful, son. These bandits…they've been known to kill and they are not to be taken lightly."

Arran turned around fully, taking in the seriousness in Qoman's eyes.

"I understand."

Qoman watched Arran as he left the room.

I only hope that your instructors are as right about your abilities as they proclaim. Good luck, son.

As Arran exited the keep through the main door, he heard someone behind him calling his name.

"Young Master Arran." It was Mindell.

"Yes, Mindell?"

Mindell hurried forward, short of breath as he held out a bundle. "I thought it wise for you to have some provisions for your trip, so I took the liberty of having the kitchen prepare something for you."

"Thank you, Mindell." Arran took the pouch, placing it in his bag.

Arran looked up to find himself the recipient of a very uncharacteristic hard stare from the servant. "You find the cretins, young master. You find them and put an end to this raiding of theirs, you hear?" Mindell's voice was strained and tremulous. His normally implacable face was wrought with more anger than Arran had thought possible of the man.

"I will do my best."

"I have a sister in Crenn'ier," he whispered, tugging at the bottom of his vest habitually.

Arran simply reached out and placed a hand on his arm, feeling a quiver of pain and anguish wash over the man's body.

Mindell's eyes dropped and never left the floor as Arran turned and left the keep.

The training grounds were easy to find. As Qoman had said, the soldiers were arriving from their morning routines and making not a small amount of noise. Arran slowed his approach as he neared the soldiers, admiring their armor and the forms they executed with their long swords. They were in perfect synchronization.

"Keep at it," a man shouted to the men and then broke away from the group, approaching Arran.

"May I help you?" he asked sternly.

"Yes, sir. I was told I could find General Relorre here this morning."

The man looked at Arran dubiously.

"And who might have told you that?"

"Lord Baelonne and Master Qoman have sent me," Arran replied sternly, trying to knock off a bit of the man's haughtiness.

The man looked Arran up and down, obviously not impressed, but quickly replied. "Follow me."

He led Arran to a central tent not far off the training circle and instructed Arran to wait outside. He entered the tent and then came back out, instructing Arran to proceed inside.

Arran entered the tent. It was well lit, with three men in the room. Arran recognized Relorre seated behind the large table in the center of the room, but not the other two.

Relorre raised his head from the papers on the desk and looked at Arran.

"So you are the Intelligence student sent to assist us on the bandit issue, eh?"

"Yes, sir."

He looked Arran over with the eyes of a cold and hardened soldier.

Does he not remember me? Have I changed that much?

"Very well, then," he said, ruffling through some papers on the table and coming up with what Arran surmised was the latest report on the bandits.

"I have sent a militia of eight men to assist the local magistrate in the investigation. You can make contact with Magistrate Cole. He can bring you up to speed."

Relorre paused, looking at Arran with disdain. "My militia is there to protect and eventually apprehend the subjects, and not to participate in the goings on of the Intelligence order. If..." He said the word with emphasis, "...you find the bloody whelps, then and only then may you work with my men to plan any apprehension. Is that clear?"

"Yes, sir."

Relorre eyed Arran with a steely glare. "I don't want them traipsing off in the countryside and ignoring their patrol routes."

"Understood, sir."

"You may requisition a horse for your travels from the stables. That will be all." Relorre returned to his papers on his desk.

"Thank you, sir," Arran replied, understanding his dismissal. He turned and left the tent for the stables.

So definitely not a fan of the Intelligence order.

Arran couldn't help but grin at the soldier's obvious disdain.

<hr>

By the time Arran had procured a horse and made his way out of town, it was early afternoon. The horse, Gallant, was fit and strong, and Arran could tell he would be able to keep a good pace. Gallant was every bit the horse Storm had been, his horse from the trip to Valoor, but it was also very clear that Gallant had been trained in the art of war. There was something about his gait and posture that told Arran this horse had seen battle.

He was told that it was a three-day ride to reach Crenn'ier, but he hoped to beat that estimate. If he could make good time this afternoon, he might be able to reach the town with only two more days of solid riding. He was sure Gallant could handle it, so he spurred the horse on to a slow gallop and headed down the southwest road toward Crenn'ier.

Arran was rewarded by his determination, and in no small part, Gallant's fitness. By midmorning on the second day, he knew he was getting close from the telltale signs of the last few miles. Farms and homesteads had begun to appear with more regularity along the road. A town was near.

"You did well, boy," Arran said, leaning forward and patting the horse on the neck.

The horse raised its head and whinnied at the attention.

Arran grinned, "You did real good, Gallant. Good boy," he cooed into the horse's ear.

Arran slowed the horse to a trot, giving the steed a break now that they were approaching Crenn'ier.

It wasn't long before Arran caught his first sight of the militia Relorre had mentioned. Four militiamen approached him on patrol. They only gave him a cursory glance as they passed and did not bother to question a lone rider.

Arran entered the town and made his way to the stables. He tied Gallant to the post next to a water trough as a young boy approached him from inside the stable.

"I'm looking for Magistrate Cole," Arran asked.

"Aye, the magistrate is usually in the town hall over there," he said, pointing across the central yard to a two-story building.

"Thank you."

Arran took out a copper ingot and flipped it to the boy. "If you could take care of my horse, please. Food, water, and stabling. He could probably also use a good brushing. I've pushed him hard the last few days."

The stable boy caught the ingot, pocketed it, and nodded.

Arran slung his bag over his shoulder and with staff in hand, made his way across the yard to the town hall. He entered and found a small, unattended desk in the center of the foyer. He looked around.

"Anyone here?" he asked loudly.

Arran heard a rustling from one of the side rooms, and a portly, older man appeared in the doorway, spectacles looking like they would fall off his nose at any moment. His hair was thin and mussed as if he had just awoke.

"May I help you?" the man said, trying to smooth down his hair.

"I'm looking for Magistrate Cole."

He looked up, pushing his glasses up his nose. "Well, that would be me."

Arran gave a small bow. "Magistrate, I was sent by Lord Baelonne to assist with the...uh...disturbances."

"Ah, yes, please come in." Cole fidgeted with his glasses again and muttered something under his breath as he lead Arran into his office.

Cole stepped around his desk and took a seat as Arran settled into a chair on the opposite side, setting his bag on the floor and staff against the other chair.

The magistrate looked at Arran for a while with obvious skepticism on his face.

"You say Lord Baelonne sent you?" It was stated as if he was not quite sure what to make of the young man sitting before him.

"Yes, sir. I'm Arran from the School of Intelligence, on commission to assist."

"Intelligence?"

"Yes, sir. Third year." Arran kept his voice calm and confident. He knew he was stretching the truth a bit since he hadn't actually started his third year, but he was trying to get past the obvious bias the magistrate was exhibiting towards him.

Arran sat patiently waiting for the magistrate to continue, but his impatience ended up getting the better of him.

"If you could fill me in on your current findings and discoveries, I will get started."

The question finally put a spark in the old magistrate and he started as if he had been napping.

"Of course, of course. I'm sorry, it's just that you are, well, so young and I guess I had been hoping for someone a bit more seasoned, given the delicate nature of things."

Arran's anger flared, but he kept it from reaching his face. Remembering Mare's words of encouragement, *They are grooming you*, Arran steeled himself and tried to break through the man's misgivings.

"I was sent for a reason, Magistrate Cole. Let us assume that Lord Baelonne and my instructors at school understand the 'delicateness', as you put it, of the situation and felt that I was best for the task, eh?"

"Of course, of course."

The man was a fidgety old guy, and it was clear the events were not something he was well suited to handle. His distress was clearly written across his face, and his demeanor was agitated.

The magistrate rummaged around his desk for a few moments, flipping through the piles of papers. Finally, he tapped a grouping, picked them up, and began reading from the top sheet. He read and flipped through the papers for several minutes.

Arran fidgeted in his seat.

Finally, Cole looked up. "There have been three attacks. Two on the road to Morc'ier, and one on the road from Saloanne. Different locations and different terrains. No obvious attack points that we could discern. The odd thing about all of this, and quite frankly, what has us all confused, are the trails. The trails from the attacks lead off in all directions. It's like the bandits split up and all ran off in different directions. We'd track them for miles before eventually losing them."

Cole paused as he took a sip of his coffee, his face wrinkled. It was cold.

Arran nodded in thought. "They could have doubled back and then used a single trail to hide their numbers."

"We thought of that, but each trail was eventually lost. If they doubled back, then to what end?"

Arran's brow furrowed in thought.

"Which attack was the most recent?"

"The one on the road from Saloanne. It was two days ago. I can have one of my men show you." He paused and pushed his glasses back up his nose in thought. "Sev, I think, he's a good lad."

Arran was a little surprised at the suggestion. "Not the militia?"

"Ha! Good luck getting them off their patrols."

Arran sighed heavily. The militia were going to be difficult. "Fine. I'd like to get started if I could. I'll need to get a room and stow some of my gear, then I'd like to head out. Can you have Sev meet me at the inn, in say, thirty minutes?"

"That will be fine. Tell Ingrid that the room and board can be charged to the town proper."

"Thank you," Arran said rising. "I might be a few days, but I'll report back as soon as I can."

Cole nodded, and Arran gathered his gear. The sound of paper shuffling and the incoherent mumblings of the magistrate followed him out the door as he headed for the inn.

Sev slowed his horse. "This is where the attack occurred. You can see where the caravan was forced off the road over here." He stopped and pointed to the patch of trampled ground in front of them.

Arran surveyed the sight. "The trails?"

"There were two trails headed in that direction," Sev said, pointing to the opposite side of the road. "The other three were on this side, all in different directions."

Arran nodded and dismounted Gallant, moving over to observe the trampled ground. He sighed in relief when he was still able to find the three trails that Sev had mentioned. They were faint, but the previous trackers had enhanced the trail somewhat and he could still make them out.

Sev leaned down over his horse. "Will that be all?"

Arran looked back over his shoulder. "Yes. Thank you. Can you take my horse back to the stables? I'll be hiking in from here."

Arran grabbed his pack and staff off of Gallant, giving him a pat on the neck, and handing the reins to Sev.

Sev nodded, then turned, and headed back towards Crenn'ier.

Arran paused and looked at the surroundings. The trails on the opposite side, he deduced, were false. That direction did not offer much in the way of good cover for a hidden camp or set of operations. This side, however, had rolling hills and a forest for miles. He decided this was the best place to start.

He picked the first trail that ran parallel to the road towards Crenn'ier and followed it until it abruptly turned and went into the trees. Noting the location, he returned to the site of the attack and followed the middle trail, which went straight into the forest. He followed it for a while, but it was almost completely straight.

Too obvious.

He returned to the attack site and then followed the trail that went along the road towards Saloanne, away from Crenn'ier. This one went a long while before turning into the trees.

If I were trying to lay a false trail but eventually wanted to circle back around, this is the trail I would use. The trees and hills off of this trail would be the most remote and...it's what I would do.

Confident in his decision, he headed off to track the trail he had chosen.

After about an hour of tracking, Arran could make out where the previous team had lost the trail. He noticed where they had spread out to look for obvious coverings in an attempt to pick the trail back up. There were markings in a vague circle for at least a hundred paces in all directions before they had obviously given up.

Arran surveyed the area. He did not have a trail to follow, but acting on instinct, he chose a direction that he would make if he were trying to circle back around and towards a central point. Closer to say, a location like Crenn'ier.

Darkness was falling and in amongst the trees, it had become difficult to see. His gift of Sight could help him stay on the trail longer than most, but he decided to stop. Some food and rest were in order. He would continue with fresh eyes in the morning.

Arran arose early and had been following his instincts for a few hours now, slowly making his way southward through the forest in the direction of Crenn'ier. He had chosen a path that was far off the main road, at least a mile by his reckoning. It would offer good concealment and hopefully he would find some signs or another trail that would lead him to their main camp. Most likely deeper in the forest.

As he was making his way up a small hill, weaving his way around the big boulders and climbing over the smaller ones, he heard a twig snap. Arran froze. All of his senses coming alive at once. Everything narrowed down as he focused in concentration.

The sound had come from in front of him and to his right, just over the rise of the hill he was climbing. Arran slowly dropped his bag and began moving forward, concentrating intently on stealth, as he made his way to the top of the small incline. Lying prone, he crept forward, and peeked over the edge of the rocks.

He didn't see anything. He lay very still, listening, and sharpening his sight as he slowly scanned the area for any evidence of the noise.

Could it have been a deer or maybe a wild boar rutting around?

He willed himself to be patient and continued scanning the area.

There!

About fifty paces or so ahead of him, he saw the faint flicker of a shadow as it moved across the underbrush. The sun was high in the sky, so the shadow was small with only the smallest of movement, but his Sight ability allowed him to follow it. After a few moments, he was rewarded. It was the movement and shadow of a man walking.

Arran took a long breath and steadied his breathing. Marking the direction, he crept back down the side of the hill, picked up his bag, and began tracking.

He easily found the track of the man after only a few minutes and decided to slow his pace. Now that he had the track, he did not need to rush.

He followed the man for several hours and then heard the sound of additional voices and stopped.

"Oi!" the man he had been tracking said as he entered the camp.

Arran had found 'a' camp, but was it 'the' camp of bandits he was looking for? He backed away from the camp until he could no longer hear the voices, covering his tracks as best he could. Using one of his old tricks from training, he climbed a tree to find a nice wide branch to stretch out on to wait out the day. He would approach the camp at night.

Arran watched as the last bits of daylight finally began to blanket the forest in darkness. He climbed down and stashed his small bag and staff in some underbrush, then slowly began making his way back towards the camp.

Longest...day...ever!

Arran found a good spot about fifty paces from the camp. It was a large tree with a good amount of underbrush for him to discreetly observe the camp.

There were five men in the camp and they looked to be in the process of cooking dinner.

"What's for dinner?" one of the bandits asked.

Another bandit stood and went over to a stack of goods laid off to the side of the camp. The pile was a mess. Boxes, bags, and various bundles were strewn about in disarray. The pile had obviously been thoroughly rummaged through.

Arran cursed at himself.

Why didn't I ask what was stolen?

"Looks like beans and rice again," said the one rummaging through the goods.

"Again?" several others moaned in unison.

"Shut it. You ain't starving are ya?" the one who Arran guessed was in charge replied.

"No, but I sure could go for some meat," came a reply.

"You'll have some soon enough. We should be done here in a few more days," the leader replied. "Master should be arriving this evening or tomorrow morning to give us our final orders."

As if on cue, Arran saw a sixth and seventh man enter the camp from the opposite side.

"What are you idiots squabbling about now?" one of the new men asked.

"Nothing, sir," the leader said. "Just waiting for your orders is all."

"Good," the new man said.

Okay, I guess we have a new leader.

This new man was tall and lean and was not dressed like the other bandits. He seemed to be a man of more means and had much nicer clothing than the rest. He carried himself confidently as he strode into the camp.

The new leader entered the center of camp and stood in front of the group of men.

"Did you get me what I asked for?"

The previous leader spoke up quickly. "Yes, Master Pim."

Like a thunderbolt and lightning quick, the man who spoke was brought to his knees with a vicious slap across the face.

The man was kneeling and whimpering, blood beginning to seep down his cheeks from three long gashes.

Pim seethed with anger. "What have I told you about using my name?"

"Sorry, sir," the man whimpered, prostrate on the ground in front of Pim.

Pim looked around the camp with disdain. "Where is it?"

The whimpering man pointed towards a cart.

Arran could not make out exactly what it was from his vantage, but it appeared to be a cage. He could not make out what was inside.

"Good. Very good." Pim's voice had become calm and menacing as he walked over to the cage. He held out his hands and waved them over the cage. "This will do well."

Pim removed his cloak, draped it over the cart, and then returned his attention to the cage. He straightened his posture and held out both hands in front of him. A soft glow began to appear around his hands. It was darker than Arran was used to seeing the students use at school. As Pim continued, a stream of the dark light snaked out from his hands, directed at whatever was in the cage.

He's using the Source!

The unmistakable squealing of a boar rose out into the night.

Pim stood, hands held out in front of him, chanting and channeling for at least five minutes before releasing the Source. He stepped backed, his shoulders sagging, noticeably drained from the effort.

"That never gets old," one of the bandits said.

Pim turned his head and looked at the man with disdain.

"Prepare to break camp and leave this place." Pim paused. "Day after tomorrow. I should have the transformation complete by then."

He's transforming the boar?

Arran's mind went into overdrive as he processed what he had just seen and heard.

Have all the incidents the school has been investigating been because a group of people, using the Source, have tainted the wildlife?

Arran shuddered at the implications. He continued watching the group as Pim sat down by the fire. Pim gazed out into the trees. His face tired and uneasy. He looked as drained as Elinda would be after casting a large spell.

Arran froze as Pim's gaze swept in his direction. He willed himself deeper into the shadows, not making the slightest of moves.

Pim's eyes narrowed as he scanned the area.

"What is it, boss?"

"I don't know. Nothing." Pim waved his hand.

Arran willed himself deeper into the shadows, and then it happened. The spark of an ability hit him, and he had to hold in his gasp. There was the burn in his chest, the flow of energy throughout his body, and then it was gone.

A gift? Now?!

Arran was close to panicking, desperately trying to mask his heavy breaths. Without any thought or effort, his vision began to blur around the edges. It flowed and moved like a dim, grey, milky shadow. The ethereal looking shadows shimmered darkly at the edge of his vision as he struggled to remain perfectly still.

Pim looked away, shaking his head. "I must be tired is all. Fetch me some of that gruel you call dinner."

Arran moved his head ever so slightly and looked at his hands. He could barely see them. Realization dawned on him.

I have just received the gift of Shadow!

His mind raced as he tried to come to grips with the new gift. He paused and slowed his breathing, taking long, purposeful breaths before letting them out. One, two, and then a third. He held the last in for a few seconds before releasing it. The shadow started to recede and his vision began to return to normal.

Arran's temper flared in frustration, cursing inwardly. He had to get out of here and return to Crenn'ier to alert the militia. They had to stop this before Pim was allowed to finish the transformation.

What if they were planning to release that beast like the ones in Freeholt?

Arran was forced to wait a long while in his position before he dared move. It was frustrating as time crawled by before the bandits began to bed down for the night. Only one guard was left on duty while the rest went to sleep. Pim was in a tent that had been erected for him behind the cart in a small clearing. Arran slowly crept back to retrieve his bag and staff. He continued to move stealthily for at least fifteen minutes before he began sprinting through the forest in the direction he hoped was Crenn'ier.

Arran ran until he thought his lungs would burst. Dawn was still at least an hour away by his guess, but he could finally see the edge of the forest ahead. He took a moment to slow his pace and catch his breath.

Bless you, precious Rayneer.

Arran smiled, thinking of his friend making him run all those miles.

Once he broke the edge of the forest, Arran could see a small farm ahead of him. He didn't know if he was north or south of Crenn'ier, but surely someone at the farm would know.

He had startled the farmer's family when he pounded on the door. After easing the farmer's anger at the intrusion, he was relieved to find that he had not been too far off. He was still north of Crenn'ier, but only by a few miles. He thanked the farmer profusely and headed off at a trot, picking up his pace as he went.

Arran looked a mess when he finally entered the town and made his way to the town hall. He was sweating profusely, his hair was matted, and there were bits of leaves and debris from his trek through the forest. He stumbled into the magistrate's office, hands on knees.

"What the bloody...?" The magistrate cut his comment short as he took in the heaving mess of the man that stood in front of him.

Arran held up a finger in a gesture that said he needed just a minute.

"I found them," he finally said between breaths.

Cole looked at him, dumbfounded.

"You found the bandits? That's great!"

"Not so great," Arran wheezed out between ragged breaths. "How much do you know about the incidents in the north?"

"The stories of wild animals attacking villagers? Not much, just the same rumors and conjecture as everyone else."

Arran regained some of his composure and stood up straight to face the magistrate. "Well, they are true. I've fought the beasts and let me tell you, they are not to be taken lightly. Three other students and I, all well gifted and talented, barely took down three of them." Arran wasn't sure if he was breaking some kind of protocol, but at this point, he didn't care.

"I believe these bandits and their leader are preparing to release one of these beasts on Crenn'ier."

Cole went pale and did not answer. Arran could tell by the man's demeanor that he was in shock.

"Magistrate! Where is the militia?"

No response.

Arran shouted, more emphatically this time. "The militia!"

Cole started and stammered out a response. "On patrol...Yes... they will be on patrol by now."

"Send your best riders out to retrieve them. We need to go after the bandits today!"

Cole sat in his chair, staring blankly at his desk.

Taking a deep breath, Arran lowered his voice and spoke as calmly and deliberately as he could, "Magistrate Cole, we need to get moving as soon as possible."

Cole blinked and then jerked to alertness. "Of course, right away." Cole then rushed out of the room, much more nimbly than Arran would have thought the man capable, shouting for anyone within earshot.

It took much longer than Arran had hoped to gather the riders and then retrieve the militia from their patrols. Arran was sitting in the town hall's meeting room trying to grab a bite to eat and drink some coffee to keep himself alert. He was studying a group of maps of the surrounding area, which the magistrate had laid out for him.

The militia leader, Captain Mollen, entered the meeting room in typical military bluster.

"What is the meaning of this?" he exclaimed. "Why have my men been called back off of their patrols?"

Arran did not look up from the maps and replied simply. "I found them."

"Found who exactly?"

Arran looked up as if the man was dull. "The bandits."

Mollen looked at Arran suspiciously. "Are you sure?"

Arran didn't respond to the question and continued. "I found their camp, and it was littered with the goods and stores that I presumed were stolen from the caravans." Arran stood up straight and turned towards the Captain. "Additionally, I overheard them speaking of a planned attack. Like the ones up north." Arran paused as recognition spread across the man's face. He changed his tone to one of more reverence, befitting of the Captain's rank. "Captain, they are planning it soon. We have no time to spare."

Arran spent the next hour bringing Captain Mollen up to speed on what he had found, the size and makeup of the bandit camp, and formulating a few strategies.

It turned out that Mollen had very little knowledge of the incidents in the north, but rumors were widespread now. Those in power had done a very good job of keeping the specifics of the incidents quiet, or, at the very least, downplayed. Mollen was surprised to hear the specifics, especially from an Intelligence student, but to his credit, he took the danger seriously once Arran explained Pim's actions with the Source. He shook his head in disbelief at the news.

After going over the maps and formulating a handful of plans based on a few different scenarios, Arran stretched. "I defer to your knowledge of military tactics, Captain. How do you want to proceed?"

Mollen looked at the maps in front of him, rubbing his eyes.

"We will attack from two fronts: One directly from the west and the other slightly southwest. The groups will stay within earshot of one another, but offer two fronts for us to attack, and force the bandits to have to defend. If we are lucky and gain the advantage of surprise, so much the better. But I must warn you, militia guards are not the most stealthy of beings."

Arran chuckled. "I might be able to help there. What if I cause a distraction on the opposite side of the camp?"

"That could work. They'll be alerted and distracted away from our advance."

Arran smiled maliciously. "Consider it done."

By the time they had finished their plans and gathered the militia, it was already past noon.

"We will need to make haste if we are to arrive before dark," Mollen said to his troops. "Let's go."

With Arran leading the way, they set off on horseback for the forest. They would have to abandon the horses once they were in the trees, but it would still save some time.

Arran was with the militia group attacking from the southwest. Mollen was leading the men attacking directly from the west.

The going was slow, but methodical. The troops had opted to wear their training gear versus the full armor they used for patrolling. One, because it was too heavy and loud, and two, there was a risk of being seen a mile away if any stray light caught the shining metal.

Dusk was just settling in when Arran quickly held up a hand for the group to halt.

"Give me a minute."

Arran moved forward stealthily, focusing on his Sight and Observance. Within a few minutes, he verified what his senses had alerted to. The camp was just ahead, and they were starting their fire for the evening.

Arran made his way back to his group and instructed them to stay put. They were to wait for his distraction. He then headed left, hoping to find the other group and instruct them of the same.

It took a while for Arran to find the other group. They had been slower in finding their way towards the camp.

"We are one man down," Mollen whispered as Arran approached. "A lad was climbing around some boulders and slipped. His ankle might be broken."

Arran nodded, then whispered, "The other group is ready. Let me circle around. Be ready for my distraction."

"What do you have planned?"

Mollen stared at the huge grin spreading across Arran's face as he slowly crept away. "That boy scares me just a bit," he muttered.

Arran worked his way around the camp, inspecting it as he went. As far as he could tell, Pim and the one bandit that arrived with him were gone. Only the five original bandits were left in the camp. Arran winced. If that were true, then Pim had finished his work with the animal in the cage.

Not good.

Arran crept his way around and to the back of the cart, where the animal cage sat on its side. He looked in and saw the grotesque, disfigured beast of what had once been a boar. It was lying down as if asleep, its sides heaving.

Deal with you later. Time to put that new skill to use.

Arran concentrated on his new ability. It came to him easily; he was pleasantly surprised. Melding into the shadows, he brought all of his senses to bear on the men in front of him. He scanned the encampment and let the new sensation of his Shadow form sweep over him.

It was a very strange sensation...looking at one's own body as if it were almost ghostlike in the shadows. He would need to consult with Klintoc as soon as he got back to school.

Quit it! Focus!

He scolded himself and returned his attention to the men in front of him. He knew what was coming, and he knew that this night would probably be the first of what would undoubtedly be many more. A time and duty when he would be called upon to kill. No one spoke of it at school, but it was there. The unspoken truth, the sordid reality of what the training was all about in the first place. Now that it was in front of him, Arran was surprised to find that he was not nervous, not hesitant in what he must do. He had seen the outcome of what these men were planning. The innocent lives that had been taken, and at Freeholt; the life that had ended as Arran knelt in the man's blood. He could stop it. He would stop it. An unnerving calm swept over him. He was ready.

Arran's plan had been to pick a target and throw a dagger for a kill from the rear of the camp. Eliminating one and giving the militia groups their diversion, but to Arran's surprise, one of the bandits decided it was time to relieve himself, and began walking away from camp on Arran's side. Arran let him pass, hidden in the shadows, then followed. Arran was awed at how easily he was able to slide between the shadows as he stalked behind the man, silent as a mouse.

The bandit stopped and before he could even unbutton his britches, Arran slipped a dagger to his throat and cut deep, covering the man's mouth. There were a few seconds of panicked struggle, but then the bandit's body began to ease. Arran slowly guided the body to the ground, just as he had been taught. Quiet, efficient and, most importantly, deadly.

That's one.

Arran returned to the cart and observed the camp. The other bandits were oblivious to what just happened to their comrade not twenty paces away. Arran drew his daggers.

The first dagger he threw caught one of the bandits in the throat. It had been an easy throw. The bandit grasped at the dagger and pulled it out in a shower of blood. His hands instinctively reaching up in a desperate attempt to try and stem the fountain of blood. His eyes glazed over quickly as his arms fell, body slumping sideways to the ground. Arran's second dagger was already in the air before the first had hit the ground, but he missed. His second target had jerked around in alarm and his dagger only garnered a glancing blow off of the bandit's head, slicing at his ear.

Arran ran forward, pulling out the dagger from his first victim. Diving left, he stabbed a third bandit in the thigh. Continuing his roll forward, he came to a kneeling stance and surveyed the battle. Two dead, one essentially battle ineffective, and two left scrambling for their weapons, but they were too late. Before the last two could reach their swords, the two militia groups stormed into the camp.

Mollen surveyed the scene in front of him.

"So your idea of a distraction was to kill..." He looked around the camp in puzzlement. "Where is the fifth?"

"Oh, that one chose a very bad time for a piss break." Arran pointed his thumb over his shoulder.

That drew some chuckles from the militia group, which Mollen quickly brought to a halt with a withering glance.

Mollen surveyed the camp. "So, you kill two bandits outright, incapacitate one, and then leave two so disheveled that our involvement was essentially mop up work? That's your idea of a distraction?"

Arran picked up his second dagger, sat down on a log next to the fire and began wiping his blades on a random piece of cloth. "Well, it didn't quite go as planned, but in the end...yeah, I guess so."

Mollen tried as hard as he could to keep his professional face intact, but in the end he had to give credit where credit was due. He shook his head in admiration. "Damn, son, that was one of the most brilliant takedowns I've ever seen."

Arran did not reply, continuing to clean his blades as the guards finished securing the three remaining bandits.

Mollen sent five men with the two unharmed bandits back to town. They also had orders to pick up their fallen comrade and return in the morning. Arran, Mollen, and the two remaining guards would stay at camp until more assistance could arrive the following day.

Arran watched the group leave. "I will take first watch. The one they called Pim, and the other were not here. I don't want to be surprised if they decide to return."

Mollen agreed and turned his gaze to the cage in disgust.

"I guess that dispels any rumors."

Arran followed his gaze to the disfigured animal in the cage.

"Yes," Arran replied gravely. "I'm not sure what Pim did, but we need to get that animal to the right authorities for investigation. We should impress upon the soldiers to keep this quiet, and maybe move it off to a more discreet location before tomorrow morning. We don't want to have to explain it to the villagers."

Mollen nodded. "Agreed. We'll do it first thing in the morning."

They had found a bowl of meat near the cage. The meat had white powder all over it, as if it had been rolled in flour. They assumed it was a drug of some sort that the bandits used to subdue the beast. Hopefully, it would last until morning. If not, they at least had some extra to feed it.

The evening was uneventful. Pim had not returned, and by the time the militia and some villagers with pull carts had arrived back at the camp, they had moved the animal cage to a safe distance. It had not awakened.

The group spent most of the morning loading up what remained of the stolen goods and clearing out the camp before heading back to Crenn'ier.

Mollen had instructed one militia group of four to stay at the camp 'in case anyone returned', which was partly true, but mainly to keep watch over the cage until they could covertly transport it back to Saloanne.

———

Arran spent the next four days in Crenn'ier as he and Mollen waited for the courier's return with their new orders from Saloanne.

Two militiamen had already set out for Saloanne, cart in tow, with some of the 'evidence' from the camp. In truth, they were to meet up with the four militia left at the bandit camp and retrieve the cage for transport to Saloanne.

By the time the courier returned from Saloanne, Arran had become extremely anxious and was ready to be on the move again.

The news from Saloanne was short and to the point.

Mollen paraphrased as he read the orders. "My militia and I are to return to Saloanne immediately. As for you..." he paused, looking at Arran. "It simply says, 'Arran has his leave and is to return to the capital as soon as possible'."

Arran smiled at Mollen.

"Leave?"

"I am from Kine. About three days' ride. I haven't seen my family in almost two years since leaving for school."

Mollen inclined his head. "I see. Well deserved, lad. Go. Go and see your family. We'll make our reports and see you on your return to Saloanne."

"Thank you."

Much to Arran's surprise, Mollen held out his hand. Arran took it.

"Best of luck to you."

Arran thanked the Captain and then turned and almost ran to the inn to gather his belongings and Gallant.

There weren't any roads that went straight towards Kine from Crenn'ier. So, Arran chose the most direct path and rode cross country for the majority of his journey. Despite this, he made good time and near noon on the second day, he found the east/west road that would take him to Kine. The same road he had left on with Qoman so long ago. The road that would take him home.

He slowed Gallant to a trot as he slowly made his way down the road. Taking in all the familiar sites of home as he drew closer. He could see Challand's family's farm off to his right as he got closer to town.

I wonder how she has been?

She could be betrothed by now for all Arran knew.

Arran rode into town and stopped short of the town center, staring at the sourcestone altar in thought. Breaking his gaze from the stone, he looked around. Not much had changed in his near two-year absence. He was glad that it was as he remembered.

Arran made his way towards his father's blacksmith shop. The familiar ringing of hammer on anvil reached his ears. He dismounted and tied Gallant to an outside post and stepped into the doorway of the smithy.

Without looking up, his father yelled above the din of his work. "I'll be with you in just a minute."

Arran watched as his father brought his hammer down for another blow.

Arran watched reverently as his father worked the metal. This could have been his life. This shop could have been his, in time.

Arran leaned against the post. "No hurry, Father."

Dale's head shot up.

"Arran!" he shouted gleefully, dropping his hammer, and scrambling out of his gloves and apron.

Dale ran to his son, picking him up in a giant hug.

Arran grunted at the strength of his father's embrace. "I'd like to still have the use of my lungs, if you don't mind."

Dale released him and held Arran by the shoulders at arm's length.

"Let me get a look at you. You have filled out!" Dale squeezed Arran's shoulders and then his arms.

"You might last an hour on the anvil now," he said mockingly.

Arran laughed. "I might at that. It is good to see you, Father."

"Come, let's go see your mother. She is going to be so happy to see you."

The two turned and headed towards the back of the shop and the doorway to the main house.

Standing in the open door, silhouetted by the light behind her, in stark contrast to the dimness of the smithy, stood his mother. His beautiful mother. Arran broke from his father's arms and walked swiftly up the stairs to stand in front her.

"Hello, Mother." His voice coming out in a hoarse whisper.

She clasped Arran's face with both her hands and gave him a kiss on the forehead, just like she did to him as a child, tears streaming down her cheeks. Then she grabbed him in a warm embrace that only a mother could give.

Arran could smell the familiar scent of his mother's hair, and the all too familiar smells from the kitchen as they assaulted his nose with memories. He was home.

INTERLUDE

Spirit was waiting in the council chamber, pacing nervously. She made her way around the hall, taking in the murals from ages past. Would a mural from this age take its place amongst the others, or was this age to come to an abrupt end before it even had the chance to make its mark?

The hour of the meeting was close, and she made her way back to her chair as the others slowly filtered in.

Once everyone was seated, Spirit rose and anxiously looked at Breanna, who nodded in recognition as if to say, 'Go on'.

"I have called this council meeting due to some abnormal behavior on Galleant," Spirit said, proud that she was able to keep her voice calm and neutral.

No one spoke, so she continued.

"I have discovered abnormalities in the wildlife. Similar, albeit to a lesser degree, to that of the incident with the sourcestone."

Kemor's face darkened, and his response was immediate. "What sort of abnormalities?"

"Erratic and rabid behavior. In a few cases, the affected have wandered into villages, attacking the humans. Most likely out of fear and confusion, but there have been several deaths."

She paused.

"Is this the only abnormality you have seen?" Kemor asked.

Spirit lowered her head and spoke softly. "It is not. It is for this reason that I have called you all here today. The occurrences have become more frequent, and the animals are showing signs of deformity. With some it is simply size, growing approximately twenty to thirty percent larger, but it is the other deformities that alarm me. Unnatural alterations to their bodies have been observed. Spines, tusks, and claws have all been modified to grotesque size and lethality. Just to name a few."

Spirit paused to take a drink.

She pointed to the tablets in front of each of the other council members. "The full observations are in my report."

Spirit looked around the table at the grave faces of all in the chamber. A few had already pulled up her report and were reading through its contents.

"Is this another incident with the sourcestone? Has it been uncovered?" Talon asked.

"It has not, Master Talon. Our efforts there are intact. The sourcestone is undisturbed and undiscovered," Spirit replied.

"So what, then?" Kemor asked. "Is this simply a natural manifestation that we are observing? Effects that are occurring naturally over time with a planet connected to the Source?"

Breanna took this opportunity to break in on Spirit's behalf.

"We also asked this question, Master Kemor. While this is the first planet we have exposed to the Source, I have come to the conclusion that these abnormalities could not be caused by the natural ambient levels of the Source. There is still much that we do not know."

Talon replied with a look of surprise on his face. "So you have been assisting in this investigation, also?"

Breanna squared her shoulders in response. "I have. Sister Spirit came to me not long after she discovered the anomalies and asked for my expertise."

Breanna winced slightly. *Only a small lie.*

"If not natural, then..." Kemor trailed off as a sudden look of realization dawning on him.

Spirit waited for Kemor to finish his thought with trepidation.

"The humans." Kemor looked up from the datapad.

"The humans," Spirit replied solemnly.

Mevan huffed. "Wait, the little buggers have already figured out how to muck about with the Source to affect biologicals?"

Spirit could see the slightest bit of admiration in Mevan's expression as he continued reading her report. "That is our conclusion. Once we began that line of investigation, it did not take long for us to observe individuals using the Source directly on the wildlife. They are quickly becoming more adept at the process and...more bold in their experiments."

Talon laid his datapad down hard on the table. "Well, that is that, then. We cannot allow this to continue. It was a bold experiment, but I believe we have to end this age before all of this gets out of hand. The humans are too rash and power hungry for this not to end badly."

Spirit cringed at the statement. *That didn't take long.*

Spirit steeled herself for one last gambit. "I do not believe such a drastic decision is warranted. Not yet. I would like to ask for more time. The contingent responsible is small, and a group of authorities at the school and at the realm capital level are becoming aware of their activities as we speak. This may resolve itself without the need to end the age."

"Ha!" Talon shouted loudly with derision. "Humans resolving human issues? We have seen this before. Resolving issues amongst themselves has never been their strength."

"I hate to admit it, sister, but Talon is correct. Humans do not have history on their side for this argument of delay," Tovin said.

Spirit shot her brother a glance, anger and betrayal on her face.

The council chamber went quiet, and no one spoke for a long while. The Patrons had precedents in place for ending an age before its natural demise, but it had only been used a handful of times. An action of this sort would reach the central realm and an investigation would be rendered.

"Please," Spirit finally said desperately. "Give the humans a chance. This age is different. I can feel it."

Kemor shook his head sadly. "I am sorry, sister. Your idea was bold, and it has shown promise. Maybe we learn from this and try again. Possibly with a different race, the humans are so...difficult and unpredictable."

Spirit lowered her head in dismay.

Why couldn't she make them see!

Talon grabbed at the sentiment. "Better to end it now and deal with the investigation, than let it get out of hand and look negligent."

Kemore stood. "Does anyone need time to deliberate before we put this to a vote?"

No one replied.

"All those in favor of..." Kemor was interrupted by the loud and distinctive ringing of the Corpellian grand bell.

"What the...?" Mevan began to say, but then every member in the chamber froze as they all felt the unmistakable opening and closing of a portal.

"Bloody hell," Mevan said, shaking his head. "That was fast."

Kemor shook his head in dismay. "They could not have known about this so quickly. This has to be for another reason." His declaration was weak and did not convince anyone.

A few moments later, a tall, lean man of middle-looking years strode into the council chamber.

A look of surprise and wonder instantly appeared over the entire group. Spirit had never seen the high counselor this intimately before. In all her time, she had only seen the man at a distance, usually during a large central realm event. This was an unprecedented visit.

Kemor was the first to respond and bowed. "High Counselor Astaban." The rest of the council stood, following the gesture.

"If we had known you were arriving, we would..." Kemor was interrupted with a wave of Astaban's hand.

"This is not an official visit."

Astaban strode towards the table with calm authority.

"Show me the planet."

"The planet?" Kemor replied.

Astaban eyed Kemor wearily. "Don't be coy, Kemor."

Spirit pulled up Galleant from the table's display.

Astaban gave Spirit a glance and then began to inspect the planet's information.

After he was done, he flipped the table's presentation away, and addressed the council.

"You are to do nothing to interfere with the planet. I am aware of the current activities, and the decision stands."

Astaban swept his gaze around the table.

"I want no gifts given that would not otherwise be normal practice. I want no direct or indirect interference with the information available to the humans. This entire process will play out under the given constraints you established upon creation of this age. Am...I... making myself...clear?"

He looked around the table. No one responded.

Evidently satisfied, Astaban continued. "I want..." he turned to Spirit. "What is a time that would be relevant for an update?"

Spirit hesitated at such a direct question aimed at her. "Bi-weekly should prove appropriate, sir. Equivalent to twelve days' central realm."

"Bi-weekly, then. I want these reports made directly to me." He paused for emphasis. "Made directly to me...in person."

Spirit looked around the table at the other council members and then back to Astaban.

Astaban looked at Spirit expectantly. "It will be you, then?"

"It will, sir."

"Very well." Astaban's demeanor suddenly relaxed as he pulled up Galleant's information from the table once more.

As he surveyed the planet, he said to no one in particular. "You are not the first to have tried introducing the Source to a mortal race."

He spun the planet around, zooming in, a look of question spreading across his face.

"How is it that I see traces of Source throughout the planet?"

Spirit leapt at the question excitedly. "That was Breanna's idea, sir. She felt that we needed to introduce a, well, for lack of a better term, a source for the Source. So, we created a single sourcestone and infused it. The gifts flow from there."

"But that doesn't account for the Source presence on the other continent and how the sentients there have manifested gifts without Patron intervention." Astaban turned his head, a hint of a smirk on his lips.

Spirit blushed and her cheeks went hot.

"What!" Talon exclaimed.

Spirit looked at Astaban. All hints of the smirk had vanished.

He is enjoying embarrassing me.

Spirit straightened her skirt absentmindedly before addressing the rest of the council members. "I introduced a small single village on the other continent, as a control."

Talon was respectful enough to not get into an argument in front of the high counselor, but his stare shot daggers at Spirit.

Spirit continued.

"You are correct, High Counselor. The gifts manifested by the villagers on the other continent do not abide by the normal parameters we set forth. As a matter of fact, the use of the sourcestone itself has almost become irrelevant. The planet itself has become...infused. By our measurements, in another one hundred years, the use of the sourcestone will no longer be needed at all. The Source levels on Galleant will have become self-sustainable. As for the control group manifesting gifts, we believe that is a natural progression, given their specific race, and natural attunement."

Astaban nodded his head and flipped the planet's display away.

"I look forward to your reports. I must take my leave."

"I'll walk you out," Spirit said hastily, not wanting to face the rest of the council until much later; after they had time to settle down since the news of the second village had been broached so unceremoniously.

Spirit and Astaban walked in silence as they made their way to the portal room. As they climbed the stairs to the chamber, Astaban turned to face Spirit.

"You have questions."

Spirit hesitated, not sure where to start.

"How did you know?" She purposefully kept the question vague to try and see where he took the conversation.

Astaban simply tilted his head at her questioningly.

That didn't work.

She rephrased the question. "How did you know about the anomalies on Galleant?"

"We see much," he said simply.

Spirit blustered forward. "But why is the High Council and you, in particular, so interested? You said yourself that we are not the first to have tried this."

Astaban hesitated, taking a few moments to himself before he answered. He did not want to divulge too much information this early, but the girl and her council had indeed accomplished much where many others had failed.

"Let us say that you are indeed not the first, but your...results have been of interest. We wish to investigate further."

"Have we overstepped?" she asked hurriedly. "Have we committed a breach in our mandate?" Her words came out rushed and eager, like a child's. She chided herself the moment they left her lips.

Astaban gave Spirit a warming smile.

"Overstepped? I would not say overstepped."

Astaban hesitated. "Let us say you have diverted from the path and we shall see where it leads us."

Spirit let out a small sigh of relief.

"I must go. I'll be expecting your reports." Astaban turned and stepped towards the portal. He turned back and looked at Spirit for a few moments, as if inspecting her, and then entered the portal.

CHAPTER 11

PIM

YEAR 1305 / JANUARY / WEEK 3

Pim was purposefully taking the long way back to his master, sticking to the small towns and less used roads. There was little chance that anyone would attach him to the events in Crenn'ier, but why chance the main routes and the bigger towns? More guards, more people, more risk. He wasn't a wanted man per se, but he had enough enemies that there could be a chance he would be recognized. He would prefer to avoid the distraction.

The crew should have already released his latest creation on the town by now, and he would probably start hearing the rumors soon.

Oh, the rumors. How I love the desperate, panicked rumors.

Pim smiled. It was not a pleasant smile. The wicked curvature of his face holding no warmth, only malice.

Wrapped up in the personal revelry of his latest accomplishment, he didn't notice the traveling salesman until he heard the hooves of the horses. He cursed himself as the salesman approached.

Stupid! Stupid.

"Good day, sir," the salesman said, coming to a stop alongside the road. "Might you be interested in anything for your travels?"

Pim hated the lilted speech of salesmen. Their cheesy and insincere pitches to sell their wares. He was about to say no when he remembered he ran out of cheese a few days past.

What the hell.

"Do you have any cheese? Maybe some wine?"

If you have some cheese, why not a bottle of wine to go along?

The salesman smiled amiably. "I do indeed."

The salesman turned and yelled to someone in the back of the covered cart. "Bring a block of the sharp and our best bottle of red."

Best bottle of red?

Pim laughed inwardly at the obvious sales pitch. He reached for his pouch to pay the man when the stupid idiot decided he wanted to strike up a conversation.

"Dumbass salesmen," Pim muttered.

The salesman turned back to face Pim. "Eh?"

"Nothing. How much?"

"Two silver."

Pim glared at the man. The slimy weasel didn't even hesitate at the offensive price.

The salesman continued. "It is a fine bottle of red."

Pim sighed.

Even if it's watered down piss, it'll be better than nothing.

"Fine." Pim handed the greedy little monger his money.

As the man hurriedly tucked away the coins, he continued with his incessant chatter. "Bad business up in Crenn'ier. Bad business, indeed. At least they finally caught the buggers."

Pim's head snapped back, looking at the salesman in alarm.

"What is that you say?" Pim struggled to keep his tone calm and inquisitive, but inside he was already fuming.

"Those bandits up in Crenn'ier. They've finally been caught." Then, as if someone might overhear them on this godforsaken road in the middle of nowhere, he leaned in dramatically.

What an idiot. Who was going to hear them out here?

Pim played the inquisitive traveler dutifully and leaned in to play along with the charade.

"There's rumor of dark workings going on. Dark they say. Best you keep your wits about you out here all alone on the road."

Like you give a rat's ass, you ignorant simp.

At least that is what went through his brain, but Pim calmly replied as nonchalantly as he could, "Thank you, I will. Good that they were finally caught. They were making a mess. Did they discover anything else?"

"No, sir, just that several were killed in the melee and a few more wounded and captured...and of course, the dark rumors."

Those idiots never released the beast!

Pim's face turned sour.

"You okay, sir?" the salesman asked, noticing Pim's sudden shift in demeanor.

"Oh, sorry, I was just thinking about all the poor people that they hurt. So useless," Pim said, shaking his head. "It angers me is all."

The salesman nodded and then turned as a woman strode up carrying a small bundle and a bottle of wine.

"Here you go, sir. We will be on our way if there is nothing else."

"No. No, that will be all," Pim said distractedly, already lost in thought.

"Good day to you then, sir."

Pim watched as the woman disappeared back into the covered cart and the salesman took the reins with a wave. The slow clopping of hooves and rattle of the cart faded into the distance.

Pim did not move for several minutes. He sat atop his horse in the middle of the road, holding the bundle of cheese and the bottle of wine. Fuming.

"Shit Shit Shit!" he yelled angrily, throwing the bottle of wine reflexively in his anger. He watched as the bottle tumbled in the air with immediate regret. He quickly began to reach out to arrest its fall with Air, but he was too slow and too angry to focus properly. The bottle finished its lazy arc and Pim watched as it smashed into the ground, spilling its precious contents onto the road.

He let out a heavy sigh. "Well, shit."

Later that evening, Pim sat at a corner table at a local inn. It was the first worthless little town he came to after the news from the salesman. He didn't even know its name. It didn't matter. He needed to think.

He stared blankly at the people gathered at the inn.

Such little people going about their petty little lives.

He took a drink of his ale and returned to the matter at hand.

The fact that there was no other information aside from the capture of several men meant a few things. First, and most obvious, was that the beast was never released. If it had, there would have been no way to keep that news from spreading. Hell, it was kind of the damn point. Secondly, and more importantly, was the capture of several of the men. Master Azra'el was not going to be happy that his men, caught alive, and with knowledge of Pim and his abilities, were now in custody. Pim shuddered.

How in the hell am I going to explain this?

He finished off his mug and held it up to the waitress for another.

As the waitress placed the fresh mug on his table, he had finally concluded that there was no explaining to do at all. He had executed the plan as directed. He made sure the camp was well hidden and that the men obeyed every precaution to avoid detection. Hell, they had been there for weeks and no one had even come close to finding the crew. When he left them, everything was in order. The men would release the animal the next day and then leave the area, just as he had.

He would state these facts and avoid trying to subvert a story to alleviate his fault. Lying to Azra'el was not something he wanted to try ever again. Pim grimaced as the scars on his back began to itch from the memory.

That is it, then.

Pim finished his fresh beer in one long pull and retired for the night.

Pim finally reached the cabin two days after learning of the failure in Crenn'ier. As he approached, there were no signs that anyone was present. The horse pen was empty. There was no smoke coming from the chimney, and even though it was near dark, there were no lights emanating from within.

He sighed with relief, knowing the uncomfortable conversation was inevitable, but he did not want to address it after his long day of riding. He was tired, and he wanted some rest.

Pim entered the familiar cabin and looked around. It felt like coming home, and in a way, it was. Every corner of the small one bedroom cabin had a memory attached to it. Some good and some... not so good.

Pim did not mind the sometimes harsh treatment imposed upon him during his training. He had endured worse. Pim was in it for the power, and in his time spent here in this little cabin, his power had grown almost exponentially under the master's tutelage.

Lighting a small candle for the barest amount of light, he went to the far corner and kicked at the bedroll and blankets. Dust billowed up in huge clouds, making him cough. He hauled the entire bundle outside and shook them out as best he could and then put them back. He was not allowed to use the bedroom, even in the master's absence. He then rummaged through the small kitchen space, finding nothing; not that he had expected to find anything, and made do with the remains of his travel provisions. Blowing out the candle, he climbed into his bedroll, reminiscing on how far he had come.

Year 1299/Month Unknown

The day was dreary; they were all dreary, and Pim stared up at the swollen, cloudy sky. It would rain soon, adding to an already miserable day. Last night had not been fruitful, and he was hungry. He rummaged around in his pockets and pulled out a single bronze coin. It would have to do for now, as he sat up and removed the threadbare and ragged piece of cloth he used for a blanket. He wondered what he could buy for his bronze today.

Pim was the unfortunate and illegitimate son of a whore. He had been raised begrudgingly at the brothel until he was old enough to strike out on his own. He had discovered at a young age that while he had never been gifted by the Patrons; he did have a small amount of skill in the use of magic. He was not sure how, but it was there, and for someone of his standing, it was beyond him to seek advice from his betters, or seek tutelage at the infamous School of Doctrine. So, he did what most orphans did with no education or means. He made his way on the streets.

In the beginning, he would perform the handful of cute little tricks he had managed to teach himself for pocket change. Push an item with a puff of air or snap his fingers for a quick spark of flame. On the bad days when his tricks no longer entertained, he was forced into petty stealing. It had not taken him long to find that he was very poor at the art of stealing. When he would get caught, which was most of the time, he would be beaten, either by the local gangs or the guards, whomever had caught him first.

Such was his life, and today did not appear to be starting any differently. He managed to get a moldy loaf of bread for his bronze and settled down to eat the decent parts between the mold under a covering in an alley. After finishing the bread, he found a decent corner and decided that today would be a performing day.

Maybe today will be better.

He did not have the strength, or fortitude to try his hand at petty thievery this day. He was still recovering from the last beating.

Pim set to performing his tricks with no success and was ready to find another location, when he noticed a man watching him intently from across the street. He was sitting at a table, drinking a coffee, and eating a fresh morning bun. Pim's mouth watered as the man tore off a piece and slowly raised it to his lips.

Pim continued performing his small retinue of tricks, running through every single one he had taught himself. When he was done, the man simply continued to stare at him. He finished his coffee, stood, then walked over and tossed a silver at him. Without saying a word, the stranger walked away. Pim stared at the silver coin in awe. He understood an opportunity when he saw it and followed the man. At the very least, he could maybe perform for another silver. At best, he might have the opportunity to relieve the man of his entire pouch.

The man walked for a long time, turning down random streets and never stopping. The rain had started and Pim was forced to continue in the cold wetness as the man sloshed ahead under his umbrella. Eventually, he stopped and looked up at the sign above a warehouse on the outskirts of town. He entered. Pim stopped across the street and watched. A short while later, a light appeared in the upstairs window. Sensing his opportunity, Pim crept over and into the warehouse to investigate. As soon as he entered the warehouse and took a few steps, he heard the almost inaudible click of the door being shut behind him. Before he could turn, he was quickly grabbed from behind, his arms deftly pinned behind his back. A sack was thrown over his head as he wriggled to get free, but the hands that held him were firm.

"Quiet, or your night ends here," came a man's gravely voice behind him.

Pim immediately ceased his struggling. He was dragged across the room and then roughly pushed up the stairs to what he assumed was the second floor, where he had seen the light. He was shoved into a chair, breathing heavily from exertion, and no small amount of fear. His hot, fetid breath not helping under the confines of the hood.

"So you want more?" The voice of a different man, smooth and refined, emanated in front of him.

"Ma...more?" Pim questioned raggedly between breaths. Pim heard footsteps behind him and began to turn his head, which only prompted a sharp slap across the face. Even under the hood, it stung sharply.

He heard the creak of a chair as someone rose, then footsteps, and now the refined voice was to his left. "What do you want? More food? More coin, perhaps? Or do you want...'Mooore'." The last word was drawn out with tantalizing emphasis.

Pim thought for a moment and then remembered how the man had watched him perform his simple tricks.

Power! The man was observing his gifts!

"I want more power," Pim said with as much confidence as he could muster.

"And what are you willing to pay for that power?"

"Anything!" Pim's answer came out quickly and without any hesitation.

"Good," the stranger said flatly.

That was the last memory Pim had until he awoke in this cabin, on the very same bedroll where he was now lying. That had been almost five years ago.

<hr>

Pim was returning from his meager morning hunting trip, cursing the need to provide for himself. Neither tracking nor hunting had ever been his strong suit. As he began preparing his meal, he saw a man approaching on horseback.

Pim stood to greet him, wiping his hands on a towel. Only a few people knew of the cabin, so this person was most assuredly a courier sent by Azra'el.

The man came to a stop and, without dismounting, pulled a sealed note from his jacket. He handed it to Pim and then rode off without saying a word.

Pim watched the man ride away until he disappeared over a rise. He looked at the note. It was simple, no writing on the outside. The wax seal had no markings and was unbroken. He broke the seal and extracted the note within.

He immediately recognized the writing. It had been penned directly by Azra'el. The note was simple and to the point.

Crenn'ier was unfortunate. Make way to Samal.

Pim read the note again and then again, teasing the meanings out of the simple text.

First, master knew about the failure at Crenn'ier and the fact that

Pim himself was now probably compromised. This assumed that the captured soldiers would confess. Pim was fairly certain, as Azra'el would be, that they would not hold out long under the 'scrutiny' of the interrogators. Secondly, it was also probable the authorities now knew that the various animal incidents were not natural, but the work of magic. Their magic. Sending Pim to stay with Samal was a way to move Pim out from underneath the inevitable prying eyes that would be seeking him until the excitement abated.

Pim had never been to visit Samal. As a matter of fact, he had only met the man on one previous encounter with Azra'el.

Could be fun.

Pim turned and began preparing for his journey.

CHAPTER 12
HOME

Arran was finishing his second plate of food as his mother began preparing another.

"I'm good, Mother." He pushed the plate forward on the table and leaned back. "They don't starve me." Arran grinned at his father, who was also finishing up his second plate.

Pai'ese stopped abruptly. Her hands coming to rest next to the plate she had begun preparing. Her original anxieties and anger from Arran's Source Day rising to the surface once more. She took a deep breath, her body stiff and unmoving.

Arran rose and went to his mother, taking her into a tight embrace from behind.

"It's okay, Mother. I'm fine. I'm better than fine," he said, trying to reassure her.

She broke his embrace and turned to sit.

The three sat at the table in silence.

"So," Dale said enthusiastically. "I think maybe it's time for a good cider and you catch us up on the past two years."

"Agreed," Arran said. "But...is Tabard's bitter any good?"

"Beer!" Dale exclaimed loudly. "You want beer? We definitely have some catching up to do." He smiled broadly. "And Tabard does indeed have a fine bitter. Does everyone feel like an evening out? There will be a lot of folks wanting to welcome you home," Dale said, looking at Pai'ese questioningly.

"I think that would be lovely," Pai'ese said. "Besides, I think I could use a bitter myself. Give me a few moments to freshen up."

As the three left the house, Pai'ese took Arran's arm in hers. They had barely walked halfway to Tabard's Inn before the townsfolk began recognizing Arran. By the time they made it to Tabard's and received their drinks, the inn had become the epicenter of activity in the town. Arran had returned!

The inn was bustling. Everyone from the mayor to family friends, and some who were not quite friends, were in on the evening's activities. Tabard himself had produced his lute and was playing for the crowd as everyone danced and enjoyed the festivities. It reminded Arran of a good weekend at the Goose.

"Seems like folks are having a good time," Dale said, taking a drink of his beer as the onslaught of well-wishers began to die down. "So tell me, son, when did you discover the wonders that is a good bitter?"

"Funny story, that." Arran told his story about finding the Singing Goose and how his tastes had slowly matured to the different ales that Tan made. His father's eyes widened at some of the more exotic flavors Arran mentioned. Finally, he told them how he and his friends frequented the inn and had made it their spot when they wanted to step away from the stress of school.

"It's like a second home. Like here, at Tabard's. You'd love Tan, Father."

"This Elinda..." His mother said trailing off.

Arran looked at his mother, noticing the mischievous look on her face.

"Oh, no." He shook his head, almost spitting out his beer. "Nothing like that. She is a good friend, Mother. That is all."

"I see."

Arran could tell that she was not done with that bit of conversation, but she let the topic go with a small smirk.

It was at that moment Challand entered the inn. Arran saw her and as she looked their way, Arran raised his mug in greeting as she hurriedly made her way over to their table.

"Welcome back, Arran!"

"Why, thank you, Challand. I have to say it is nice to be back. How have you been?"

Challand nervously straightened her dress. "I have been well. You look...well yourself."

Pai'ese eyed the two youths with a gleam in her eye. "Dale, why don't you invite your wife to a dance?"

Arran's father blanched at the offer. He was not what one would call...a dancer.

"But..." He did not get to finish the sentence as Pai'ese rose and took her reluctant husband's hand.

"Come, dear." She gave him a quick glance and then moved her eyes ever so slightly back at Arran and Challand.

"Oh." He took one last drink of his beer and let himself be led out onto the dance floor.

"Would you like to sit?" Arran offered with a gesture.

Challand nodded and before she could even finish sitting, asked eagerly, "What did you think of the school?"

Arran was surprised at the question, but then quickly remembered that Challand was the only other person in their village that had attended, and she seemed eager to hear about his experiences.

Arran leaned forward and whispered, "It's amazing."

"I know, right!" Challand leaned back, raising her head, lost in thought. "I loved it."

Arran was confused. "So why did you return? I always thought you wanted to come home."

Challand looked at him with sad eyes. "I didn't want to return. I wanted to stay, but we could not afford multiple years of training." She sighed. "I had learned enough to be of use back home, so I returned."

Challand had not been sponsored as he had been and therefore the burden of school tuition would fall on her family.

"I never knew."

"No one did outside my family. Everyone was led to believe I had chosen to return on my own. I so wanted to stay, Arran. I loved it there and I could have learned so much more."

Arran reached across the table and grasped her hands in his.

"I'm sorry, Challand. I really am."

Challand accepted the gratitude and then slowly looked up with a mischievous grin, her initial exuberance returning.

"Which is why you are going to tell me everything!"

Arran laughed. He waved to the server for another round and began; starting with his arrival in Meitellen, finding his way to the school, and meeting Elinda.

Arran stopped, thinking about something, then decided to continue. "Was Master Bronsel, the librarian, there when you attended?"

"The old dour guy behind the giant table, spectacles perched on his nose as he stamped books?"

"That's the one." Arran told his story of checking out his first books, the accidental courtship walk with Elinda, and then the discovery that he had lost the book.

"You lost the book, courted a noble, and had no clue?" Challand's eyes began to water she was laughing so hard.

"Not a single clue. I was terrified on both accounts."

Arran took a drink of his beer and sighed contentedly. "Elinda reminds me of you. Pretty, smart, and with a devilish sense of humor. Hell, you turned that last scheme of mine on me somewhat good."

"She sounds amazing. I'm more interested in...Mare, was it? Being a priestess with her demeanor...she seems like an interesting person."

"That is one way to put it. Mare is one of a kind. She may be unconventional, but she is a good friend and, if I'm honest, the smartest person I've ever known. Wicked funny once you get to know her."

Challand sat back, cupping her drink in both hands, and taking a long contented breath.

"It certainly sounds like you have found your way."

Arran thought for a moment and simply nodded.

"You know...I think I have. Want to know what the most surprising part of it is? I think I'm really good at it. I haven't told my parents yet, but I've already been evaluated to year three. I was put up for early evaluation this past term."

Challand leaned forward in surprise. "A full term early?"

Arran nodded, a huge smile spreading across his face.

"That's amazing, Arran. I didn't even know they did that!"

"Mare thinks they are grooming me or something like that. For what, I don't know, but I don't really care. It allowed me to come home much sooner than I expected after my commission."

Challand looked quizzically at him.

"Oh, did you not hear about commissions?"

Challand shook her head.

"After finishing year two evaluations, I became eligible for commissions. The instructors approved and now I can take on commissions for Aaeu'din. It is a way for me to pay back the tuition to Lord Baelonne."

"So you finished this commission before coming here?"

"I did. It was a simple scouting mission, nothing major. They start us out easy. They'll get more involved once I progress."

Arran didn't like lying to Challand, but he did not want to go into the actual details of the events in Crenn'ier.

"A commission already?" Pai'ese said as she and Dale returned to the table and sat down.

"It was nothing, Mother," Arran said nonchalantly as he took a drink of his beer.

Pai'ese stared at her son suspiciously, knowing him too well that it was most certainly not 'nothing'. She'd let it drop for now.

Challand finished her drink and rose. "I should be going. I'm sure others would like to welcome you home. It was good seeing you again, Arran. Thank you for the stories."

Challand left and made her way over to her family's table.

"That one is bound to find a good lad one day," Dale said offhandedly, hiding his smile behind a drink of beer.

"Father, no. Just stop."

"Just saying, son. She's not the catch I landed in your mother, but she is a fine young lady."

"Leave him alone, Dale," Pai'ese said, slapping his hand.

Several hours later and after far too many bitters, Arran was led home by his mother and father. He sluggishly made his way to his room, barely having time to notice that not a single thing had changed since he left, before collapsing on the bed from exhaustion and beer.

Pai'ese stood in the doorway to Arran's room and watched as her son fell into a deep sleep.

Dale came up behind her and wrapped his arms around her waist.

In a soft whisper, "He is turning into a fine man."

"Yes...Yes, he is." Pai'ese softly closed the door.

⸻

The following morning started with a major headache, and his mouth was as dry as a desert. He closed his eyes and willed himself for more sleep, which would not come. The pounding of his head dominating all else.

"Ugh," he groaned as he rose and sat on the edge of the bed, head in his hands.

He dressed, then slowly walked around his room, brushing his fingers across the odds and ends of his youth, and the memories they held.

A knock came at the door.

"Come in."

"I thought I heard you up." The door opened as his mother took a step into the room.

Arran groaned. "Barely."

She wrinkled her nose at him with motherly disdain. "You obviously haven't learned the lesson of too many beers yet?"

Arran ran his hands through his hair. "Not yet, evidently."

"Go get cleaned up and then come on down. A good breakfast and a walk will do wonders."

After breakfast, Arran and his mother went for a walk. The breakfast had indeed done wonders for his hangover, and he was hopeful that his mother's advice of the walk would do the same. His head was still a pounding mess.

"So tell me about school." Pai'ese did not address him directly, and nonchalantly brushed her hand across some flowers at the side of the path.

"It's a lot of running, weapon training, sparring, meditation and forms, classes on every topic imaginable..." He trailed off.

"Sounds positively dreadful." She turned to him and smiled broadly.

Arran laughed.

"Yeah, not exactly the skills one learns in Kine, and a far step away from blacksmithing."

"Anything stand out?" Pai'ese gave a slight tug on his arm, guiding them along a path that led out around the pond.

Arran thought for a few moments.

"I went out to some training for four weeks with a fellow student, Cass. She was gifted from Bestia, taught me a lot about hunting, tracking, traps, snares, and survival in the wilds. I liked that. The solitude of living off the land was peaceful."

"Four weeks..."

Arran hesitated, not wanting to lie to his mother.

"The last week was a combination of all that training, coupled with a live exercise of me being the prey to two other students." He saw her grimace and quickly added. "With practice blades, of course."

"Did you win?"

"As a matter of fact, I think I did."

Pai'ese nodded approvingly.

"Have you received any additional gifts during your training?"

Arran stopped, his arm falling from hers as he turned and looked at his mother with mild shock.

Pai'ese did not react to his sudden stare. "You don't have to look so surprised. I didn't always live in Kine. I know a thing or two about manifested gifts."

Arran eyed her suspiciously. "Oh?"

She tilted her head with raised eyebrows. "A little."

They continued their walk. "My first gift was actually on the road to Saloanne. We were camping overnight, and I went for a walk in the forest. I found a trail and began tracking it for something to do. I received Stealth that night."

Arran paused. His mother giving no indication of surprise at the revelation.

"Not too long afterwards, I received the final two common gifts of Observance and Sight during school training. It was considered unusual to have received all three so quickly, or so I was told."

Arran paused again. No reaction.

"Most recently, during my commission, I received the gift of Shadow. That one is uncommon."

Arran paused again, studying his mother intently. She was taking all of this surprisingly well.

They walked for a while without speaking, the only noise the crunch of their shoes on the gravel path.

Pai'ese stopped and turned to Arran. "So the commission was not a simple scouting exercise, then?"

Arran was taken aback at the remark.

"Why would you say that?"

"Gifts are usually manifested under extreme circumstances. When one is focusing intently, and using a combination of gifts at the same time, no?"

"How?..."

She looked at him askance. "Again, not always from Kine."

Arran hesitated.

"There were a few...exciting moments during the commission. I came close to being caught while I was observing a campsite of individuals I was tasked with tracking. It was then that I received the gift of Shadow."

Pai'ese smiled at her son.

"Individuals...at a campsite," she said slowly. She could see how uncomfortable the conversation was for him. He was hiding something that he could not tell her. She let the conversation go and hastened their walk.

They made their way back home by mid-morning. Arran went up to his room while his mother cleaned up the breakfast plates and began preparing for lunch.

A little while later, Pai'ese stepped to the bottom of the stairs and announced, "Lunch is ready."

"Coming!"

Arran was up and headed for the door when he remembered the photos. He went to his bag and grabbed the pouch and headed down.

"Smells great," Dale said, washing his hands.

Lunch was, of course, delicious as they all sat contentedly in front of their empty plates, sipping at their tea.

"Mother, I found a photo at school while I was researching a fellow Intelligence student. According to Lord Baelonne and Qoman, she was the only other Intelligence gifted student from Aaeu'din. She was supposed to be amazingly gifted, a prodigy in her time." Arran reached over to the pouch on the table.

Pai'ese froze, a sudden look of panic spreading across her face.

As Arran set the pouch on the table, he noticed her distress. "Mother? What is the matter?"

Dale straightened up with a look of concern, reaching his hand across the table to hers. "What is it, Pai'ese?"

She didn't reply. She looked at Arran; her face furrowed as she held out her hand for the pouch.

She took it, hands trembling.

Dale rose. "Pai'ese, you're scaring me. What is the matter?"

Pai'ese took a deep breath and pulled the two photos out of the pouch.

She unfolded the first photo, and her eyes immediately began to water. A single tear falling down her face, then another. Her gaze never leaving the photo she now held before her.

"Pai'ese?" Dale asked again with desperation, trying to elicit a response.

Pai'ese looked up, wiped her face with a towel, and then stood.

"Go to the sitting room, please. I'll be there in a minute." Pushing back her chair, she left and went upstairs.

Arran looked at his father in confusion, but they did as she asked, and went to wait for her in the sitting room.

Pai'ese stood in front of the mirror in their bedroom, palms flat on the dresser, with the photo spread out beneath her hands as she breathed heavily. She had hoped that this day would never come. Prayed even. Every day since Arran's Source Day. She took several long, deep breaths to calm herself. She looked down and then picked up the photo and held it up again. Her stare bore the hurt and anguish she had thought she had forgotten. She looked at it for several long moments before finally folding it back up and placing it in her pocket. She wiped her eyes and then went to her nightstand, moving it aside. Kneeling down, she pried up the floorboards that had been secured so many years ago. Inside was a box, grey with years of dust. She reached down and removed it, setting it gently on the floor beside her.

She brushed some of the dust off the top and then rested her hands on its surface, closing her eyes in reverence.

Rising, she went to her dresser and retrieved a key from her jewelry box. Grabbing the box, she went downstairs to unburden herself of the secret she had buried long ago.

Pai'ese entered the sitting room, setting the box on the table, and taking her chair.

She looked at her husband and her son. Both looking back, deep concern etched on their faces.

Her beautiful boys. Would they understand? Would...no...could they forgive her?

"What I'm about to tell you both, I have never told another soul. No one." Her voice quavered as she spoke.

Pai'ese took a deep breath, then took out the photo that Arran had given her, handing it to Dale.

"That is a photo of me. A photo from very long ago. A photo..." She hesitated. "...of a young woman who does not now exist."

Dale looked at the photo in confusion. "How is it you if you say she does not exist?"

Arran turned to his father, his voice flat and even. "Father, I found that photo in the archives at school. It is over one hundred years old."

Dale looked at Arran and then at Pai'ese, in confusion.

"That photo is of me and my fellow students..." She stopped suddenly and then corrected herself. "...my friends. We had it done while I attended the school..." she paused, inhaling sharply. "...one hundred thirty-one years ago." She looked up, eyes wet. "My given name was Sai'el." She pointed at herself in the picture. "That is me and I was gifted by Talon. Same as Arran."

Arran stared at his mother in disbelief, rising from his chair.

"This makes no sense! How can you be Sai'el? She is dead!" Arran began pacing around the room, frantically trying to make sense of what his mother had just said.

Pai'ese inclined her head and said wryly. "Not yet."

Arran stopped and looked at his mother, dumbfounded.

"How can you be so...so calm?"

"Sit down, Arran!" Her voice was stern, and it had not been a request. "You are making me nauseous with all your pacing."

Arran sheepishly returned to his seat with a loud thump.

"If the photo is that old, how old were, um, you when it was taken?" Dale asked.

Pai'ese leaned over to look at the photo again. "If memory serves, I was about twenty when that photo was taken." She began pointing at the others in the photo. "That is Gale, Stephan, Brent, and Stella."

Dale did the figures in his head with a look of shock. "That would make you one hundred and fifty years old!" He gasped.

"A hundred and fifty one." Her reply came without any hesitation, calm and matter of fact.

"So if you are still alive, are they..." Arran trailed off, remembering the book and its tragic ending.

"They are all dead." She lowered her head with a long sigh.

"Mother, this makes no sense. How?"

"That, my son, is a very long story."

Northern Valoor
Year 1178/Month Unknown

"Seriously, Sai'el. Why are we on this crap commission?" Stephan groaned for the twelfth time by her count since they had started.

"I told you already. It's a good commission, it pays well, and the local magistrates want it dealt with swiftly. Their local militia won't go near the beasts after the last mauling. We're here to clean it up, grab a payday, and go home."

"I still think it's rubbish. Stupid bears," Stephan grumbled.

That was thirteen.

"Noted. Now let that be the last of it."

"The cave entrance should just be up ahead," Stella informed the group.

"Good..." Stephan began, but Sai'el cut him off.

"Serious time. Everyone be on alert. I don't want any surprises." The command in her voice was clear.

The group had been together long enough to know that tone. Now was not the time for any more questions.

Sai'el jerked her head forward towards the cave. "Stella, go on ahead and report."

"Be right back."

Sai'el looked around at her team as they readied themselves. When her group was not on a mission, they could be quite the handful. Especially Stephan, but over the years they had formed a cohesion that made them one of, if not 'the' elite teams in all the realms. They worked together flawlessly, each knowing the other's strengths and weaknesses, anticipating each other's moves and, most importantly, trusting each other. There was no other group she wanted by her side when an engagement began.

Stella came jogging back lithely a few minutes later. "The entrance is clear. Definite activity, though. There are a lot of tracks leading in and out of the cave."

Sai'el stood. "Okay, let's form up. Stephan, you know what to do."

"Yes, ma'am."

The entrance to the cave was large, wide enough for all of them to enter shoulder to shoulder if they wanted. Instead, Stephan led the way, with Sai'el and Stella right behind. Gale and Brent brought up the rear.

About one hundred paces into the cave, it began to curve to the right and their light from the entrance began to fade.

"Brent, some light. Keep it faint," Sai'el commanded. She could see in all but the darkest of areas, but her comrades did not have her gift of Sight.

They had been slowly tracking the cave for almost two hours when Sai'el called for a stop.

"Let's take a break and ration up. Grab some water. Looks like this cave is going to be a pain in the ass to search."

Stephan removed his helmet, sweat rolling down and into his eyes. "Is it just me, or is it hot in here?"

"If you didn't need all that armor..." Gale punched him in the arm.

"Hmmph. You'll thank me when I'm holding the beasties from getting at ya."

The group smiled at the now familiar banter between the knight and the priestess.

Up until now, they had only found one junction in the cave. They marked it for future investigation and had continued on the main path. The cave was like any other Sai'el had seen, but for some strange mushrooms. They grew in clumps where the dampness was most prevalent, and they had a shimmering glow about them. Brent, who was their botanist, did not know what they were and excitedly collected some for future study.

Stella peered down the cave from the direction they had come. "We have been in here a long time. The tracks out front all indicate bears, but this is a long way for them to travel, don't you think?" Stella glanced sideways toward Sai'el. "Usually you can find a den or at least a spot where they bed down much sooner."

"Agreed," Sai'el replied with a frown. "Something is definitely queer about this."

The group continued, marking three more junctions, but stayed on the main path, which suddenly made a sharp turn to the right.

"Psst," Sai'el hissed, signaling the group to halt. She made a motion to herself and then forward. She would investigate the turn.

She braced herself and stepped into the shadows, the dark edges of ethereal smoke embracing her.

She peered around the corner, and about two hundred paces ahead, she could see a faint light. She crept forward, all of her senses on alert.

As she neared the light, she could now see that the path emptied out into a large chamber. The light was brighter now and she could make out a shimmer on the floor in the middle of the chamber.

Water? A pond maybe? Is this where you have wandered?

Staying on the right wall, she inched forward, taking in the vantage of the left side of the room. She was now only a few paces from the chamber entrance, and it was indeed a pond in the center of the room. The room appeared to be circular, with no visible exits from her vantage point. The light seemed to be coming from above, but she could not see the top of the chamber.

She inched backwards, then shifted sides, and repeated the maneuver on the left. This time, when she was about ten paces from the chamber entrance, she saw them. Three sleeping brown bears were on the right side of the room.

One of the bears was absolutely massive. She could not tell its exact size since it was lying down, but its bulk was imposing.

That one is going to be a bitch.

The other two were smaller than the first one, but still impressively large.

She continued forward to clear the rest of the room as best she could. As far as she could tell, those were the only three in the room. No other exits. She inched backwards and made her way back to her group.

Using hand gestures, she held up three fingers. Then she held up one finger, gestured large and pointed to Stephan, indicating he would take the large one. Occupying the largest or at least the biggest threat to the group was his job. She held up two fingers, indicating the second target, and pointed to herself. Then she held up three fingers and pointed to Stella and Brent. They nodded in assent. Gale would stay at the rear and heal as necessary for the entire group during the engagement.

Sai'el stepped back into the shadows and made her way up to the chamber entrance, her team following closely behind. She entered the room and made her way around the right wall until she was within two arm's length from her target.

Blades already drawn, she inched forward and without any hesitation plunged both daggers through the back of the bear's neck. It rocketed up with amazing speed, its roar gurgled as it tried to scream out. Sai'el was forced to jump back and to the side, her daggers still embedded in the bear's neck.

At the sound of the gurgled howl, the other two bears were instantly awake, clambering to their feet with astonishing speed.

The second Sai'el had plunged her daggers, the rest of the group went into action.

Stephan ran towards the largest of the three as it was rising, shield and sword raised, as he let out a battle cry. As the bear rose to its full height, Stephan's eyes went wide in amazement.

"Aren't you a right big one!" Stephan yelled again as he ran towards the beast.

Stella and Brent were on the remaining bear as it rose, and a bolt of fire erupted from Brent's hands as Stella's arrows began piercing the beast. They looked like small pins in a doll against the massive size of the bear. The bear roared in anger and sprinted at the two. This time Brent kept the fire burning, and a stream of flame hit the bear head on. It stumbled, the smell of burnt fur and flesh began to permeate the room. The bear had stalled, but slowly began to resume its pace towards Brent.

"Watch out!" Stella shouted, dropping her bow and drawing out her daggers. She rushed towards the bear. She raked the beast down its side with both daggers as two parallel lines of blood appeared. The beast didn't even react to her strike as it continued towards Brent.

The bear was almost upon Brent as he dove to the side, but he was too slow. The bear caught him midway through the dive with a viciously hard blow, raking three deep gouges in his chest. The force of the blow sent him tumbling backwards. He hit the wall with a sickening thud and the cracking of bones. He lay crumpled, one arm and leg twisted at an unnatural angle. He did not move.

Stella was slashing and dodging the bear that had just struck Brent, as Gale went into action, trying to assess and heal Brent.

The second her hands began to glow, the bear snapped its head around and stared at Gale with malevolent yellow eyes. Stella desperately stabbed and raked the bear with her daggers; but nothing she did could take its attention away from Gale, who was desperately trying to keep Brent alive.

"Gale!" Stella shouted as the bear broke from her and charged at the healer.

Gale barely had time to turn when she heard her name and the bear was upon her. It leapt, its full weight coming down on the priestess, burying her beneath its bulk as its massive jaws ripped into her body. It lifted its head and roared ferociously, shaking its head. Spit and gobbets of flesh and blood went spraying through the air. Then it plunged its head downward again and bit Gale's neck, nearly severing her head from her body.

Stella, enraged, ran and jumped on the bear's back trying to drive the daggers into its neck like Sai'el had done, but the beast was a writhing mass of muscle, and she was tossed off to the side, rolling to a stop a few paces away.

Sai'el heard the shout from Stella and she looked up just as Gale was buried beneath the bear. Sai'el had managed to retrieve one of her daggers from the first bear's neck and began harrying the beast with strike after strike. Slowly, the bear was finally beginning to falter, the loss of blood and difficulty breathing finally catching up to it. She leapt upon its back, pulled out her second dagger, and then viciously sliced upwards from both directions beneath the bear's throat. The great beast heaved, let out one last gurgled roar of blood, and then fell to the ground.

Sai'el looked up and quickly assessed the situation. Brent and Gale were down. Stephan was holding the large bear at bay, but he wasn't doing much damage. It was all he could do to dodge and swipe as best he could, all the while giving ground around the perimeter of the room. She focused on Stella.

Damn, stupid girl!

Sai'el watched as Stella jumped upon the beast's back, only to get tossed to the side. Sai'el leapt from the back of the dead bear and ran to assist Stella.

Stella shook her head to clear the stars in her vision, and got up on one knee. The bear, seemingly satisfied and done with Gale, turned its head and stared at Stella. It howled and charged.

Stella jumped to her feet and dove as it leapt, the bear's claws missing her by inches. Sai'el joined her and the two positioned themselves to attack on two fronts.

The bear's head turned back and forth, looking at both of them. Shaking its head in a roar, it began to walk forward, head low and growling, but it was evident to Sai'el that it was beginning to feel the effects of its wounds. The bears were huge and they could take a lot of blood loss before succumbing.

"It's getting fatigued," Sai'el said. "Continue to bleed it so we can go help Stephan."

"But, Gale." Stella was sobbing. Her hands trembling as she held her daggers.

Sai'el looked at her companion, tears of her own beginning to form.

Not now, she scolded herself.

"I'll take lead and you follow."

Stella nodded.

Sai'el stepped forward, grabbing the bear's attention.

"Over here, you wretched beast!" Sai'el hissed.

The bear tried to run at her, but stumbled, and Sai'el was upon it, stabbing at the sides of its neck and leaping away. Stella was right behind her as she stabbed the front flank and side of the bear, but in a sudden move, the bear twisted and swiped at Stella with its other paw. It wasn't a powerful hit, but the beast's claws had done their damage. Stella stumbled backwards, grasping at her chest and stomach. Rivulets of blood seeping between her fingers as it cascaded down her body and dripped to the floor. She fell to her knees.

"NO!" Sai'el screamed and dove at the now nearly dead bear, stabbing it in desperation and anger. The bear was no longer moving, but she continued to stab it relentlessly.

"Sai'el!" a hoarse shout coming from Stella.

Sai'el turned to her, as Stella nodded her head towards Stephan.

She looked up, and Stephan was beginning to lose his battle. He needed help. She ran towards the massive bear to aid Stephan.

Stephan was beginning to fatigue. He knew it and he could almost see in the bright yellow eyes of the bear that it also knew it.

The bear was big, but it wasn't as fast as the other two. That alone was the reason Stephan was able to last as long as he did. The bear lunged, swiping its paw, and Stephan was easily able to dodge it, but he stumbled. His foot had hit something big behind him as he dodged. As he fell to one knee, he saw the bloodied body of Gale lying on the ground. Her head nearly severed and lying sideways towards her shoulder, as if she were stretching her neck. He looked in horror at his friend. The other side of her neck was completely gone. He faltered. That was all the big beast needed, and it was upon him.

The big bear pinned Stephan to the ground with one massive paw upon his shield. The shield protected him from the beast's claws, but it did nothing about the now immense weight that was crushing and pinning him to the ground.

The beast roared and then engulfed Stephan's head in its gigantic maw, helmet and all. The sound of teeth grinding on metal, some cracking on the hardened steel, filled the room that was otherwise eerily silent.

Stephan squirmed beneath the bear as a faint glow began to emanate from his entire body.

Sai'el watched, helpless.

Perseverance. He's using Perseverance!

Understanding dawned on Stephan as the bear bore down on him and through the stench and foulness of the bear's mouth, Stephan called upon Tovin. Perseverance was the strongest and most draining of his abilities. Yes, it could empower him with great strength, but he could only maintain it for the amount of time his body could endure. His previous best was eight seconds.

The glow surrounding Stephan grew as Sai'el raced towards the giant beast and leapt upon its back. It didn't even flinch, engrossed in the effort to get past its armored opponent.

Stephan grunted in pain as his body was imbued with Perseverance's blessing. He slowly pushed at his shield in an attempt to leverage the bear to the side. He was somewhat successful, but the bear's grasp upon his helmet did not falter. The bear's paw slid off of Stephan's shield. Stephan was now dangling like a dog's toy from his mouth. He swiped at the bear's neck with his sword, which only seemed to enrage it more. The bear shook him effortlessly, like a rag doll. Stephan's eyes widened just in time for him to understand his situation, and then his neck snapped. His body went limp and with one last shake of the beast's massive head, Stephan's body separated from his neck and went flying across the room.

Sai'el screamed in fury as she ran up the back of the beast.

Reaching the bear's head, she spread her arms wide and drove both of her daggers into each of the bear's ears, instantly piercing its brain.

The chamber fell silent as the great beast's brain ceased to function; no longer sending messages to its body and incapable of roaring in pain. Stephan's head dropped to the floor from the bear's mouth with a sickening splat, and clang of metal. The bear's eyes began to glaze over as it slowly began to stumble before toppling to the ground as its legs gave way.

Sai'el yanked her daggers from the bear and jumped off the side as it fell, rolling. She was kneeling and breathing heavily.

She got up and limped over to Stella, kneeling at her friend's side.

"Remove your hands. Let me see to the wound."

Stella removed her hands, and Sai'el threw open her shirt to get a look at the wounds. She had almost been completely disemboweled from the strike. Her armor doing little to protect her from the bear's strike.

"No!" Sai'el shouted. She ran towards the packs they left near the entrance to the chamber.

Returning, she began throwing items out of the bag until she found the gauze and vial of blood coagulant. Dousing the wounds on Stella's chest and stomach with the coagulant, she then began pressing the clean bandages to the wound.

"It's okay, Sai'el," Stella whispered quietly.

"No," she whimpered. "No! No! No!"

Stella reached out and laid a hand over Sai'el's. "Look at me."

Sai'el continued applying pressure to her wounds, then stopped and looked into her eyes. Blood and spittle bubbled from her mouth.

Their eyes locked and Stella gave the most imperceptible of nods, as she let out one last long breath.

Sai'el let her head fall to her chest, and she sobbed, unable to remove her hands from her fallen friend's chest. She didn't know how much time had passed as she knelt there next to her friend, but eventually she slowly stood, and she screamed. It was a scream of pain, and of anguish at the loss of her friends. She screamed so loud and for so long she felt her lungs were going to burst, and her throat became raw from it.

Panting heavily, Sai'el noticed the light in the room begin to brighten. She stared up at the ceiling through blurry eyes at the chamber's light source. At the top of the chamber was an upside down obelisk, hanging like a stalactite. It continued to glow brighter and brighter until, all at once, it let out a long beam of bright light that struck Sai'el in the chest. She gasped, eyes going wide in shock as the warm light embraced her, consumed her. She couldn't move.

Surprisingly, it did not hurt. It was warm, like the rays of sunshine when you step out of the shadows on a cool day. The burst did not last long, maybe a few seconds. When it released her, she stumbled to the ground in utter exhaustion. She panted for breath as she fell to her knees.

What the hell?!

She stared up, looking up at the obelisk, which was slowly returning to its original brightness. As it did, she noticed it had markings of some sort on the sides, but she could not make out what they were.

She placed her hands to her chest, checking for any injury or burn that it might have inflicted upon her. Nothing. Even her gear was still intact.

She closed her eyes, head slumping forward to her chest in exhaustion. After several minutes? Hours? She did not know. She finally raised her head and surveyed the room.

So much blood. Her friends' blood.

She allowed herself to weep again. She wept until she had no more tears to give and then spent the next hour laying her friends out in a respectful row at the entrance to the chamber. Once done, she placed a blanket over each body and then knelt before them, numb.

Eventually, she picked up two bags, slung them over her shoulder and left the cavern.

Pai'ese sat back, slumping in her chair and wiping her eyes.

Dale rose and went to Pai'ese's side, placing a hand on her arm.

"Are you okay?"

She smiled up at him and marveled at her husband's concern.

"Yes, I'll be fine. It has been a long time. Giving those memories voice was more emotional than I thought it would be. You would think a hundred plus years would dull the pain." She gave a wan smile, patting his hand in appreciation.

Arran ran his hands through his hair, trying desperately to come to grips with the story. "I have so many questions." He looked at his mother questioningly. "This can't be. It...it's too much." Arran stood and walked out of the room. The sound of water pouring quickly followed. Then another. Arran returned and placed a glass next to his mother.

In the silence that fell, Pai'ese began to question her decision to divulge the secret. She could see the anxiety and frustration on their faces. She had to press on and get them to the end of her story, but first, she needed to know.

"Can you ever forgive me?"

They both looked up and stared at her.

A deep expression of hurt spread across Dale's face. "Forgive?" He looked away and then back. "What is there to forgive?"

Pai'ese looked at them both with desperate eyes.

"I've lied to you. Lied to you both. All of these years."

Dale shook his head vehemently. "You never lied."

"Okay then, at the very least, I deceived you by omission."

Dale continued shaking his head, took a long breath. "Pai'ese. You are the best person I have ever known." He looked down and then back up at her lovingly. "You made me a better man, and you raised a fine son. This...story...does not change that. It's hard to believe, mind you, but it does not change the person I know or the way I feel for you."

Pai'ese let out a breath she had not known she was holding and looked at him through blurry eyes. She rose and went to the couch, gesturing for them to sit beside her. She put an arm around them both in an embrace and they sat. They remained in each other's arms for a long time.

Pai'ese finally withdrew and wiped her cheeks. She rose and returned to her seat opposite them, straightening her dress.

"All right then, what questions do you have? If I am to make you understand, make you believe, you need to know it all. Ask your questions."

Arran and Dale looked at one another, neither knowing where to begin.

Pai'ese sighed.

"Surely you have something? I mean, I just told you that I'm one hundred fifty one years old. Maybe start there?" The mocking tone of her voice broke the tension.

Dale raised an eyebrow. "That one 'is' high on the list."

"All right then, let us start there." She picked up the glass and took a drink. "The short answer is, I don't know. Not for sure, but I suspect it was the obelisk. I believe it gave me a gift. A gift of life? Immortality? I don't know. But I'm convinced that the obelisk was of the Source and it gifted me...something."

Now it was Arran's turn to respond incredulously. "A strange obelisk in a cave that gifted you?"

Pai'ese gave him her best mother's glare.

Arran withered and shrunk back. "Sorry. Sorry. Go on."

"As I said, I believe the obelisk gave me a gift. Trust me, I do not come to this conclusion lightly. I have spent years investigating individuals with gifts without Patron intervention. There are not a lot, but they are there. How does that happen if not by some other mechanism? My interaction with the obelisk in that cave is the best plausible answer."

"Did you go back to the cave and investigate it?" Arran asked.

"I tried. I spent no small amount of time trying to find that cursed obelisk again, but I never did. I couldn't even find the original cave or any other evidence that would lead me back. It was like it never existed."

Dale's curiosity perked up. "It just disappeared?"

"I don't know. It could still be in that mountain for all I know. What I can tell you is that there is not a way in. The cave was gone."

Arran fidgeted before asking his next question. "What did you do after the cave? The ummm...fight?"

Pai'ese sighed.

"I went to the magistrate that held the commission, told him that it had been completed and begrudgingly took payment. I took a cart back to the cave the next day and retrieved my friends. Once I had the arrangements made for them to be returned to their families, I disappeared. I went as far from that place as I could, wandering south from town to town, doing odd jobs along the way until I hit the ocean. I wanted to forget. Leave it all behind me. Eventually, I began moving around again. That was when I discovered the first person with a gift who had not been directly gifted by the Patrons. The discovery brought back all of my questions again and it nagged at me. It had been almost five years since the cave, but I went back north and began investigating, as I mentioned."

"You never returned to the school or reported back?" Arran asked.

"I did not. I was done with the school. I was so angry at the death of my team, and for what? A commission? It all became so senseless to me and I was done. The enthusiasm and youthful excitement were gone. All I saw was death. The thought of trying to put another team together and continuing on without them was too much." Pai'ese sunk back into the chair after the statement.

Dale quickly tried to redirect the questions. "When did you figure out that you...weren't...you know, aging?"

Pai'ese looked up. "That took a while. I investigated for any trace of the cave for a long time. Eventually I tired of it all. The investigation, the questions, and all the nagging doubts that plagued me. I grew frustrated. So, I quit. It felt like a betrayal to my team, my friends, but I had grown weary of the task. I began to wander again from town to town like I had in the beginning."

Pai'ese paused and took another sip of water. Looking at the two of them, she saw the eagerness in their eyes. The same eagerness she now felt in finally relieving herself of this long-held burden.

She continued.

"It had been about ten years now, and the town I was staying in had a very bad flu outbreak. Everyone was sick...it was bad. I assisted as best I could, but then I noticed that the sickness did not come for me. I began thinking back over the past years and it occurred to me: I had never been sick in all that time. Not once. As the years passed, I began to pay more attention to other little things, like injuries healing slightly faster than normal, and in the end, that I was not aging."

"But you are aging now." Dale immediately caught his blunder and stammered, "I mean in a good way, of course."

Pai'ese laughed.

"I am at that. I believe the gift expired, for lack of a better term, when Arran was born. I don't know why. The timing of his birth and my noticing of normal aging effects were pretty close. For instance, I had never had this before." She ran a hand through her hair, combing it back to show the locks of grey. "And I was well over a hundred by the time I found my way to Kine."

"Why Kine?" Dale asked.

"Sentimental, I suppose." A reverent muse to her voice. "I was from Morc'ier and the area felt like home. Kine was small enough and out-of-the-way, so I decided to stay awhile."

Pai'ese paused and looked lovingly at Dale.

"Then I met you. I was ready. Ready to stop wandering and settle down. I am actually grateful that the gift relinquished itself upon Arran's birth. I loved you. I loved having a family. I had given no thought to how I was going to explain not aging, once you and others began to notice, but thankfully, I was normal again and it felt good."

Arran stood up, resuming his thoughtful pacing around the room. "So my Sourcing Day. My being selected by Talon. That wasn't just a fluke. It's true, I am the son of Sai'el." He stopped, staring at his mother in sudden realization.

Pai'ese looked lovingly at her son and reached out for his hand. Arran crossed the room and took it.

"You remember my reaction? When that sigil of Talon appeared? I was so furious when you were gifted. I did not stay hidden for decades to finally settle down and have a family only for my son to be gifted by Talon. I did not want that life for you. Yet here we are."

Pai'ese looked at her son. "Your life is yours, and while I wasn't happy about it, I had to let you make your choice. My question for you is...are you happy?"

Arran hesitated as he thought about the question. He thought about his training, his friends, and all of his gifted abilities. He thought about all he had learned, the excitement, and sense of accomplishment when he received his gifts, and trained with them. He raised his head with confidence.

"Yeah. I believe I am."

Pai'ese sighed, not a disapproving sigh, but one of acceptance. "Then that is all that matters. Come, sit back down."

Pai'ese reached into her dress pocket and retrieved the key.

"I came close to burning all of this and melting the weapons down in your father's smithy many times over the years. I never found the will. These items are the few that remain of the connection I have to my friends, to my past. Silly, I know." She inserted the key, unlocking the box.

She raised the lid and took out the garment that lay on top. It was a black leather cloak with cowl. She held it up, handing it to Arran.

He took it reverently, holding it up in admiration.

He ran his finger across the material. "This is magnificent."

"Try it on. It is enchanted and should fit you. At least I hope so. I don't know if gear enchantments actually expire."

Arran swept the cloak up and around his shoulders, pulling the cowl up and over his head. Sure enough, within seconds, the cloak had lengthened and altered to fit his broader shoulders.

Pai'ese nodded in admiration. "It looks good on you."

She continued to pull out additional gear, delicately laying it all out on the table. Boots, leggings, tunic, bracers, mask, and belt. All the garments were leather, black with dark mahogany brown accents. It was a perfect matching set.

Pai'ese looked at the assembled gear on the table. Memories washing over her as she stared at the equipment.

"Everything is enchanted to varying degrees. Some have enhanced protection, others have gift enhancing abilities." Pai'ese slowly brushed her fingers across the garments.

"Mother, this is remarkable. That gear, even now, would be considered opulent."

"Only the best for team Sai'el," she muttered softly.

"What was that?" Dale asked.

"It was something that Stephan would always say. 'Only the best for team Sai'el'. His family was fairly wealthy, and he made sure to pick up any cost we couldn't afford ourselves."

She shook herself out of her reverie and then looked at Arran, a huge grin spreading across her face.

"Now for my pride and joy."

Pai'ese reached back into the open box and, on the bottom, lay a bundle carefully wrapped and tied in cloth. She pulled it out and handed it to Arran.

Arran gasped excitedly as he felt the weight of what lay wrapped in the bundle. He sat down and began untying the leather straps. He gently unfolded the bundle and inside were two of the most exquisite steel blades he had ever seen. They were simple in design, with two short cross guards of steel matching the blade. The grip was of braided leather with a simple circular pommel. The entire surface of the blades was etched in fine runes and markings. He picked them both up admiringly and hefted them in his hand as he stood.

He executed a few basic forms as he tested their weight and balance. They were a little longer than he was used to, but knew that this would only enhance their lethality. Given their size, they were also lighter than they should be.

"Nice forms," his mother said approvingly. "What do you think?"

"These are...I...wow," he replied.

"They are all yours. Everything."

"Mother, I could not." Arran shook his head. "You said yourself that these items were a connection to your friends."

Pai'ese looked at Arran sternly, which quickly turned to defiance.

"If my son is going to take the path of Intelligence, he is certainly going to have the best gear available. Besides..." her tone taking a more somber note. "I can think of no better way for 'us' to honor them than you accepting this gear in their memory."

Arran lowered his head. "Thank you, Mother."

Arran began admiring the blades again and sat down next to his father, handing one to him.

Dale gave a low whistle of admiration. "This is some fine craftwork. How did you come by them?"

"Not easily. It took us a long time to find the right craftsmen that could forge them." Pai'ese paused. "Do you recognize the metal?"

Dale continued to turn the blade in his hand, feeling at the edge and running his fingers over the etchings. "It's not normal steel, that is for sure. The etchings are too fine. Plus, the weight isn't right." He looked up. "I honestly don't know."

"Star metal."

Dale looked at her questioningly. "Star metal?"

"You know about shooting stars at night? Well, it turns out those are actually rocks falling to earth. Some, very few mind you, are found and the metal in them is far superior to normal steel. Star metal."

Dale returned his attention back to the blade in admiration. "I've never heard of such a thing."

"Not many have. It took us a long time to gather enough metal, find the right forger, and then pair him with the right enchanter. They had to work together to etch the symbols. Those enchantments increase the blade's durability and strength. They can hold up against the largest of swords and they stay sharp for a very, very long time. Test it."

Arran tested the sharpness of the blade with his thumb and sure enough, even after years of storage, they were still extremely sharp. Sharper than his current set of blades and he sharpened them frequently.

Pai'ese watched as Arran admired the blade. "They could probably use a little touching up, though. Luckily, I just happen to know a good blacksmith who can probably do that for you fairly cheaply."

Dale grinned. "First thing in the morning. I'll have to take it slow and experiment with the metal a bit, though. Wouldn't want to rush in and do more damage than good."

Arran placed the blade back on the wrappings and fell back into the couch. "This is all too much. First your story and now all of this," he said, gesturing at the pile of gear on the table. "I don't know what to say."

"That sentiment alone is enough. I came very close to telling you both my story many times over the years, but it never seemed appropriate. Never the right time or for the right reason. Now...you..." She pointed at Arran lovingly. "...have given me both."

Arran was awestruck at the magnitude of the gifts.

Pai'ese rose suddenly. "I am hungry. We are well past supper. Let's eat."

The familiarity of dinner allowed time for Dale and Arran to process everything that they had been told that afternoon. They asked a spattering of small questions throughout the meal and, after dinner, they all retired back to the sitting room.

They sat in silence, enjoying the contentedness of a nice meal, sipping warm cider next to the fire, and the presence of each other's company. Arran was the first to break the silence.

"I should probably head back to Saloanne soon. The lord will be anxious to hear my personal account of the commission. I don't want to take advantage of his generosity in letting me come home."

Both of his parents nodded in agreement.

Pai'ese cocked her head at him. "Can you tell me what happened? On the commission?"

Arran hesitated for just a fraction of a second before remembering who his mother really was.

"Of course." He told his parents everything that he had discovered at the bandits' camp.

"This...Pim. You saw him do this?" Anger in her voice.

"I did."

"Arrogant magic wielders!" she spat. "All this time, and they still try to outshine their predecessors with their hubris."

Pai'ese was fuming. Arran and Dale were taken aback. Neither had ever seen such anger on her face before.

Arran tried to calm her down. "We will stop them, Mother. The evidence I was able to gather will surely lead us to them."

"Serious business," Dale said, shaking his head. "Men like that won't be taken so easily."

After the commission story ended and the mood had died down, Arran filled the rest of the evening with his own stories of the last few years. He recounted his arrival to Meitellen and the tale he shared with Challand about Elinda and the book. His parents laughed as hard as Challand.

Arran yawned. "I should probably get some sleep. I'd like to get up early and head out."

Sleep did not come easily that night. Arran's mind was reeling from all that he had learned, but eventually weariness overtook him and, much to his surprise, he slept well.

———

Arran arose before dawn and readied himself for his trip, packing his bag. He took a long look around his room, gathered himself, and headed downstairs.

Arran smiled as he entered the kitchen, his mother already up and cooking breakfast. A bundle of food was prepared and lying on the table.

His father entered just as Arran was finishing his plate. He laid the bundle containing the daggers on the table, wiping his brow.

"These two are something else, Pai'ese. I would have loved to meet the man who created them."

Arran placed the bundle in his bag reverently.

"I honestly don't know how I'm going to explain all of this gear when I return. I'll need to make do with my own until I can figure out an explanation."

Pai'ese looked at him sharply. "You tell anyone that asks that they were a gift from a friend of the family and leave it at that."

"A gift like this from a friend of the family...in Kine?" his eyebrows raising.

"Keep it simple and let them wonder. They'll confuse themselves before ever coming close to the truth."

"Maybe." He shook his head. "Guess I should be heading out, then." Arran stood and hugged his mother. "Please tell Challand I said goodbye."

"I will."

Outside, Gallant was nervously stamping at the ground, eager for the upcoming trip. Arran stowed his bags and mounted.

He looked down at his parents.

"I'll return as soon as I can."

They watched, arm in arm, until their son disappeared around the corner and out of sight.

Coastline/Atre'lien Realm
Year 1305/Month Unknown

Faysciellen jumped out of the bow of the boat, splashing calf deep in the cold surf. She let out a quick breath at the shock of the cold. She grabbed the bow end rope and began hauling the boat to shore. The cold water was biting hard at her bare feet and lower legs by the time she was able to pull the boat ashore. The air was chill, but not too harsh.

Winter still.

She allowed herself to rest and let her toes sink into the soft sand, wiggling them for some warmth. She lifted her head to the sun, relishing the feel of precious land beneath her.

Precious land.

She dried off her feet and donned her boots now that she was out of the water, and finished pulling the boat up and into the tree line. Even with the chillness in the air, by the time she was done, she was sweating profusely. She drank the last of her fresh water. She would need to replenish it soon.

She took her time hiding the boat amongst the foliage. Satisfied with her work, she gathered her bag, bow, and quiver and headed inland.

Even in the midst of full winter, she could tell that this forest was plentiful. She could have shot several rabbits and squirrels during her journey, but water was her priority and she wanted to find a stream or other source before nightfall. After several hours of trekking, she was rewarded. The faint gurgle of a brook or stream had beckoned her. She drank her fill and then refilled her waterskins. She rested by the water, admiring the forest. Many of the plants and trees were familiar to her, but there were some she did not recognize.

She found a spot to bed down on not too far from the stream and then went out to hunt for dinner. After she finished her meal, she lay down next to the small fire to stare up at the stars through an opening in the canopy amongst the trees. In the morning, she would head further inland and search for signs. Signs of the strange people from her dreams.

After several more days of travel and tracking, Faysciellen discovered a small village. Their signs in the forest were hard to miss, and it had been easy to follow the trail back to its origins.

She observed them for several days. They looked similar to the strange people from her dreams, but with dreams, it was always hard to tell.

She discovered that these people were not so dissimilar to her own. Despite their odd appearance, they were hard workers, tending to their fields or their craft, and took great care of their children. They laughed and played, and it was clear that they were a close community, not unlike her own village.

One evening, she observed that the entire village had gathered in the town center. There was food and dancing in what seemed to be some sort of celebration or maybe...some kind of ritual? Whichever the case, they ignored the winter chill and celebrated well into the evening.

After several more days, she concluded that she could learn no more from this village. None of these people appeared to have any talent. She could make out their faint auras, but they were all weak. Not once during her observations did she encounter anyone ever using a talent or displaying any sign of even possessing a talent.

She would travel further inland. Surely, someone in this land had to possess 'some' talent. Her dreams had been correct so far. Why not in this also?

CHAPTER 13
SECRETS
YEAR 1305 / JANUARY / WEEK 4

Arran arrived in Saloanne three days after leaving home. He knew he needed to get back to Meitellen and inform the authorities, but he kept the pace smooth and moderate, taking the solitude afforded by the trip to process all the events of the last two weeks. He spent the days lost in thought, and the evenings meditating, memorizing the events, and stitching them back in place so that he could faithfully recount them with accuracy.

Arran made his way to the stables, dismounted, and handed Gallant's reigns to the stablemaster, giving the steed an appreciative pat on the neck.

"He is a fine horse. He performed admirably."

The stablemaster simply grunted in response and began unbridling Gallant as Arran removed his gear.

Giving Gallant one more pat on the neck, he left the stables and headed for Relorre's tent. Arran was informed that the general was at the keep this morning, and so he made his way up through the gardens.

Mindell greeted him on his arrival and led him to the same sitting chamber as before, quietly closing the door.

Lord Baelonne, Qoman, and Relorre entered a short while later, deep in conversation.

They each took a seat, giving Arran only a cursory glance, as if to say, 'We'll be with you in a moment'.

Arran went to the window and waited while the others conferred in hushed tones.

After they finished their conversation, Arran was motioned to join them and took a seat next to Qoman. Lord Baelonne poured himself a cup of tea, gesturing if anyone else would like a cup. Everyone declined.

Baelonne stirred the sugar in his tea as he sat in thought, his mind changing gears to the topic of the current meeting.

"Nasty business in Crenn'ier," he began, blowing across the cup.

Arran straightened. "Yes, my lord."

"Our only lead is this fellow...what was his name, Qoman?"

"Pim, my lord."

"Pim...what do we know about this man?" Baelonne said, looking at Relorre.

"Not much. We've made inquiries, but no one has ever heard of him. I don't think he is from Aaeu'din."

Baelonne sipped gingerly at his tea and then turned his attention to Arran. "I want you to leave immediately for Meitellen and report to the authorities there. No doubt there will be some very serious meetings at the highest levels with what you have to tell them."

"Yes, my lord."

"Tell them that we have increased our patrols and will continue our inquiries about this Pim. If we discover anything, we will send word immediately." Lord Baelonne sighed, the weariness of the situation plain upon his face.

"Yes, sir. I will head out immediately to procure passage."

"No need." Baelonne answered. "You will have use of my personal ship. It will cut a few days off of your journey and we require discretion with the transport of the beast. Nasty thing that, I'll be glad to be rid of it. Anyway, this information is close to a week old and we need to make haste. The captain has already been informed."

"Of course, my lord." Arran stood and gave a small bow.

Arran grabbed his gear and turned to leave.

Baelonne stood and turned. "Son." His tone became serious. "Be wary. These men, whoever is behind all of this...they do not know of you, but I fear that they soon will."

Arran nodded curtly and left, closing the door behind him.

Baelonne stared at the closed door. "Do you think the boy is up to the task?"

"By all accounts, he handled himself well in Crenn'ier," Qoman said, turning to Relorre. "Praise from Captain Mollen in favor of the Intelligence order is not easy to come by."

Relorre grunted in agreement.

"Very true." Baelonne returned to the stirring of his tea, deep in thought.

The trip back to Meitellen was as swift as Lord Baelonne had predicted. They arrived on the morning of the third day. The sight of Meitellen still awed Arran as the ship entered the central harbor. He leaned on the rails of the ship, once again admiring the great city.

Arran thanked the captain and left. The beast was being held until nightfall, awaiting arrangements from the school for transportation into the city. Upon arriving at the school, Arran went straight to his room, putting his mother's gear in his chest, and then went to find Instructor Shia.

Arran was relieved to find the instructor easily. She was speaking with Kallion in the training courtyard.

The two stopped their conversation as he approached.

"Arran. Good to see you back. Did you just arrive?"

"Yes, ma'am. I need to speak with you."

Shia noted the uncharacteristic seriousness of Arran's tone and demeanor.

"Is everything okay?"

"No, ma'am. It is not. There have been...discoveries during my commission, and I have been instructed to inform you immediately."

"I see." Shia looked at Kallion questioningly, who only shrugged. "Let us go, then."

Arran took a seat opposite Shia once they had made their way to her office.

"Now," Shia began, "What has you so troubled?"

Shia watched as Arran raised his head, the anguish of what he knew clearly written across his face.

"I know what is causing the incidents."

Shia's face turned dour as Arran began his report.

Arran started at the beginning of his commission and told the instructor about the entire series of events that he had so painstakingly memorized. Shia did not interrupt, letting the story unfold so that she could take the whole of it before asking any questions.

"After that I was given leave to visit home for a few days, made my way back to Saloanne, and then Lord Baelonne sent me back here to inform you."

The instructor did not speak for several long moments, parsing through the information that Arran had just revealed.

"You saw this man, Pim, using the Source on the animal?"

"Yes, I only saw it once, but he spent a long time channeling, at least five minutes, and it must have been extremely taxing. When he was done, he was so tired I thought he was going to collapse. That was when I left. When I returned with the militia, the animal was fully disfigured and feral, as we have seen before. It is still on the boat. I instructed the team to wait for dark and further instructions. If you could send for arrangements."

"Of course." Shia got up and went to her attendant. Closing the door, she retook her seat. "Was the animal fully maligned after the first channeling?"

Arran shook his head. "I don't think so, but I could not be sure. I could not see from my vantage and I left quickly after."

The instructor sat back in her chair as she stared into the fireplace for several minutes, letting the hypnotic dance of the flames calm her mind as she thought about the details of the report.

Returning her gaze to Arran, she said, "You did well. That was a bit more exciting than most first commissions." She gave Arran a wan smile. "Trouble seems to have a way of finding you."

Arran did not reply.

The instructor rose and gestured at Arran.

"Speak of this to no one." Shia smoothly led Arran to the door, already lost in her thoughts again as she did so.

"Yes, ma'am."

She ushered Arran out of the door and then addressed her assistant. "Please send word to Master Klintoc. He is to return immediately."

"Country!" Mare said excitedly, placing her tray of food on the table. "Welcome back, commission boy. So how was it? Anything exciting?"

Arran smiled and tried his best to act normally. "Not really." He covered his expression with a fork full of food.

Mare tilted her head and looked at him suspiciously.

The two were shortly joined by Rayneer, Elinda, and Bran. Arran answered their questions benignly, but he knew he was not fooling his friends. They knew him too well and, to their credit, Arran was relieved that they did not press him for details.

They retired to the Intelligence common room as everyone laughed and joked as they always did. Arran desperately tried to enjoy the moment and let it distract him, but he could not.

Arran stood and yawned. "I think I'll call it a night." He headed for the door.

Bran jumped up. "Not that way." He smiled broadly.

"You are a third year now. Time to claim a proper room."

Arran stopped as the comprehension dawned on him. He had almost forgotten. The first genuine smile of the evening spreading across his face.

Bran helped Arran gather his belongings from the old dorm room and then made their way to the first door of their dorms.

Bran held up a small bronze medallion, which had an image of a dancing jester. "We'll have to get you one of these tomorrow, but we can still go up and get you settled in this evening."

Arran looked quizzically at the medallion. "A jester?"

Bran shrugged. "Someone must have a sense of humor."

Bran held the medallion up to the door, which unlocked with a click. He pushed it open, and they entered.

Inside was a fairly unremarkable sitting room, much smaller than the main common room. It had two chairs next to a small fireplace and a table with four chairs in the back left of the room. A set of stairs led to the second floor at the back right.

Bran led Arran up the stairs and into a hallway that led to his left.

"There are ten rooms on this level. There is a second level, but it hasn't been kept up since this floor hasn't been full in quite a few years."

Bran began walking down the hallway, pointing to the first door on the left.

"That would be Klintoc's room. He's the only graduate I know that still keeps a room here."

They walked past two more doors and then Bran stopped, gesturing.

"This one is mine and if you want the one across the hall, it is open."

"Sure, that sounds good."

Arran approached the door, and a saw a small placard affixed next to the door. It read 'Shade'.

Arran looked at Bran, who simply shrugged.

"Someone must have named the rooms at some point. Mine is 'Hollow'." He pointed to the placard next to his room door.

"When we get your medallion for the main door downstairs, they will key it for this room as well."

Arran opened the door and entered. The room was about half the size of the dorm rooms downstairs, but still quite large given that it was only for one person. To the right was a bed twice the size of his old one, two nightstands, and a chest at the foot, similar to the ones in the dorm rooms, only much bigger. On the back wall of the room was a dresser with six drawers and a mirror. The left side of the room had a small corner fireplace with two sitting chairs. A writing table and chair with a bookshelf finished filling out that side of the room.

Arran and Bran crossed the room and laid his belongings on the bed.

Arran sat down on the bed, bouncing up and down a bit. "This is almost luxurious compared to our normal rooms."

"I know, right?" Bran looked around appreciatively.

"Well, I guess I'll leave you to it, then. Washroom is at the end of the hall, same as downstairs."

Bran paused at the doorway and turned back.

"You know...if you need to talk about anything..."

"I know." Arran stood up from the bed and began fumbling with his bag on the bed. He turned. "I appreciate it. I just need some time."

Bran's head dipped almost imperceptibly as he left, closing the door.

Arran looked around the room, hardly believing it was his. He went to the chest at the foot of the bed and unlocked it. It worked the same way as the chests in the dorm rooms. He grabbed the bag with his mother's gear and placed it in the chest. He placed his other clothes in the dresser and then leaned his books on the top shelf of the bookcase.

After cleaning up, Arran lay in the dark, sprawled across the bed. His thoughts going over all the events of the past weeks, desperate to try and make sense of it all until sleep finally overtook him.

Nedar/Atre'lien Realm
Year 1305/February/Week 2

Faysciellen had finally found what she had been seeking. She had discovered a town much larger than the first and, to her relief, individuals with significantly more powerful auras.

There were two individuals in the town who had auras powerful enough to give off the faint glow she had come to know meant talents. The first was a middle-aged, large woman with perpetually rosy cheeks. Faysciellen liked her. She was always pleasant and patient with all those around her, especially the children. Faysciellen quickly discovered that she was their healer.

A small child had fallen from a tree and suffered a severely injured arm. A break, or at the very least, a fracture. Faysciellen observed as the woman healed the young boy. A faint glow radiated out from her hands as she worked. Her touch and behaviors with the boy were soft and tender. She hummed softly to the boy as she worked. It reminded her of Cassien, the healer from her own village.

The second individual ended up having the talent of Earth. He was a tall, gangly man, and it took much longer for Faysciellen to discover his talent. He had the aura about him, but she could never see him use any talent. Then one day, as he passed a house with a wooden garden bed hanging from a window, she saw it. He let his hand pass over the frail and drooping plants with a light caress. A soft glow emanated up from the dark soil as the plants were quickly rejuvenated, as if enjoying a warm summer day. Faysciellen's village had several Earth talented individuals, and she knew he would be busy soon enough. Spring planting was not far off for the farmers.

Now that she had finally found some people with talent, she decided that she would stay here a while. She would observe and rest...and maybe, just maybe, she would dream.

The night still had a small bite of winter to it and Faysciellen grimaced at her stiff limbs as she sat up. She glanced at the now dead fire, looked up at the morning sun peeking through the trees and then cursed herself, recognizing how long she had slept. It was at least an hour past dawn.

She stood, stretching her arms high and releasing the night's tension, when she heard a rustle.

She quickly grabbed her bow and nocked an arrow, scanning for threats.

It did not take her long to find the source of the disturbance. As she pointed her bow in the direction of the noise, she heard a small gasp emanate from the brush ahead.

Faysciellen leveled her bow and focused, drawing in a long breath, her vision narrowing and becoming extremely keen as she peered at the source.

At this short distance, maybe twenty paces, her talents allowed her to easily make out the figure of a small girl kneeling behind the shrubs. Her hands covering her mouth and eyes wide as saucers.

Faysciellen lowered her bow and set it on the ground. She raised her hands to show no other weapon.

The young girl did not move. Faysciellen decided to take a more welcoming posture. She bent down to her knees, sat back on her feet, and rested her hands in her lap. She waited patiently.

The movement was slight at first, then slowly began to grow in confidence. The small girl began to fumble with the sling pouch across her chest. She pulled something out and then began edging her way out from behind the brush, holding whatever she had removed high in her hand.

In a high trembling voice, she spoke. "Hello. Are you hungry?"

Faysciellen was far from fluent in these people's tongue, but she had learned a few words and recognized this one as a greeting.

Faysciellen struggled as she tried to form the strange word in her mouth. "Elo."

The young girl giggled. "You talk funny."

Faysciellen pointed to her mouth, then to her ears, and shook her head.

The young girl frowned, not understanding. She shook her head. "I don't understand."

Faysciellen swore under her breath in frustration.

Best warrior hunter in her clan and she couldn't speak to a child.

Faysciellen again pointed to her mouth, then shook her head.

"You can't speak?" the young girl replied.

Faysciellen did not know what the girl was saying, but she did not believe her hand gestures were being understood. She decided on another tactic.

"I cannot speak your language," Faysciellen said in her own tongue.

The young girl gasped at the use of the strange language she had never heard before.

Faysciellen pointed to her mouth again and shook her head.

The young girl stared at Faysciellen with fascination, a look of concentration on her face, then she smiled. "You don't speak realm common." Her face blossomed in sudden realization.

Emboldened, the young girl moved forward and asked, "Food?" She raised her hand. A small mushroom lay in her palm. She pointed to her mouth and made like she was chewing.

Faysciellen took the mushroom from her hand and ate it. She had already foraged some of these mushrooms from the forest and eaten them, so she knew that they were edible. Besides, it was an easy way to let the little girl think she had helped her.

The little girl grinned triumphantly and said the word again. "Food!"

"Fewd," the word came out clumsily as Faysciellen tried to pronounce it.

The little girl giggled again.

"My name," she pointed to herself, "is Sofie."

"Sofie," she said again and pointed to herself.

Faysciellen pointed to herself and said, "Faysciellen," in her native tongue.

Sofie beamed at the foreignness and beauty of the name.

"Fichellan," she tried.

The two looked at one another for a few moments, then the little girl sprang to life.

"How about...Faye," she said, pointing to Faysciellen. "Sofie," she pointed to herself and "Faye," pointing back to Faysciellen.

Faysciellen bristled at the truncation of her name, but she also realized having a more pronounceable name in this land could be useful.

"Faye," she said, pointing to herself, and nodded.

Sofie grinned, obviously quite pleased with herself.

"I have to go home." Sofie pointed back towards the town. "Home."

Faye nodded in understanding.

"I'll be back," Sofie said, gathering herself and turning to leave, not sure if the strange woman understood her meaning, but she would come back. She would most definitely be back.

Sofie ran from the small clearing. "Best day ever."

Faye watched Sofie leave and then cleared her camp as best she could and headed deeper into the woods, farther from the town.

In the morning, Faye got up well before dawn and went to the town. She wanted to investigate if the little girl had told anyone. If she had, several of the adults would surely follow.

A short while after dawn, Faye spotted Sofie heading out of town into the woods, but not towards the camp from the previous day. Sofie continued until she was out of sight of the town, then turned and headed straight towards the old campsite. Faye watched warily to make sure no one was following. No one did.

Sofie reached the old campsite and began whispering for Faye.

"Faye! Are you here?"

Faye strode silently into view as Sofie was about to shout again.

"There you are! I thought maybe you had left."

"Food?" Sofie asked.

Faye nodded, and Sofie produced a paper bundle. Faye took it.

Inside were two fresh and still warm pieces of bread with butter slathered between them. Faye looked up at the little girl and smiled.

Faye bit into the bread, and she closed her eyes in delight. It had been a very long time since she had fresh bread and butter.

Sofie watched her intently as she ate. "Good food?"

Faye thought for a moment, then replied, "Good."

Sofie pointed to the partially remaining slice in Faye's hand.

"Bread." Then she gently reached out and dabbed her finger on the bread and then licked her finger. "Butter."

Faye hesitated a moment, then said, "bred budder."

Sofie smiled and nodded her head.

Sofie spent about an hour with Faye that second day, eagerly running around, pointing, and telling her the names of various objects. Faye was slowly picking up the strange language, and by the time they were done, she had learned some basic conversational skills. Every time Faye used a new word or was able to stammer through a simple conversation, Sofie would clap exuberantly and let out a squeal of youthful laughter.

The interchange between the two continued like this for two weeks. Sofie had confirmed the talents of the two individuals in her village. The older lady's name was Karine, and the man was Fennel. Faye continued her observations, watching the people go about their daily lives and Sofie would visit, answering any questions she had. By now, Faye could carry on a basic, albeit very stilted, conversation.

Faye had grown fond of the young girl. Her exuberance and willingness to keep her secret had been a blessing. She enjoyed the time with the young girl and had learned much, but the town was not what she was seeking. She needed to move on.

Faye watched Sofie with fondness as they were enjoying some nuts and berries. With an ache in her heart, she stated. "I leave."

Sofie looked up quickly with sadness in her eyes. "Why?"

It was the simple question of a child. So direct and earnest. "Must..." She hesitated, looking for the word. "Travel."

Sofie lowered her head as her eyes began to tear up.

"I don't want you to go."

Faye reached and pulled Sofie into a hug. She could feel the tears on her neck as Sofie gripped her tightly in the embrace. Faye held her at arm's length and wiped away a tear of her own and gave her a pained smile.

Faye pulled her bag close and began to open it. "Have gift."

She pulled out a deep red cloth similar to the one Faye wore on her own head. Her mother had made it for her, specifically for the trip. 'Remember us' her mother had said when she gave it to Faye.

The cloth had gold trimming and was embroidered with intricate designs. Faye handed it to Sofie, pointing to her own head band.

Sofie took the cloth and fingered it lightly, surprised at the softness of the material and intricacy of the patterns.

"Thank you."

"Welcome."

Faye straightened up on her knees. "Sofie? Where big town? Bigger than home..." she hesitated as she tried to recall Sofie's village's name. "...bigger Nedar."

Sofie wiped her eyes and blinked a few times.

"Carfellin is pretty big. It is that way and many days' trip on foot."

"Carfeeleen. Much bigger Nedar?"

Sofie immediately perked up at the question, wiping her face with the sleeve of her dress. "Oh yes. There are so many people, and it is surrounded by big walls. Oh, and the tallest buildings I've ever seen! My father took us last year, for the New Year's festival. It was wonderful."

Faye sat back on her heels, relieved. "Thank you, Sofie."

They sat in silence for a while, Sofie caressing the cloth gift while Faye watched, wondering what her mother would say about the gifting. She would approve, Faye concluded.

Faye leaned in and lightly placed her hand on Sofie's. Neither spoke as Faye rose and began gathering her belongings to leave.

When Faye was done, she looked down at the small girl who had become so valuable to her these past two weeks. A friend in this foreign land, a tutor of all things. Faye had hoped that she would find the right person to speak with when the time came. Who could have guessed it would come in the form of a little girl?

Faye reached down and brushed a loose strand of hair over her ear. "I not forget Sofie."

Sofie's head never rose as she stared at the cloth in her hands. In the softest of whispers, she replied. "Please come back."

Bending to one knee, Faye gave her one last hug. "I return when can."

Faye stood and took a deep breath, looking off in the direction that Sofie had indicated, and slowly began to walk away. When she reached the edge of the clearing, she glanced back over her shoulder. Sofie remained in the same spot, slowly folding the cloth lengthwise and then wrapping it upon her head and tying it into a loose knot, wearing it as Faye did. When she had finished, Sofie gave a sad wave, tears once again streaming down her face. Faye gave a quick, single wave in return, and then disappeared into the foliage, her own eyes blurring as she pushed herself into a run towards Carfellin.

INTERLUDE

Spirit stopped in front of the mirror and fidgeted with her hair for what had to have been the third or fourth time.

"You look fine," Breanna said behind her.

Spirit turned and sighed.

"I'm not so much concerned about my appearance as much as I dislike making this trip to the central realm. It annoys me."

"What is so bad? You go, give your report, and come back."

Spirit gave her a sardonic smile. "Everything. The people for one. All of their pomp and politics. Everyone so full of themselves, 'Oh look at me, I live in the central realm'," Spirit said in a mocking, low voice.

Breanna chuckled.

"Plus, you would think the central realm would be some grand and beautiful city. I don't know how it started, but it's just a collection of buildings where over the years one egoist tried to outdo another and you end up with this grotesque montage of architecture. Do not get me started on the realm offices. That building is like someone had a favorite cave, then tried to glitz it up."

Breanna chuckled and then tilted her head mockingly. "So what you are saying is that you are not a big fan of the central realm? Noted."

Spirit huffed. "Just let me get it out so I can move on."

"Fair enough."

Breanna gave Spirit several moments as she watched her calm down.

"Are we good?"

Spirit took a deep breath and let it out slowly.

"Yes. See you when I get back. Thanks, Bree."

As Spirit made her way to the door, Breanna jumped up and ran over to Spirit. "Oh, wait!" Then she pretended to straighten a length of hair. "I found one out of place."

Spirit slapped her hand away and left. Breanna's light laughter followed her down the hallway as she made her way to the portal room.

Spirit shivered as she appeared out of the portal and into the central realm offices. The cold wave of the portal transfer slowly fading as she stepped down off the platform.

"Welcome back, my lady," said the steward of the portal room.

"Thank you." It was a perfunctory reply, and she knew the man did not deserve it, but she wanted to get this over. She headed off in the direction of the high counselor's office.

Astaban's office was at the end of a long hallway that ended in a t-junction. His office was in the middle of the junction straight ahead, with offices spreading down the hallways in both directions.

Spirit took a breath, still somewhat in awe of the man on the other side of this door. She steeled herself and knocked.

"Come in," came a reply from the other side.

Spirit entered to find Astaban sitting in a chair next to a small fire, legs crossed and reading. He gestured for her to sit down in the chair opposite him. This was a break from the formal meetings of her previous visits, where he sat behind his desk.

Astaban was preoccupied with some other work and held up his hand. "One second, please."

Spirit sat and waited for Astaban to finish with the document. He signed it and then set it aside on the table next to him.

"Refreshment?" he asked, again breaking from previous protocol.

Spirit was quickly taken aback, but answered. "Yes, please. Tea, if you have it."

"Of course." Astaban snapped his fingers.

A man appeared from a side door and Astaban asked for a pot of tea.

Spirit handed Astaban her sheaf of papers that entailed the previous week's report. A digital copy was of course available, but Astaban had requested early on that she provide him with a physical copy. Much like having an actual fireplace in his office, he preferred the tactile. She had approved of the sentiment so close to her own.

Astaban took the papers and set them in his lap without looking at them.

"Give me your personal interpretation of the reports, please."

Again, breaking protocol. He usually would read the report, ask a few questions, and then she would be dismissed.

What is going on here?

She repeated the request, not sure what to make of it. "My interpretation?"

"Yes. Tell me, in your own words...about this." He tapped lightly at the papers in his lap. "I want your interpretation, your thoughts, and analysis."

Spirit sat silently for a few moments, gathering her thoughts.

"The humans, as you are aware, now know that the animal deformities are not natural and, in fact, well...man-made. They do not know who, but the name that Talon's disciple uncovered is already providing leads for them. I do not believe it will be long before they uncover the individuals." She paused, gauging Astaban's features. The man was as blank as a stone wall.

The side door opened, and the steward entered, placing the tray of tea on the table between them.

"Thank you," Astaban said. The steward bowed and left.

Astaban leaned over and began pouring two cups of tea. "Continue."

"The incidents thus far have been small, but the rate and geography of the newer ones indicate they are gaining confidence, despite the recent setback in Crenn'ier. The group behind the manifestations has to know, or at least have to understand, that they cannot stay hidden forever. They are going to be discovered. Their leader is clever and is a very skilled magician. How he was able to come about the tainted power is still unknown, but he is driven. I believe he has an underlying agenda that we have yet to discern." Spirit paused as Astaban's left eyebrow ticked up. It was the first indication from him that she had said anything of importance. "My guess is that they are using this time of anonymity to hone their skills for some greater cause. Thus, time is the issue and by spreading the incidents out, they introduce confusion, chaos."

Spirit paused and took a sip of her tea.

"Interesting. Humans have such a breadth of emotions that can consume them. It can drive them to the heights of altruism, or to the depths of egoism, and everything in between. Fascinating species."

Spirit watched as Astaban took several sips of his tea, never taking his eyes off of hers. Her eyes narrowed as she saw a flicker of amusement cross his face.

"You already know everything in that report, don't you? You don't really need me to report to you at all." Her words came out wholly more inappropriately than she intended. There was no shortage of venom.

Astaban chuckled, which only angered her more. He held up a hand. "I mean no offense, and in answer to your questions, the answer is yes on both accounts. I already know the contents of your report, but I also am of the opinion that I still need you."

Spirit frowned at his response. They sat for several long moments before Astaban spoke, breaking the awkward silence with a reluctant sigh.

"I have another source of information, as you may have deduced. As such, I generally already know what you have in your reports.

But...I still require your services. You may forgo the written reports if you wish, but your analysis and interpretations are still needed and wanted. Let's say I value a diversity of opinions and I find your analysis to be keen."

Spirit's anger ebbed a bit with Astaban's last remarks, and she asked, "Do I know the other source?"

Astaban did not answer.

"Realm politics," she muttered softly.

Astaban smirked at the comment behind his cup as he took another drink.

"Sir. If you require my analysis, have you or...the other, found out how the humans are using the source in this manner? We have not been able to sort out their methods. It's a twisting of the natural source that we cannot..." she trailed off.

Astaban's face grew serious. "For another time. I would like you to continue your investigation on this path, though." He set his tea down very gently and deliberately on the table and rose. "This has been a very pleasant visit. I, unfortunately, have some other appointments."

Spirit rankled at the curt dismissal before acquiescing. "Of course." She rose, placing her cup next to his.

"Until next time." Astaban turned for his desk.

Spirit made her way back to the portal room and for home.

What was Astaban up to? The informality of this visit and his candor was a huge break from protocol. I need to talk to Bree.

The cold wave of the portal transfer swept over her as she entered for home.

CHAPTER 14
STRANGE MEETINGS
YEAR 1305 / FEBRUARY / WEEK 3

Week 3 of First Term

It had been three agonizing weeks since Arran's return. First term for third year had begun, and he was still having trouble concentrating on his training. Between the events in Crenn'ier and the revelations from his mother, his focus and temperament had become less than enthusiastic.

He hoped that this afternoon's practice session with Klintoc would be just the type of training that he needed. It was not.

Klintoc sheathed his daggers. "We're done here. Let me know when you get your head on straight, boy." Klintoc growled under his breath as he left. "Waste of my time."

Arran heard the comment and cursed at himself. He hissed in disgust, whirling in anger, desperate to hit something...anything.

With most of the afternoon left, he went for a punishing run, followed by two rounds on the obstacle course, desperately throwing his body into physical exertion in an attempt to release his frustration.

Kallion stepped up behind Shia as they watched Arran come in from the obstacle course in a tousled mess. "The boy is frustrated."

"As are we all." There was no empathy in her voice.

"But you are purposefully withholding information that he needs to reconcile the events. The not knowing is eating at him and if you don't give him something, he is going to burst."

"He's not ready."

"Not ready?" Kallion hissed and stepped in front of Shia. "Seriously? The boy and his friends dispatched the threat in Freeholt with ease, and the work he did on his commission was exemplary. He made sound decisions and earned not easy praise from the realm militia. Who outside of Klintoc has performed to this level in recent years? Tell me!"

Shia did not reply and could only hold his eyes for a moment before glancing away.

Kallion continued in an almost hoarse growl. "He and his friends have turned this school's training into the most efficient cross disciplinary regimen I have ever seen. You are coddling him, Shia, and this protectiveness is doing more harm than good." Kallion was breathing heavily and several groups of students had stopped their training to look over. Kallion did not hold back his look of scorn. "Aargh, it's like talking to a stone." He stomped away.

Shia watched Kallion leave, knowing that he was right, but at the same time reluctant to make the decision she knew she had to make.

That evening, mind made up, Arran made his way to the common room. As he entered the room, he turned and slowly closed the door, garnering the full attention of the group.

Facing his friends, he said quietly, "I have something I need to tell you."

"About damn time." Mare replied flatly. "You have no idea how close I was to beating it out of you." She gave him a wry grin that Arran could not return.

Elinda placed a hand on Mare's arm. "I believe what Mare is trying to say is that we know something happened, and that we were waiting for you to come to...you know, when you were ready..." she trailed off.

"I know." He slowly crossed the room and sat down. "I am sorry, but I was instructed by Shia not to speak of it."

"Shia..." Mare said with disgust.

"Shush, Mare," Elinda reprimanded.

Arran stared at the floor. "It's about my commission." He raised his head. "It was not as simple and uneventful as I have let on." He hesitated and turned his attention to the fire, unable to hold their gaze. "I discovered the cause of the outbreaks, the incidents like the one encountered in Freeholt."

"The hell you say," Mare replied. "In Aaeu'din? But..."

Arran held up a hand, cutting her off.

"Let me get this out, Mare, please." His eyes pleading as he looked at her.

"I was commissioned to track some bandits that had been disturbing a major trade road. Find the bandits and then report to the militia on duty. That's it, simple enough. After a few days of tracking, I was successful, but what I found was not a simple bandit camp. There was a magic user, a mage? Maybe a priest? I don't know. He arrived at the camp while I was observing. They had a wild boar locked in a cage and he began channeling at the animal. It was agonizing to watch, as I came to realize what I was witnessing. I rushed back to inform the militia and the next day we raided the camp, capturing a few of the bandits...the rest were killed. The magic user was not present, and the animal was still in the cage. It had been fully transformed, just like the ones we encountered at Freeholt. I believe they were going to release it on the city of Crenn'ier the following day."

Arran finished, taking in a long breath. The crackling of the fire the only sound in the room.

Elinda rose and moved over to sit next to Arran, wrapping an arm around his shoulders.

Bran was the first to speak. "Did you recognize the magic user?"

"No. But one of the bandits did call him by name once, Pim."

Bran's forehead wrinkled as he muttered the name, "Pim...Pim... that name sounds familiar for some reason. I can't quite place it, though."

"So you come back, report to Shia, and she clams you up. No wonder you've been moping around lately," Mare said.

"Mare!" Elinda exclaimed.

"I'm just saying that's a lot of baggage to carry around with no one to talk to."

"Yeah," Arran said quietly.

"During the raid..." Rayneer said, trailing off.

Arran looked at his friend, understanding what Rayneer was asking, and replied, "Two."

"Two..." Rayneer repeated solemnly.

Mare stood seething. "As if the discovery that some halfwits are mucking around with some sort of dark magic wasn't enough, you had to kill not one, but two men. And then! In their infinite wisdom, they put a gag order on you? Idiots. How in all the hells did they expect you to process all this?"

Arran finally gave the smallest hint of a smile as he watched Mare storm around the room. "Not well, as you so delicately mentioned earlier."

Finally, talking to his friends, despite Shia's direct orders, was exactly what Arran had hoped for. The release of tension was like a cool salve on an open wound.

Arran sat in the dining hall, picking at his meal as the dull hum and chatter of the other students going about their normal activities washed over him. It was calming, in a way. After unburdening himself the previous evening, he was relishing the first decent night's sleep he had enjoyed since returning to Meitellen. Elinda was the first to join him and she let the quiet monotony of the meal speak for her.

Rayneer and Mare arrived a short time later, and the group eased their way back into their normal banter, letting the previous night's revelations sit idly off to the side, to be discussed later.

Bran was last to join as he hurriedly picked his way through the other students and sat down.

He held up a finger, taking several ragged breaths, and then leaned over the table to speak privately. "I know where I heard that name before."

"What name?" Rayneer asked.

Bran gave him an exasperate look. "Pim! The magic user from Arran's story last night. I know where I heard that name before." His voice was excited as the others finally understood his excitement.

"And..." Mare said, gesturing with her hand to continue.

"My father's court mage, Lajor. I remember overhearing him speaking to a man in my father's stables once. He called him 'Pim', which I remember thinking was a peculiar name."

"You're sure?" Arran asked.

Bran raised his eyebrows. "Pretty sure."

Arran shook his head. "Well, this sucks."

"What?" Rayneer asked.

"I think we need to let Shia know, but if we do, it kind of reveals that I've spoken to all of you...specifically against her orders."

"We could say it was just me," Bran said.

"I'm not sure that helps. I still disobeyed her orders."

Elinda straightened, her posture becoming resolute. "I think we go as a group. We already have part of the story with the incident in Freeholt. It would make sense that you told us all."

"I agree," Mare said, looking around at the others.

Everyone nodded.

Arran let out a long sigh and looked at his friends, the solidarity of everyone's decision firm upon their faces.

Arran got up from the table. "Okay, let's do this. No better time than the present. It's still early, and the instructor is probably still in her office. I'm sick and tired of all these secrets."

The team entered the foyer to Shia's office, and Arran turned to look at everyone in the group. No one faltered, and he knocked on the door.

"Enter," came a distracted reply from within.

The group entered the office and moved as one to stand in front of the instructor's desk. Shia looked up over her spectacles, her eyebrows raising.

She removed her glasses, holding them askew in one hand. "To what do I owe this honor?"

Arran steeled himself to reply, hands clasped behind his back.

"Ma'am, I know you told me not to discuss the events in Crenn'ier, but I felt the team, given its previous experiences and knowledge, would be able to assist. As it turns out, Bran believes he has some information that might be of assistance."

Shia did not respond.

Bran edged forward to speak. "Ma'am. When Arran mentioned the name Pim in his story, it bothered me. It sounded familiar and then this morning it finally came to me. About a year ago, I overheard my father's mage, Lajor, speaking to a man I did not know in the stables. He called the man 'Pim'. They finished their conversation and shortly thereafter, Pim left. I do not recall ever seeing him again."

Shia stared at Bran for a long moment and then began cleaning her spectacles in thought.

"A year ago?" she finally responded.

"Yes, ma'am."

"And you are sure that the name you overheard was Pim?"

"Yes, ma'am. I immediately recognized the name when Arran mentioned it during his story. Remembering the exact circumstance of the memory finally came to me this morning."

"I see."

The room was silent for several long moments. Arran stepped forward from the group to address his instructor.

"Ma'am, I take full responsibility for my actions and disobeying you. My friends did not coerce me in any way, quite the contrary. They never asked or pushed me for any information surrounding the events."

Shia gazed upon Arran admirably, one corner of her mouth twitching up sarcastically.

"My young man, I'm surprised it took you this long. If you had not told them, I would have been more shocked." She turned her attention to Bran. "Thank you for the information. I will see that Lajor is questioned on the matter. Is that all, or are there any other dark secrets the group would like to share with me?"

Arran's face flushed. "No, ma'am."

"Very well, then." Shia returned the spectacles to her face and went back to the papers on her desk.

Taking their cue, the group turned and left the office, looking quizzically at one another, not exactly sure what had just happened.

Once they were down the hall and out of earshot, Mare stopped and turned, forehead wrinkled in confusion. "Did we just get complimented after breaking a direct order from an instructor?"

"I think we did," Rayneer responded.

"Hmm...just checking."

Carfellin/Atre'lien Realm
Year 1305/March/Week 2

It took Faye three days to reach Carfellin. She had easily found the main road that Sofie had mentioned. There were a lot of travelers and they did nothing to hide the noise of their passing. There were a wide variety of caravans with various goods moving in both directions from the city. Faye stayed well back from the main road within the cover of the trees and followed in the direction of the full carts.

Spring was now in full bloom, and today already felt more like summer. She found the familiar scents of the flowers and the freshness of the season soothing.

As she came upon the city, she watched the proceedings of the main gate from afar for the remainder of the day.

The city was indeed large. She had no idea how many people to expect within the walls. The gate was tall and wide. The surrounding walls were not overly tall, but high enough to keep out all but the most determined of individuals. The woods surrounding the city had been cleared away, with the tree line beginning no less than a hundred paces from the wall.

The main gate was open and guarded during the day. Guards dutifully inspecting the long line of people requesting entry into the city. As night fell, the gates were closed and passage in and out trickled to a halt. Faye decided to walk the perimeter of the city and began circling from the safety of the trees, looking for weaknesses or opportunities.

Faye knew she was eventually going to have to venture into the city if she wanted to continue her search for the faces in her dream. Trying to go through the main gate during the day was out of the question. Her language skills were not up to the task. Climbing the wooden walls would not be difficult, but there was a risk that she would be seen by the patrolling guards on the battlements. In the end, she decided this was her best option. She would simply need to time it correctly with the patrolling guards.

Over the wall it is.

She made her way to the backside of the city and waited for darkness. This part of the city smelled of filth, but she had noticed the patrols were scarcer here. When a guard did pass by, they did not tend to linger, passing through the section quickly.

Faye watched as several guards made their way past her intended location on the wall. There were several naturally small ledges in the wood and the planks were also wide enough apart for handholds.

Just like climbing a large tree back home.

She watched as the guard passed her spot and then dove out of her cover to run the distance to the wall, springing herself upwards for the first foothold. She hit it perfectly, sprang up again to another handhold and then grabbed the top edge of the wall.

Holding herself perfectly still, she listened for any alarm. None came.

She eased her head above the rim of the wall and looked in both directions. The guard that had passed was well down the walkway now, back to her. Moving quickly, she hoisted herself up and over the top of the wall and then quickly dropped down beneath the patrolling walkway. She took a moment to catch her breath and listen. Hearing nothing, she made for the closest building she could find. She wrinkled her nose. She hadn't thought the stench of the city could get any worse, but she had been wrong.

How do these people live this way?

Faye repositioned her headband to cover her mouth and nose.

Staying in the shadows of the buildings and alleyways, she slowly began to make her way towards the more central section of the city, inspecting the buildings as she went. Stables, warehouses, and a few artisan shops seemed to dominate this section of the city. A few people wandered the area, but it looked like most everything had been closed down for the day.

Carefully making her way through the back alleys, she began to smell the scents of food as she neared the central section of the city. Peering down an alley, she noticed the streets had become far more crowded. She removed her headband from her face and replaced it back on her head, taking in a long, blessedly clean breath of air.

"By the gods," she muttered as she relished both the breath of clean air and the aroma of freshly baked bread. Her mind going back to that first gift of bread and butter Sofie had given her.

She inched her way up the alley, staying in the shadows as best she could. She made it about halfway and crouched behind a barrel. She peered out to see a door to a tavern or inn across the street and half of its front window. People were milling about on the street, but paying the alley no mind.

Faye grimaced at her poor line of sight. She needed to get closer to the street. She tested the weight of the barrel and found that it appeared to be fairly empty. It was solid, but not too heavy.

This should do nicely.

Staying behind the barrel, she lifted it, and began inching forward along the wall.

Once she got as near the entrance to the alley as she dared, she stopped and knelt down with her back to the barrel, breathing heavily from the exertion.

She scolded herself, slamming a frustrated fist on her leg.

I have neglected my training. This should not have tired me so.

Once she regained her composure, she flipped her hood up over her head and peered around the edge of the barrel. The tavern was in full view now, and she could make out the patrons inside. She slowly began scanning the various people that passed by. Most simply passed her by in idle talk, while two lovers stole a kiss in the doorway of a closed shop. Faye smiled at this, remembering her own first secreted kiss.

She continued her observations for another full hour. She did not, to her dismay, observe any auras of note.

It is but the first night, and it is a big city.

Faye was just about to sneak back down the alley and out of the city when she saw the movement of a man in the window of the tavern. Her trained eyes picking up the movement and involuntarily moving to observe.

It was an older man, dressed in a normal cloth tunic, pants, and a large cloak, cowl up. As he sat, he lowered the cowl and leaned his cane against the chair next to him. She stared at the man for several long moments. Faye could not decide if the man had no aura at all or if it was so weak as to be undetectable. Then she saw it. His aura flickered into existence and then slowly dimmed to...nothing. It was as if his aura was faintly there and then...he was simply...blank.

Not possible! Every living thing had some measure of faint aura.

A waitress arrived and took the man's order. Then, without hesitation, the man turned and looked straight out the window in Faye's direction.

Faye ducked behind the barrel instinctively, her heart instantly pounding in her chest.

He was just looking out the window. There is no way he could see me through the lighted window, across the street and in the shadows of the alley.

Faye took a breath and slowly peered back around the barrel. The waitress had arrived and delivered the man's drink. He could be seen thanking her, and then, without any hesitation, he looked back out the window in Faye's direction, raised his mug, winked, and took a long draft.

Faye ducked behind the barrel and was instantly on the move. She retraced her steps through the back streets and alleys, up and over the wall, and ran as fast as she could to the tree line and beyond. She stopped only long enough to grab her hidden gear and then ran until her panic finally began to subside. She slowed herself to a walk, breathing heavily.

"What just happened?" She muttered to herself. "How had that man even known I was there?"

She took a few moments to assess her bearings, then headed off to find a suitable site to bed down for the night.

Faye could not sleep. She eventually rose before dawn, absently gathering her breakfast as she strolled through the forest. She found some mushrooms, the same kind that Sofie had given her at their first meeting, and she smiled at the memory. The walk had calmed her, and after finding a pouch full of the various berries, nuts, and mushrooms, she made her way back to camp.

Eating slowly, she recounted the previous night's event with the old man. The uncanny way in which he had 'seemed' to see her. She stressed the word 'seemed' to herself because she was still not convinced his gesture was meant for her. It was unnerving for sure, but it could have been directed toward anyone on the street.

The man's aura though...that still bothered her. The way it flickered in and out, that wasn't natural. In the short glimpses she had, when it was absent, it felt...wrong.

How can anyone or anything...not have an aura? Even the trees and the grass had a faint aura of life about them.

To encounter a human or Elf without any aura at all was unthinkable.

Whoever he was, she finally decided, he was to be avoided. She was here to find the individuals from her dreams and the answers she desperately hoped they possessed. They, at least, had auras and it was them she wanted to find. Best to avoid this man.

Her mind made up, she lay back down to wait out the day and get some much needed rest for the upcoming night.

Faye made her way back across the wall and chose a location on the opposite side of the city from the previous night's reconnaissance. Hopefully, the man made a habit of frequenting the same tavern and would be avoided this night.

She had also decided on a different tactic for this evening's observations. She was on a flat rooftop of a two-story building. Locating a suitable spot along the low wall of the roof, she settled in. Her line of sight into the building across the street was limited, but her vantage up and down the street was greatly increased. This gave her a much better opportunity to view more people at once.

She had arrived earlier in the evening and the streets were much more active. So far, she had only seen one person of note who possessed a strong aura. It had been a middle-aged woman dressed all in white. The people of the city bowed their heads to her in deference as she passed.

Maybe a priestess or other person of faith?

Either way, it was not a face she had recognized from her dreams.

Faye knelt down and put her back to the wall of the rooftop to take a break, eating some berries and drinking from her small waterskin.

Should she stay here or move to another part of the city?

She decided to stay a little longer and turned around to peer back down over the street below. She had just settled into a comfortable position when she noticed the same old man enter the tavern across the street from her.

Faye cursed as she ducked down behind the wall.

Ferd'e!

She sat for several minutes, trying to decide if she should leave the city for the night or find another location. Neither was going to satisfy her curiosity, she thought, so she turned to peer back over the edge of the roof.

The man was sitting idly by the window again, drink in hand, just as he had done the previous night. Then, without hesitation, he once again raised his mug in her direction and looked upward...towards her!

Faye gasped and ducked behind the wall again, resting her forehead upon the wood, beads of sweat forming on her brow.

"You have traveled far, young lady." The voice came from behind her and in her native language.

Faye spun, her dagger out and pointing at the source of the voice.

Leaning against some crates, completely at ease and with his mug still in his hand, was the old man. He idly took a drink, as if meeting in the middle of the night on a rooftop was the most normal thing in the world.

Faye did not move a muscle. The dagger held solidly out in front of her, unsure of how to respond.

How does he know our tongue?

Neither spoke for several long moments.

The old man took another drink then set the now empty mug on the crate beside him.

"I'll have to compliment the tavern keeper on his beer. That is a particularly good bitter." He sighed, brushing his hands together.

The two locked eyes again, and Faye strained to discern the old man's aura. It was still flickering in and out of existence, and she could not make sense of what she was seeing.

"What you are?" she finally said in a hoarse whisper.

"Ah, you speak some of the common tongue of this land. How clever of you."

"What are you?" she said again, correcting herself.

He looked at her questioningly, as if taking her measure.

"I am just a man, enjoying the fresh air, some ale, and a conversation with a very interesting young lady."

"How you get here?" Faye asked, lowering her dagger but keeping it unsheathed and ready.

"Why, I simply came up the stairs." He pointed to the door on his left.

Faye looked at the door and responded. "Too fast."

The old man smiled at her.

"Let us say that I am not without...I believe talent is the proper term, no?"

Faye winced at his reply.

He has talent but no aura? That didn't make sense!

Faye shook her head. "Not possible."

"Yet here we are."

The man sat in silence, as if understanding that she needed time to digest the information he had just given her.

"Why do you follow?" Faye finally asked.

"You intrigue me. Your aura shines like a beacon to my eyes and I wanted to meet you."

Faye narrowed her eyes at him, "You have talent of..." She did not know the term in the common tongue, so she finished in her native tongue. "...the talent of the Aura sight?"

The man replied in common. "Yes. I have the talent of Aura sight."

"But you no...ooora." Faye struggled with the new word.

"Let us say I can 'hide' it. Do you know this word?"

Faye nodded. It was not an ability she had ever seen or heard of before, but at least it could plausibly explain his flickering aura.

"I would love to sit here with you all night, but my mug is empty." He leaned over and picked up the empty mug as he continued. "And I really would like to have another."

The old man stood and stretched his legs, grabbing the cane Faye had not noticed laying atop the crates.

He locked eyes with Faye and spoke calmly and decisively. "You will not find your answers here."

Faye looked at him in astonishment.

Did he know of her dreams?

"You should move on." He turned towards the door.

"Stop!" Faye said, more forcefully than she intended.

He turned to face her.

"What name?" She was desperate for anything to extend the conversation.

How could he know?

His brow furrowed at the question. He did not answer for several long moments, as if pondering whether he wanted to answer.

"I do not have a name in your tongue, but here, in this land...I am called Anders." He turned and disappeared into the door.

Faye rushed to the door in desperation, but he was already gone. She ran back to the edge of the roof and began surveying the street below. She scanned the street frantically, looking for the man to reappear.

She stayed on the rooftop long into the night, watching the street and the tavern window, but he was gone. Vanished into the night.

"Anderz," she said quietly to herself.

Faye had returned to her camp and mulled the words from Anders over and over in her head. 'You will not find your answers here. You should move on', he had said to her. Fear, doubt, and confusion all roiled in her mind, crashing into one another, as she tried to make sense of the encounter.

How could she trust the man? Was he purposefully trying to lead her astray? If he did know of her dreams, was that another talent that she did not know of? Was he powerful enough to stop her? Did he want to stop her?

All of these questions and more plagued her as she paced around the camp.

Faye eventually began to grow weary and lay down. She needed to rest and gain a clearer mind to work through it all.

The early light of dawn was the last thing she remembered as sleep finally overtook her.

Running, not from fear, but desperation. Desperation to be somewhere, towards something. The woods were thick. Branches and shrubs slapped across her body, leaving long welts upon her skin. Thorns drew blood and her clothes were ripped and tattered. A road. It had a sign. The road split and went in two different directions. She ran towards it. She could not understand the writing. The words pointing right glinted, and she took off in a blur. She ran. She ran like she had never run before. Back into the woods. Exhaustion overwhelming her, but she ran on. Ahead, the trees were thinning, and she could finally see the edge of the forest. She ran to it, breaking through with exhaustion and exhilaration. She was atop a large hill and before her, far in the distance, was a city. A huge city. Nestled along the banks of a mighty river and beyond it, the wide expanse of the ocean.

Faye awoke with a sudden jerk. Dagger instantly up and ready, her heart beating rapidly in her chest. Her clothes were wet from sweat and her hair was damp from it. She quickly examined herself. No blood, no welts, and her clothes were fine. She scanned the area, no threats.

"A dream," she muttered to herself in relief, sheathing her dagger.

She sat for several minutes, letting her heart rate return to normal as she recalled the dream.

This was her first true vision since coming to this land. She had begun to wonder if she would ever have one again. If she would ever be given some direction beyond the few faces from her previous visions.

In her dream she was running as if drawn, desperate to reach some unknown destination. She had found a road, but what road?

The road had a sign, but the letters were a jumble to her, and she did not know their meaning.

Faye rose and decided to gather some breakfast, letting the sereneness of the activity calm her thoughts. She walked and went over the dream again and again as she thoughtlessly gathered the various berries and nuts.

The sign is the key.

But which road? Which sign? How was she to find it?

There was only one main road that she knew of that could possibly be traveled enough to warrant it splitting in two directions. The road to Carfellin. She would follow the road away from Carfellin to see where it would lead her. The sign was the key, and although she did not know what the foreign words meant, the image was clear to her. She would easily recognize it again when she saw it.

CHAPTER 15
HARSHIN
YEAR 1305 / MARCH / WEEK 3

Week 7 of First Term

First term for third year was almost halfway done, and over a month since Arran and his friends had addressed Shia with their information about Pim. A month of infuriating information void. Shia had not called upon them or even mentioned the topic.

The term and his usual training was proving to be nothing short of monotonous. The enthusiasm of the previous term was gone. The effects were still there, students training together, learning from one another, but Arran's heart was not invested. The only highlight of the term so far had been his handful of sessions with Klintoc. After the initial disasters earlier in the term, Klintoc had begun to train him again when he was available. The training was primarily for Arran's new Shadow ability. After Klintoc began to show him the subtleties of the gift, he realized how clumsy he had been when he first used it in Crenn'ier. The sessions were slow, and the gift was much more difficult to master than his others, but he was making progress. The ability's effectiveness and duration were steadily creeping forward.

Arran was panting heavily as he dodged a blow from Rayneer, then pivoted for a strike to his leg, which he also deftly dodged. "I'm going to go insane if we don't get some answers, or at least some kind of information."

Arran held up his hand to call a stop to the sparring session. He wasn't in the right frame of mind and if he wasn't careful, even in a sparring session, a blow from Rayneer could prove quite painful.

The two friends walked over to the water barrel for a drink.

Rayneer agreed, as they sat down. "I only know what I've been told, but you lived it. I get your frustration, but you have to trust them." Rayneer's gaze trailed up to the office windows of the instructors.

Arran looked at his friend, knowing that he was right, but did not reply.

"Let's go store our gear and go for a mind-numbing run. I promise to make you forget about this business, if not for a little while."

Arran smiled wanly back at his friend.

"Sure."

<hr>

The following morning during breakfast, a school steward approached the dining table and addressed the group.

"Instructor Shia has requested your presence," he said flatly.

Mare widened her eyes in the expectation of more information and then sighed.

"When?"

"As soon as possible," he replied indignantly and promptly turned to leave.

Mare sniffed as she watched him leave. "That one is a right brat."

"Finally," Arran said. "Maybe we will get some answers, if not some new information. It's driving me mad."

"Calm down there, Country. She probably just wants to glean some more information from us. Not that we have much more to offer."

The group left the dining hall and made their way to Shia's office. Shia's assistant ushered them forward. Rayneer looked at the others and then knocked on the door.

"Enter."

They entered to find Instructor Shia sitting at her desk with Klintoc on one side, and a man Arran had not seen before standing on the other. They were looking over some papers in front of the instructor.

The group filed in and stood in front of the desk.

The three did not acknowledge the group for several moments, finishing their discussion in hushed tones.

Shia removed her spectacles and pushed back her chair, rising and placing her hands on the desk in front of her.

"This is Counselor Mintare from the Meitellen High Council." She gestured to the man Arran had not recognized.

"Ladies," he said with a small bow of his head to Elinda and Mare. "Gentlemen."

Everyone reciprocated the greeting politely, if not a little uneasily.

Shia reached for some papers on her desk and continued. "Counselor Mintare is in charge of the investigations for the council and our liaison."

Shia inspected the top sheet and then handed it to Klintoc. He gave it a cursory scan and then nodded to Shia as he handed the paper back.

Shia turned back to the group. "We have a commission for you."

They all looked at one another and then back at Shia.

"All of us?" Elinda asked.

Shia looked up reproachfully. "Yes. The council, Klintoc, and I believe it would be prudent to send all of you, given your previous experiences in Valoor."

Elinda looked at Arran, who shrugged his shoulders.

"We believe Harshin to be an area of interest. There have been no reports of any 'disturbances'..." stressing the last word uneasily, "...as of yet, but we would like for you to investigate and report your findings. Especially if they resemble anything like Valoor or Crenn'ier. It could only be a matter of time, given it is the only region yet to report any incidents."

Shia looked over the group of students one by one, studying their reaction to the sudden news of the commission.

"You will pose as a group of friends on holiday. Harshin caters to many vacationers, so you should not have any issues blending in. Keep your associations with the school hidden."

"How and to whom are we to report our findings? The distance to Harshin…" Mare trailed off as Shia held up her hand. She reached into her desk drawer and produced two rustic and well-worn leather bound journals. They were both fastened with a leather strap, a silver button holding them securely.

Shia handed one of the journals to Mare. "You will use this."

Mare took the journal and turned it over in her hands, then looked back at Shia questioningly.

"It is a missive journal," Shia replied. "Write your reports in the journal. Once you have finished, close, and retie the book. Those words will then appear in its sister journal here." She tapped her finger on the other journal.

"Once the words have been read here, and the journal closed, both journals will then be erased. The missive is not tied to any one person, so any of you may use it."

Mare looked at the journal again, this time in fascination and admiration as she caressed the leather and twirled the clasp bindings in her fingers.

"They are exceedingly rare and expensive." Mare looked up to find Shia staring at her intently. "Please try not to lose it."

Mare quit tampering with the book and held it to her side.

"Are there any more questions?" Shia asked.

"Funds?" Arran asked uneasily, unsure of the protocol for such a commission.

Mintare stepped forward and laid five pouches on the desk.

"You may use these funds at your discretion. It should be enough to keep you for at least two months and cover your expenses."

"Are there to be any rules of engagement should we discover anything?" Bran asked.

Klintoc stiffened at the question. "Your rule is not to engage. Report your findings and await further instruction."

"Yes, sir."

Shia scanned them all in turn. "If that is all, you should go and pack. You are to leave as soon as possible."

The group stepped forward, each taking one of the pouches provided by Mintare, and left the office.

———

As the door shut behind the students, Klintoc spoke, eyes still watching the door.

"Do you think they suspect anything?"

"The fact that we are sending them all together is suspicious, but no, I do not think they suspect our true intentions," Shia replied.

Mintare walked around the desk to face the other two. "You really believe the boy is in danger?"

Shia shrugged noncommittally. "After Crenn'ier, I think it is highly probable that whoever is behind this most likely knows of his involvement by now. I am uneasy at the mention of Lajor's involvement and his relationship with this Pim fellow. I know he had a plausible explanation when we interviewed him, but I'm not convinced. Even if it is not Lajor, I am convinced that we are dealing with someone of similar power and means. Sending the group to Harshin is a prudent move."

Klintoc chuckled softly to himself. "Who knows? We may even garner some insight as to how widespread the influence of this seditious faction really is. That group attracts trouble like bees to honey."

Shia turned her head and looked at Klintoc scornfully.

He shrugged.

"Do we have eyes on Lajor?" Mintare asked Klintoc.

"I do. Two operatives are tailing him sporadically to avoid suspicion, but I do not have much confidence of them revealing anything.

If Lajor is involved, we've tipped our hand by divulging Pim's name to him. He will be wary now."

"Keep at it," Shia said. "We need him to become comfortable again. Return to his normal routines."

"Do you really believe someone of his stature could be behind this? I know that you have no liking for the man, but this?" Mintare asked.

Shia did not answer for several long moments.

"Lajor was...is, an extremely talented mage. His talent and skill were never in question when he was here at the school. His temperament, his lack of restraint, and disregard for the rules and authority... well, let's just say he was always his own worst enemy. On several occasions, his temper and actions almost got him dismissed. When he was passed over for the second time to join the school council, he left under, shall we say, unfavorable terms."

Mintare could feel the heat and distaste of the man rolling off of the instructor. There was something personal there.

Shia continued. "He harbors a lot of resentment toward the entire establishment here in Meitellen. I'm not saying that he is behind all of this, but he does have the magical means and potential motive. Above and beyond his own narcissistic love of power."

Mintare nodded his head. "The rumors are beginning to gain traction. The council is extremely wary about how much longer we can maintain our ruse and keep this all a secret. We have a lot of worried councilmen who want closure, and quickly."

Shia prickled at the underlying politics of the comment. "As do we all, but I understand. We will let you know when we have any additional information."

Mintare bowed his head appreciatively. "I will take my leave, then."

"As will I," Klintoc said.

As the door shut quietly behind them, Shia was left alone with her thoughts and she did not like where they were taking her.

If Lajor or someone like him was behind this, how long before the secret to this ability of transformation is revealed? Once it was known, there would be no way to keep it from those that would use it for personal gain and/or chaos.

She sat and closed her eyes, rubbing them in a vain attempt to remove the exhaustion. The world as they knew it was on a ledge and they were perilously close to tumbling over.

Year 1305/April/Week 3

The trip to Harshin took just over three weeks. Arran had tried to book the Wayfarer, but Harshin was unfortunately not on their schedule. They ended up booking passage on a similar vessel and while the captain and crew were as equally amiable, Arran missed the companionship of Cid and the Wayfarer's crew.

The morning was sultry as the boat made its way down the Seitellen. Arran and Elinda stood at the prow of the ship as they approached the city of Harshin.

Harshin was a large city, second only to Meitellen. It was the last city on the river Seitellen before it emptied into the ocean. Due to its southern climate, it was a favorite tourist attraction for its ocean views and soft, white sand beaches. While tourism was extremely popular, it was Harshin's docks and point of entry on the southern-most part of the continent that drove commerce. Only the Seitellen and Eitellen emptied into the ocean and only Harshin boasted the channel depth and docks for the larger vessels needed for trade around the continent's coastal regions.

Arran leaned over the rail and took in the smells of the ocean breeze coming up the river. He could taste the saltiness in the air.

"The land down here is exotic and robust," Elinda remarked as they stood, admiring the lush views as the ship slipped easily down the river. "The forests are different, more dense and lush. They have a word for it, but it escapes me."

"Jungle," Mare said as she approached. "It's a variant from the old tongue, Jangala."

Elinda turned. "Yes, that's it. It's magnificent."

The three remained at the prow, taking in the city as the ship maneuvered its way to the docks.

"What's the plan, then?" Bran asked as the group stood on the docks, looking around. "Stay in the city proper or out along the coast?"

Everyone looked at Rayneer. "What? Oh..." He laughed at himself. "Of course we have to stay on the coast, right?"

"Can we afford it?" Arran asked.

Elinda winked. "I've enough to cover any difference we may need. Besides, we're on vacation."

Mare took Elinda's arm in hers. "Always pays to have a princess around."

Elinda huffed at the old joke. "I'm not a..."

Mare tugged on her arm, interrupting her as the group headed out of town.

They found a cabin rental about a half mile from Harshin city proper that had three rooms. It was not directly on the beach, but instead sat on a small rise behind the beach cabins. The unobstructed views of the ocean were well worth it.

Rayneer stretched out in a lounge chair and put his hands behind his head. "Not bad for some third year's. Not bad at all."

"Don't get too comfy there, big guy," Arran said. "We've got work to do."

"Doesn't mean I can't enjoy the colors of that sunset now, does it?" He tilted his head towards the ocean.

Arran leaned over the balcony railing, taking in the vast ocean. He watched as the sun slowly dipped below the horizon, painting a myriad of colors on the water's surface and in the clouds above. It was a spectacular sunset. He then sat down in silence, enjoying the relaxing moment.

CHAPTER 16
OLD FRIENDS
YEAR 1305 / MARCH / WEEK 4

Pim strolled through the west gates of Harshin. It had taken him quite a few weeks to make the journey, but he was finally here. He walked the streets without much purpose, taking in the all the sights and sounds as he slowly made his way towards the heart of the city. He didn't have anywhere specific to be or anyone to meet...well, that wasn't exactly true. He knew that if Azra'el told him to meet Samal, eventually he would be approached by someone. So, with this in mind, he wandered until he found the busiest and most popular section of town. Finding an inn to his liking, he settled in and waited.

He spent several days wandering about the city and enjoying the shores. He had to admit; the beaches were beautiful in this region. Eventually, though, his assumption proved correct. He was enjoying a nice, post dinner wine at his table when a woman walked up and sat down opposite him. She did not say a word. She simply looked at him with an unnerving dead stare. She was pretty in a sort of rustic way. Dark hair, brown eyes, and tall for a woman. Not exactly Pim's type, but he wasn't known to be picky with his women. He simply smiled and sipped his wine as she continued to stare at him.

They sat this way for a long time, so long in fact that Pim had finished his wine.

"May I interest you in a wine? Ale, perhaps?" Pim waved a hand at the server.

"No," she said flatly as the server approached the table.

"I'll have another glass of wine and an ale for the lady."

"I said I didn't want anything."

"I heard."

"So why..." she trailed off as a wry smile spread across Pim's face.

"To get me talking. Clever."

Pim bowed his head at the compliment.

"My name is Pim, which I'm sure you already know. You are..." he let the question trail off.

The woman did not answer. She had only been instructed to approach and assess the man. If need be, return without him. It was her decision. He was definitely calm, maybe too calm. There was something about him though, simmering beneath the surface. A confidence? Or was it arrogance?

The server returned with their order, eying the two suspiciously, as they didn't even acknowledge her presence. They appeared to be in some kind of staring contest. She dismissed it like she always did. Eccentric rich bodies down south on vacation.

The woman waited until the server had departed before finally answering. "Lia."

Pim held up his wine in salutation. "Nice to meet you, Lia."

Lia picked up the ale and took a long draw, hoping she had made the right choice.

Lia led Pim directly into the trade and industrial section of the city. They eventually came to a small apothecary shop. Pim stopped and looked at the tiny shop as Lia entered. She held the door expectantly behind her and then turned.

"You coming?"

Pim smiled and entered the shop. The assault on his nose was immediate, hitting him before he had even crossed the threshold.

The mixture of an untold number of herbs filled the air with a pungent fragrance. Above it all, a hint of lavender. She walked purposefully to the back of the shop before the door had closed. Pim followed slowly, observing the variety of products in the small shop as he passed.

"Quite the nice assortment you have collected."

Lia didn't respond and walked through a door behind the counter and into a room with several tables. Various equipments of the trade were neatly laid out atop each. The room was clean and tidy. The tables appeared to be the work benches used for any necessary preparations for the shop's wares.

Pim nodded in appreciation at the professionalism of the shop.

Lia looked back at him and started up a set of stairs at the back of the workroom.

"This way."

Pim followed and at the top they entered a large, single room roughly the size of the shop below. It was warm and inviting, with a central fireplace, several couches, and chairs. Two beds peaked out from behind a privacy screen, tucked neatly near the back wall of the room. The furniture was set up in such a way so that each arrangement spoke to a specific purpose. There was a desk against the wall to his right, and a man sat studiously going over what Pim assumed were the shop's journals. As below, everything was tidy and in its place. He was impressed. He himself had never been this well organized, but he could definitely appreciate it.

Maybe I'll hire someone one day.

Lia went over to the man and whispered something in his ear. The man finished what he was writing, neatly blotted the paper, and then closed the journal. He placed the writing quill in its holder and turned.

Samal was older than Pim by at least twenty years, tall and lean with a polished, educated refinement about him. Pim knew that Azra'el favored Samal. He was a thoughtful and methodical man. Samal was recruited not only for his belief in their cause, but also for his formal training and teachings at the vaunted school. He took to the master's trainings with a serious precision, in stark contrast to Pim's brash and unorthodox approach.

'Results are results, no matter how they look', Pim had always said when he found himself comparing the two.

Pim smiled and walked over to Samal, extending his hand in greeting, which Samal rose and took.

"Good to see you again," Samal said, moving to one of the couches by the fireplace.

Pim took a seat opposite.

"How are operations going in your region?" Pim asked. "May I be of any assistance?"

Samal inwardly winced at the straightforward question. He forced down his annoyance. "That is very generous of you, but I believe that Lia and I have the operations under control. You should enjoy the city and the beaches during your stay. You have arrived at a fortuitous time. The peak of our season will begin soon."

Pim straightened his vest habitually and looked about the room as he replied. "That sounds perfect. I could use a nice vacation."

"Well, then," Samal said, placing his hands on his knees and rising. "If you don't mind, I have appointments to attend."

"Of course." Pim remained on the couch, bringing his gaze back to Samal. "There is the matter of my being sent."

Samal sat back down. "I am aware."

"If there is anything, anything at all I can do to assist…" Pim attempted his best genuine smile, but it did not reach his eyes. "You will let me know, yes?"

Samal returned the perfunctory smile with one of his own and pretended to give the question serious thought. "Perhaps. Let me think on the matter. I'm sure Lia and I can find a way to make use of someone with your…talents."

"Excellent!" Pim rose. "I love the place you have here."

Samal stood and began a slow walk over to the stairs. Stopping just short of the entry. "Please let us know if you need anything."

"Thank you." Pim lowered his head in deference and then proceeded down the stairs to leave.

Formalities out of the way, now I can get down to business.

Pim casually left the shop, the small bell tinkling at his exit.

Samal parted the curtains and gazed out the front window, watching as Pim walked down the street below.

"Keep an eye on that one," he said. "It will not take long for him to intrude upon our business here. I want to make sure we assuage him of those thoughts."

Without a word, Lia turned and left.

Pim did not immediately go back to his inn. He instead took a very random and circuitous route around the city, eventually making his way to the seediest part of the city, the docks. He could probably follow Lia himself, but there was the chance that he could be seen and he did not want to overplay his hand too soon. So, he would do the next best thing and find a local who would blend in and have her observed. He was sure that they would have him observed also, but he could deal with that. It would not be the first time, nor the last, that he would need to deal with a tail.

He settled in at a particularly nasty-looking tavern called 'The Black Sails' and ordered an ale. The ale was crap, but he forced himself to sip at the bitter concoction while he observed the patrons. There were the normal dock hands and sailors, but he was not interested in them. He was looking for someone local, someone he knew would know the area and be of the ilk to make a little money, even if it were on the shady side.

It did not take long before a group of four men entered the tavern and settled down at a table across the room. They were loud, obnoxious, and obviously comfortable with their standing in the tavern. They mercilessly hounded the young waitress, who cringed at their every advancement as she took their order. No one lifted a finger to assist the poor girl.

Pim smiled.

They will do nicely.

Pim waited for them to be very near the end of their first round of drinks and then ushered for the barmaid. He ordered their second round. As she delivered the fresh mugs of ale, she pointed in Pim's direction. He lifted his mug. The thugs stared at him menacingly, but did not turn down the free ale.

After taking a few draws from his mug, one of the four rose and came over to Pim's table.

Ahhh...the leader emerges.

The man came to the table and sat down hard on the chair opposite Pim, his mug splashing a bit of ale on the table as he did.

He stared menacingly for several seconds. His words came out in a harsh dialect that Pim did not recognize. "What'r you playing at?"

Pim's face was the picture of innocence as he replied. "Playing at?"

"What...do ya want?" The man pronounced each word slowly and even more harshly than before. His demeanor turning even more surly.

Pim was impressed.

Yes, you will do just fine.

"I am in need of, shall we say, services that I believe a man of your skill and cunning might be able to provide." Pim pretended to take a small sip from his mug, watching the look on the man's face turn from anger to questioning.

"What kinds of services?"

"I need someone followed and her whereabouts reported back to me. Easy and simple. Five silver a week until I have the information I need." Pim estimated that the man would most likely counter with ten.

"Fifteen."

An ambitious one.

"Eight."

The man did not hesitate. "Ten."

Pim did not respond for a few moments, as he pretended to wrestle over this last offer before replying, "Ten it is, then."

The man grinned wickedly. It was as if smiling was a foreign concept to his weathered features. It was not a pleasant sight. "Who we tailing?"

"Do you know of the apothecary in the trade district? Small shop near the middle of the street?"

"Rings a bell."

"There is a woman, dark hair, tall. You can't miss her. I want to know where she goes. I need her followed constantly, no slacking off, even if she leaves the city."

The man rubbed his chin thoughtfully, as if following her outside the city was somehow more difficult. "Might cost ya extra."

Pim replied smoothly. "Why don't we agree that we can discuss any additional funds based upon the quality of the information?"

The man pondered for a moment and then agreed.

"Good." Pim pulled out his pouch and handed five silver across the table discreetly.

The man looked at the amount angrily. "We said ten."

"Five now, and I'll give you the rest at the end of the week. I will be here every two days for your report, paying you twice a week, as agreed."

"Hmmph." The man took the five silver, returning to his table.

Pim left the unfinished mug on the table and exited the tavern to wander about the city. He was, after all, on vacation.

Year 1305/April/Week 3

Pim left his inn and ambled down the street towards the merchant section. It had been three weeks since he hired his wayward counterpart and his own routine had become a familiar friend. For those three weeks, he had been the most bland, unassuming person he could imagine, keeping his days habitually boring. He awoke late, left the inn, bought some fresh fruit or maybe a morning bun from a vendor, then made his way down to the beach where he sat and read a book, or at least pretended to read.

Pim loved the 'cat and mouse' game of being tailed. Keeping to the same routine allowed him to become very familiar with not only the area, but the other people who frequented said area. He had thus far identified three different tails. They did not repeat from day to day. Three tails, different each day, but the idiots followed a shared pattern. They followed him from the same distance and always stopped at the same location when he went to the beach.

Amateurs.

Pim put down his book and stretched his arms above his head, taking in the morning sun and ocean breeze. This really was a nice place. He could now understand its allure, and maybe even see himself moving here one day.

One day. Maybe. There is still work to be done.

Pim was already thinking about the report he would receive this night. The previous report from his shady friend had been the first positive news he had received thus far. Lia and another tall man, Samal, Pim had guessed, looked like they were preparing for a trip. Pim's hopes had been on edge for two days. With any luck, this would be a trip to their field operations, exactly what he had been waiting for.

Pim finished his morning at the beach, took lunch at one of the myriad of taverns sprinkled along the shoreline, then visited several random merchants to finish out his afternoon. He bought a new book, which he could not have cared less about, for a show of earnestness in his endeavors. He made his way back to his inn, ordered a glass of wine, which he sipped slowly and methodically, had an early dinner and then retired to his room to wait for darkness.

Pim peered through the slats at the window of his room to the street below. Seated two shops down, in front of a now closed tailor merchant's establishment, was this evening's tail. He looked bored.

Perfect. Nothing to see here.

Pim made his escape out the back of the inn. He had a surly, if not informative, friend to meet.

Pim entered The Black Sails and scanned the room. He did not see his contact, so he settled into a table and ordered some of the shitty ale.

This is really bad. How hard is it to have decent ale?

Wincing, he took another sip and set the mug down.

The leader of the group Pim had hired entered a few minutes later, and made his way over to the table and sat down. He stared at Pim's mug.

Pim sighed and then motioned the barmaid over.

This seemed to placate the man, and he lowered his head to speak confidentially. Why, Pim did not know. There was no way anyone could overhear them amongst the clamor in the room.

"The two I spoke of's last time," he said, halting to make sure Pim was following along.

Pim nodded his head.

"They went west out's the city to a small farming village called Kiel. They's obtained rooms at the local inn and then immediately's left. They's headed straight west of town and into's the jungle."

The barmaid arrived with his mug, and he took a long draw before continuing.

"The jungle is thick there's, and the two went's in a fair distance. I could's not tell how far, but it were at least a good's hour before's they came to a small camp." The thug stopped and took another long draw from his mug.

"Tell me about the camp. What did you see?" Pim tried his best to hold back his excitement.

Pim watched the man curiously as he paused, an almost pained expression on his face as he tried to remember the specifics. "There were a crude cabin, prob'ly a single room and small shack. They rummaged about, doing what, I do not know. Then they's fed what was, I believe, some animals in the shack. I weren't able to see in, but I did hear'em. They sounded big. All sorts of yelps and howls. Then they's left. Went back's to the inn. They's came back to the city in the morning."

Then, to Pim's utter astonishment, the man pulled out a sheaf of paper.

"I drew a map." He handed the dirty parchment across the table.

Pim took the paper, still shocked that the man had this much foresight. He scanned it. It was crudely drawn, but he believed it would be serviceable enough for his purposes.

Pim was almost shaking with pleasure at the news. Taking a moment to gather himself, he slowly reached into his pouch and produced ten silver, handing it to the man.

"For your thoroughness and effort. I will no longer need your services."

The man greedily grabbed the silver and smiled a grotesque smile, his brown fetid teeth showing his appreciation.

Use some of that for a new toothbrush. Stupid sod.

The man quickly tucked the silver away, finished off his mug in one long draw, and left.

Pim went over his options. He could leave tonight, but arriving late at the inn would make him stand out, memorable. No, he would show discretion and leave in the morning, arriving like any other traveler. That decided, he left the dingy tavern, hoping never to make its acquaintance again.

"Just one more day," Rayneer and Mare begged in unison.

Bran and Arran shook their heads.

"We've had our enjoyment. We need to investigate some of the villages around the city and see if we can gather any information," Arran said.

Mare looked pleadingly at Elinda for help, but she only shrugged her shoulders.

"Arran is right. We need to at least get some work done and send a report back before Shia gets suspicious."

Mare huffed.

Arran leaned over the table at the map they had procured. "We'll pick one of the closer villages and be back here before the end of the day." It was a vain attempt to placate the two, he knew, but it was the best he could do for now.

He pointed to a small village just west of Harshin. "Here. We'll start there and see what we can find."

A short time later, and after no small amount of grumbling from Mare and Rayneer, the group was ready to head out.

"Do you want to ride or walk?" Elinda asked.

"I vote walk," Bran said. "I don't know about all of you, but I think my legs could use a break from the vacationing."

"Agreed," Rayneer said.

"Walk it is then," Arran said.

The walk was pleasant and Arran had to admit it was good to get out and stretch his legs. They followed a small cart path that wound its way through alternating fields of tall grasses and newly planted crops. As the group entered the village proper, Arran observed it was not too dissimilar to Kine. It was pleasant, quiet, and unassuming. Just another farming community amongst many. The only difference was the bustling market at its center. The town was obviously prospering due to its close proximity to Harshin.

"Feels a bit like home," Arran said to no one in particular.

"Nice place," Rayneer agreed.

"Market seems busy. How about we start there?" Elinda said. "Split up and meet at the inn, in say, about an hour?"

Everyone nodded as they slowly dispersed.

Arran peeled off to the right and headed over to what appeared to be one of the fruit vendors. It was only mid April but this far south it appears that the season for fruit was at least a few weeks ahead of the northern realms. The scent of fresh apples, oranges, and a variety of melons assaulted his nose. Most of the produce from this village would end up in Harshin, but some would, undoubtedly, be shipped northward. But right here, right now, this was about as fresh as one could hope for.

Arran walked up to one of the vendors. "Cup of mixed fruit, please."

Arran casually watched as the vendor quickly began gathering a variety of fruit on his cutting board. "How is the village doing so far this year?" Arran picked up a melon from one of the bins and gave it an approving sniff.

The vendor smiled warmly as he continued cutting the fruit.

"The weather has been especially mild and the season moderately wet. As you can see, the crops have responded well. I believe this will be a very good year."

Nothing seems to be bothering this man, at least.

Arran smiled amiably as he paid for his fruit. "Good day to you, sir." He slowly meandered away as the vendor greeted his next customer.

Arran picked his way through the crowd, casually glancing at some of the other vendors. He plopped a delicious piece of melon in his mouth and had just started to chew it when he froze.

Walking into the marketplace, without a care in the world and just the hint of a smile on his face, was Pim.

Arran stood transfixed, his pulse racing

"Are you okay there, lad?" one of the vendors asked.

Arran quickly gathered himself, and his attention snapped back into focus as he turned and smiled at the vendor. "I'm fine. I thought I saw an old acquaintance is all."

Arran slowly moved out of the market, looking for the nearest shadow he could find between two buildings. He slid out of sight and then entered the shadows. His vision narrowing through the ethereal fog, but never leaving Pim.

Pim had never seen Arran at the campsite near Crenn'ier, he was sure of it, but it would do no good to have him catch Arran staring at him from across the market either.

Arran watched as Pim strolled through the marketplace, stopping at a vendor for some fruit just like he had done, and then went to the inn. All of this in as casual a manner as if he were nothing more than a common vacationer out for a stroll, taking in the countryside.

Arran's mind was racing. He closed his eyes, releasing the shadows, and took a long, deep breath.

"Stay calm!" he muttered, berating himself.

He took a few more breaths and opened his eyes. He scanned the market and found Bran first. Forcing himself to stay slow and casual, he worked his way over to Bran, popping fruit in his mouth to try and add to the effect.

Arran held out the cup for Bran. "Piece of fruit?"

"Uh...I guess." Bran looked at Arran warily. "Why are you acting so weird?"

Arran shrank at the criticism, cursing himself. "I was going for calm and casual."

"You might want to work on that a bit. You look freaked out more than anything. What's up?"

Arran took another piece of fruit from the cup and used the time to continue collecting his thoughts. As he was doing so, Elinda had sighted the two and came over to join them.

"What's up with him?" Elinda asked Bran.

"Not sure yet."

"I'm not deaf, you know?" Arran said.

Arran looked at the inn, then turned his attention back to Bran and Elinda. "Pim is here," he said under his breath.

It took a few moments for the realization to hit them, and then both sets of eyes went wide.

Elinda's response came out as a muted squeak. "The magic user from Crenn'ier?"

Arran nodded.

"Are you sure?" Bran asked. "I mean, it's been a while, and you only caught a glimpse of him and even so, that was from a distance."

Arran had to admit both points, but after a moment's deliberation he said, "I'm sure."

Elinda looked around worriedly. "Where is he now?"

"He went into the inn."

Bran poked Arran in the shoulder to get his attention. "What's he look like? I'll go over and have a peek, eh?"

"Tall, lean, black hair and he was dressed neatly, like a low to middle noble, brown and green."

Bran grabbed the cup of fruit from Arran. "Okay, you two gather the others and find a conspicuous spot in the market to hang out. We're vacationers...try to act like it." He punched Arran in the shoulder. "I'll be back shortly."

Bran spent a few more minutes in the market, wandering aimlessly as he finished the fruit and then made his way over to the inn. He went directly to the bar, taking a seat and ordering an ale. He deliberately did not look around the room as he did his best to pass himself off as a man of leisure, just a normal guy grabbing a mug on a nice, warm day.

After his drink arrived, Bran drank for a bit and then slowly turned to face the room. He casually began to survey the room, never lingering on any one spot for long. Pim was sitting in the corner with a drink of his own and it looked like he was...talking to himself? Bran moved his gaze around the room before coming back to Pim. Sure enough, he looked like he was muttering under his breath, completely ignoring his drink. Pim's expression turned very odd, almost distraught. He appeared to become agitated as he continued to mumble to himself.

Weird.

Bran let his eyes continue around the inn, not wanting to get caught staring. He leaned his back against the bar, sipping at his ale, while keeping Pim in his peripheral vision. He was about to order another, when Pim stood up, leaving his drink untouched, and headed up the stairs to his room.

Bran quickly finished his drink and left the inn. He made his way over to the rest of the group, who had settled on one of the tables in the center market area.

"So what did you see?" Arran asked urgently.

Bran shook his head. "He sat in a booth for a while, muttering to himself. He looked agitated. He didn't touch his drink and then he went upstairs to his room."

"Agitated?" Mare asked.

Bran shook his head. "I don't know. It was strange, he was behaving oddly. Agitated is the only word I can think of that fits."

No one spoke.

Arran took a breath and addressed the group. "First things first. I think we need to send word to Shia via the missive. Secondly, we need to keep an eye on Pim. How about Rayneer, Mare, and Elinda head back to the cabin and send the missive? Bran and I will stay and keep an eye on Pim. Once all of you have word back from Shia, come back here and we'll figure out our next move."

Everyone nodded in solemn agreement.

After the others had left, Bran turned to Arran. "We should split up. We shouldn't be seen together in case one of us is compromised. He probably won't suspect two tails and no sense taking a chance."

"Agreed."

Bran eyed the buildings across the market opposite the inn. "I'll watch the front of the inn from across the yard, and you cover the back."

Arran left the market via the main road before circling back around to the back of the inn. His skin tingling with adrenaline.

CHAPTER 17

DARK DISCOVERIES

YEAR 1305 / APRIL / WEEK 3

Night had fallen and Arran found himself perched atop the inn, surveying the rear of the building. He reached into his pouch and pulled out some dried venison.

Going to be a long night.

He ate half of the portion and moved to put the rest back in his pouch, when the back door of the inn opened, a thin sliver of light spilling out. The door closed quickly and silently. There was not a breath of sound as Arran sat tensely in place; then the soft whisper of footfalls. A figure emerged from beneath the eaves. He wore a dark cloak, cowl raised, hiding his features. The figure paused for a moment, peering in each direction, then headed straight out across the fields and towards the woods.

Jungle. They call it a jungle here.

Arran hesitated a moment, not sure what to do.

Is that Pim?

Arran was unsure.

Well, shit!

Arran quickly made up his mind and began climbing down. He kept his distance as he followed, focusing intently on silence and stealth as he crouched low, dropping to the ground at the slightest hint of the man turning or altering his gait. Arran's Stealth had become his most acute skill, and his movements were easily masked by the soft grass of the field.

The man stopped near the edge of the jungle and looked around, as if trying to determine his bearing. Arran threw himself down to the ground, heart thundering in his chest. The man hesitated a few moments and then proceeded. Not ten steps later, Arran lost all sight of the man as he disappeared into the dense undergrowth of the jungle. Arran hastened his steps to catch up.

The pace slowed considerably once they entered the jungle. The man, Arran still unsure if it was Pim or not, stopped periodically, changing his course more than once.

After about an hour, Arran stiffened as the man picked up his pace and headed confidently forward. A few moments later, Arran understood why. The man had found a small clearing in the midst of all the foliage. The clearing was not very large, maybe fifty paces across, and was somewhat circular. There was a small cabin, and a shed with a crude table and a firepit near the center.

The man walked up to the table and laid a hand on the surface almost reverently. With his other hand, he removed the cowl. Arran focused intently, increasing his sight from the hiding spot outside of the circle clearing.

It was Pim!

Arran watched as Pim entered the cabin. Arran could hear him rummaging around for a few minutes before exiting and heading towards the small shed. He peered in through the slats. The shed was locked with a heavy bolt and chain. As Pim moved his head from side to side, desperately looking for a better view of the shed's contents, Arran could just make out the faint rustling of straw and the heavy breathing of animals. Seemingly satisfied, Pim turned away from the shed and Arran could just make out the wicked smile spreading across Pim's face.

Not good.

Pim did not stay much longer at the site, evidently discovering what he had come for and left. Arran followed him back to the inn, where Pim entered again through the back door and disappeared.

Bran turned around quickly, hand going to his sheaths, before realizing it was Arran coming up behind him in the alley.

Bran watched Arran approach, his face grim. "What?"

"Pim left out the back entrance and went into the jungle. There is a campsite about an hour's walk in. They have a shed with at least one animal captured, if not more. It was exactly like I saw at Crenn'ier."

Bran's shoulders slumped. "So it is as we feared, then. He is here to continue his work."

"It appears so, but I don't think the campsite was his. When I was following him, he looked lost a few times, and when he finally found the camp, he inspected it like it was the first time he had been there. We may be dealing with more than just Pim."

"Great."

"You mind if I catch a little sleep?" Arran asked. "I don't believe he will be going out again tonight, and one of us should get some rest. Wake me after a few hours and I'll take over."

"Sounds good." Bran watched with dismay as Arran disappeared down the alley to find a spot to rest.

Dawn was only an hour old when Arran saw Rayneer, Elinda, and Mare coming into town. He stepped back into the alley and gave Bran a light shake on his shoulder.

"The others are back."

Bran nodded and wiped the sleep from his eyes as he rose.

Arran exited the alley, catching Rayneer's eye. He pointed to the tavern across the yard from the inn. Rayneer nodded.

The tavern had a reputation for good ale, but the group had also heard it had very fine food, especially breakfast. They settled down at a table near the front window to keep an eye on the inn across the yard.

The group talked amiably about various mundane topics until after the barmaid had delivered their plates of pancakes, eggs, bacon, sausage, dark toast, and fruit.

Rayneer eyed the food greedily.

"Think we ordered enough?" Mare said sarcastically.

Rayneer looked up with a grin. "I'll let you know in a few minutes."

Mare sighed and placed a piece of toast and some fruit on her plate. "Men and their stomachs."

Arran began fixing a large plate for himself. The venison from the night before had long ago served its purpose. "I take it you heard back from Shia?"

"We did," Mare said. "It was almost immediate. That missive is remarkable." She took a bite of toast before continuing. "They were surprised to hear Pim had made his way this far south and they are sending Klintoc and two others our way immediately to deal with him. We are to observe and gather intelligence until they arrive." She gave a very disapproving glare. "We are not to engage."

"Typical," Bran said in disgust, mirroring Arran's own angry scowl.

Arran lowered his voice angrily. "It will take them weeks to get here!"

Elinda placed a hand on Arran's arm. "Patience. We will have plenty to do until they arrive."

"We think that Pim might not be acting alone," Bran said between bites, looking over at Arran and nodding his head towards the others as if to say, 'Tell them'.

Elinda sat up straight in anticipation. "Did he meet with someone last night?"

Arran shook his head. "No." He then spent the next few minutes recounting the previous night's events.

Elinda sat back and forked at a piece of fruit on her plate in thought. "It's not a bad assumption." She turned her gaze back to Arran intently. "All the more reason we gather more intelligence while we wait for Klintoc and the others to arrive."

Arran slumped in resignation and nodded his head begrudgingly.

Bran gestured out the window. "He's leaving."

Everyone turned their heads to look out the window at the tall, dark-haired man leaving the inn.

Mare's face scrunched unapprovingly. "That's him, eh? He may try to put on airs of wealth with the clothes, but that haircut and gait say otherwise."

"I'll follow," Bran said, wiping his mouth off and rising.

"How will I find you if he goes back to Harshin?" Arran asked.

"Meet me at the central market before sundown and we can swap out. Best if you get some rest today and be fresh for the evening watch."

Everyone agreed.

Bran poked Rayneer in the back as he left. "Wait for me to get well away from town before you all leave. Rayneer sticks out like a rotten apple."

Rayneer grunted and then began attacking the remainder of his plate.

The following two weeks were as wearisome as Arran had ever endured. The routine of following Pim day and night became tedious and uneventful. Pim had to be the most patient man Arran had ever seen and watching him go through the same pattern day after day had become frustrating. For all intents and purposes, Pim was acting like he was just another vacationer, enjoying the peak season of Harshin and its sights.

Bran was the first to observe a break in his routine. He observed Pim as he took a very circuitous route to the trade district of Harshin, where he ended up at an apothecary. Bran watched Pim enter the building, spending an abnormally long time inside before emerging with a small bundle.

"What do you think?" Bran asked Arran that evening during their scheduled change.

"I don't know. Did you get a look at the owner?"

"I didn't stay after Pim left and I couldn't see inside. The windows were darkened."

"Hmm...let's keep it as a possible lead, but stay on Pim. Agreed?"

"Agreed."

Arran made his way to Pim's inn and settled in to his now customary perch atop the building. From this vantage, he could see and hear anyone leaving via the front or back of the inn. He was resigned to what he thought was another long night of boredom when he heard the faintest of movements in the back alley. Arran crept over and peered below. A cloaked figure was making its way down the alley.

It was Pim. Arran was sure of it. Anxious for anything to break the monotony, Arran began his descent and followed the figure.

Pim was cautious. Arran had been forced to use his Shadow ability more than once as he followed. Pim made his way to the trade district, never straying from the back alleys and streets. He finally stopped and hid in an alley across the street from an apothecary shop.

Gotcha!

Arran watched patiently while Pim intently eyed the apothecary. Not long after, a tall man, similarly cloaked as Pim, exited the shop with a woman. She was dressed in very functional leathers, all browns and light greys. Each had a large backpack on their back and the man carried an additional bag at his side. They locked up the shop and proceeded down the street, Pim watching their every move and then following in the shadows.

Arran chuckled to himself. The irony of Pim trailing the two from the shop, and he himself trailing Pim, did not escape him.

It soon became evident the two shopkeepers were headed out of town. After procuring two horses, they headed for the road, which would take them to the village of Kiel.

———

Arran trailed silently along behind the shady caravan as they arrived in Kiel in just under an hour. The two shopkeepers did not stop. They continued riding straight through the small village and out through the fields on the far side, just as Pim had done. Arran went straight for the woods, heading directly to the campsite. He didn't need to trail them now; he was confident of their destination.

The shopkeepers strode into the camp and, as they did, low howls and snuffling growls began to emerge from the shed. The pitiful sounds were so deep and resonant, Arran had to wonder as to the size of the creatures within. The woman began unpacking the bags and organizing the contents on the large table near the front of the cabin while the man threw some wood in the firepit. Once he was done and, without hesitation, he held out his hands and executed a precise stream of flame to light the fire.

Arran's eyes shot up in amazement. So now they had two magic wielders in the mix.

Juussst great.

Off to Arran's right, and just in his peripheral view, he saw a slight movement. Arran focused his attention in that direction. Pim had arrived. He remained sheltered within the thick undergrowth, evidently content to watch the proceedings.

What are you up to?

The woman continued to unpack the bags. The majority of the contents were large packages of what appeared to be meat. They were wrapped like one would get from a local butcher shop. Once all of these packages were laid out, the woman then produced several jars from her backpack and placed them at the end of the table.

The tall man shed his cloak and laid it down near the firepit. "Feed the animals while I prepare."

The woman did not reply and simply began unwrapping the

meat. Once she had about half of the meat laid out, she reached for the jars and began sprinkling small amounts from each on the meat. When finished, she went over to the shed and unlocked the front door. The shed was large, at least half again as tall as Rayneer, and at least twenty feet across. The hinges creaked in protest as she pried open the large doors.

Arran focused and peered into the shed in the dim light, but what he saw was as clear as day. There were three side-by-side cages in the shed. Each as tall as the shed itself, taking up the entirety of the shed's width. Inside each cage was a malformed and disfigured animal. They were almost unrecognizable. Arran knew one of the creatures. It was one of the large cats from the local jungle, and the other two were some variety of the tree-dwelling creatures native to the area. Mare had told them the difference between the smaller and larger species of the animals, but he could not remember the names. These two creatures were massive, with wide torsos and broad shoulders. They sat squat on thick, muscular legs. Arran suspected that if they stood, they would barely be able to stand erect in the tall cages.

All three animals intently eyed the woman with unnatural, yellow glowing eyes as she opened the door. To Arran's surprise, their menacing growls and howls actually diminished as she opened the doors. She began feeding the treated meat to the creatures. Each animal ravenously tore into the meat, consuming huge chunks in single chomps. The whites of the creatures' teeth gleamed as they sliced through the flesh, consuming it. When they would finish one piece, the woman would toss in another. The creatures devoured everything in mere minutes.

Arran had no doubt if those cages were opened, the three creatures would maul the two shopkeepers, and begin rampaging through the camp, feasting on anything that happened to be in their path. He cringed at the thought, remembering Freeholt.

Arran turned his attention to the tall man who had taken a meditative pose next to the fire, closing his eyes. He remained this way for at least another fifteen minutes before opening his eyes and rising.

"Are they ready?" His voice was clear and smooth. Nothing like Pim's nasally, high-pitched tone.

The woman did not look up from her lap where she was sharpening her knives. "Yes." She gestured with the knife in her hand to the cages and the three creatures. All were lying on their sides asleep, or more likely passed out from whatever she had put on the meat.

The man uncurled his tall frame to stand and slowly strode over towards the shed. "With any luck, this will be the last session, and then we can proceed."

Proceed to what? Were they prepared to unleash these three beasts on the town of Kiel as Pim had been prepared to do in Crenn'ier? That would be a very ugly scene.

The man took a deep breath and held out his hands in front of him. He intertwined his fingers in a complex configuration and began to hum. The humming rose and fell in volume as he slowly began swaying to the rhythm of his own music.

Ever so slowly, Arran began to see faint whispers of smoke begin to form around the man's hands. The smoke turned darker and darker as it grew into a writhing ball of dark energy, enveloping his hands. As he held the mass of energy in his hands, his humming slowly diminished and with the smallest twitch of his fingers, black tendrils of the dark mass shot out at the cat-like creature. The creature lurched up as if struck by lightning, every muscle clenching in a tight spasm. Wherever the black tendrils struck, it began to spread out, eventually creating a sort of cocoon around the animal. That was the only way Arran could think of to describe it. The mass pulsed and undulated around the creature like the ripples on a pond. The man continued unabated, keeping a constant stream of dark energy feeding his creation. As the energy was absorbed into the poor animal, sections of the cocoon would begin to dissipate, but the man was diligent and with the smallest gesture from his hands, a new flow would move to strengthen the spell. Gradually, the creature's muscles began to relax as it sunk to the ground. It did not stir. The man continued to pour the dark energy into the animal as Arran watched the creature transform right in front of him. Every muscle of the creature became enlarged and spines began to form along its back. As the spines emerged, they turned backwards towards its tail, creating a crest along its back. Its claws grew in length and girth as they curved down to their lethal points. Finally, Arran watched in both horror and fascination as the creature's fangs slowly elongated, pushing out and protruding up and down out of the creature's mouth.

The man's humming slowly died away as the ball of energy gradually dissipated from his hands. The tendrils of dark energy lazily breaking apart and wafting away like smoke from a dying fire. His hands fell to his side, shoulders slumping in exertion as all the dark energy slowly vanished.

The woman came to him and helped him over to the fire to sit. She looked at the man dubiously.

The man sat down wearily. "I'm fine, Lia. I just need a few minutes to rest and then I can continue."

Arran watched on through the rest of the evening and into early morning as the man, now utterly exhausted, finished the same ritual on the other two creatures. All three creatures were now at least twenty percent larger than they were before. They all had random, various extra protrusions like scales or spines on their bodies and their claws and jaws were vastly enlarged. But for Arran, the most eerie aspect by far were the creatures' eyes.

Their eyes were now a much brighter yellow and glowing menacingly. Arran thought they were asleep, but their eyes were open and blankly staring out from the cages. They were so bright! As if someone was shining a light behind a piece of yellow glass. They sparkled and, if not for the current context, could have been thought of as beautiful, but all Arran saw was raw malice. A hatred and a hunger to kill.

"Store the rest of the provisions. Tomorrow night we will finish this." the man said.

Lia did as she was told, secured the shed, and put out the fire. They slowly made their way out of the camp, with the man leaning heavily on Lia for assistance.

Arran watched them leave and then focused his attention on Pim.

He was still there, obviously having seen everything Arran had. Pim waited for at least ten minutes before scrambling out from his cover and walking through the camp over to the shed. He peered in.

Pim then turned and went to the table. "Tomorrow it is, then," he said silently to himself. That same wicked grin spreading across his face.

Arran watched Pim leave, trying to process all the information he had just seen and heard.

The tall man and Lia were dark magic users, like Pim, but they weren't working with Pim? Pim was spying on them, just as he was spying on Pim. It didn't make any sense. Arran looked at the shed and could hear the creatures stirring inside. Whatever game Pim was playing at could wait. Only one thing was for sure: They needed to stop whatever was to take place tomorrow.

Arran left the campsite and returned to the cabin. Dawn had expired with the morning already turning unseasonably warm. Arran was sweaty, dirty, and tired by the time he arrived. Elinda, Mare, and Rayneer were at the kitchen bar when he walked in. They all turned as he made his way to the couch.

"Don't you dare sit on that couch!" Elinda said.

Arran stared at her, then looked himself over and sighed. She was right. He looked and smelled like he had just returned from a hard day's training. He turned and strode towards his room without a word.

Arran lounged on the couch, where he was now allowed to sit, recapping the previous night's events as he finished his meal. Everyone listened intently, not interrupting as the tale unfolded. When he was done, Mare was the first to respond.

"Is it possible Pim knows the apothecary and this girl? We know he went to their shop. Do they all know each other? And Pim is not supposed to know about their operations and he is snooping? It would explain him following them without their knowledge."

Arran shrugged his shoulders. "I don't know...maybe? If they do know one another, why have groups obviously working to the same ends and behaving so independently? It seems counterproductive."

The group mulled it over. Elinda's tapping foot the only sound in the room.

Suddenly, the tapping stopped. "Information," Elinda said. A dawn of recognition spreading across her face as she quietly finished her thought. "Someone else is guiding them. Someone with a plan, the means, and the skill for all of this." She gestured widely with both hands. "By keeping the groups isolated, each group only knows their piece, not the whole. The leader controls the information."

"It's a decent theory," Rayneer agreed. "But what is Pim up to, then?"

Elinda's foot resumed its rapid tap, tap, tap on the floor. "I don't know. Maybe it's nothing more than curiosity..." she trailed off for a moment before continuing, "Could be jealousy? Arran, you said the work of the magic user looked to be more advanced than Pim's, right?"

"I think so. The creatures the apothecary transformed were far larger, and definitely more complex from what little I could see. He also worked on all three in one night. Pim was barely able to achieve one lesser transformation back in Crenn'ier before totally exhausting himself."

"So, this apothecary is stronger...quite a bit stronger." Elinda descended back into silent thoughtfulness.

"Where are you going with this Elinda?" Mare asked. "Internal rivalry? That could work to our advantage."

Elinda shook her head in uncertainty.

"This is all good, but what do we do about whatever is supposed to happen tomorrow...I mean, today?" Bran asked. The group fell silent and as he looked around; he was sure everyone was thinking the same thing, but reluctant to give voice to the thought.

Arran caught Bran's eye and nodded. "We are going to have to stop it. Whatever 'it' is." The expressions on everyone's face turned grim. He watched as his statement took root. No one looked up at him. "Klintoc and his team will not be here in time. It has to be us and...we will be disobeying another direct order."

"They are not going to be happy," Mare replied. "Trust me, I've had my fair share of not following direct orders over the years. Our little faux pas with Shia a few months ago will seem childish compared to this."

Bran rose, joining Arran and placing a hand on his shoulder reassuringly. He turned with a mischievous smile. "So we play this smart. We will inform them of the new information and our intentions of observing and only taking action if needed."

"And when they reply with counterorders?" Mare asked.

"I believe we missed that response. We will have already left for the campsite." Bran's smile broadened.

Mare smirked. "I love it!"

Rayneer fidgeted in his seat, nervously shaking his head. "This is a very thin line we walk. We need to be absolutely sure of their intentions and any possible danger. Otherwise, we come off as bungling amateurs."

Arran nodded at his big friend and then scanned the group, catching the eye of each in turn. Everyone nodded in ascent.

"All right, then. Everyone gear up. We'll send the missive and leave within the hour."

Arran gazed down at the open bag on his bed. This would be the first time he wore the gear that his mom had given him. He reached down and stroked the smooth leather of the chest piece in admiration.

Bran entered and closed the door behind him, throwing his bag out on his bed. Sneaking a glance over his shoulder, Arran watched as Bran began laying his own gear out. Arran began the same, laying each piece out reverently. Noticing the sudden silence, Arran turned to face Bran. Bran held a glove in one hand and was silently staring at the gear on Arran's bed. His mouth was agape at what he saw.

Bran quickly covered the two steps over to Arran. "What is this?" he whispered.

"Oh...just a gift from an old friend. It was given to me while I was on my commission."

Bran's right eyebrow shot up. "Just a gift? I know quality pieces when I see them and those look to be of extreme quality. That must be some friend."

Arran looked at the gear on the bed and said silently, "Yes." Arran's eyes traveled across the assembled gear. "Yes, it is. I cannot explain right now, so please do not ask."

Bran slowly nodded. "But you will definitely need to explain all of this once we are done." Bran picked up one of the gauntlets and turned it over in his hand before setting it back down and returning to his own gear.

Once the two were outfitted, Bran gave a low whistle at the sight of his friend.

"Stop it." Arran punched him in the shoulder on his way out of the room.

The response from the rest of the group was no less surprising than Bran's.

Elinda and Mare both poked and prodded Arran, circling him as they examined the gear.

"This is some serious, high-quality work," Mare said approvingly. "What enchantments do they have?"

Arran shrugged his shoulders. "I'm not sure exactly. At least not all of it. I didn't have time to inquire when they were given to me."

Mare laughed incredulously. "You didn't have time to inquire about the enchantments of the wealth of gear you were given?"

Rayneer held one of the daggers in his hand, running his fingers along the runes while inspecting it appreciatively.

"And you mean to tell me all of this was gifted to you?" Rayneer said, handing the dagger back to Arran.

"As I said. They were a gift, and we are going to leave it at that. Can we get on with our more pressing matters, please? Mare, are you ready to send the missive?"

Mare stared at him and then huffed. "Yes, they will get the short version of last night's information and that we are continuing our investigation."

"Everyone ready?"

The group nodded in unison.

"All right, then. Mare, send the missive, then meet us out front. Let's go!"

The group headed out cross-country, straight for the jungle and the campsite, avoiding any roads. As they entered the jungle, the group stopped to take a much needed drink. The day was hot and the oppressive humidity of the jungle only added to the discomfort.

Arran led the group slowly and meticulously through the jungle towards the campsite. He halted the group at a spot he felt was a safe distance from the camp.

"Bran and I will go scout ahead. Hold here." Arran and Bran headed forward without a whisper of sound as they made their way through the underbrush of the jungle.

"What are the odds you think we are going to have to fight?" Elinda asked to no one in particular, her hands restless in her lap as she rubbed them nervously.

"I don't know," Rayneer replied. "This whole thing is so messed up. What are the odds of us running into the same guy Arran saw in Crenn'ier? It feels like we are being manipulated. It's too coincidental. I don't like it."

"Orrr..." Mare said, lingering out the word as she turned. "Our dear friend, Arran, has the gift of trouble."

This brought a small uneasy chuckle from the other two, breaking the tension. The three sat in silence until Arran and Bran returned.

"No one appears to have arrived yet," Arran said, sitting down next to Elinda.

"Not too surprising, it's not even mid-day," Mare said. "These shady bastards will probably wait for nightfall."

Bran took a seat next to Rayneer. "Maybe. If they plan to unleash the creatures on the town like the other incidents, they are best served when the townsfolk are out and about, not inside for the night. More chaos."

"Which is why we are going to play this nice and patient," Arran replied. "Bran, can you watch the camp and let us know when someone arrives? I need some rest."

Bran left to patrol the campsite and the immediate area as Arran laid down and closed his eyes.

It had felt like mere minutes before Elinda shook him awake. Bran was returning. Arran sat up groggily.

Bran knelt down. "The apothecary and the young woman have arrived."

The news shocked Arran awake as his adrenaline rose at the news. "That was fast."

"You've been asleep for three hours," Mare said mockingly.

"What? Really?"

"You snore." Mare kicked him in the leg. "I thought you were going to give our position away."

"If those two are here, it means Pim is probably not far behind. Did you see him?" Arran asked.

Bran shook his head. "I came back here as soon as those two arrived." He gestured over his shoulder. "What's our next move?"

No one spoke. Once again, Arran could guess what was running through everyone's mind. They were about to cross a line. If they set out and had to take action, this was the point of no return, but instead of uncertainty, he was greeted with grim determination.

"Bran and I will go back to the camp to keep an eye on the two and look for Pim. I just know he is going to follow them. Once we know the playing field, I'll come back and lead you three to a spot closer to the camp. Thoughts?"

No one spoke, their eyes telling Arran everything he needed to know.

Bran and Arran headed back to camp and as they got nearer, Arran motioned for Bran to go left as he went right, concentrating intently as he entered the shadows. The sun was still high, but the dense jungle provided more than enough shadows for him to operate.

He could hear the faint voices of the two in the camp as they spoke through the shadows. He ignored them, focusing his attention on the terrain around the camp, looking for Pim. As he neared the small opening into the campsite from the meager path he had originally followed Pim through the previous night, Arran finally caught sight of him.

Arran stopped to watch as Pim slowly and casually walked right up to the camp and entered the small clearing. Foregoing all pretense of concealment as he had the night before.

Pim stopped several paces into the clearing and watched the other two with amused eyes. He cleared his throat, announcing his presence.

"Ahem."

Two heads shot up in Pim's direction as he casually waved a hand and continued his leisurely stroll into the campsite.

"I should have known," the apothecary said.

"So nice to see you too, Samal, and you also, Lia." Pim gave Lia a polite nod as he came to a halt a few scant paces from Samal.

Arran could see the crack appear in the older man's facade. Anger replaced all niceties, and an intense loathing was etched across his face and in his words. "What are you doing here?"

"Why, to offer assistance," Pim said in a kindly sing-song tone.

"We are doing just fine." Samal's voice was hard and scathing.

"I see that." Pim gestured towards the shed. "That is some very fine work. Are they ready for Kiel?"

Samal glared at Pim for several long moments, an intense hatred in his eyes. Pim took one slow and measured step forward and stopped, giving Samal a slight bow.

"How may I help?" Pim asked innocently.

Samal continued glowering at Pim as if trying to measure the man's true intentions. Lia stepped forward and to Samal's right, her fingers twitching on the hilt of her dagger. Smiling the entire time, Pim never broke eye contact with Samal, and did not acknowledge Lia's movement.

The three stood there for several long moments, the tension thick and palpable.

Then, with a lightning quick thrust, Pim's right hand shot up and out of his cloak, his dagger thrusting upwards.

Samal was caught completely off guard, his hands never having a chance to even try to deflect the blow. The dagger came up under Samal's chin, piercing up and into the man's skull. The casual lethality of the strike stupefied Arran as he watched in horror. Pim held the knife firm and tilted his head as if in fascination of what he had just done.

Lia gasped and went to draw her own dagger, but Pim was ready. He thrust out his left hand and a tremendous force of air caught her full in the chest, violently throwing her aside. She flew backwards from the attack, smashing into the doorframe of the cabin so hard it shook the entire structure. Lia's head snapped back at the force of the impact with a sickening crack. Her eyes rolled back as she slumped to the ground.

Pim never moved. The dagger remained in his hand as he slowly finished plunging the blade upward until the hilt was resting under Samal's chin. The man was surprisingly still alive and attempting to speak, but all that came out were bloody gurgles. Blood and spittle poured out of his mouth as Pim continued to hold him upright. Pim once again tilted his head in morbid fascination as he watched the light slowly fade from Samal's eyes. Then, with uncharacteristic reverence, Pim slowly eased the man to the ground.

As Pim finished gently laying Samal on the ground, he pulled out his dagger. "Poor, poor, Samal. You always thought you were sooo much better with your education and your nobility." Pim's mocking tone was soft and menacing as he wiped his dagger across the man's chest.

"I suppose master will not be pleased to find out you lost control of your creations. It was only good fortune that I was here to assist and salvage something of worth from this day." Pim stood, a wicked grin spreading across his face as he maliciously licked the small remainder of blood off his dagger.

Arran watched the scene unfold, horrified at the sheer brutality and ease with which Pim had executed the man.

He cannot be allowed to continue!

Arran slipped out of the shadows and worked his way around to Pim's back. He stepped into the clearing for his throw. Bran must have seen him and burst out of the treeline, catching Pim's attention.

Pim jerked to attention and stepped backwards, half turning to run when he saw Arran's first blade leave his hand. Pim rolled as Arran's dagger flew harmlessly past and struck the cabin with a loud thunk, falling to the ground.

Whether from Lia hitting the cabin or the sound of Arran's dagger, he was not sure which, Arran heard the creatures in the shed begin to stir. Loud growls and angry grunts began emanating from within. The cages rattled within the shed as the beasts began hurling themselves against the bars, chafing at their confinements.

Pim turned his head at the noise and smiled wickedly. He leapt to his feet, running towards the shed with Arran following just a few paces behind. Bran sprinted into the campsite after them both.

Pim swiped his left arm in a wide gesture from right to left, and a massive slice of air swept out in front of him, shattering the shackles and chains of the doors to the shed. Splinters of wood and metal flew through the air at the impact.

Arran caught up, grabbing at Pim's cloak, but he shrugged it off as he jumped, his hands pushing downwards as he leapt. The burst of air propelled him forward and up as he landed roughly on top of the shed. Arran stumbled forward from his lunge as Pim's cloak fell to the ground.

Pim turned and smiled at Arran in mocking glee.

"How abouts we have some fun?" Pim's eyes gleamed, as if this was all just a game. Without any hesitation, Pim made another swiping gesture of his arm, demolishing the locks to the cages.

CHAPTER 18

A LITTLE HELP

YEAR 1305 / MAY / WEEK 2

Arran stopped dead in his tracks. Pim laughed maniacally from atop the shed.

"I have some new friends I'd like to introduce you to."

Arran began slowly backing away from the shed as the clatter of the cage doors' destruction died away. He saw Bran out of the corner of his eye to his right and Mare, Elinda, and Rayneer enter the clearing to his left.

There was an eerie silence for several heartbeats as Arran continued his slow retreat from the shed. Time seemed to slow as Arran watched the three beasts shake their heads. He wasn't sure if it was from the drugs wearing off, or the explosion of their confinements, but they were definitely more aware. They sniffed the air tentatively.

Arran was about halfway across the clearing when a huge blast of wind rushed across the campsite, slamming into Pim. A horrified look of confusion appeared on his face as he was lifted off the shed and thrown brutally into the cabin. He fell to the ground, landing atop a pile of wood at a horrific angle. Arran heard a loud crack of bone as Pim reached out for his left arm. A jagged, broken bone protruded through his shirt sleeve, just beneath the elbow. Pim screamed in agony as he stared at his arm. His entire lower arm hung limply at an impossible angle. He howled in agony again, tears of pain streaming down his face before he lifelessly fell to the ground, passing out.

Arran turned to Elinda, arms still extended in front of her, panting from exertion.

Alarmed by the cries of agony and use of magic, the beasts burst into a frenzy. One of the large apes threw itself at the cage door, bashing it with its huge shoulder. The door flew off its hinges and hurtled outwards, barely missing Arran. It bounced and clanged across the clearing in a mangled heap of metal, as the beast burst out of the cage in a single leap.

Apes...that was what Mare had called them.

The creature was enormous, nearly half again in height of a grown man. Its chest and torso were impossibly massive. Arran watched, partly in awe and fascination, but also fear, as the creature's front arms slammed repeatedly at the ground with incredible strength. Arran felt the earth shudder under the massive impacts. Its claws tore and ripped the earth, creating deep furrows as it twisted and hurled itself about as if in some kind of macabre dance. It then stopped abruptly, raised its head, and let out the most horrific roar Arran had ever heard. The deep howl reverberated in his chest as he stumbled back another few steps.

The surrounding jungle erupted in a cacophony of noise as hundreds of surprised and frightened creatures took off in all directions. A mass of birds rose and disappeared en masse, out of sight over the trees.

Rayneer ran forward and placed himself between the creature and Arran. He raised his sword as the sounds from the jungle faded, leaving only the sound of the huge beast's pants and snarls. Huge fangs dripped with saliva and its yellow eyes narrowed, now focusing intently on Rayneer.

Another cage door rattled and clunked to the ground as a second beast, similar to the first, lumbered its way out of the cage, echoing the howl of the first. They swatted at each other with gigantic paws that were larger than a man's head, as if they intended to fight. They both grunted back and forth, as if communicating, then turned and focused their gaze on Rayneer.

There was movement to Arran's right as Bran began moving in, catching the eye of the creature on his side. It eyed him warily as Bran motioned with his daggers as if saying, 'Over here, come on'. It worked. The creature turned, taking a small step forward, then with uncharacteristic speed for a creature of its size, pounced from a still position, launching itself in the air straight at Bran.

Bran dove to his left, escaping the beast; rolling and coming up to his feet in an instant.

Chaos erupted. The second creature lunged at Rayneer, but he was ready and sliced at the creature's arm as he turned and evaded the beast. It shrieked in pain as dark black blood oozed from the wound. The creature's gaze turned crazed, and it shook its head again and howled, spittle flying in every direction. It lunged, but at the last second turned itself as Rayneer attempted another swipe of his sword. The huge claw slapped at Rayneer, leaving four large gashes in his sword arm. He did not have his normal metal gear, only hardened leather, and the claws ripped through it like cloth. Rayneer grunted and looked down at his wounds. He reaffirmed his grip on his sword and stood at the ready. Rayneer's face hardened as the 'Warrior rage' in him exploded like thunder. Using his offhand, he sprinted the short distance with lightning speed and punched the creature in its face. The beast rocked back, several of its teeth shattered from the blow.

Mare and Elinda began maneuvering farther into the camp, desperately trying to find a way to assist the group. Mare focused her attention on Rayneer and the injury on his arm. Her hands began to glow as she heard a low growl emanate from behind her. She and Elinda both turned their heads as they saw the third creature, this one much different from the other two, slowly exit its cage. It was a jungle cat of some kind, or at least, used to be. All they saw now was a malformed and disfigured beast, hardly recognizable as once being of this world. Its feline mouth turned backwards into a snarl, long canines snapping, as its tail swished angrily in long, side-to-side strokes.

Arran watched his two friends engage the creatures and was about to run to Bran's aid when he saw the large cat-like beast exit its cage. He turned and ran at the creature, yelling with all his might. Arran barely had time to think as the creature turned its head, taking two impossibly quick steps towards him, and lunged. Arran ducked and went into a forward roll under the beast as it flew above him, its claws barely missing him.

Mare and Elinda moved away from the fray. Each desperately trying to find ways to assist. Mare's healing spell for Rayneer had been interrupted by the cat, but she had at least stopped most of the bleeding. She turned her attention towards Bran.

Most of Elinda's spells were too broad in nature to be of much assistance in the one-on-one fights. She was not precise enough to use them in the close combat melee of her friends. She grimaced in frustration.

Bran dodged the huge beast as it came at him in another lunge and rewarded the creature with two swipes of his daggers across its back. His strikes skittered almost harmlessly off the hardened hide and unnatural fur. It howled in rage as it turned and began running at him again. Bran cursed at the ineffectiveness of his strikes. The wounds had been superficial at best.

Bran steeled himself as the beast continued forward at a run instead of lunging at him. As Bran pivoted into his dodge, the beast slowed and twisted with him, swiping Bran across his chest and throwing him backwards to the ground. Bran grunted in pain as four large swaths of blood erupted from his chest. The gashes were not deep. His armor protected him from the worst of it, but they were damaging enough, and they had hurt. The beast howled and began to charge again as Bran was regaining his footing. He braced himself, feigned a dodge left, then twisted right. This time he caught the creature off balance and Bran lunged to stab it underneath its arm. As he did, he felt the satisfying feeling of the dagger finding purchase and he pushed his thrust forward, plunging the weapon deeper. Before he could fully imbed his dagger, his upper body stopped as if it had hit a rock wall. Bran's eyes went wide with amazement and then pain as the realization hit him. The beast had somehow executed a lunge of its own, using its other paw and four claws. All four were now embedded deep into Bran's opposite shoulder and upper arm. The two combatants were locked together, each impaling the other. Bran grunted and pushed forward with his entire body. The creature easily had the size and weight advantage, but it was caught in an awkward position and began to stumble and then fell. Bran grimaced in pain as the two landed and the creature's claws finished their path through his shoulder and upper arm in a wet slurp of blood. Bran screamed in pain as the Warrior overtook him. He brought his head down in a vicious blow right in the center of the beast's face. The beast shook its head and momentarily staggered, but that was all Bran needed. With a grunt of agony, he was already pulling out the dagger after his head blow. Mustering all his strength, Bran thrust it through the side of the beast's neck. The beast's eyes widened and stared up in confusion as it tried to breathe, tried to howl, but it could not. Bran withdrew the dagger and stabbed again and again. He stared into its yellow eyes, not five inches from his own, until the yellow glow faded to pitch black.

Bran grunted in pain as he fell forward in an exhaustive heap on top of the beast. He tried to roll off, but came to the horrible realization that he was still impaled on its claws. He felt someone try to pick him up.

"Hold still," Mare said. "I'm going to have to pull you off of those claws, but we need to do it smoothly or it could tear your arm off at the socket."

Bran could only mumble in exhaustion and pain. He felt so tired, and his eyes began to droop.

"Stay awake!" Mare yelled and positioned herself directly above and behind Bran, grasping his arm right below where the claw had entered his shoulder.

"This might hurt a bit." She began counting. "One...two..." And without warning, she pulled as hard as she could straight back and up.

The claws pulled away from Bran's shoulder with a sickening, sucking slurp of blood as Bran and Mare fell off to the side of the creature. Bran didn't so much as whimper at the process, his eyes becoming glassy and unfocused as he passed out.

Mare began muttering to herself as she inspected the wound and went to work. "Stop the bleeding. Repair internal vessels and move out. Then move on to internal muscle and ligament damage..." Her hands began to glow as she poured herself into her spells, concentrating on the shoulder wound first, placing both hands on the wound.

Elinda watched as Mare knelt next to Bran and returned her attention back towards Rayneer. The battle was intense and fast-moving. The only spell she had thus far dared to try were small bursts of air to try and throw the beast off balance to give Rayneer an opening or reprieve. Fire was out of the question and while she had landed some ice spells, the strength she dared use in such close proximity to Rayneer only shattered against the beast's tough hide. Despite the use of Air, which was her strongest and least exhaustive spell, the constant exertion of her smaller spells was starting to fatigue her after her spell against Pim.

Pim!

Pim awoke to blazing pain. His head and his arm were groaning in agony. He grunted and opened his eyes. The sudden light was like staring at the sun and he quickly snapped them shut. He listened intently as the ringing in his ears subsided and the sounds of the world returned. There was fighting. A lot of fighting. He could hear the snaps of magic and the periodic grunts of pain and exertion. The faint whistle of a sword being swung and then a guttural roar of anger and frustration. He smiled weakly.

Good.

Slowly, he peeked out through slitted eyelids. It was blurry, but he could at least see movement now. He very slowly worked his eyes open, letting them adjust to the light.

Must have hit my head. Filthy little girl. She'll get hers.

He lay very still as he let the rest of his body regain awareness. As his vision improved, he could see that all three beasts were out and the meddlesome group was, unfortunately, holding their own. He spared a slow glance down at his arm. It was bleeding where the bone had punctured the skin on his forearm. He tried to move it protectively across his belly and was immediately reprimanded with a shock of pain.

"Arrggh..." Pim grimaced in pain, letting out a pitiful yelp. He looked up, frightened that he had given himself away. No one had noticed and he let his muscles ease. His breath was ragged and quick as he recovered from the lance of pain.

Need to get out of here.

He tested his legs and feet.

Well, at least they are working.

Using his good arm, he reached across his body, closed his eyes, and clenched his jaw tight, readying himself for the pain. Ever so gently, he grasped his injured arm at the wrist and began sliding it slowly across his chest.

"Uggh...Arggh. Shit, shit, shit..." He grimaced at the pain through clenched teeth, jaw aching from the exertion. His elbow was ruined, and it berated him for the change in angle and motion, but he continued. Once he had the arm across his chest, he leaned back, panting from exhaustion and pain. He could feel his body desperately wanting to lie back down. 'Just rest a bit' it was trying to say.

No!

With his good arm, he leveraged himself up and began pushing himself backwards across the ground to the rear of the cabin. Every movement sent a piercing shot of pain up his injured arm. He went slowly at first, not wanting to draw any attention to himself, but the group was too busy with the creatures. He hastened his pace, ignoring the pain, and finally made it to the back of the cabin, where he propped himself up against the back wall, sweat pouring down his face and brow.

He looked back down at his arm with disgust.

This is going to be a pain in the ass.

With his good arm, he drew his dagger and cut off the ragged sleeve of his injured arm, and managed a loose wrap around the injury. He cradled it in position with his good arm. Placing his legs beneath him, he pushed up and back against the wall to stand. Stars blurred his vision as he stood and he fell back against the wall for support until the dizziness passed.

He took one last look around and then stumbled forward, disappearing into the jungle.

Elinda turned and took two strides towards the cabin, glancing to where Pim had fallen...he was gone. She frantically looked around as Rayneer narrowly escaped another huge swipe from the beast. She returned her attention back to the fight and thrust out her hands, striking the beast in the knee with a small burst of Air as it tried to catch Rayneer off guard after he stumbled. It was the reprieve Rayneer needed to regain his balance, and their dance continued.

Arran crouched as he and the cat slowly circled one another. It was fast, and it had a much better reach than Arran had anticipated.

He had already received two wounds: one on the arm, and another on his right leg. The one on the arm was not serious, but the leg wound would slow him. It was going to need stitches or a good spell from Mare. He could feel the warm blood as it trickled down his limbs.

Arran feigned a lunge forward with his one remaining dagger, and the cat flinched. Arran took two steps back and to his right, anticipating a counter when his foot suddenly twisted in agony as he fell. He looked down to discover he had stepped on the cage door that had been thrown from the beast's initial escape from the shed. The cat instantly flew into a run, pouncing straight at him. Arran went to roll from the attack, but his leg would not follow. He looked down. His foot had become twisted in the mangled bars of the cage door and he was stuck. He grunted and brought his dagger up to meet the attack of the cat.

The cat was at the apex of its lunge, snarling in anticipation of the kill, when, out of nowhere, an arrow flew into its side, knocking the beast slightly to Arran's left. As it landed, he was able to roll aside just enough for the weight of the great cat to miss him by mere inches, An arrow was embedded into its side, right behind its left shoulder. Arran did not hesitate and quickly rolled towards the cat and drove his dagger all the way through the beast's neck. It did not so much as twitch at the impalement. There were no throes of death. It simply lay there, a pool of black blood spreading out around its head.

Arran bent and untangled his foot with a groan of pain. It was twisted badly, and he gingerly rose, testing to see how much weight he could manage. He turned and looked out into the jungle where the arrow had originated. He focused his sight and peered deeply into the overgrowth until he spotted a hooded figure half hidden behind a tree. The figure rose and slowly stepped aside from behind the foliage. Arran nodded, and the figure nodded back.

Arran glanced back to see Bran on the ground, Mare holding him in her arms, and Rayneer still battling his beast. Arran turned to the stranger and held up a hand with one finger as if saying, 'give me one minute'. The stranger nodded.

Arran began hobbling as best he could to Rayneer's aid. Rayneer saw him coming and turned the beast so its back was to Arran's approach. As Arran drew nearer, he dove forward into a roll coming up behind the beast, slicing at the backs of both heels. It roared in pain and kicked backwards, catching Arran's shoulder and sending him reeling backwards. The damage was done, however. No longer able to hold its massive weight upon its back legs, it toppled and fell as it tried to move. Rayneer was on it in an instant. With one smooth swing of his sword, the creature's head was severed from its body, rolling to a stop a few paces away. Blood sprayed from the wound, covering Rayneer from head to toe in the black viscous fluid.

Arran looked up at Rayneer with a grimacing smile. "Thought you could use a hand."

"I had it," he said, grinning behind the mask of gore that covered his face. Only the whites of his teeth and eyes were visible.

Arran pointed his finger at his face in a swirling motion. "You should...you know, do something about that look you've got going. Not very appealing."

Rayneer gave him a tilt of his head as he wiped gore off his face, flicking it to the ground with a muffled splat.

Arran looked over at Elinda, who was slowly lowering herself to her knees in obvious exhaustion. Her face was covered in sweat and her hair lay in tangles around her head, which was matted to her face and neck. She blew out great, gasping breaths that puffed her loose, dangling hair in rhythmic pulses.

Rayneer helped Arran up, gingerly holding his arm across his chest from the shoulder the beast had kicked. He hobbled over to Elinda. "You good?"

Without looking up, she replied, "I'll be fine."

Arran placed his hand on her back for what small amount of comfort it could give. Then he and Rayneer made their way over to Mare and Bran. Elinda slowly rose to join them.

It was a gruesome sight. All Arran saw around them was blood. A lot of blood. It soaked the ground. The bright red of Bran's blood and the dark black blood of the beast was everywhere, mixing and congealing on the ground.

"How is he?" Rayneer asked, kneeling.

"I believe I have stopped the bleeding, but he has lost a lot of blood. Over time, I can knit the wounds, but I cannot replace his blood. We will have to wait and see."

Elinda approached, scrambling with her pack. She pulled out a small vial of red liquid. "Have him drink this."

Mare took the vial and stared at it questioningly. "What is it?"

"It's a boosting potion. It should help him heal faster."

"A healing potion?" Arran asked in disbelief.

Elinda knelt again from exhaustion. "Kind of, but not like what Mare does. It cannot heal directly like Mare's abilities, but it can boost the body's natural healing process. Speed it along. If he has lost a lot of blood, this should help him replenish it faster." She panted, catching her breath. "As long as we keep him hydrated."

Arran's mouth was agape. "That is amazing! You made this?"

"With the help of my instructor, yes. It's only apprentice level, but better than nothing."

Mare took the vial and dribbled it into Bran's mouth as he unconsciously swallowed.

"Who is that?" Rayneer said, looking back towards the front of the campsite.

Arran turned to look at the stranger, who had entered the clearing a few steps in from the jungle, approaching no further.

"That is a very good question," Arran replied.

<hr>

Arran and Rayneer slowly walked across the campsite towards the stranger, stopping a few paces away.

The stranger was fully hooded, but now that he was closer, Arran was able to discern more details of his rescuer. It was a woman with extremely fine features and piercing grey eyes. She held her bow at her side, un-nocked.

"Ello."

Arran and Rayneer looked at one another, both baffled at the woman before them, and her strange dialect.

"Umm...Hello," Arran replied.

Arran looked at the now dead cat and pointed at it. "Thank you for the assist."

"You welcome."

Arran turned to Rayneer again.

"Don't look at me." He shrugged his shoulders.

Arran turned back to the stranger. "Where are you from?"

"Far away. Across many waters. Far."

Arran looked at her questioningly. He thought for several long moments, then asked. "You are from an island...in the ocean?"

"I-land?" She pronounced the word as if it were two.

"Yes. A small land located out in the ocean." Arran tried to explain with his one good hand, to no effect.

She shook her head. "Not small. As big as here, I think, but I not seen all."

Both men's eyes went wide. Rayneer held up his hand in a stopping motion. "There's another land as big as Galleant out there, somewhere?"

Arran's face was a mask of confusion. "The world's a big place? Pretty sure we haven't seen it all. Possible I guess."

Arran returned his gaze to the stranger and asked, "So there is another land across the ocean with other humans?"

"No humans."

Arran and Rayneer exchanged startled glances.

"Not human? How is that..." Arran trailed off as the stranger lowered her hood.

With the hood fully removed, Arran was able to take in the stranger's full beauty and foreign features. She was quite possibly the most beautiful woman he had ever seen in his life. Her silken blond hair was pulled back tightly on her head into a long braid that fell down her back. Her slender neck had several tattoos running down both sides, disappearing beneath her tunic, presumably onto her back. She turned her head to the side and Arran finally saw her most distinguishing feature, her ears: they were larger and longer than a human's, and were tapered at the top to a soft point.

"Not human. Elf."

By now, and for many reasons, Arran's and Rayneer's eyes were wide with wonder. Neither could speak.

"That one awake," the stranger said, pointing back towards the cabin.

Arran and Rayneer both turned their heads in the direction of the cabin. Lia was trying, unsuccessfully, to rise.

"You want me shoot? Poison fast. Good."

Arran held up his hand. "No. No shoot."

The three made their way over to Lia and held her down. It wasn't difficult. She was still groggy and probably concussed from the blow she took.

Arran turned to Rayneer. "Do you have anything to tie her up?"

Rayneer was about to answer when the stranger knelt down as she reached into her pouch. She produced a length of rope and began tying Lia's hands and feet.

Arran rose and raised his eyebrows. Rayneer gave him a weak smile.

Arran shook his head. "Seriously. You need to clean your face."

Once the stranger was done, they walked back to the others. Mare was still tending to Bran. She scowled at them.

"Help me get him up on the table. I'm tired of sitting in all this blood."

Once Bran was gently placed on the table, Elinda looked at Arran and then at the stranger. "What is her name?"

"Her name?"

"You haven't even asked her her name?" Elinda let out an exasperate sigh.

Elinda approached the stranger. "I am Elinda. What is your name?"

"I Faysciellen. You call Faye."

Now it was Elinda's turn to be surprised at the stranger's dialect. She turned towards Arran and Rayneer.

Arran's expression replied with as much confusion as Elinda held on her own face. "Don't ask us. She says she's from another continent. Came from across the ocean. She says she is an Elf? Elven?" Arran shook his head in confusion. "I'm not sure which, but definitely not human." Arran pointed to Faye's ears emphatically.

Elinda slapped his hand down. "Idiot. Don't point like some child." She turned back to Faye. "It is nice to meet you, Faye."

Elinda huffed and turned back to Arran. "Now, was that so hard?"

Arran did not reply.

"Your friend hurt bad." Faye pointed at Bran on the table.

"Yes," Mare said warily as Faye approached.

Faye looked over the wounds. "You good heal. This good." She lightly touched and probed at Bran's wounds.

Faye reached into her pouch and pulled out a jar.

"Put on. Will help heal fast. Help..." she struggled for the words, "...outside. Also below."

Mare took the jar hesitantly and opened it up to see what looked like a simple cream. She sniffed at it, wrinkling her nose at the pungent smell. "This will help heal him externally, as well as internally? Inside? Below?" Mare said, correcting herself.

"Yes. Put on and..." Again Faye stopped struggling for the right word but making a motion with her hand, wiggling it up and down.

"Ahh, rub it on and it absorbs into the skin?" Mare looked at the salve again in appreciation. "Absorbs and moves down into the internal wound? Impressive," she muttered.

"Absorb mean down, yes?" Faye asked.

"You are going to have to show me that recipe," Elinda said, stepping up between the two and glancing into the jar.

Mare raised the small jar. "Thank you." Then she began rubbing the ointment on Bran's wounds.

Elinda's face darkened. "Pim is gone." She pointed to the side of the cabin where Pim had fallen.

Arran sighed. "That's just great." He was tired, still bleeding from his wounds, hobbling on a bad ankle, his shoulder was going to be massively bruised, he met a stranger from another continent that wasn't human, one of his best friends was lying on a table unconscious, and now Pim had escaped. He looked at the group, shoulders sagging. "We are not going to hear the end of this. You know that, right?"

"Want to try and track him down?" Rayneer asked, looking around.

Arran sighed, looking despondently at the surrounding mess. "He could be anywhere by now, and tracking him would take too much time. I think we need to figure out all this mess and report in. The longer we wait, the worse it's going to be."

Rayneer followed Arran's gaze. "I say we leave the carnage for tomorrow. We are in pretty bad shape right now."

"You're probably right. Mare? Can we get Bran back to the cabin?" Arran asked.

"I don't think so. He needs to rest and when he wakes, he's going to struggle to get on his feet. Maybe tomorrow, if we are lucky. It will all depend on how well Elinda's potion and Faye's ointment work. We'll have to wait and see."

Arran nodded and thought for a few moments.

"Rayneer, Elinda, and I will go back to the cabin and send a missive explaining the situation. We'll be back tomorrow bright and early to try and tend with the rest of this." He turned to Faye. "Faye, can you stay here with Mare and Bran for now?"

"Yes."

Arran gave Mare a questioning look. "You good?"

Mare glanced at Faye and gave a weak smile. "We will be fine."

"Tomorrow I would like to hear more about this other land of yours," Arran said, trying to smile amiably.

"To-morow."

Arran hobbled to the table and looked at Mare. "Can you maybe help out this bum ankle before we go?"

Faye watched as three of the people from her dreams left the camp. She had finally done it! She had found the faces from her dreams! Faye could not help the broad smile that followed. The elders will be pleased. Now that she had found them though, she began to understand the 'why'. She knew that they needed help, but from what, she had not known. Now she saw. Now she understood that something was happening here in this land and she had been sent to assist. The beasts were unnatural.

Faye sat next to Mare by the small campfire, who was taking a break from her healing vigilance over her friend.

The two sat in silence for a long while, watching the fire.

Her eyes never leaving the fire, Mare's voice broke the silence with a whisper. "Why come here?"

Faye turned to her as Mare continued.

"The others mentioned you were from another continent. Why travel so far from your people?"

Faye turned her gaze skyward. Mare looked up. Faye's face was soft and contemplative, grey eyes unblinking as she stared at the sky. She did not answer for several long moments. "I...dream. All you." Faye pointed, first at Mare, then to Bran and finally in the direction the others had left.

Mare's expression turned to one of confusion. "You traveled across the ocean, to a strange land because of...a dream? Because you saw us in your dreams?" Mare shook her head in disbelief. "We humans would call that foolish. Most humans do not believe in dreams. They are just make-believe stories of our minds." Mare pointed to her head. "While we sleep."

Faye tilted her head, uncomprehending. "Dreams, important. My dreams much important. Many dreams real. When I dream you, my people...my old ones, see danger. Danger only I follow. I come help."

Mare thought for a few moments, trying to piece together what Faye was trying to tell her.

"You are talking about true foretelling. Seeing the future, or at least a piece of it. I've read about it but..." She hesitated. "Humans have had a few individuals who could...dream." Mare shook her head in disbelief as she silently tried to recall her studies. "True foretelling though...humans have never had that powerful a gift. No one has even come close to the level of detail you are describing. The timing, the depth of information, and the detail...that is nothing short of amazing."

Faye nodded in understanding. "I have good talent?"

Mare looked at her questioningly, then understood. "You call your dreams a talent?"

Faye nodded, as if that were obvious.

Mare chuckled softly. "We call them gifts."

"Ahh. Talent is same then, yes. My dreams are gift."

Mare looked at her incredulously. "And yes. Your gift is very good. We would call that an extremely powerful gift."

"You have gifts. You heal. Very good...impotent."

Mare chuckled at the mispronunciation. "Imporrrtant." She corrected. "Yes, I am a healer."

Faye mouthed the word again. "Impoortint."

Mare smiled. "Much better."

Faye glanced up at Bran on the table. "All friends have gifts?"

"Yes. We all have gifts. Different, though."

Faye nodded in thought.

"I come, my gift show me help. We all here have gifts. Not your people share gifts to help others?"

Mare sat for several long moments thinking about the simple question and the underlying wisdom it implied.

"No," she finally replied. "We do not always share our gifts to help others."

Faye's brow furrowed. "Why this?"

"Because humans can be very selfish."

"Selfeesh? I not know."

"It means someone who only thinks for themselves and not others."

"Ah, selfesh. Let us..." Faye pointed to Mare, "not selfish."

Mare sniffed at the thought. "Easier said than done." She tossed a small stone into the fire, sending a sparkle of embers up into the night sky. "You have just discovered one of the most common of human traits. Selfishness."

The two sat in silence for a long time as the evening wore on. They both tended to Bran, giving him water and small bits of food any time he awoke. They also made sure Lia had water and a small bit of rations before Mare finally fell asleep. Faye watched over them all, gazing at the night sky, wondering where her dreams would lead her next.

The trip back to the cabin was slow and arduous. The group was still exhausted from the fight, but they hurried as best they could. No one spoke until they were out of the jungle. They quickened their pace now that they were on more even and untangled ground.

"Who do you think she is?" Elinda asked.

"I don't know..." Arran replied, trailing off. He had run the story through his mind over and over as they trudged through the jungle, and he still found it unbelievable. It was like something out of a children's book he could find in Quil's store.

"I don't know what to believe about a whole other continent of non-human people. That kind of information would shake a lot of people up." Arran grimaced as he stumbled, sending a jolt of pain through his shoulder as he tried to catch himself. "She would probably become some kind of prized catch. Can you imagine what the school, the realm council, and who knows who all else would try to do with her? All digging at her for information and ways to exploit it."

"That's a bit pessimistic," Rayneer said.

Arran shook his head sullenly. "My faith in the goodness of humans is kind of low at the moment."

Rayneer had no response.

They hurried on as best they could in silence until they started to see signs of civilization again. It was not quite dawn as their cabin came into view. Arran held up his hand, and the group came to a stop.

"Did someone leave a light on?"

"Not likely," Elinda whispered.

Arran motioned forward, and the group worked their way to the side window beneath the kitchen. Arran peered over the windowsill to see a man seated on the couch. His back was to Arran and his cowl was up.

Arran jumped as a loud voice echoed up from the room. "Get in here, you three."

Arran ducked quickly back below the window and looked at Rayneer and Elinda in surprise. Then his shoulders sagged as slow recognition spread across his face.

Arran looked at the other two in resignation. "Klintoc."

The trio walked into the main room, standing as far back as they could from Klintoc. The famed Intelligence agent lowered his cowl and stared at the three bedraggled and, quite frankly, sorry-looking threesome.

"What the hell happened to the three of you? And where are the other two?" Klintoc asked, looking towards the door.

Arran, Elinda, and Rayneer exchanged glances.

Elinda's eyes kept to the wall just over Klintoc's shoulders as she meekly replied. "Back at the camp, sir."

"The camp you were to be watching?"

"Yes, sir."

"The camp, I'm going to assume, that turned into more than a mere observation and information gathering order?"

Arran put a hand on Elinda's shoulder. "Yes, sir." Elinda's whole body sagged and Arran helped her to sit. She rested her elbows on her knees, head in her hands.

Klintoc's eye's traveled from one to the other not saying a word. He let the silence build.

Two other agents entered the cabin, standing stoically just inside the door. Klintoc looked over at them.

"Anyone else about?"

The female of the two shook her head. Klintoc returned his gaze to the three students. The time for discipline was later. He needed their report so that he could get moving.

"Out with it, then."

Arran asked for some water, which one of the other agents brought, and then he began retelling the events of the previous evening. He started with their arrival at the camp: Pim's murder of the apothecary, the fight with the beasts, Bran's injury, the capture of Lia, and escape of Pim. Arran left out any mention of Faye. He wasn't sure why. It was on the tip of his tongue and then it was gone. Tell them now or tell them later. He didn't see that it mattered, and he needed more information.

"We left Mare to care for Bran while we returned to send a missive updating Instructor Shia," Arran concluded.

Klintoc was silent. His face stony and impassive as a statue.

Arran did his best to remain just as impassive. Waiting for the next question, but he had to be honest with himself...he was nervous as hell.

He's too silent. Was he mad? Was he just thinking about what to do next? Say something!

Klintoc rose from his seat. "Elinda, can you send a missive explaining everything as it was just told to me, please?"

Elinda nodded.

"Good. Arran, you will guide us to the camp, and Rayneer, I want you to stay here with Elinda in case anyone else decides to...drop by. I'd like to have a word with this Lia you spoke of." Klintoc turned and headed out the door.

Arran groaned, looking at Rayneer and Elinda. Rayneer shrugged, almost apologetically, and Arran slowly headed out, following Klintoc.

Arran wearily approached the three agents as he begrudgingly began the return journey of the one he had just finished. The sun was halfway through its morning ritual and dawnlight bathed the land in front of them. Klintoc handed Arran a flask, and he eagerly drank the cool water.

Finishing, he held the flask out. "Thank you."

"Keep it. Here, have some of this."

Klintoc handed Arran a hearty portion of dried meat. Arran took to it as greedily as he had the water. The water and meat did much to alleviate his hunger, if only a little, and give him some much needed energy. He was still bone-tired though and Klintoc must have noticed.

The pace was kept even and unrushed, even though Arran could tell that the three agents were eager to survey the scene and interrogate Lia.

As they neared the camp, Arran stopped and pointed. "It's just up ahead." He spoke a touch more loudly than he needed, hoping that Mare and Faye would take the hint.

The three agents stopped as they entered the camp, surveying the carnage of the fight before them. Arran rushed over to Mare and Bran. He gave her a wry smile. Faye was nowhere in sight. Arran hadn't noticed that the three agents hadn't followed him in and turned to see the stunned looks upon their faces.

Klintoc was first to move and walked over to Bran, placing a hand on his forehead.

"How are you, brother?"

Arran was more than a little shocked at the heartfelt display from Klintoc. Gone was the brusqueness of one of the most feared men in all of Galleant.

What was it Mare had said? Layers...

Arran smiled inwardly, a new spark of appreciation forming for the man.

Bran tried to raise himself and was halted by Klintoc's firm hand. He didn't resist. "I am doing better, sir." His voice was weak and not convincing. "Mare here is a hell of a healer."

Klintoc turned to Mare and gave the slightest twitch of his head in appreciation.

Did Arran just see Mare blush? He couldn't be for sure, but then true to her nature, the Mare he knew was back.

She huffed and began tending to Bran's bandages. "Men are fine if they do what they're told."

Klintoc's head reared back, eyes going wide as he gaped at Mare. The female agent behind him stifled a laugh with her hand.

Klintoc turned and glared at the agent. "Something to add, Pon'fre?"

Pon'fre shook her head and removed her hand, desperately trying and failing to hide her grin while still softly chuckling.

Klintoc shook off the slight and his firm countenance reasserted itself.

"Where is the prisoner?"

Mare gestured towards the cabin. "Over there. She is not going to be much help for a while. She took a nasty strike to the head and was out of it most of the night. We gave her some food and water when she was awake, but she hasn't been very coherent. I gave her a few heals, but my guess it will be a while before she's in any shape to answer any questions."

Klintoc grunted at this as he looked at the tied figure in front of the cabin.

Klintoc turned to Arran. "Take us through it."

Arran walked over to the shed and began with how Pim had shattered the cages with an Air strike he had never seen before.

"It was like he sliced the cages with a sword that was as wide as all three cages, but using only Air."

"I've seen it before," the second agent said. "Very powerful spell, but it takes a lot of energy and a strong Focus gift to wield it with such precision." He knelt, inspecting the locks and how efficiently the Air slices had destroyed them.

Klintoc reached out and felt the cold metal of the cages. The bars were thick. It had been a powerful spell. "Could it have been the same person you saw before?"

The agent did not answer, lost in his own examination.

Klintoc turned. "Tilkin?"

Tilkin jerked back from his internal thoughts abruptly. "What? Oh, no, I don't think so. The person I knew of was quite old. I'm not even sure he is still alive. If we can find this Pim, I could probably identify him, to be sure."

Arran guided Klintoc through the rest of the fight as the other two agents began gathering all the bodies in the center of the camp. Tilkin then went through the cabin and what was left of the shed to make sure there was no other evidence. He dropped everything of note in a pile next to the bodies.

By the time they had cleaned the camp of all evidence, there was a fairly large pile in the center. It was almost noon now and Arran could barely stay on his feet, despite Mare's help.

Klintoc went through the pile of evidence sparingly. Apparently not finding anything of importance, he rose. "Pon'fre, Tilkin, you stay here. Take our samples, then once it's dark, burn this lot." Klintoc surveyed the dead creatures and miscellaneous items. "I don't want to attract any undo attention to this spot if we can help it."

He turned to Mare. "Can Bran and the prisoner travel?"

Mare frowned, but nodded her head. "We'll probably need to take frequent breaks, but I think they can manage it. I think getting indoors and in a bed will do them both good anyway."

As the group was leaving the site, Arran casually looked out into the jungle. He was pretty confident that Faye was watching them, and he hoped that she understood the need to stay hidden for now and that they would be back.

Arran's eyes opened, and he heard the sound of dishes clinking. There was a soft murmur of voices coming from the common room. It had taken twice as long as it should have getting back to the cabin the previous day with Bran and Lia in tow. Once Mare had them both set up in their beds and had given them a sleep tonic, Arran made his way to his own bed before nightfall. He was asleep within moments of his head hitting the pillow.

Arran stayed in bed for a while longer, looking out the window and letting himself come to full wakefulness. By his measure, it was maybe a few hours past dawn and he had slept close to fourteen hours.

He eventually crawled out from beneath the blankets and threw his legs over the side, wiping his eyes. He placed his elbows on his knees and rubbed his hands through his hair, recalling the last few days, and then it hit him like a wave. An awful wave. He wrinkled his nose.

"What is that awful smell?" He sniffed the air only to realize...it was him. Arran looked at his grimy armor and the now ruined sheets of the bed. He swiftly began to undress, noticing that his wounds were nearly imperceptible. Mare must have come while he was asleep. As he lay his gear over the back of a chair, his eyes widened in wonder. He picked up his pants. The tear from the cat's claw...was gone. He turned the piece of clothing over and over in his hand. It was whole again. He picked up his shirt. It was not part of the gear his mother had given him and, sure enough, there was a tear in the upper arm where his wound had been. He softly whistled in appreciation.

I need to make sure I ask Mother about these enchantments.

After cleaning up, Arran rejoined the group in the common room.

"Welcome back to the land of the living," Mare said.

Arran ignored her, the smell of breakfast instantly making his mouth water and his stomach complain loudly. He went to the kitchen counter and began fixing himself a plate, immediately eating one bite of everything for every portion that made it to his plate.

Plate and juice in hand, he made his way over to the couch and sat down next to Elinda, who gently held a cup of coffee between both hands. Arran began to eat loudly and, after a few bites, realized everyone was staring at him.

"Wha'th?" he said over a mouthful of food.

Mare shook her head and muttered. "Men."

Arran swallowed and then forced himself to take a more measured approach to his meal for the benefit of all.

Mare, Elinda, Rayneer, and Klintoc were the only ones in the room at the moment. The other agents were nowhere to be seen and Bran was probably still in bed recovering.

Klintoc took a sip of his coffee. He stared blankly over his cup at the trio. "So, what aren't you telling me?"

Arran glanced sideways at the other three as he finished chewing, and then back to Klintoc. "I'm not sure, sir. I believe I've told you everything that happened." He feigned as if he was trying to recall any additional information.

Klintoc eyed Arran suspiciously and then turned to Elinda. "Is there anything else that I should know?"

Much to Arran's surprise and astonishment, Elinda did not falter in her reply. "No, sir. I don't believe there is."

"I see." Klintoc took another slow sip of his coffee.

"I spoke with Shia via the missive last night, and we feel it is best if all of you lie low for a while. Enjoy Harshin for a while and most importantly..." Klintoc paused for emphasis, "...try to stay out of trouble."

No one replied, all eyes roaming everywhere in the room, except at Klintoc.

Klintoc threw a pouch of coins on the table. "This should afford you some extra time. Keep the missive and we will contact you with new instructions." He rose.

"You're already leaving?" Arran asked, consciously trying to keep the relief from his voice.

"As soon as Pon'fre returns with some new clothes for the prisoner."

Mare frowned.

"We will keep her comfortable, do not worry, priestess. It is a private vessel and she will be well tended to. I give you my word."

Mare only replied with a disdainful "Hmmph."

Arran thought he saw a smirk beginning to form on one side of Klintoc's mouth as he turned and began walking towards the bedrooms.

A few hours later, they all stood on the porch of the cabin as Klintoc's group made their way back to Harshin. Not until they had disappeared into the throng of other travelers and vacationers did anyone speak.

Elinda's gaze never left the road as she stared down the road. "We just lied to Klintoc and an instructor."

"Yeah," Rayneer replied.

Mare put her arm around Elinda. "Feels good to be just a little bad, doesn't it?"

Elinda leaned into the hug and shoved. "You are a bad influence."

"And I say again, it feels good, doesn't it?"

"You are incorrigible."

Mare shrugged. "I've been called worse."

Arran and Rayneer laughed at the exchange as they all went back inside.

"Now what?" Rayneer said, hefting the bag of coins on the table and then peering inside. "Wow. There is enough in here to last at least another month, and that is in addition to what we still have. Whatever we decide, money is not going to be an issue."

"I need to go back and get Faye. Then...I've been thinking..." Arran trailed off as everyone gathered around in the common room.

"Oh, I have to hear this." Everyone turned as Bran stood leaning against the doorway to the bedrooms.

"I thought I told you bed rest," Mare said angrily.

"I'm a bad patient. Anyway, it feels kind of good to be bad, eh?" A broad grin spreading across his face as he gingerly walked to one of the chairs with Rayneer's help.

Mare glared, but in the end, had to smile at the joke, even if it was at her expense.

Arran looked at Bran. He looked pretty good, given it had been less than two days since the fight that left him fighting for his life. The periodic heals from Mare, the boost potion from Elinda, and Faye's cream must have worked their wonders. He was, at the very least, several days, if not a full week ahead of what should have been normal healing. His color was back and the mere fact that he had strength enough to walk was nothing short of miraculous.

Arran got up and walked over to place a hand on Bran's good shoulder. "Good to see you up and around." He turned to gather his gear and shouted over his shoulder as he left. "We'll talk when I get back." He heard a few muttered assents as he began jogging off once again towards the beleaguered campsite.

Bran winced as he changed positions in the chair. "So, where is my food?"

Arran made good time on his way back to the camp. He was feeling much more like himself. The rest, Mare's healing, and his massive breakfast all working together in their own kind of magic. As he cleared the jungle and stepped into the campsite, he was surprised at the thoroughness of the agents. A darkened stain in the middle of the clearing was all that remained of the evidence. The shed had been toppled, leaving only the cabin as the sole erect building.

He crossed to the cabin and looked inside. It had been gutted. Not a single piece of furniture or any other objects lay inside. It was completely empty.

Arran heard the faint steps behind him as he turned to leave the cabin. He smiled warmly. "Hello, again."

"Ello."

He looked around. "They destroyed almost everything."

"They are complete. Not much here now."

Arran nodded. "I guess I should have asked before, but...do you want to come with us?"

Faye did not hesitate. "I must yes. I need follow now I find."

Arran still did not understand the 'why' of her need to find them, but that would come later. They needed to leave this area behind them.

"Do you have anything you need to bring?"

Faye trotted lithely over to the edge of the clearing and grabbed a bag hidden within the undergrowth.

"This all."

Arran admired her simplicity. Bow, arrows, knives, and a satchel. She had traveled across an ocean and had undoubtedly been trying to find them for quite some time, and this was all she needed.

Arran turned with a gesture of his head. "This way, then. Let's go."

***

It was midafternoon by the time Arran and Faye returned to the cabin. Bran looked even better than he had earlier. Arran suspected a hearty meal and a little more of Mare's healing had a lot to do with it.

To Arran's surprise, and embarrassment, he had forgotten that the group had not all been formally introduced. They spent some time making all the proper introductions, telling Faye a little about themselves.

With Faye's permission, Mare relayed her story. She told them of her dreams and her suspicion that Faye had a gift of true foretelling.

Faye did not ask many questions, remaining silent for a good portion of the conversation as everyone else talked, observing. She marveled at the casualness of their discussions and how easily they laughed with one another. Her people, of course, laughed and enjoyed merriment, but the humans were different. More...direct and easy of nature.

After they finished the evening's meal, they all gathered out on the rear balcony to enjoy the sunset.

Arran tentatively interrupted the silent contemplation of everyone as the sun passed below the horizon. "As I was saying earlier. I've been thinking..."

Everyone turned his direction.

"Anyone feel up for a trip?"

Rayneer's brow furrowed. "A trip? As in, do the exact opposite of what we've been instructed to do...again?"

Arran held up a hand defensively. "Hear me out."

Rayneer scowled. Arran knew his stalwart friend did not like disobeying orders and the lies they had already told were weighing heavily on him.

"Here is how I see it: We just lied to Klintoc and basically the School of Doctrine for Faye. We now know her story and her reason for being here. She foresaw the dark magic and the danger it has put us all in." Arran hesitated before continuing. He was unsure how the others would take his next statements. "I don't feel that running her off to the school authorities and the council of Meitellen is the right move. Sure, it's probably the easiest way, but what about her? We need to think this through. Her secret is going to come out. Another race? From another continent? This is huge." He paused again, trying to judge everyone's reactions. "What are our options? What is the best way to reveal all of this new information and, more importantly, her? What is best for Faye?"

No one answered.

"Hiding her here amongst a city of this size is not going to be feasible for long. There are too many eyes and ears for that idea to go horribly wrong. What about...we go somewhere more remote. More out-of-the-way? Somewhere like...Kine?"

Everyone remained silent as they thought about Arran's proposal.

"I have to say, Country, that isn't the worst plan you've come up with."

Elinda looked at Faye and then back at Arran. "I hate to say it, but I think I agree."

Rayneer shuffled uneasily in his seat. "I agree." Everyone looked at him in surprise.

"I'm a little ashamed to admit..." Rayneer stared at the floor, then cleared his throat before continuing. "I had not thought about Faye's welfare. Protecting her identity until we have thought this through is the right thing to do."

Faye set her cup down on the table. Everyone turned. "You trouble for this? Is necessary?"

Arran's expression softened as he nodded towards Rayneer. "As Ray said, it's the right thing to do. Besides, we get in trouble all the time."

Faye's expression remained impassive, obviously not under-standing the joke. She was clearly uneasy.

Arran finally turned to Bran. "How about it? Any thoughts?"

"I'm good. Besides, I think I've had my fill of this place for a while." He winced in an attempt to shrug his shoulders.

Arran got up and began pacing along the railing.

"Arrraaan..." Mare said. "What else?"

He turned to face the group. "We could use some advice and I think I know just the person to ask."

"This mysterious 'friend' of yours, maybe?" Bran asked.

Arran smiled wanly, not sure how he could obtain advice from his mother and keep her secret.

Figure that out later.

Arran ignored the question and rubbed his hands together. "It's settled, then. We are going to need passage to Saloanne."

"I'll check tomorrow," Rayneer volunteered.

The remainder of the evening was spent in uncharacteristically uneasy conversation before everyone retired.

CHAPTER 19

DECISIONS

YEAR 1305 / JUNE / WEEK 1

Rayneer went to town early and easily found passage north for later that day. The trip to Saloanne would take almost two weeks as the ship had quite a few stops along the way, but they could make it safely and, more importantly, anonymously. The excitement of the new adventure and trip north was surprisingly therapeutic. Everyone desperately wanted to question Faye about her home continent, her people and, of course, her gifts, but on the ship there were too many opportunities for eavesdroppers. So, they spent the two weeks as normal, unobtrusive, tired vacationers returning home after a trip to Harshin.

The gangplank lowered, and Arran led the group down to the docks of Saloanne. He looked around to get his bearings, then headed up the old familiar passage to the rear of the main keep. He thought back to the day he had first traveled this road and the beginnings of his journey to Meitellen and the school. It seemed like a lifetime ago.

"What are you thinking?" Faye asked as they walked.

"Hmm?" Arran replied, coming out of his reverie.

"You look...thoughtful," Faye replied with a slight hesitation, making sure to find the right word. Even with the hesitation, Arran was amazed at how far Faye had progressed with her language skills. While they did not talk of anything of importance on their boat passage, they did spend a lot of time in conversation. Everyone told stories of their homeland, growing up, customs, and the like. Faye absorbed everything. She was like an eager young child learning something new. She only needed to hear an explanation once, and she seemed to be able to remember it perfectly. Arran smiled.

Before long, she'll speak common better than me.

"I was remembering." He gestured up the road with a tilt of his head. "The first time I came down this road. It was not long after my Source Day. I had never been far from home before and within two weeks I was gifted, tested, traveled to the capital, met the lord, ate dinner with the lord, and then down this road to a ship that would take me off to school. That was about..." Arran hesitated a bit, "...two years ago." He finished with a shake of his head. "It hardly seems possible that it has been that long."

Faye did not reply. Arran had noticed that Faye did not always reply after someone spoke. Either it was something in her culture, or they had an uncanny sense of understanding when nothing 'needed' to be said. Either way, he found it refreshing.

They continued to the top of the hill and then Arran led them off on a side path that took them around the keep, skirting the lush gardens.

"These are beautiful gardens," Elinda said approvingly as they made their way around the keep. "How many are there? The flowers and designs have already changed twice, I think."

"There are eight gardens around the keep, each with their own theme, types of flowers and...shrubs and stuff? I'm not much for plants," Arran replied.

Elinda smiled. "Eight is impressive, though. I would like to visit them properly sometime."

"As would I," Faye said with admiration.

Arran hastened his pace. "Another time, perhaps. I'll ask for a grand tour and escort, but for now, I want to get away from all these people. It makes me nervous for Faye."

"Another time, then." Elinda took Faye's arm in her own. "We shall hold him to that promise, won't we?"

Faye chuckled shyly behind her hand and nodded in agreement. Faye enjoyed the humans and their odd ways of friendship. A comment such as this would elicit sharp retorts and be held as offensive in her culture, but not with the humans. Humans somehow considered these remarks a deep act of friendship, understanding that it was meant as a friendly jest. A comment or statement with meaning that only close friends would know and understand and that this intimacy is where the jest originated.

Faye watched as the nuance of the conversation played out across Arran's face.

"Not you, too?" he said to her dejectedly.

Faye regained her composure and expressed herself with another human gesture she had learned and shrugged her shoulders.

Elinda smiled approvingly. "We girls have to stick together."

Arran sighed and looked at Rayneer and Bran, who both decided that the ground and their boots were far more interesting at the moment.

Elinda leaned over and whispered in Faye's ear. "When Arran is anxious, he is an easy target for a little fun. Mare is the best at it, but I have my moments." She gave Faye's arm a little squeeze.

Arran decided it best to ignore the taunts. He continued leading them around the keep and down the main path to the garrison.

Arran stopped when they got to the bottom of the path. "Stay here while I go and see if I can requisition some horses."

Arran walked into the barracks and over to the command tent. He didn't know if General Relorre would be in, but surely there would be someone that could approve a requisition for horses.

Arran approached the tent and announced himself for Relorre. A few moments later, he was admitted and saw the familiar site of the general busy at his desk covered with papers and maps. He looked up and smiled, getting up from his chair and extending his hand in welcome.

"Good to see you again, lad."

Arran took his hand, a little surprised at the gesture. "Thank you, sir."

"What brings you back to Saloanne? Do you have another commission so quickly? That last bit of nasty business was only a few months ago."

"No, no. Nothing like that. I'm on...well, I guess you could call it a small side mission of sorts." Arran winced inwardly. He hadn't thought this part through.

"Side mission?"

"Yes, sir." Arran tensed as Relorre hesitated for what seemed like an eternity.

"We are traveling as a team and I have a few others with me. I was wondering if I could requisition a few horses? If you have enough to spare, my lord."

"Hmm...how many do you need?"

"Six if you have them. It might be a month or so before we make it back this way, though."

Relorre was thoughtful for a few moments before replying. "We should be able to handle that. After Crenn'ier, we doubled our patrols, but it has been eerily quiet recently. We have the horses to spare. Let the stablemaster know and I'll make sure the requisition is completed." Relorre motioned to one of his attendants.

"Make sure six horses are requisitioned to young Arran here."

"Yes, sir," the attendant said with a quick salute, and hurried away.

"Will you be in Saloanne long? I would love to hear a full account of the Crenn'ier commission over dinner if you have the time. You did quite the job impressing Captain Mollen."

"Not presently, sir. We are anxious to continue. Perhaps on the return trip?" Now that he had the horses, Arran was anxious to leave. The last thing he wanted was to get bogged down at the capital and an extended stay with the nobles.

"Of course, of course."

"Thank you, sir."

Relorre bid Arran farewell, returning to the mountain of papers on his desk as Arran left the command tent for the stables.

———

Mare nudged Rayneer and tilted her head towards the militia compound. Rayneer turned and saw Arran and another man leading six large, beautiful horses their way.

Rayneer whistled in appreciation. "He'll just run off and see if he can requisition a few horses, eh?"

Arran stopped and began handing the reins to his friends as the stablemaster did the same. Arran thanked the man. He gave his normal, muttering grumble and tromped his way back towards the stables.

Rayneer and Elinda began petting and admiring their steeds.

Elinda's eyes were wide with excitement. "These are magnificent! How did you manage such fine horses on short notice?"

Arran's face grew hot. "I...uh...might have made an impression with the militia during my commission. I guess the general still remembered me. I was even able to get Gallant here, back." Arran patted the horse on its neck, as it whinnied appreciatively.

"You just went in and asked the general? Good will, indeed." She shook her head. "You never cease to surprise, Country. I'll give you that."

Arran's face then grew alarmed as he noticed Faye standing as far away from her horse as the reins would allow.

Arran went over and took the reins from her trembling hands. "Faye? Have you ever ridden a horse before?"

Everyone turned.

Faye's face was stricken with fear and question, all at the same time. She eyed the horse warily and then back to Arran.

She shook her head nervously.

Arran scolded himself. "I didn't even think to ask."

"I'll show her," Elinda said quickly, stepping over next to Faye. "We'll take it slow and I'll teach you as we go. Don't worry."

Faye nodded, but it was clear that she was not very comfortable with the idea.

They spent some time loading up and getting to know their horses while Elinda worked with Faye. Slowly, her fear began to turn to curiosity, allowing her to become somewhat comfortable with the horse. It wasn't long after that Elinda was able to get her up and in the saddle. After a few shaky starts, the group slowly began to make their way through Saloanne and finally out the main gate.

With every step they took away from the city, Arran felt a measure of tension leave his body. As the constant fear of Faye's discovery diminished, the excitement of seeing his parents again overtook his anxiety.

They rode the rest of the afternoon, making camp in a small valley off the road.

The fire was crackling amiably as the group finished their meal, enjoying the warmth of the flames.

Faye shifted uneasily on the ground in obvious discomfort.

"You'll get used to it," Elinda said. "You are too tense when you ride. You need to loosen up and let your body move with the horse. Once you have that, you'll be far less sore after a ride."

Faye grimaced as she shifted again. The group all nodded and chuckled as they watched her, all of them remembering their own first horse riding lessons.

"Faye?" Elinda asked.

Faye turned to Elinda with no reply.

"What is your home like?"

It was the first real question anyone had asked of Faye's home since they had met.

Faye hesitated, not at the question, but in thought.

Arran could not help but stare at her fine features. In the light of the fire, there was almost a glow about her. He had been so anxious since they left Harshin; he had almost forgotten how beautiful she was. Her hair, the high cheekbones, and fine features. She was radiant. That was the only word Arran could think of.

"Quit gawking, you three," Mare retorted. "You act like you've never seen an Elven girl before."

Arran, Rayneer, and Bran all turned their heads to Mare, and she shot them with the hardest 'Don't be stupid' glare Arran had ever seen.

Arran sheepishly lowered his head. "Right. It's just...she's...well you know..." Arran stopped speaking as Mare doubled the intensity of her glare at him. He instantly decided he better stop speaking before he said anything more embarrassing.

Faye smiled at the exchange. "My village is very different. We live in a valley full of trees near the mountains in the north of my continent. I traveled very far to the south before I made my journey across the great waters."

"I still can't believe you crossed the ocean by yourself," Bran said, flexing his injured shoulder.

"My village is different than here. We do not have buildings like here, we build and live in the trees. All are connected. Our village is a part of the trees this way. We only cut what we need from the trees and plant back two of what we take. The forest has grown large over many years."

"The trees must be huge," Arran replied.

Faye nodded. "Much bigger than here. We have..." She placed her hand on the ground.

"Ground? Earth?" Mare asked in an effort to help.

"Earth, yes. We have Earth gifts in my village that make trees grow."

"How many people are in your village?" Elinda asked.

"I do not know your numbers well. How many is this?" she said, holding up both hands and all ten fingers.

"Ten," Elinda replied.

"And how many is ten more of ten?"

"A hundred."

Faye thought for a few moments and held up her hand with all five fingers. "This many hundred, I think."

"Five hundred? That seems small for a village that has been

around for so long."

"Maybe there is more than one village?" Arran asked.

Faye shook her head. "Only one, we know. We have traveled far. Never found any others on our land."

Arran's brow furrowed in confusion. "If the Elves have been around as long as humans, it is surprising that there are not more of your kind. Humans have spread across most of our continent."

"Yes. Humans appear blessed with many children. My people only have one child in their lifetime, maybe two...sometimes none, but we live long and so our numbers do not increase like humans."

Arran and Elinda exchanged glances at this, and then Elinda hesitantly asked, "Faye, how old are you?"

Faye's eyes twinkled at the question. "I wonder when you ask. First, let me ask, how old are all of you and how do you measure?"

"We measure our time in months and years," Mare replied. "Thirteen..." Mare held up ten fingers, then added three more. "Thirteen months to a year, measured by the great star Callista." Mare looked up into the night sky and pointed to the large star. "When Callista reaches full high in the sky, that marks one year from the last."

"I see." Faye thought for a few moments. "We also use great star, but we call it different in my tongue and we measure it as a cycle. One cycle is your one year."

Mare nodded and looked around the group. "We are all between the age of..." she trailed off, not really knowing the age of everyone in the group but made her best guess, "...twenty to twenty-two cycles." She showed Faye the counts with her fingers.

Faye nodded in understanding. "How many is..." Faye held up all ten of her fingers again and then asked, "...four more?"

"Forty?" Mare said in disbelief. "You are forty years, um, cycles old?"

"That is close, yes."

Arran gasped. "You are the age of my parents!" Arran's mouth hung open and his eyes went wide. "But you're so, you look so..."

Mare glared at him again and threw in a punch for emphasis.

"Ow! What?" Arran replied. "She looks our age!"

Everyone was silent for a few moments before Mare asked Faye quietly. "Faye, how many cycles do the Elves normally live?"

Faye thought for a few moments and then replied evenly. "Four to five hundred of your years, I think."

Everyone gasped. Faye looked at them questioningly.

"Is that long for humans?"

Arran was the first to regain his composure. "Uh, yeah. Humans rarely live to one hundred with most many tens of years...cycles, less than that."

"I see," Faye said thoughtfully. "By these measures, I am much younger than you, in my people's eyes."

Mare did the math in her head. "She's right. By this math, she wouldn't even be midlife by the time we reach eighty years old."

The night air had finally lost the heat of the day and the faint crackle of the fire replaced all conversation. The slow, methodical snores from Bran began to fill the void. Elinda and Faye stifled a laugh, and soon everyone began to settle down next to the fire.

Faye lay on her back and stared up at the night sky, as random embers from the fire shimmered upwards with the smoke from the dying fire. She gazed at the twinkling stars, before slowly drifting off to sleep. Content that she had finally fulfilled her dream and found good companions...maybe even friends.

The group rode steadily onward to Kine over the next three days, enjoying each other's company. The conversations became easier and Faye began to find that she appreciated and even enjoyed the openness of the humans. They spoke easily among themselves. Faye found the concept of so many different customs and traditions amongst the humans fascinating, asking many questions which the human contingent returned in favor, asking her many of their own.

The group had just crested a small rise in the road and Arran pointed off in the distance, smiling broadly. "Welcome to Kine."

The group of six rode into Kine, garnering a few wary stares from the locals until they recognized Arran. They would wave enthusiastically and then went about their business as usual.

"Friendly folk," Rayneer said.

Arran took in a long breath, as a sense of pride washed over him. "Yeah, we're a pretty easygoing group of people. 'A friend of yours is a friend of mine' kind of thing."

The group made their way through town as the slow rhythm of sound from the smithy rang out in the distance. Arran smiled inwardly at the sound.

The group dismounted and walked around to the front of the shop. Arran took a step just inside the entry. "You should probably reheat that now, old man."

Dale looked up. At the sight of Arran, he smiled. "You are welcome to come and try to do better!" He quickly put down his tools and walked briskly over to hug his son.

"Good to see you again so soon. Your mother will be overjoyed."

"We were coming through the area and I thought we could stop by." Arran turned, sweeping his hand towards the rest of the group. "Everyone, this is my father, Dale."

There were a few waves and 'Pleasure to meet you' greetings, which Dale reciprocated. "Come, come inside. Oh, but go around to the front of the house. Pai'ese will not be pleased if I led you all through the shop and dirtied her floors."

Elinda laughed. "Of course."

Arran led the group around the shop and to the front of the house, where he opened the door to the familiar smells of his mother's kitchen. He could hear her puttering around, no doubt cleaning or dabbling with some new recipe.

He led the group into the common room as everyone spread out. Arran continued into the kitchen.

"Hello, Mother."

Pai'ese turned with a start. "Arran! I had not hoped to see you again for some time."

"We were in the area and I thought we would stop by for a visit."

She gave him a quizzical look. "We?"

Arran smiled. "Yes. Come on, I want to introduce everyone to you and Father."

"Give me a minute. I'm totally unpresentable to guests at the moment." She began wiping her hands on her towel and then straightening her hair.

"You are fine. Come on." Arran reached out and took her hand, leading her into the common room.

What happened next surprised everyone. As Arran led his mother into the room, there came an audible gasp from Faye as she quickly stepped forward and knelt on one knee in front of Pai'ese.

"Honored One," she said reverently.

Everyone was stunned into silence until Faye finally rose and took a step back, head bowed.

"Arran?" Pai'ese said uncomfortably. "What is happening?"

Arran stood in shock and looked at Faye. "I don't know." He crossed over in Faye's direction. Her head was still lowered. "Faye? What is going on?"

Head still bowed, she answered, "It is proper to pay respect to one of such power."

Slowly, Faye raised her head nervously, and once again looked at Pai'ese, then at Arran.

"This is your mother?"

Arran raised an eyebrow. "Yes."

"You did not speak of her status."

"Status?" several spoke up at once, repeating the statement in surprise.

Arran shook his head emphatically. "We are...no status." He held her gaze and repeated. "No status. She's just my mom."

Faye looked confused. She swept her eyes back to Pai'ese, then back to Arran, and then back to Arran's mother again.

"How can this be? I only see one aura as strong." She shook her head incredulously. "Elder in my village. She has most respect. She is our spiritual leader and decides much with the elders in all things. High status."

The room went silent again but only for a moment as Dale

walked into the room and with enthusiasm said, "Great! Everyone is meeting one another. What did I miss?"

Every eye in the room was immediately on Dale as he slowly shrank back from the attention, visibly uncomfortable. "What?"

Pai'ese felt the unease in the room and took control. "Maybe we should all sit down. I'll fix some drinks and we can go through the introductions."

This seemed to break the tension, as they now had something to do and everyone began to move. Dale brought in some additional chairs from the kitchen to accommodate everyone as Pai'ese set a pitcher of lemonade and glasses on the table, pouring everyone a glass.

Everyone fidgeted until Pai'ese took a seat.

Pai'ese stole a quick glance at Faye as she settled into her chair. She still had a look of awe on her.

She must have Aura sight...in due time.

She turned to Arran. "I believe introductions are in order?"

"Oh, yes. Sorry, everyone, this is my mother and father, Pai'ese and Dale."

Everyone nodded in greeting. Faye bowing her head and placing her hands to her forehead, fingers interlocked into a sign or gesture of some kind.

"Mom, Dad this is..." Arran gestured to each of his friends as he went around the room, "...Elinda, Rayneer, Mare, Bran, and Faye."

Pai'ese smiled graciously. "It is a pleasure to finally meet you all. Arran spoke very fondly of you all during his last visit. You are always welcome in our home."

Pai'ese's warm generosity and obvious genuineness permeated the room, and Arran could feel a little of the tension ease away.

Pai'ese straightened her skirt and then gave Arran a stern, motherly stare.

She spoke softly and firmly. "So, what is the real reason you are here? Kine isn't exactly on the way to anywhere and you went out of your way to come here. This isn't just a cordial visit, is it?" Her eyes darted to Faye and then back to Arran.

Arran withered under her gaze and the tone. "No."

Silence.

Pai'ese maintained her eyes on Arran as he visibly faltered at how to start this conversation.

"Faye is...she is not from around here."

"Understatement of the year," Bran muttered under his breath.

Arran turned to Bran with a glare and he muttered, "Sorry."

"I gathered," Pai'ese responded flatly.

Arran looked at Faye and the two locked eyes. Faye nodded in understanding, hesitated, then slowly reached up and removed the cowl from her head.

To Arran's surprise, his mother hardly reacted at all, save for a small wrinkle between her eyebrows. She tilted her head and took in the foreign features of the young girl inquiringly without comment. Arran's father, on the other hand, gasped, his mouth agape.

Pai'ese slapped him on the arm. "Close your mouth, Dale. You'll give the young thing a fright."

Pai'ese continued to look at Faye and muttered under her breath, "I guess old Santal was right after all..."

Everyone looked at her questioningly. Pai'ese snapped out of her reverie, not aware she had spoken aloud, and shook her head. "An old sailor I once knew, he was a drunk and most considered him half mad, but he spoke of another continent, west of Galleant, and it had a strange people. No one believed him. Just another sailor story, like mermaids and sirens. Fanciful tales to spice up their drink."

Rayneer's eyes went wide in wonder. "We knew about another continent?"

Pai'ese shook her head. "No one knew for sure. Several voyages tried but never came back. Santal claimed he was the only survivor in his tale. The seas west of Galleant are turbulent except for short periods between seasons, as the stories go, and the voyage was said to be very long. People eventually just gave up. At least I thought so..." Pai'ese looked back at Faye with admiration.

Faye gave a slight nod in acknowledgment, and then Dale gave out a low whistle.

Pai'ese returned her eyes to Arran, raised her eyebrows, and tilted her head as if to say 'Continue'.

Arran gathered himself and looked at his friends. No one knew that he had already told his mother a good portion of the story or that she was indeed his 'mysterious' friend. But with the revelation of Faye already out, he began. It was easier than he thought it would be, and he found that he was eager to get the full story out.

Arran spent the better part of the next hour going over the group's trip to Harshin. He spoke of their orders south from Shia, mouthing his suspicions that it was only to get them out of the way; eventually finding Pim, the campsite, and finally the ensuing battle, and then meeting Faye.

Very calmly, Pai'ese took a deep breath and then bent to grab her glass, taking a very slow and deliberate sip of her lemonade. She looked at Faye.

"Faye, why did you call me 'Honored One'? Why do you believe I have such power?"

Faye fidgeted for a few seconds before answering. She had not fully exposed the extent of her talents to the strangers yet, but knew that if she was here to help, she would need to trust them. A small amount of tension released from her shoulders as she answered.

"You have strong aura. Very strong."

Everyone turned to look at Faye.

"You can see auras?" Arran asked.

"Yes. It is one of my...gifts," Faye glanced at Mare questioningly.

Mare gave a small nod, acknowledging she had spoken correctly.

"So you have gifts?" Arran said, looking thoughtful, then continued, "You are gifted from the Patrons? Spirit, Tovin, Talon..." He trailed off looking at Faye who was shaking her head, her eyebrows furrowed.

"I do not know these...Patrons. We are born, our gifts reveal themselves, usually at an early age, and then we nurture and perfect them over time. Is this not the same for humans?"

"I...uh..." Arran stammered in an effort to try and process her statement.

Elinda came to his rescue. "Allow me?" She looked at Pai'ese for approval. She was not exactly sure why she felt the need for her approval, but it felt...right. There was something about Arran's mother. Strength wasn't quite right, but a sense of inner power, a calm wisdom.

Pai'ese nodded and Elinda explained to Faye the ritual of Source Day, the various gifts given by the seven Patrons, and then how humans are tested. She told of how those, usually the strongest in the Source, end up training in Meitellen; while others are either too weak for training, or simply choose not to go. She did admit though, that this was rare.

Faye listened intently to Elinda, and when she was done, she asked, "So not all humans have gifts?"

This brought a chuckle from most of the group.

"Not even close," Rayneer replied. "Can you imagine if every person on Galleant had gifts? It would be utter chaos."

Everyone muttered their agreement and shook their heads.

"Have you met your Patrons?" Faye asked?

No one spoke.

"We have not," Pai'ese said, taking control of the conversation.

Faye shook her head in confusion. She would need to think about this and let the elders know. Were her people's gifts granted by these Patrons all this time, and they simply did not know it?

"Faye, what gifts do your people have?" Pai'ese asked.

"I..." Faye hesitated, not sure how to answer or if she should answer. Divulging her gifts for the sake of her quest was one thing, but fully disclosing her village was another.

Pai'ese noticed the wariness in her hesitation and immediately knew that she had crossed a line. She raised her hand with a gentle smile. "I am sorry, Faye. That was inappropriate for me to ask. How about your gifts? You have told us of your Aura sense. Do you have any more?"

Faye's expression eased, and she was visibly relieved. "Yes. I have the gift of..." Faye looked at Mare, unsure of the term she had used.

"Foretelling," Mare said. "The way she described her dreams to me, I believe it is the gift of true foretelling. Her ability has a lot of depth. 'A lot of depth,' and it is very specific in its predictions. I do not know of any human that is even close to a foretelling skill of this strength."

Mare looked at Faye. "Would you mind if I explained your story?"

Faye shook her head, looking relieved at the offer.

Mare told the group of Faye's foretelling. Her story of the four of them and how very specific and accurate it ended up being.

"That is remarkable," Pai'ese said. "Do you have many foretellings of this nature?"

Faye shook her head. "Most are small. Not important. But they are almost always true. My people have trust in them over the cycles."

Faye looked around the room and then back at Pai'ese. "I continue?"

"Oh, yes, I'm sorry."

"My other gifts are with bow...hunting. I have talents...gifts with this skill. I can be silent, think clearly, focus, and even slow down for important shots."

Arran understood all the gifts she mentioned, but one. "Slow down?"

"Yes. Everything around me slows for a short time. I do not miss when using this gift, but it can...I tire quickly if use too long."

"You can slow time?" Arran gasped, looking at everyone else in the group as they all shook their heads. No one had ever heard of such a gift.

"Yes," Faye said. "It only for a short time but I learned to use it well. I am considered one of the best hunters of my village." She straightened up proudly as she finished.

"I bet you are," Rayneer said admiringly.

"The shot on the cat? At the campsite?" Arran asked.

Faye nodded. "Yes."

Pai'ese took another sip of her drink as she let her gaze sweep around the room. The tension of silence at Faye's revelations began to build. The discovery of a new race with gifts not presented from the Patrons, and unbeknownst to the humans...it was life-changing, culturally and personally. She was just about to speak when Mare broke the silence before her.

"Please tell me, Lady Pai'ese. How are you still sane after raising Arran all these years? You must have the patience of Patron Kemor himself."

Elinda stifled a chuckle and was about to admonish Mare when Pai'ese gave a very unladylike snort of laughter.

Pai'ese leaned forward and whispered conspiratorially, but loud enough to be heard by all. "He was a handful, that is for sure. We'll talk later."

Arran groaned and put his head in his hands.

Mare beamed. "Oh, I already like you more than you can say. I want all the embarrassing stories I can get on Country here." Mare patted Arran on the shoulder affectionately. "Coming here was the best idea ever!"

Pai'ese crooked an eyebrow. "Country?"

"Just my little nickname. You should have seen him those first terms in Meitellen. As lost as a puppy. We'll talk later," Mare mimicked with a wave of her hand. Everyone laughed as Arran shrunk into the chair in an attempt at escape.

Rayneer slapped Arran on the back and between snorts of laughter said, "It was your idea to come here. You had to know that Mare and Elinda were going to talk to your mother. The price had to be paid."

It took a while for everyone to regain their composure and stop laughing. Mainly due to quite a few more jokes at Arran's expense.

"Dear?" Dale said, leaning over to his wife.

"Yes?"

"Some food maybe? It is getting a bit late."

"Of course, of course." Pai'ese replied, wiping a tear from her eye.

Pai'ese looked around the room at her son and the group of individuals he had found and befriended. She felt a pang of sorrow, remembering her own adventuring group.

Friends like these are what make it all worthwhile. I would not have traded those experiences for anything.

Pai'ese rose and straightened herself out. "So, as my very stomach-driven husband has so casually reminded me, it is about time for dinner. Anyone interested?"

The replies echoed around the room.

"Aye!"

"Yes, ma'am."

"Oh gods, yes."

Pai'ese looked at Faye and her eyebrows furrowed, "Faye, dear, do you have a headband or something a little less conspicuous than a full cowl you could wear to, um, maybe disguise your obvious...?" She pointed delicately at her ears. "Kine is a very welcoming village, but I don't think we want to rush them in to interspecies discussions this evening, eh?"

Faye smiled at Pai'ese, "Yes, my lady. I think that would be wise as well."

***

Dinner at Tabard's Inn was a series of ordering food, everyone explaining the dish to Faye, and then Faye experimentally tasting it, generally to everyone's delight or horror, depending on her reaction. Luckily, her assessments were mostly favorable, pushing the tensions aside, and giving everyone a respite to enjoy the evening's merriment.

Arran found it very interesting watching someone experience the most common and mundane of foods and drinks for the first time. Dishes that he and everyone else took for granted. It was the source of much conversation and laughter throughout the meal.

"I cannot eat more." Faye leaned back in her chair, placing a hand on her stomach. "Thank you for a most good and...different meal."

"You are welcome," Pai'ese replied, taking a moment to observe everyone at the table. She was very proud of her son. She had not thought the camaraderie of her team could have ever been duplicated, but here in front of her were the makings of a group of friends with just the right mix of skills and personalities to rival it.

Smiling out of her reverie, Pai'ese began, "We should probably talk about accommodations. Faye...I think it would be best if you stay with us while you are here. Will the rest of you be okay here at the inn?"

Elinda approved enthusiastically. "Oh yes! It is quite cozy here. I like it."

"That means small and quaint," Mare said.

Elinda brushed back her hair haughtily. "Small and quaint equals charming."

The two stared at each other for a moment and then laughed. The rest of the table enjoying the two girls' jibes. Everyone except Faye.

Faye had still not become accustomed to the human's form of friendly wit and the nuances of the quips. Her brow furrowed as once again she watched what should have been hurtful comments turn into laughter.

Pai'ese saw the girl's confusion. "What is wrong, Faye?"

Faye turned to Pai'ese, her expression turning from confusion to one of question.

"They spoke ill of one another...but it is funny?" She shook her head. "This I still do not understand. Is not funny with my people."

Pai'ese raised her head and leaned back chuckling.

Pai'ese leaned closer and kept her voice low. "Now I understand. Culturally, we humans find teasing each other with small insults a form of...how shall I say...friendship, yes. When two humans are very close, the kinship and understanding of one another can be used to tease. It actually strengthens their relationship."

Faye shook her head emphatically. "I have seen this. How can you tell hurtful from...tease?"

Pai'ese chuckled softly. "That is very difficult to explain. Friends... just know." She paused. "Humans can be difficult..." She paused as if to continue but became lost in the thought of her old team and their personalities.

Difficult doesn't even come close.

It was then she noticed Challand edging her way over to their table from across the inn. Pai'ese gestured with her mug for her to come over.

Arran saw his mother's gesture and followed it, seeing Challand. He rose his mug along with his mother's. "Challand! Join us?"

Everyone turned to see the newcomer, and like a bolt, Rayneer immediately straightened in his chair. As she drew near, he rose, politely proffering Challand a chair at the end of the table.

"Thank you," she said, a little embarrassed at the attention.

Mare turned to Elinda and whispered. "He ever jump like that to get you a chair?"

"Not once."

"Hmm...That's what I thought." Mare eyed Rayneer suspiciously.

Rayneer returned to his seat, his full attention now firmly set on Challand. Mare rolled her eyes.

Challand smiled as she sat and turned to Arran. "I did not expect to see you so soon again," Challand said.

"We are just passing through, taking a small break. Would you like a drink?" Arran raised his hand for the server.

Challand looked around the table warily before Arran realized introductions were in order.

"Sorry, Challand, these are the friends I spoke of before...from school."

Arran made all the introductions. Rayneer very formally bowing from his seat, uttering a very polite, "Good day, Miss Challand."

Mare nudged Elinda in the side. "Is he blushing?"

Elinda squinted her eyes. "I think he is. I believe our young knight may be smitten. Interesting...he has adamantly rebuffed all manner of courting from his parents."

Mare and Elinda were not the only ones to notice this subtle interaction, and the smallest hint of a smile tugged at the corners of Pai'ese's mouth as she raised her mug.

The group fell into easy conversation, Challand regaling everyone with several of Arran's exploits.

"He gave you a flower!?" Mare laughed incredulously.

"A yellow rose. I had to follow clues for a week! It was actually well thought out." Challand chuckled to herself. "It was equal parts frustrating and endearing. I honestly didn't know what to do."

Pai'ese eyes went wide at the story. "When did this happen? I never heard of this story."

"Not long before his Source Day, I think," Challand replied.

Pai'ese looked askance at her son, shaking her head with a smirk.

"Yes, yes, yes," Arran said, waving his hands. "That's enough about me."

Mare wiped a tear from her eye. "Oh, there can never be enough of this."

"I should be heading home," Challand said. "It was nice to meet all of you. Please come by the farm if you have the time. Mother and Father would be happy to see you again, Arran."

"I will," Arran promised as Challand rose to leave.

Rayneer rose also and stepped around the table to pull out her chair, leaning in close as he did. "May I escort you to the door?"

Challand looked surprised and then looked at Arran, who just shrugged.

"Thank you. That would be lovely." Everyone watched as the two slowly walked off towards the door. The distance was not far, but the two made the short walk last as long as they could.

Pai'ese smiled at the exchange and the beginnings of youthful attractions. "We should probably be headed home as well."

Rayneer returned to the table and sat down, finishing his drink as everyone stared.

"What? She's nice."

No one replied. Mare finally stood and lowered her arm to Elinda and in the most girlish voice she could muster, "My lady, may I escort you to the innkeeper? We are in great need of a room. I feel that I may swoon from all of this excitement." She feigned as if she was light-headed, raising her arm to her forehead.

The table tried to hold back their amusement with little success.

Rayneer frowned at the exchange. "Nice. A man shows some politeness, and he gets chastised. A man is a brute, and he gets chastised. There is no winning with you."

Mare flicked her hair back haughtily with a toss of her head. "As it should be." She took Elinda's arm in hers as they strolled towards the bar.

Faye squinted her eyes in concentration and then turned to look at Pai'ese.

Pai'ese affirmed her suspicion. "Yes. More of the same."

Faye sighed in resignation. "I do not know I will ever understand this custom."

Later that evening, Dale entered the bedroom and immediately saw that something was bothering Pai'ese. He sat on the bed next to her and placed his hand on hers.

"What has you so worried?"

Pai'ese looked up, but her gaze was elsewhere for a second before she focused on her husband. "It's Faye."

"She seems like a nice girl."

"That isn't the problem." She patted his hand in hers. "She's not human, Dale. It changes everything. Humans are not alone. And if you think we have issues with people not getting along now in this world, what will it look like if we introduce a new race of people? It frightens me."

"Why should people care? Either you are a good person or you are not. Human or..."

"Elf," Pai'ese finished for him.

"...Elf."

"Not everyone is like you, Dale. A lot of people do not have the capacity to see past the difference. They see different and immediately develop a dislike or even a hatred for it." Pai'ese squeezed his hands and leaned forward to place a kiss on his forehead.

"It is one of the reasons why I love you so."

"So what do we do? How can we help?"

"I believe we need to take her to Meitellen. The school, maybe? Which, of course, will lead to the council, and then who knows what will happen to her? I just don't know. There is a part of me that wants to tell her to go home and we never speak of it again. Safe for everyone and go back to not knowing, but...I think that is naïve." Pai'ese stared down at their hands. "Take into account her story, her dreams, and how she knew of the danger Arran and his friends were in..." She trailed off in frustration at her indecision. "Her people are going to be discovered, eventually. I can try to convince myself to ignore her, her people, and her reason for being here, but it doesn't feel...right."

Dale narrowed his eyes.

"What?" she asked.

"You said 'We'..." he remarked. "...we take her to Meitellen."

Several moments passed before Pai'ese replied.

She sighed heavily. "I did. I'm not sure about it, though. If I do, I would need to divulge my past. I could use that standing to help protect her from the politics that are inevitable. I just don't know, even that isn't a guarantee. Who knows, maybe it would do more damage than good?" She let the question hang pleadingly as she lay her head on his shoulders.

"What should I do?" she whispered.

Dale stroked her hair for several moments before answering.

"Whatever you believe is right," he finally answered. "Let me put it this way. In your long life, have you ever done what your conscience said was right and regretted it after?"

Pai'ese looked up at Dale thoughtfully and shook her head.

"So, when you believe you have figured out what is right, that is what you do. Regardless of doubts." He kissed her forehead softly. "Come, despite all the thoughts I know you have running through your mind, it will not be resolved tonight." He pulled her in closer as they eased back down on the bed.

They lay in each other's arms for a long while, Dale holding her until her slow, rhythmic breathing told him she had finally fallen asleep. With a finger, he swept a lock of hair from her face before closing his eyes and falling asleep beside her.

Several days went by and Pai'ese watched the stress and memories of the harrowing events in Harshin ebb slowly away from Arran and his friends. Bran was healing well and he and Rayneer had begun helping Dale in the smithy. The work helped Bran and did wonders with the recuperation of his shoulder and arm. 'You take to the craft well', Dale had told him. Dale was eager to share his knowledge, and both boys found themselves curious and became eager learners of the craft. Pai'ese smiled as she observed Arran content to watch from the side, as his old chores became a source of enthusiasm for his friends.

One afternoon, and to no one's surprise, Rayneer had Arran take him to Challand's family farm. It had become very clear the two were more than a little taken with one another. Challand's mother and father were absolutely beside themselves when they learned Rayneer was a knight 'and' a noble. They were constantly inserting themselves in an effort to encourage the pair, which in the end suited the two of them just fine.

Elinda, Mare, and Faye spent the majority of their time with Pai'ese. A good portion of this naturally centering around the kitchen. Faye, it turned out, was the only one interested in the art of cooking. Pai'ese listened and observed as they would sit and drink tea in the afternoons. Pai'ese had been astonished to learn that Faye was almost forty years of age! Her race was indeed different and unique.

After spending a few days with the girls, Pai'ese was very impressed. They were all unique, had strong self-confidence, and good countenances. Elinda was thoughtful in her opinions. Mare was more straightforward and a bit brazen, but there was intelligence underneath that sharp tongue. Faye...Faye was usually silent and observing, not in a bad way, but with fascination and an eagerness to learn. She would only offer her opinion if asked, and it was usually always very astute.

It was on the morning of the third day when Pai'ese had finally made her decision. She just needed to know one last thing, and if she was honest with herself, it was the most important.

She was first up as usual and preparing for the morning meal as she heard someone enter. It was Faye, as she had hoped.

"Good morning," Pai'ese said, looking over her shoulder.

"Good morning, Lady Pai'ese."

Pai'ese half turned. "I told you. You do not need to call me that."

"I know, but is proper."

Pai'ese busied herself at the counter, accomplishing nothing, and then let out a long sigh, throwing the towel over her shoulder.

"Faye, I need to ask you something. It is very important and your answer could decide how we will continue. Do you understand?"

"I do. I have been waiting your decision. The rest look to you for guidance."

Observant, indeed.

She wiped her hands on the towel as she took a seat across from Faye.

"Do you want to go home? Your family, your friends, they must all miss you by now and be extremely worried."

Faye looked directly into Pai'ese's eyes for several long moments, her grey eyes unblinking as she contemplated the question. Pai'ese almost looked away as the gaze began to unnerve her, when Faye tilted her head slightly to the side as a child might when confused, easing the tension of the moment.

"I ask myself the same question. Over and over since I arrived here. I have received no dreams to guide me after I find Arran and the others. Never have I been in such need and my dreams not guided me."

Faye paused, and her gaze drifted down to her clasped hands on the table as she sat deliberating. Her expression ran through a cycle of emotions as she wrestled with her thoughts. Finally, she looked up with conviction and continued.

"Do I want to go home? Yes. I miss my family, my friends, my home. The comfort of my village and my people. This all is true, but I believe my dreams have stopped for a reason. This decision is my own. I must make this decision for myself. I must do what 'I' feel is right."

Pai'ese shuddered, remembering her conversation with Dale. *'Have you ever regretted what your conscience has told you was right?'*

Faye hesitated, then she replied, voice trembling. "I believe I should stay. I want to stay. It is hard to say. I have dreams of Arran and the others for a long time before I finally acted. To see them alive in the waking world, as in my dreams..." She paused. "...assisting them as I did against the evil, it changed me. Give me direction. I believe there is more. That there is more for me to do and this is not at home. It is here."

Faye focused her grey eyes back on Pai'ese intently and spoke with utter conviction. "I wish to stay."

Pai'ese held her gaze firmly and reached across the table. Holding Faye's hands in her own, the two sat with hands clasped, their decisions made.

Pai'ese was impressed with Faye's honesty and admission of such private thoughts. It steeled her for what she knew she must now do.

"Come," Pai'ese finally said, standing up. "Let us prepare for the day and tonight we will speak with the others."

"That was another fine meal, my lady," Rayneer said with a mocking bow from his seat across the table.

Pai'ese feigned a curtsy from her chair, "Why, thank you, sir knight."

Mare rolled her eyes. "That boy is so smitten you could have boiled pine cones and he would be happy right now."

Rayneer did not take the bait of the comment and just slid his chair back contentedly.

Pai'ese rose. "If everyone is done, please get comfortable in the other room. Arran, would you please help me clear the table?"

He replied awkwardly. "Sure." An uneasy feeling worked its way through his stomach as he felt that there was more to this simple request.

After everyone had left and Arran was placing the dishes on the counter next to his mother, she grabbed him softly by the arm.

"Arran," she said quietly. "I want you to know that I think we should take Faye to Meitellen."

Arran did not answer.

"And...I am going to go with you."

"But...what...why?" the words coming out in a jumbled stammer.

Pai'ese fully turned towards her son and grabbed his hand in hers. She held his eyes for several moments.

"I will be going as Sai'el."

Pai'ese watched as the ramifications of the statement hit him. Astonishment, fear, and surprise rolling like waves across his face.

"But...that means you have to tell..."

"Yes. I've given it a lot of thought and the time has come. I can do more good for you, your friends, Faye, and discovering whoever is behind these incidents if I do this. It will not be easy, but my hope is that my standing of old will still hold sway with the school and the council. If that doesn't work, I know a good number of secrets. One or both should give us the leverage we need. Faye will need someone on her side with these groups."

"But what of everything you've done and gone through to protect yourself?" Expressions of concern and fear replacing all else.

"I will be giving up the facade that I've built. This is true, but not the life I have built. I have already spoken with your father and he is in agreement. This is the right thing for me, for us, to do."

Arran shook his head, not fully understanding this new strategy. He had hoped to receive his mother's advice, but...

"Are you sure? Introducing Faye 'and' the legendary Sai'el back from the grave? That is going to be a lot for them to take in all at once."

Pai'ese's expression turned confident, a sly smirk forming. "Oh, don't worry about that. I've dealt with these groups before. I know how they think and how they act. I'm sure not much has changed. I think I can handle them."

Pai'ese pulled Arran into a hug and then held him at arm's length by the shoulders. "Let's go introduce Sai'el to your friends, shall we?"

Pai'ese and Arran entered the sitting room with several conversations already in progress.

Bran flexed his shoulder. "I think I am regaining some strength. Maybe we should include blacksmithing in our training when we get back to school."

"Good luck with that," Rayneer said with a laugh.

Pai'ese sat in her chair as Arran went to stand near his father.

Pai'ese spoke firmly, gathering everyone's attention. "I think the time has come for all of us to make a decision on where we go from here."

The room died down instantly, all eyes now intently focused on Pai'ese.

"Firstly, I would like to discuss Faye. She and I have spoken and we believe we need to take her and the story of her people to Meit-ellen. She believes, and I happen to agree with her, that if she is going to continue to assist you in uncovering the secret behind the incidents, keeping her hidden will prove too much of a hindrance."

Pai'ese let the statement hang, giving everyone a moment to think.

"Thoughts? Objections? Concerns?"

"So many," Mare said, alarm in her voice. "I was kind of hoping that we help her get back to her land and people, if I'm honest. I'm concerned about what will happen to her if we present her to the school and council."

"We discussed this and I have a plan that will hopefully help with that, but before we get to that, does anyone else have anything to add?"

"I'm pretty much concerned with the same," Rayneer said matter-of-factly. "People with a lot of power are going to want access to her, possibly use her for their own gains. I don't know how, but..." He trailed off.

Arran grimaced inwardly, remembering his own pessimistic statement in Harshin of the same and Rayneer's jibe.

He gets it now.

Arran swept his gaze around the room at the expressions of concern on his friends' faces. It was a testament to their quality and genuine concern for Faye, which mirrored his own, and for that, he was profoundly grateful.

Pai'ese continued. "Your concerns mirror my own, but I believe this is where I can help. I will be going with you to Meitellen and I will act on her behalf, as her ward, for lack of a better term."

"Lady Pai'ese," Rayneer instantly objected. "You are a fine lady..." he hesitated before he finished, his expression turning to one of embarrassment, "...but these are powerful men."

Pai'ese responded sternly. "I am aware." She stopped, admonishing herself at the sharpness of the reply. "I'm sorry, Rayneer, I did not mean to offend. Your concern is valid." She took a deep breath before she continued. The point of no return. She glanced at Dale and then at Arran before returning her attention back to the group resolutely. "But...I will not be going as Pai'ese, wife of Dale and Mother of Arran of Kine. I will be going as Sai'el, the highest ranking Intelligence agent the school has ever produced."

Looks of astonishment and confusion instantly appeared on everyone's faces. Arran wasn't sure who all knew of Sai'el, but he could see Bran working it out in the moments that followed. Realization suddenly dawned across his face. Arran knew that of everyone in the group, Bran was the most intimate with his obsession of the legendary figure. He and Bran had talked endlessly about the deeds of the legendary Sai'el and her group late at night in their dorm room.

"You are Sai'el?" Bran's reply was one of obvious incredulity. "The one from Arran's book? Not possible! Sai'el disappeared ages ago!"

"Over a hundred years ago, yes," Pai'ese responded.

Bran did not respond, the absolute firmness of her response silencing any retort.

"It...is a very long story."

Pai'ese retold a much shorter version of her story to the group than the one she gave Dale and Arran, and the room exploded with questions.

"There is a sourcestone?"

"You're over a hundred years old?"

"Why did you hide?"

"Not possible!"

"All right, all right, everyone," Pai'ese said, raising her hands.

Arran stepped to the corner of the room, retrieved his bag and placed it on the center table. He opened it up and began to pull out the gear his mother had given him for everyone to see, placing the daggers on top.

Rayneer looked at the gear, then at Pai'ese. "This was yours? You are the mysterious friend?"

"I am." Pai'ese reached out and picked up one of the blades, twirling it in her hand effortlessly. The small, practiced move did not go unnoticed.

"This gear is worth thousands of gold," Bran said.

"A lifetime of work, blood, and eventual heartbreaking death. I am aware of its physical and emotional worth." She placed the dagger back down on the pile mournfully.

"My lady," Mare began hesitantly. "I have no reason to believe you are trying to deceive us, despite the enormity of your story, but convincing us and convincing the school and council are two entirely different levels of trust."

A small and confident smile spread across Pai'ese's pursed lips. The smile reached her eyes as they narrowed almost evilly. Arran shivered.

"I have my ways. You must trust me on this. I have only the well-being of all of you first and foremost in my thoughts. Once we can get everyone past Faye's arrival, and my identity established, I hope to switch the focus back to finding the source of the corruption. That is the greater issue at hand and it is in this that we must concentrate our efforts."

Pai'ese could see that there was still doubt and confusion written across their faces. She had hoped to avoid using a direct display, but had prepared for the eventuality.

She rose. "Follow me." And between one heartbeat and the next, she disappeared into the shadows.

Gasps erupted from the room.

"A simple Shadow walk," came a voice from across the room. Pai'ese reappeared behind them.

Everyone turned in surprise at the sound of her voice.

"Simple!" Bran exclaimed. "It was like you just disappeared. I've never seen anyone have a Shadow form that complete! Not even Klintoc!"

"Well, to be fair..." Pai'ese said, returning to her seat. "...I've had a couple of lifetimes to perfect it."

"Close your mouth, dear," Pai'ese said softly, turning to Dale.

"I...I mean...I've never..."

"I know." She patted him on the arm lovingly.

The rest of the evening was a flurry of questions. Much to Pai'ese's surprise, the majority of the questions turned out to be historical in nature. Mare was fascinated learning about events and culture from a firsthand account from over a hundred years ago. The others quickly joined Mare in her enthusiasm with several of Pai'ese's stories making the group erupt with laughter.

Eventually, everyone began to tire, even with all the excitement, and they agreed to resume any and all conversations the following day.

"Aren't you coming to bed?" Dale asked.

"In a moment, I want to tidy up the kitchen, so it's not so bad in the morning." She could still see the confusion mixed with wonder in his eyes. "It's still me, Dale. My gifts do not change what we have."

"I know. It was just...a surprise is all. You told me...I knew in the back of my mind...but to see it."

Pai'ese just nodded her head in understanding as he turned and left.

Pai'ese began clearing up the dishes when she saw Faye enter the kitchen out of the corner of her eye. She turned.

"Before the...sourcestone?" Faye said questioningly. "Were you as powerful as now?"

Pai'ese shook her head.

"I was very good, but not as...well, powerful isn't the right word, exactly, after the sourcestone. I would say my gifts became more effective. My skills didn't have any additional strength or power, but they were...easier, more...complete. A mere thought, quick as that. Like tonight. Other gifts came to me over the years, but mainly it was the ease and effectiveness of my gifts that was the biggest difference."

Faye nodded her head in understanding. "It is the same with my people. The truly talented always act with such grace and ease."

Satisfied with the answer, Faye gave a short bow and left.

<hr>

The following morning, everyone arrived early and eager as Pai'ese prepared the morning's breakfast. New questions, unasked from the night before, sprang up in conversation as they ate.

Pai'ese looked upon the group and she saw the same youthful enthusiasm she remembered with her friends long ago. It was invigorating, she had to admit.

Once breakfast was done, and the questions had died down to a trickle, Pai'ese addressed the group. "So, everyone is together on this? We must act together and with common purpose."

Everyone nodded.

"When do we leave?" Rayneer asked.

"I suppose we could leave anytime we wish. We could use today to prepare and leave tomorrow if everyone is in agreement. I only have one thing left to do...well actually, the three of you to do." She pointed to Arran, Rayneer, and Bran.

"Tomorrow, then?" She swept her gaze around the table.

Everyone agreed.

She turned towards Dale. "How many shovels do we have?"

"Shovels?"

Pai'ese raised her eyebrows and tilted her head at him.

He recovered and quickly replied, "I believe I have two."

"Good. You three." She pointed again to the three boys. "I want you to take the shovels and go to the tree in the orchard. Arran knows the one. On the north side of the tree, take ten paces straight north and dig. They are about six feet down if memory serves."

Arran looked quizzically at his mother. "What is six feet down?"

"Just a few things I hid long ago. Chests, to be exact. There should be seven chests buried there. One medium-sized chest with an Intelligence sigil on the top and six smaller ones. Bring the medium chest and one of the smaller ones. Leave the rest and re-bury them. Make it nice and tidy so no one will stumble upon it."

Arran, Bran, and Rayneer all looked at one another.

"Buried chests?" Bran said, with no small amount of amusement. "As in, like a buried treasure?" His head swiveled back and forth between the other two.

"Kind of. Now off you go," she said with a wave of her hand.

The three retrieved the shovels and headed out, forgoing the cart, as they all thought it was too suspicious. As if walking out into the orchard with shovels in hand wasn't suspicious enough.

They found the spot and sure enough, about six feet down, they found the first chest. It was the bigger one Pai'ese had told them to retrieve with the Intelligence sigil on top. They found the other smaller chests, retrieved one and then covered up the hole, sprinkling leaves and other ground cover around to hide their work.

Both chests were heavy, the smaller one belying its weight in such a small size. Rayneer carried the larger chest, while Bran and Arran alternated with the smaller one on their way back.

Pai'ese saw them coming from the window and stepped outside.

"Take them to the shed, please." She turned and went back into the house.

By now, everyone knew the boys had returned and headed for the shed, following Pai'ese, who now held a small keychain in her hand. She entered the shed and then closed the door behind them once everyone was inside.

Pai'ese turned to the three girls. "Can one of you provide some light, please?" To her astonishment, all three girls quickly produced small globes of light in their hands.

She grinned appreciatively. "That will do." She looked at Rayneer. "Could you place that on the table, please?" Rayneer lifted the chest with ease and placed it on the table. Pai'ese then leaned down, picked the largest key on the chain, and unlocked the larger chest. Everyone peered over as she raised the lid to the chest, eager to see its contents.

On top was a well-oiled leather sheet, which she pulled away to expose a neatly folded set of gear. She pulled the gear out and set it aside on the table next to the chest. It was a full set of gear, from boots to cloak.

Next were three bundles of leather, bound and tied with thick leather strips. She picked each one up reverently and placed them on the table.

Lastly, on the bottom of the chest, snugly tied and tightly packed to cover the entirety of the bottom of the chest, were what looked like large coin purses. Bigger than one would carry, but maybe the size used by a merchant or store owner. She pulled out six purses in total and placed them alongside everything else on the table. Each one giving a muted clank as she set them down.

Pai'ese paused and looked over the contents of the table, nodding her head in satisfaction. She picked up the cloak, unfolded it, and held it up in front of her, inspecting it. "Not bad at all, given it has been underground for so long."

"Can I have a look?" Bran asked.

She handed the cloak to Bran.

Pai'ese pointed to a smaller table on the side wall. "Arran, could you bring that other table over?"

Arran pulled the table over, as Pai'ese began unfolding and placing the gear out along the second table. It was indeed a complete full set of gear.

"This is really nice," Bran said admiringly. "Not as nice as what you gave Arran, but still...."

"This is my original set of gear. The set I gave Arran replaced it.

Like you said, it's not near the quality of Arran's, but it is still quite good. It will serve my purposes."

Next, Pai'ese gently began untying and unwrapping the three bundles. Inside each was a book.

"What books are those?" Arran asked, bending over to get a better view.

"Journals," Pai'ese corrected him. "One is mine and the other two are Brent's and Gale's. Stella and Stephan were not very keen on writing." She opened each journal to inspect it, flipping through the pages.

"Still in good reading condition. Good."

She bundled the journals back up and bound them back with extreme reverence.

Lastly, she hefted one of the purses, opened it, and poured the contents on the table. The coins clinked out across the table with a sound only gold coins could produce.

Everyone gasped at the sight of so many gold coins spread out before them.

"How...how much is this?" Arran stammered.

"Back then, a pouch like this held about five hundred gold pieces." Pai'ese picked up a few of the coins. "Look here, though." She handed a coin to each of them. "Back then, the gold coins were much thicker. They've gotten thinner over the years, so maybe each bag is two or three times that now?"

Mare did the math, taking into account the other pouches. "So, we're looking at six to nine thousand gold here on the table?"

"That would be my guess as well. There should be another ten bags in the smaller chest."

"Ten more bags?" Arran exclaimed. "That's..."

"Twenty five to thirty thousand gold in total," Mare replied quickly. "Depending on how many coins are in each and what they exchange for now."

"Mom, we could have lived forever on this! You and Dad would not have had to work!"

"True, but that would have defeated the whole 'I'm in hiding' part of my story over the years. That kind of money tends to attract attention. How do I explain a hundred years' worth of accumulated gold without some fanciful story? Besides, we lived comfortably. We never wanted for anything."

Faye reached over and picked up one of the coins. "This is valuable?"

"Very much so," Pai'ese responded.

"We have this in my village. We use for decoration."

"Humans also use it for decoration, but also for trade."

Faye looked at the coin again and then dismissively returned it back to the table.

By mid-afternoon, everyone agreed that they would be ready to leave in the morning. Each person had a portion of the gold to carry with the rest stored in the small chest. Everyone readied themselves for travel.

Rayneer anxiously headed out the door. "I will be back in time for dinner." No one asked him where he was going. They all knew.

Rayneer rejoined the group before dinner and sat down.

"Rayneer?" Bran asked.

"Yeah?"

"What is that on your arm?"

Rayneer looked at his arm. Tied right below his shoulder was a yellow silk scarf.

His cheeks flushed in a sudden burst of pink. "Challand gave it to me before I left."

Bran chuckled and shook his head. "You have got it bad."

"Yeah. I'm going to have Father send a formal courtship invitation when I get home."

"Seriously?" Bran's eyes went wide in surprise and then genuine affection for his friend. He patted him on the back. "Good for you."

"Yes, I'm happy for you, Rayneer," Elinda said.

Mare entered the room from the kitchen, took one look at Rayneer and said, "What's with the frilly scarf?" Everyone smiled.

Arran loved the company of his friends and he was genuinely happy for Rayneer, but he needed some time alone. Everything was moving so fast. He made his way through the kitchen and out the door.

"Dinner will be ready soon!" Pai'ese shouted to him as he left.

Arran waved his hand over his shoulder and continued walking. He didn't know where he was going, but ended up at the tree in the orchard, just as he did in his youth. He sat down beside the tree, facing west to watch the approaching sunset.

A few minutes later, he heard footsteps approaching and turned. It was Faye.

"I saw you leave."

"I just needed to think." He looked at her, managing a weak smile. "Plus, I don't make it back home often and wanted to enjoy this spot. I would come here a lot when I was younger."

"It is a good...spot." Faye smiled back.

Arran returned his gaze to the sunset. "I hope we are doing the right thing for you and...well, for all of it. It seems like everything has gotten bigger, more dangerous, and complicated. Life seemed so simple not that long ago."

Faye did not reply and then, much to Arran's surprise, she sat down next to him and placed a hand on his.

"I felt the same way when I left my village. Life was simple. Then I left. It was hard when I arrived here. Then I met all of you, discovered the corruption, and the final meaning of my dreams. Now we head off to a city the size of which I never imagine." She paused contemplatively. "'This is life and be glad for it'. That is what my father would always tell me when I was troubled."

Arran gave an almost imperceptible nod as the two fell into silence, enjoying the myriad colors of the sunset. Arran turned his hand over and took her hand in his, fingers intertwining as they watched the sun slowly disappear beneath the wave of grasses and over the horizon.

On a small hill, outside a small village, an old and ancient entity smiled.

EPILOGUE

Astaban walked over to the mirror and pulled on his robe. He chose the dark cobalt brocade with gold trimming and embroidery for the day. It was his favorite. He turned sideways, admiring the lay of the robe, and ran his hands down the sides of the textured fabric, flattening unseen wrinkles. Astaban was not a particularly vain man, per se, but he did take a certain pride in his appearance. Satisfied, he strode out of his personal chambers, heading for his office.

It was still early in the central realm and there were few about in the halls as he made his way. He nodded politely at all who passed, and uttered a 'Good Morning' to those he recognized. He was a stern leader, he knew this of himself; but he was also fair, and did not have the rude or egotistical temperament of many in the central realm, despite his lofty office.

He had a philosophy: 'Paying respect garners respect', and it had served him well.

Astaban opened the door to his office and deftly shrugged out of the robe, carefully draping it over the mannequin behind the door.

Astaban's office was the largest in the central realm, but it was not the most ostentatious. The room was roughly rectangular in shape, deeper than it was wide. The back quarter of the room was his main office space, with only a desk, chairs, and a few shelves to the side. It was purposefully positioned at the back of the room by design. When someone came to see him, they had to traverse the entire length of the room to address him. It was a guilty power play.

In the middle third of the room were two large couches facing one another, with a table in between. Two fireplaces flanked the couches on the walls to either side. The space could easily accommodate a group of ten. The remaining front section of the room was more intimate. It housed a small lounge with two chairs and a fireplace in the corner on one side, and in the opposite, was his small personal library with a table and chair.

The walls, floors, and furniture were all of dark woods from across the galaxies. Wherever one looked, they were treated with a variety of hues, textures, and designs from the myriad of cultures under the domain of the central realm. Blacks, tans, and browns dominated the color scheme, with splashes of greens and reds filling out his chosen pallet. 'Subdued elegance' he had often been told, and that suited him just fine.

Astaban turned and was immediately surprised to find that he was not alone. Seated behind his desk, feet propped up in obvious impertinency, was an aged man sipping a drink.

Is that beer?

Astaban was immediately incensed at the disrespect.

"Who, may I ask...are you?" Astaban demanded, storming across the room in long strides.

"Oh, quiet down, Astaban," the old man said. "We need to talk."

Astaban reached the chairs in front of 'his' desk and looked at the man disdainfully.

"Please remove your feet from my desk," he said vehemently.

The old man looked at his feet, sighed, and lowered them, resting his drink on the desk. "We need to speak about this planet of yours."

Astaban's fury was still peaked and he reiterated, "Who are you?"

The old man's eyes narrowed. "I have become fond of this form and so I decided to meet you in person. I would have thought you'd be happy to see me."

Astaban frowned.

This form?

The old man smiled as he watched the slow dawning of realization begin to spread across Astaban's face.

Would you prefer I speak to you this way? Come.

The now familiar voice resonated in Astaban's head ominously.

The old man chuckled.

Astaban's head jerked in surprise, and his eyes widened. He blinked several times before regaining the old man's gaze.

The man's face was now placid, almost serene.

This Galleant has intrigued me. We need to talk.

Astaban's face went pale, and he grabbed the back of a chair to steady himself.

"Best if you take a seat before you fall and hurt yourself," the old man said with a gentle smile.

Astaban took a few deep breaths, then slowly maneuvered around the chair and sat.

The old man let several long moments pass, sipping at his drink, while he waited patiently for Astaban to regain his composure.

A cat, seemingly appearing from nowhere, sauntered to the desk and began circling Astaban's legs. Astaban looked down, unable to process this new intruder in his office. He could feel the low resonation of its purrs as it circled from one leg to the other. Then, without any hesitation, it jumped up onto the desk. The old man held out his hand as it crossed the width of the desk and began head-butting his palm and fingers. The old man pressed back, and then began stroking its short, rusty-striped fur from head to tail. It flopped to its side in the center of the desk, rolling and purring in sensory pleasure.

Astaban could only stare in stunned silence at the surreal scene in front of him. In a soft, hoarse whisper he finally broke the silence. "You..." He swallowed hard before continuing, "You are He?"

"I am," the old man replied, taking a sip of his drink thoughtfully as he lightly scratched the cat behind its ears.

"Technically, I am 'It', since I do not have a gender, but yes, I have taken the form of a human male, so 'He' is situationally appropriate."

"And..." Astaban pointed to the cat.

"Oh. This is Keedith. I found...no, that is not the right of it. Keedith found me, I believe is more accurate. I've never shared company with a cat before. I have found it most enjoyable." He patted the cat on the head as if to emphasize the relationship, and Keedith chirped in response.

Astaban did not know how to continue. No one in the history of the realms had ever 'seen' the Creator. His position, this very office, existed for the sole purpose of communication with the Creator, but those interactions were extremely rare. The handful of recent contacts being the first interactions in a very, very long time. Deciding deference was probably the best course of action at this point, he dropped down in front of the chair, prostrating himself, with his hands clasped to his forehead.

The old man huffed in derision. "Oh, do sit up. How are we to have a serious conversation with you on the floor?"

Astaban raised his head and peered over his clasped hands. The old man gestured back to the chair. Astaban complied.

"Good. Now, let us talk about this planet of yours."

ABOUT THE AUTHOR

D.A. Putman is an emerging author, publishing the first novel in a trilogy with the A New Age of Man in 2024. He began writing down ideas and concepts of books since the 1990's and finally put pen to paper in 2022. You can visit him online at DAPutman.com for more information on this book, upcoming works, maps, and his ongoing blog for more about his untraditional journey to author.